# LAURENCE HOWARD

# THE CROSS OF GOA

Published in Great Britain by Winchester Boson Publications

ISBN 978  0  9573623  0  7

Cover Design by Edward Howard

# Acknowledgments

When I set out on this journey I had absolutely no idea where it was going to take me. Even less of a notion of how much time it would take to reach my destination.

First I thank, with all my heart my long suffering wife, Angela, for her undying support, her constructive criticism and her encouragement which helped me so much when the going was tough.

My children deserve a massive thank you: Elizabeth, my eldest daughter for proof reading the first few chapters and then my youngest, Natalie, who continued with the proof reading; a special thank you to my son Edward who designed the book cover and also set up my illustrations for printing.

I should like to thank my cousins Ann Sadighian, Peter Didcock and Tim Didcock for their support and belief in me and to Frances for her invaluable help with rigging and other seafaring details.

My colleagues in the Trade Finance Department of an American Bank were an inspiration: Thank you to Shahid Khan for his encouragement, Mohsin Shafi for introducing me to Islam, Harunur Rashid, Barry George, Brian Cubitt, Prakash Kale and Ayse Barker for their valued friendship and support.

*For my wife...Angela,*
*with all my love and eternal gratitude.*

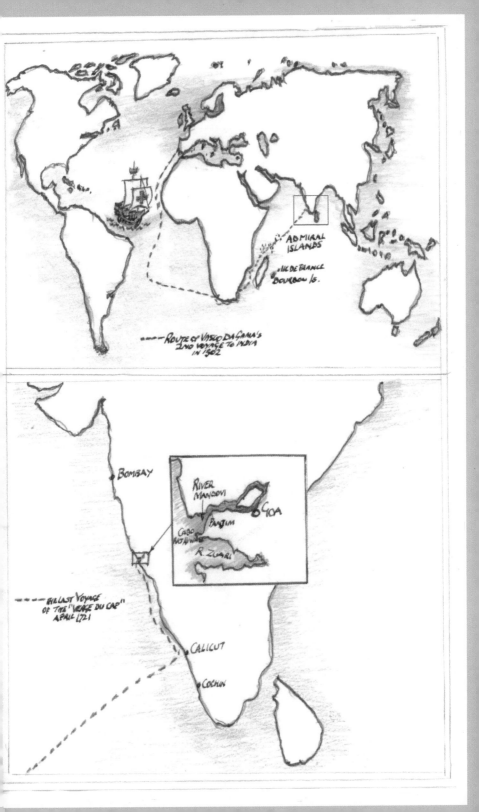

ADMIRAL
ISLANDS

ÎLE DE FRANCE
BOURBON Is.

ROUTE OF VASCO DA GAMA'S
2ND VOYAGE TO INDIA
IN 1502

BOMBAY

RIVER
MANDOVI

PANJIM

GOA

CABO
RAJIWADA

R. ZUARI

THE LAST VOYAGE
OF THE "VIERGE DU CAP"
APRIL 1721

CALICUT

COCHIN

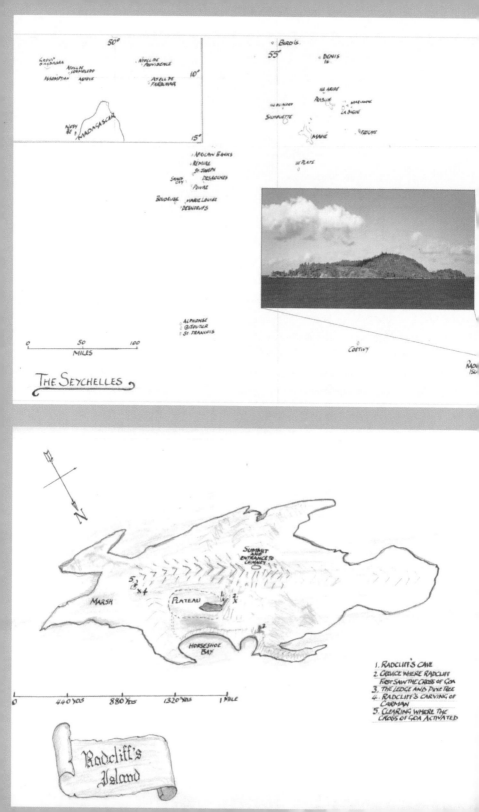

THE SEYCHELLES

50°
GROUP D'ALDABRA
ATOLL DE FARQUHAR
ASSUMPTION
ASTOLE
ATOLL DE PROVIDENCE
10°
ATOLL DE FARQUHAR
NOSY BE
MADAGASCAR
15°

BIRD IS.
55°
DENIS IS.
ILE ARIDE
PRASLIN
MARIANNE
ILE DENIEUSE
LA DIGUE
SILHOUETTE
MAHE
FELICITE
ILE PLATE

AFRICAN BANKS
RÉMIRE
ST. JOSEPH
SAND CAY
DESROCHES
POIVRE
BOUDEUSE
MARIE LOUISE
DESNOEUFS

ALPHONSE
BISSOUTER
ST. FRANCOIS

COETIVY

RADCLIFF'S ISLAND

0        50        100
MILES

North

N

SUMMIT AND ENTRANCE TO CHIMNEY

5
×4

MARSH

PLATEAU

1
2 ×

3

HORSESHOE BAY

0    440 YDS    880 YDS    1320 YDS    1 MILE

1. RADCLIFF'S CAVE
2. CREVICE WHERE RADCLIFF FIRST SAW THE CROSS OF GOA
3. THE LEDGE AND PINE TREE
4. RADCLIFF'S CARVING OF CARMAN
5. CLEARING WHERE THE CROSS OF GOA ACTIVATED

Radcliff's Island

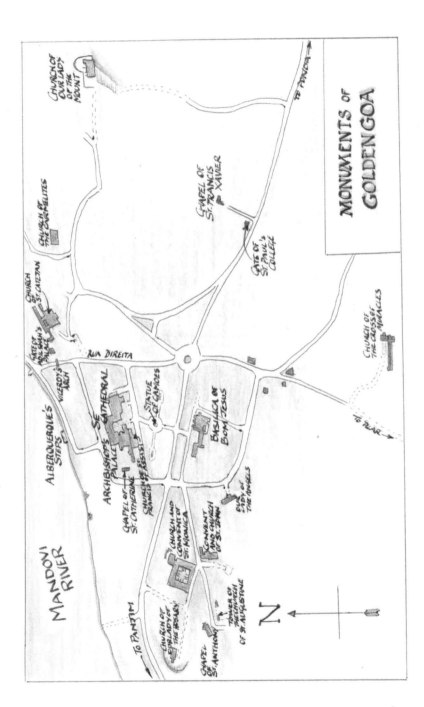

MONUMENTS of GOLDEN GOA

RADCLIFF'S ROUTE THROUGH AUSTRALIA

BARCALDINE · ALPHA · BOGANTUNGAN · ROCKHAMPTON

THERESA CREEK

TAMBO

AUGATHELLA

QUEENSLAND

CHARLEVILLE

BRISBANE

CUNNAMULLA

BOURKE

R. DARLING

NEW SOUTH WALES

NYNGAN

WEST WYALONG

WAGGA WAGGA

SYDNEY

R. MURRAY · ALBURY

WANGARATTA

VICTORIA

MELBOURNE

# Prologue

Ten thousand years ago in the shadows of the Pontus Mountains of northeast Turkey, as the great ice sheets covering Europe were retreating an expansive green basin spread out towards the distant horizon. Although frequent heavy snowstorms blanketed the region an increase in the global mean temperature was enough to sustain a consistent thaw.

Within a mountain cave a small band of hunter-gatherers sheltered from one such blizzard. A fire burned close to the cave entrance. It had burned for as long as anyone could remember, keeping the air temperature just above freezing. The cave entrance had been blocked up to shield them from the icy wind, which had been raging since the last full moon. Their food stocks were dangerously low.

The women, ten adults and two juveniles, all clothed in gazelle or goatskins, clustered around one woman who was lying naked suckling her newborn baby. Those sitting close were either caressing the child or the mother's hair whilst the others swayed rhythmically to a beautiful gentle melody sung by an older woman. Her sweet voice resonated hauntingly within the high vaulted cave, holding the final note of her song effortlessly its enchanting beauty melding with the wind to be carried away across the snowfields.

A man, clad in skins with thick matted hair and beard approached the women. He clasped a stone axe in one hand. He removed his skins and gently draped them over the woman and child then leapt upon a rock in the centre of the cave. Naked, revealing a multitude of scars on his limbs and torso, he held his arms high and cried out in a gloriously lyrical tongue: "I have a son! Praise be to El Shaddai! We thank you Lord for this gift!"

Twenty men rose up and roared out in unison and beat their chests repeatedly.

He turned and faced his men. "We must get to work," he bellowed, his face glowing. "We have another mouth to feed...." his sudden joyous laughter reverberated within the cave; they all guffawed and cheered with their chief, "...and our home needs enlarging!"

That night, excavating deeper into the mountain with stone and antler tools, they made a momentous discovery that would change the course of their lives forever. The chief had dislodged a rock at the rear of the cave. The dim light from the fire reflected on a yellow, shiny stone. Excitedly he chipped away more rock, calling his men to join him. The glowing yellow stone covered the entire back wall of the cave. Prising a lump of the strange material from the wall he brought it over to where the women were gathered and offered the piece of yellow stone to one nearest him.

She took it. The small piece of glowing yellow rock was heavy in her hands. She passed it around for the others to feel then carefully laid it beside the mother and baby. The mother weakly caressed the rock, loving the feel of its smooth surface. The others looked on in silence, captivated by its strange hypnotic lustre.

"What is it, my husband?" she asked feebly.

"We shall name it 'Shanék Ur' ('Shining Rock')." He dropped his chopper, took his son in one hand and the rock in the other and held them both up high. "Our son will also be named 'Shanék Ur'." His great voice boomed within the confines of the cave. "This is a new beginning for our people. My son and his descendents will lead you to a place which will be warmed by the sun and where food is plentiful. This I prophesy in the name of El Shaddai."

They worked the yellow rock by first hammering it into a multitude of decorative shapes. Later they discovered that by applying differing intensities of heat to the material it was affected in strange ways; their compulsive cognitive quest to unlock its secrets had begun.

Their great fires burned close to the cave entrance. Directly above the fireplace a wide natural twenty-foot chimney expelled the smoke through a crevice in the mountainside. Winds whipped and gusted up from the basin below blasting oxygen into the fire's heart generating tremendous heat. On clearing away the ashes of one such fire they discovered a small quantity of the yellow stone had melted into the grooves and cracks of the hearth.

Successive generations experimented with the stone, subjecting it to higher temperatures then cooling it over measured periods of time. Skilful, highly intelligent eyes watched and noted the patterns and shapes that formed, detecting subtle colour changes as the stone heated and cooled. Then for one tantalising moment the stone appeared translucent and, fleetingly, they glimpsed a pathway into its secret heart.

They recorded the results of these experiments meticulously on clay tablets using rounded symbols and curved characters, representations of the patterns and shapes that emerged in the yellow stone during the heating and cooling processes.

It was Shanék Ur IV who finally led his tribe onto the plains. This delayed but inevitable transition was timed to coincide with the return of the great herds of aurochs, gazelle and goats.

Other tribes moved on with the herds. But Shanék Ur IV wisely listened to the elders of the tribe. They settled within four days walking distance from their mountain and supplies of their precious yellow rock.

This innovative group built fences and walls to corral smaller herds of livestock, grazing them on separate pastures surrounding their settlement. They improved the seed yield of a type of grass they had learned to harvest, domesticated beasts to turn large grinding stones producing greater quantities of flour and continued to experiment with 'Shanék Ur' devising efficient furnaces with giant bellows to generate the high temperatures required.

Global warming intensified. The retreat of the ice sheets and glaciers accelerated causing the planet to heat more rapidly leading ultimately to 'runaway' climate change. Sea levels rose with dramatic suddenness. The Atlantic Ocean flooded the Mediterranean Sea inundating the lowlands and gouging deep canyons into the soft sedimentary rock. Sea water eroded a channel two miles wide across the land, now the Bosporus, and crashed with cataclysmic ferocity into the deep basin beyond.

Shanék Ur V and his people could hear the thunderous rumble; the ground trembled under the force of that gigantic waterfall six hundred miles away on the farthest corner of the basin.

The mountains that towered over their settlement were covered with deep fresh snow. Giant cracks formed crisscrossing the mountain ridges and slopes.

Small streams were flooding into raging torrents carrying fallen trees and other debris aloft on the raging white water.

"I shall climb the mountain and try to see what is happening," the chief announced clasping his staff sensing the apprehension building in his people.

A twelve year old boy, nicknamed No'ah, stood abruptly from behind the goat he was milking and watched his father stride across the lush grassland until he was just visible on the foothills to the mountain. Driven by a sudden surge of fear for his father he called out to five men working close by: "We can't let him go alone. We must follow him."

When they reached the mountain they could see their chief, a black speck against the snow, trudging half way up the slope. Ahead of him the rock face rose sheer.

It was the boy who saw snow tumbling from high above the rock face. The cracks in the ice sheet had widened.

The chief looked up as lumps of snow and ice fell around him. Instinctively he turned and took flight.

The snow and ice on the ridge broke away and slid over the rock face in one spectacular sheet. The chief was half rolling half scrambling to get away from the millions of tons of snow that was about to engulf him. The avalanche hit the slope just a few feet behind him. The impact pushed everything before it catapulting their chief into the air.

The boy and the other men watched helplessly as the horror unfolded. "Father!" the boy cried out in despair.

His father landed upon the top of the surging mass of snow tumbling at terrifying speed down the slope. With legs and arms flailing as if caught in a torrent of water he rode upon the snow until it reached the bottom of the slope, about a hundred feet from the boy.

The boy could see his father struggling to free himself from the stationary mound of snow when tons of ice rammed into the back of it. His father vanished.

"I'm coming…I'm coming…father!" he shrieked.

The men chased the frantic little figure clawing his way up the slope. They dug with frenzied determination into the mound of ice and snow.

The boy, with his head visible above the rim of the hole he had dug, heaved out a great clump of ice. He sagged watching it roll down the slope gathering speed and size, its deep track cutting a deep trench through the snow.

Gasping for breath he lifted himself up, grabbed at the white tomb with frozen hands and dug with all his might.

"He's over here!" One of the men cried out, waving his arms.

They could not get to him fast enough, hauling themselves over the mound of ice, and immediately joined him digging around the protruding arm. They reached his head. The boy cleared away the snow from his nose, mouth and eyes as the others dug deeper to free his body and limbs. They dragged their chief to the top of the mound. The boy pushed on his father's chest then blew his breath into his gaping mouth.

Finally the great man coughed and made a deep wheezing intake of air. He coughed again. But this time blood dribbled from his mouth.

Two men took off their skins and covered him. All five men and the boy carried the injured man back to their village.

"My son," the chief gasped as they neared the village. Men and women were rushing to meet them. "I have much to tell you, my son." His breathing was laboured and painful. "But time is very short…"

"Rest father…don't talk…"

"This cannot wait…" he grimaced as he coughed "…I saw…a flood coming. It will be upon us very soon. You must act immediately. Build rafts and get everyone and everything onto them. Save the animals and seeds…" He was seized by a bout of coughing.

His wife arrived by his side and helped take him into their small hut and lay him beside the fire. His son knelt beside him.

He clasped the boy's arm firmly. "Listen, my son…you must act now to save our people. There's no time to lose. Listen to the elders…" He lifted himself up, his arm shaking under the strain, his eyes piercing into his son's. The boy was struck with terror seeing the expression on his father's face; he wanted to scream and run.

"But above all trust in our Lord Sumer…" he said in a long sigh as he slowly reclined onto the bed. "He helped us survive…" his voice just a whisper. The boy put his ear against his father's mouth. "...the ice for generations. He will help you now...but only if you believe in Him with all your heart and soul."

His body was racked with a fit of coughing. Blood oozed between his teeth. The boy wanted to cry. The father sensed it and took hold of his arm again. "This is your great test, my son. You must be strong and be their leader. Take our people to another place. Go now. I will be seeing my Sumer now but never forget, my son that I shall always be with you." His grip on the boys arm gradually slackened. "Goodbye son..." He coughed once then he was still.

The boy fell onto his father's chest and sobbed. He could hear his great heart fading until it beat its last. But with that deathly silence he felt his father's strength surge into his body directing his thoughts to the urgent needs of the clan. He kissed his father's noble forehead and dashed out of the hut.

The group fled to higher ground with raging torrents threatening to cut them off from their ancient mountain home.

They built rafts from uprooted tree trunks. Each raft had a central mast, which held a single sail of skins and supported the thatched shelter. Saving as many creatures and plants as possible they harnessed the fierce westerly wind that ripped across the basin and set a course for the distant mountains and their ancestor's cave.

The creation of that great inland sea...the Black Sea...brought devastation, death and destruction. The waters were poisoned. With inadequate food Shanék Ur VI was forced to abandon the cave. He led his people south over the mountain range and into the unknown.

Their slow, laborious trek over three hundred miles of snow covered mountain passes and deep barren rocky valleys took several months to complete. They followed the southward course of a large, fast flowing river...the Tigris...which broadened in its meandering path across the fertile plains. Their journey ended on a stretch of land sandwiched between the Tigris and the Euphrates; its soil doubly enriched by sediments and minerals brought by the two great rivers.

Shanék Ur VI and his people were the forefathers of the great Sumerian civilization that was to develop on that land.

It was the alchemists of that civilization, heirs to their ancestor's discoveries, who finally uncovered the incredible hidden powers and properties of the yellow stone. These secrets were lost for over three thousand years until the 'Poor Knights of Christ and the Temple of Solomon' (the Knights Templar) discovered them hidden in the underground vaults beneath Solomon's Temple. Outlawed and persecuted by the church these warrior monks bestowed some of their sacred treasures to the Knights of Christ, who preserved them within a golden ark disguised as a cross.

This cross was secreted aboard Vasco da Gama's flag ship bound for India in 1502. The cross' powers were later to become legendary. It was known as the 'Fiery' Cross of Goa.

*Jesus Said:*
*"Let one who seeks not stop seeking until he finds. When he finds, he will be troubled. When he is troubled, he will be astonished and will rule over all."*

*"Whoever drinks from my mouth will become like me; I myself shall become that person, and the mysteries will be revealed to him."*

The Gospel of Thomas
Text adapted by Elaine Pagels and Marvin Meyer

# PART ONE

# CHAPTER 1

It was 23rd February 1502. A brilliant full moon burst from behind a cloud flooding Lisbon's narrow back streets with its cool sensuous light. Sharp teeth of shadow cut mystical patterns across the streets and roofs and climbed their way up the walls. Stars cluttered the heavens, hanging like coruscating snowflakes, falling slowly, eternally from the cosmos. A welcome southwesterly breeze thwarted any possibility of a frost, instead bringing with it the promise of spring.

The streets were packed with small wooden dwellings hastily built to house the perpetual influx of country folk seeking fortune in the city. Churches, which had once dotted the countryside surrounding old Lisbon had been absorbed, along with the grand stone mansions, eclipsed by the clutter of new houses. The second floors of the houses overhung the narrow streets, offering perfect concealment to any nefarious character of the night. It also provided cover for those forced to operate clandestinely, those who endeavoured to elude the prying eyes and ears of the Inquisition.

The Inquisitors had commandeered a small church on the outskirts of the city. Within its ancient stone walls, two soldiers dragged a young man into a small room at one side of the altar. They dropped the broken, partially clothed body into a chair. His head lolled lifelessly on his chest. Blood dribbled, slithering like a dark snake from the corner of his mouth.

A black robed, aged cleric rose like a raven from behind a worn oak table. A fat, solitary candle flickered upon its polished surface. It illuminated the cleric's face from beneath, his chin and nose resembling an open beak about to rip apart the carrion before him. His bony hands clawed at the edge on the table, pulling him around until he could reach out and touch the prisoner's face. The young man's blood caked face was bruised, swollen beyond recognition. A thin finger lifted an eyelid and the young man's eyeball rolled upward into his head.

The cleric nodded to one of the soldiers, who left the room and returned with a bucket of water with which he doused the prisoner.

Consciousness brought with it agony. The prisoner screamed his broken hands and fingers burning from being crushed in the mill wheel. He tried to focus, tried to open his lids just enough to see. Although his vision was blurred he could see the eyes of the Inquisitor, burning hatefully down into his own.

"You will confess," the cleric demanded then cackled; the sound sharp and parrot like. "You're apprenticed to that heretic Federico de Silva. Your loyalty to this devil will condemn your misguided soul to everlasting damnation. You must renounce this man and all his evil… you must do it now, before God. You are dying, Miguel. This is your last chance to cleanse yourself before you rejoin your maker."

Delirium took the prisoner unto semi-consciousness. Anaesthetised from pain he watched his persecutor's diseased mouth open and close with a detached fascination: his five decaying teeth, the three protruding from the centre of his lower jaw overlapped the two at the top whenever his jaws met. He could feel the cleric's warm breath on his mouth, his pulverised nose sparing him from the stench. The old man's head became the pike he had caught the evening before. It amused him to watch his jaws moving, like the pike gasping for life dangling on the end of his line.

The pike would still be in the bag by the door to his home by the river. A vision of his wife came to him. Joy engulfed his soul. He could see her sitting on the front porch of their wooden hut by the stream, her chubby small hands busily sewing; she looked up at him, her enchanting smile broadened, her eyes sparkling in the sunlight. A blanket of warmth and peace enveloped the prisoner's body.

"Confess, Miguel," the cleric's tone harsher. Time was running out. "What is your master doing? We know he has a commission from the King. What devilish business is he into? What kind of golden calf is he making? Answer….!"

A brilliant light appeared to the prisoner. It beckoned to him; filling his spirit and dominating his nervous system. There was no more pain …no more suffering. He had proved himself worthy of the man that he had worshiped; the man that he loved more than his own father.

"What is de Silva doing?" the 'Raven' shouted frantically, both eyeballs about to pop from their sockets. "Help me to destroy this man," he beseeched, softening his tone suddenly. "He reveres the ancient heretical order of the Templars," he explained in a last attempt to reason with the young man. "His ways are insidious and perverse. Help me put an end to his evil doings and you will receive absolution…"

Miguel's swollen and broken, bloody mouth opened hideously wide, white teeth smashed away from crushed gums were embedded in his tongue. Air wheezed from the scarlet and black orifice. The cleric turned his ear closer to the gaping hole to hear his confession.

"Baphomet!", Miguel managed to whisper followed by a burst of chilling, hysterical laughter that gurgled up through his blood. He choked.

The cleric staggered backwards as if stabbed in the heart. His contorted face frozen in an expression of amazement and disbelief.

A soldier smashed the hilt of his sword onto Miguel's skull. He died instantly. The look of triumph and joy on the young man's battered face stunned the cleric. He slumped into his chair.

# CHAPTER 2

That night five men hurried stealthily through the narrow stinking Lisbon back streets. Their lightness of step was precision timed to resemble one person running through the night. They dodged the drunks and whores jumping open drains fouled with raw sewage, their capes brushing the flaking plaster walls of the overhanging two story buildings. Their hands clasped sword hilts ready for ambush from any doorway or street corner.

Fifty yards behind a bare foot young boy of about eight years old, his shirt and pants torn and ragged, sprinted to within sight of the men and ducked immediately into a doorway. Malnourished, exhausted and gasping for breath he clasped tightly in his small, grimy hand two pieces of silver that the priests had given him. It was enough money to feed his dying mother, two sisters and himself for another week. The priests had promised him more if he could bring back useful information about the men he had been told to follow.

Ahead the men had turned left at a crossroads. The boy crouched in the shadows of a doorway until two drunken, laughing women of the night passed him by leaving in their wake a heavy odour of cheap wine and strong perfume. He hurled himself to the corner where the roads crossed and gingerly peering round.

The street was wide with one side of it bathed in moonlight. The men were clustered in the deep shadow of a large three story mansion fifty yards down the street. The taller one, his face gaunt with deep sunken eyes and a goatee beard, checked furtively up and down the street.

Deep shadow and door recesses covered the boy who slithered and crawled to within six feet of the men. Standing within a narrow doorway, his bony body pressed as thin as possible against the door, he fought to control his gasping breaths.

A small door built into one of the massive doors of the mansion creaked open. The taller man leaned forward. The boy heard him utter a strange sounding word then they all disappeared within.

The boy dashed to where the men had stood. He recognised the door instantly. It was the King's master goldsmith's house, an immense edifice stretching across the block with its back yard opening onto the street behind.

Federico de Silva ushered his guests through the lower rooms of his house and out into a covered workshop. The yellow glow from the smith's furnace lit up a covered workbench and reached out far into the cobbled backyard and reflected upon the shiny hindquarters of two immaculately groomed chestnut mares harnessed to an open wagon their reins tied to a railing adjacent to the stables that ran along one side of the yard. Four other horses, saddled and ready to ride stood just visible tied to a rail on the opposite side of the yard close to the double gates that opened onto the street behind. One snorted and stamped impatiently, its hooves clipping the cobblestones.

"You have come at a most unfortunate but opportune moment, my friends," the old man announced sadly.

"Take us to the Cross, de Silva, if you will" the taller man demanded. "Time's not on our side."

"I'm aware of that Lefrage, my friend. I sent my apprentice Miguel on an errand this morning. He has not returned."

"*What!*" Lefrage exploded. "The Inquisitors have him. He'll talk! No one can withstand their devilish ways...."

"I trust him, Lefrage," the old man snapped.

"But he is young! He will be tricked by their cunning and devilish methods!"

"I trust him. They've had him only one day..."

"Trust him or not, they will extract what they want from him. If they find out about the Cross now.... at the eleventh hour... all will be lost. Everything...!"

"Get a grip of yourself, man. We've time enough to see our work through. The Cross is finished and safely hidden inside. I'll take you to it in one moment. First, you must all witness something very special."

"We can't waste time, de Silva," Lefrage persisted.

De Silva glared back at him. "You will do as I command."

The old man immediately eased the tension with a kindly smile then fixed each of the men with his wide bulbous eyes, masking deep concern for Miguel.

"What you are about to see is a phenomenon no other mortals have witnessed since ancient times." The stooping old man beckoned them towards the far end of his workbench away from the furnace. Six clay tablets, each 10ins square, lay under the glow of a heavy silver candelabrum with an ancient form of writing, clearly depicted, cut into the top surface. It was Sumerian cuneiform, one of the earliest forms of written language.

"These tablets were rescued, with other secrets and priceless treasures, from Jerusalem by the Knights Templar in 1127. As you know, our brotherhood is responsible for their safekeeping. They are evidence of a 'Truth'...the 'Truth' that everyone seeks and yearns to experience...a

21

'Truth' the church has suppressed and successfully denied its flock from knowing and is hell bent on keeping it from them.

"Anything and everything that threatens the Church's blinkered doctrine will always be destroyed: like the great library at Alexandria, the countless martyrs of the brotherhood burned on stakes and the Cross....anything slightly 'heretical' they will destroy if they possibly can! Maybe four or five hundred years from now things will be very different. Everyone should know this 'Truth' by then. God willing!

"What you are about to witness, gentlemen..."

"Get on with it, de Silva," Lefrage demanded.

"*What* you will see..." the old man continued, "will astound you beyond your wildest imaginings." A broad grin pulled the skin tight across his wide noble brow erasing momentarily the deep furrows etched by time and deep concentration. His old craggy face creased up around twinkling eyes. He guided them back to the workbench opposite the furnace and removed the canvas covering a one foot square closed iron box.

The furnace lit up one side of the box; it glowed a rusty orange and black. Rods had been fixed to the left and right sides of the box and were bent towards each other, almost meeting at the centre. Below the gap between the rods a raised platform had been erected above the centre of the box.

"Using the formulae given in those tablets I have unlocked an in-credible power."

"For pities sake hurry man...!" Lefrage nervously craned his neck towards the exit of the yard. "I'm sure we were followed. Fetch the Cross now, de Silva, and we can be on our way to the docks."

"Relax, my friend...." He lifted a calming hand and shook his craggy head. "I've never known you to be so nervous...!"

"I've never been on a more important mission, de Silva! The King himself entrusted me with this huge responsibility. I must... we must not fail."

"We're all here on the King's business, Lefrage..."

Federico de Silva looked away into the furnace, remembering his incarceration in Toledo castle, deep in Spanish Castile, two years before. He had been seized in Seville for assisting 300 Conversos Jews to escape from the Inquisitors. He grimaced, feeling again the excruciating agony of the garrotte. Just as they were about to turn the screw for the last time; just before his neck would have snapped like a twig, twelve members of his brotherhood, the Knights of Christ, suddenly burst into the torture chamber and snatched him away to safety. They had hacked their way through the whole castle guard to reach him and vanished into the night without a single casualty. He gazed up into the night sky, forgetting the five pairs of anxiously watching eyes that surrounded him, and gave thanks to God for his deliverance.

He coughed, embarrassed slightly by his lapse. "The timing of this last process requires absolute precision," he continued. Using a pair of tongs he extracted a crucible containing molten gold from the furnace and placed it carefully onto the elevated platform on the iron box just beneath the gap between the two rods.

A blinding flash arced across the gap for several seconds enveloping the crucible. The men retreated in alarm. One stumbled, knocking over the candelabrum, which clattered onto the cobbled floor. The man replaced it on the workbench.

De Silva waited for several seconds before partially immersing the crucible into a vat of cold water for two seconds. It hissed, steam billowing up from the vat.

"It's vital that I retain that colour within the metal as it cools," he explained, removing the crucible from the water.

All the men stared intently at the cooling gold, eager to see the colour de Silva had alluded to. Lefrage glanced over to de Silva and gave him a bewildered shrug of his narrow shoulders.

Returning the crucible into the furnace he waited for the molten gold to return to the colour he wanted then offered it once again to the iron box. The same intense flash followed, but this time all the men stood their ground. He cooled it again exactly as before. De Silva's skilled eye could see into the heart of the precious metal.

"Look! See that colour?" They all gathered keenly around the crucible again, the liquid gold still radiating immense heat. The air was filled with the acrid smell of molten metal. "It must never be lost..." He spoke with a concentrated passion that compelled them all to stoop over the crucible. The heat forced them to back away.

Eight times the old man repeated the heating and cooling process. A blinding flash of light sent them reeling backwards. He looked around at his shocked but captivated audience. Perspiration dripped from his nose.

"Watch closely!" he demanded, with all the drama of a magician. He lifted the cooled, blackened crucible in his gloved hand and, with ease, rested it on the anvil next to the furnace. He was amused to see their expressions change from mystification to incredulity and then to disbelief and finally to sheer amazement as the transition took place. The men gathered around him, crouching closer, to inspect the contents of the crucible.

One prodded it with a finger and examined the substance stuck to his fingernail. "It's a white powder! It's like freshly milled flour!" he announced to his comrades gaping around him.

"Come on, de Silva. Where is it?" Lefrage demanded, reaching for the iron box. "What happened to the gold?"

"Don't touch that!" he screamed.

Lefrage leapt back with his hands in the air. He laughed nervously trying to regain some composure. He looked around at the others and to his relief they had all shrunk back covering their faces with their forearms.

"What are you trying to prove?" Lefrage asked full of indignation. He pointed at the powder. "What is this, de Silva?"

"Exactly!" de Silva grinned with delight at his friend's utter bewilderment and confusion…wanting to aggravate him to the limit.

"Well! What is it?" he glared back. "We haven't time for your schoolboy games!"

"That's what it is!" de Silva stated, nodding his head gleefully, gazing at each of Lefrage's four men in turn. Within their dumbfounded expressions there was a hint of concern for their leader who was about to explode with anger and frustration.

"*What*!" Lefrage screamed.

"What it is!" He giggled.

"I asked *you* that!" he exclaimed his eyes bulging with exasperation. "Tell me de Silva. What is *it*?"

"Manna."

"Manna! Manna. What the devil is Manna?" Lefrage pleaded, wanting only for this embarrassing game to end and they could get the Cross and be on their way.

"Manna is ancient Hebrew for 'What is this?'!"

Lefrage's jaw dropped open. He shook his head forcing a wan smile. "Very funny de Silva!"

De Silva laughed heartily, affectionately putting an arm around his friend's shoulders.

"Come! Let me show you this," directing them to the end of the workbench, chuckling as he went and pointed to the six tablets. "The people who inscribed those marks on the clay tablets knew the power of gold," as he spoke the five men gathered around the candelabrum and studied the strange cuts in the clay. "These people had acquired these secrets from an unknown tribe that had come from the north. The Egyptians mastered this alchemy thousands of years later. They called the powder 'mfkzt' or 'white bread'."

"White bread…!" Lefrage sneered.

"What does it taste like?" another asked.

"Sweet; just like honey." De Silva looked at each in turn. It delighted the old man to see his audience utterly confused and captivated. "Over the centuries the craft was absorbed by the Israelites," de Silva continued. "When Moses led them out of Egypt to Mount Horeb, it was Bezaleel, the master craftsman, who built the Ark of the Covenant. Moses had said that the white powder called 'Manna' was 'the bread which the Lord has given you to eat' but when Moses came down from

Mount Horeb and saw them before the golden calf he said to them, 'You have not kept the covenant, and so the Manna is being taken from you'. "All of you know the words: 'Give us this day our daily bread'. They all stared at him stupefied. "Yes! The 'Lord's Prayer'...Jesus was a craftsman too! Jesus said: 'He who has an ear, let him hear what the Spirit says to the churches. To him who overcomes I will give some of the hidden Manna to eat'."

"Are you saying" Lefrage scoffed, "that Jesus had known this...that gold could be turned into...this powder?"

"These secrets were employed by the Pharaohs in building the pyramids, by Moses in the making of the Ark of the Covenant and by King Solomon in building the Temple in Jerusalem." De Silva paused, watching them closely as each of the group struggled to take in these revelations. He noticed that they all held that entranced, captivated look of expectancy seen in the eyes of small children.

"Here," he tapped the fifth tablet with his index finger, "these marks explain what would happen if I continued to heat and cool this 'powder'."

"It would become gold once more?" Lefrage suggested hopefully.

"No," he chuckled.

They waited.

De Silva held them in suspense.

"It vanishes!" he said with perfect timing. "It disappears completely!" he declared his face screwing up with joy.

"*What!*" a short rotund individual shouted. He glared at de Silva with an expression of utter disbelief and complete frustration. "I have strived as hard as the others to grasp and understand your methods and what you are saying to us, de Silva." His open, scholarly face tipped to one side sceptically and his sharp eyes narrowed mistrustfully. "Can you honestly state that you actually performed this experiment?"

"Yesterday evening!" His joyous, self-satisfied smile stretched from ear to ear. "I divided the white powder into two portions. When I continued heating and cooling one of the portions there was a flash of brilliant white light.... then it vanished! ...as predicted on the clay tablet!"

De Silva held out a glove to the astonished man.

"Go on, lift it…" he grinned nodding towards the crucible.

He pulled on the glove and clasped the crucible, expecting to bear the full weight of the gold.

"My God!" he shouted in astonishment. "It's as light as an eagle's feather!" His eyes bulged with excitement. "Unbelievable!" he shrieked, shaking his head.

"Shhh ! Shut up you fool," hissed one of his comrades.

"Hurry man," pleaded Lefrage. "This is all very interesting but if the Cross is ready, de Silva, we must get it loaded onto the wagon…"

25

turning his ear towards the arched entrance to the yard. He raised a finger to his lips. "Quiet..!" he whispered. He crept towards the wagon and then continued with long gangling strides to the arched gateway, unlatched the gate and peered up and down the street. He returned to the others and shrugged his shoulders.

"A stray dog, possibly?" suggested de Silva jovially. "But you're right to be cautious, my friend. We will succeed in fulfilling the Kings mission, never fear! You will not disappoint our King or the great Admiral da Gama. He sails on the next tide, does he not?"

"For pity's sake, de Silva," Lefrage hissed throwing his arms in the air. "Why don't you shout it out from the roof tops....tell everyone about your Cross whilst you're at it!"

"It's common knowledge, Lefrage. Everyone knows that King Manuel has commissioned his new Admiral to recapture Calicut."

"Yes, I know. But keep your voice down." Lefrage flapped his hands rapidly up and down, his long neck craning as if readying to take off.

De Silva laughed. "You...you look like a constipated duck...you'll worry yourself to death, man! All will be well," he added, patting him firmly on the back. "You'll see."

"The sooner we get the Cross to the Admirals ship, the happier I'll be. Federico...answer me this: why, in heavens name, are they taking this cross to India? It's hardly the safest place following the massacre of Cabral and his men at Calicut! There has never been a worse time...!"

"That's precisely why the Cross will be safe. It will be the last place those devil Inquisitors will think we have hidden our most treasured secrets. A new fort has been built at Cochin to receive the Cross. India is the future, my friend. Our King was wise to foresee its great potential as a trading gateway to Asia, the Orient and the newly found islands called the Japans. A magnificent cathedral is to be built and the Cross is to be housed within it."

"Why would those natives massacre our men?" Lefrage asked. "Aren't they supposed to be converted? Aren't they Christians?"

They heard the slap of bare feet running on the cobblestones outside.

"I knew it," Lefrage glared at de Silva. "For the love of God...*get the cross!*"

Without another word Federico de Silva carefully emptied the white powder into a golden box, the size of small jewellery box, and deftly soldered on the lid.

"All of you follow me. Oh, Lefrage! Bring those clay tablets... carefully!"

With the golden box in one hand and the candelabrum in the other he led them inside to a small room stacked with empty sea chests. A ladder and a coil of rope lay behind the door. De Silva pulled a stack of chests away from the middle of the room to reveal a trapdoor.

"Someone open it up, please."

One grabbed a ring handle. The four-foot square door opened with ease on its well-greased hinges. He laid it flat on the floor. De Silva held the candelabrum over the hole, its flickering light glinting upon two golden objects on the floor seven feet below them. He released a rope fastened to the wall. The rope passed through a pulley wheel at the end of a crane like arm. The arm swung out over the open trapdoor.

"Hurry man! Hurry!.." Lefrage held the pulley rope awaiting instructions.

"You..!" De Silva pointed to one of Lefrage's men. "Bring that ladder and coil of rope," pointing to the spot behind the door. Placing the candelabrum and the gold box on the floor, he lowered the ladder into the hole and threw the rope down. "Lefrage...follow me down into the cellar," he commanded taking off his shoes. "First, remove anything metallic from your person and take off your boots and stockings. Bring the clay tablets, though," he smiled sardonically up at Lefrage. He picked up the box, took one of the candles from the candelabrum and descended the ladder.

The two sections of the golden Cross lay side by side before the two barefoot men. The base was an open rectangular box of gold. Next to it sat the jewel encrusted Cross, suspended upon four swan neck supports that rose up from the corners of a flat solid gold surface, the lid to the base section.

Lefrage gaped in breathless awe. "Fed...er...ico!" each syllable uttered an octave higher than the last. "It is magnificent. The craftsmanship... the beauty... What a design! It's extraordinary! It's intoxicating, de Silva! More wondrous than a newly born babe," he added holding his arms up in joyous admiration.

The flame of the candle flared momentarily in a draught, dancing and playing on the golden surfaces and glinting upon the jewels in a mesmerising and dazzling multicoloured display of reflected, sparkling light. The bejewelled Cross had four intricately carved flaming suns, with rubies and diamonds at their hearts, shining from the ends of each jewel encrusted solid gold crosspiece; lines of tiny rubies, diamonds and sapphires radiated out along each tongue of flame. Each crosspiece was of equal length, measuring fourteen inches from tip to tip; a golden circle of Celtic design encompassed the intersection, bisecting the crosspieces. At the intersection there was an interlocking pentagram, traced in small diamonds, with a large diamond shaped crystal at its centre, representing the eye of God.

The four golden supports had a minimum width and thickness of half an inch solid gold, representing the four elements: Earth, Fire, Water and Wind. They gracefully curved up from each corner of the lid to cradle the Cross beneath the intersection. The Cross was held suspended four inches above the lid of solid gold which was one and one quarter inches thick. Two golden hands reached out from opposing sides of the lid, palms downward, each index finger extended, almost touching, leaving a quarter inch gap over the epicentre of the lid. The gap between the fingers was also directly below the crystal at the centre of the Cross.

The base was made from resinous acacia wood lined inside and out with pure gold. It was fifteen inches long by nine inches wide and nine inches high and stood upon four stubby legs, two and half inches high. Four gold rings had been moulded into each corner of the base to accommodate the carrying poles. An intricately decorated rim had been fashioned around the top of the base half an inch wide and half an inch high to receive the lid and upper section and hold it fast. When the Cross was complete with both sections in place it stood 30 inches above the ground.

De Silva took the tablets from Lefrage and placed them carefully inside the base.

"Hurry de Silva," Lefrage implored. "Get the Cross assembled and onto the wagon. We can't waste any more time!" Lefrage attempted to lift the top section. His joints popped under the strain.

"Wait! Do what I tell you when I tell you to do it! Patience, my friend! We must act with the utmost care from now on…you'll never lift that top section without help…" he sniggered "…but we can cheat a little." He handed Lefrage the small box of white powder. "Place it in the centre of the lid."

He did so.

"Now lift the upper section."

He lifted the top section with ease and held it a foot above the base.

De Silva gripped Lefrage's arm. "I need to replace the box of powder inside the base section. When I take it away you will bear the full weight of the top. Do not drop it. Once the top section is in place we must be extremely cautious," he said raising his voice for the others to hear, his words echoing within the empty cellar adding greater gravity to what they were about to attempt. "From the moment the Cross is complete it can never be touched! Are you ready, Lefrage?"

He straightened his back and braced his legs and nodded.

De Silva removed the small box of powder.

Gravity exerted its full force upon the solid gold. The top section dropped.

Lefrage arrested its fall an inch above the base section. His arms and fingers were stretched to the verge of dislocation; his legs buckled under the incredible load.

"Hold it. Good man. Lift it a fraction higher. Come on, Lefrage! I must get the box inside the base. *Lift…! Just a fraction more…come on!*"

Lefrage's veins in his neck protruded like knotted string. The sharp edges of the Cross and the supports cut into the flesh of his hands. His breath hissed out from between tightly clenched teeth. Lefrage concentrated his effort by looking up through the trap door, willing his shoulders, back muscles and legs to give him more lift. He wanted to scream but instead a deep growl gargled from his throat.

"Up..! Up...! Hold it..."

Lefrage held for one more second, the muscles in his face contorting and twisting with the strain. Banishing the agony from his mind he held on for another second.

"Lower it, Lefrage," he said at last. "Slowly..."

Lefrage's head shook with the strain; his eyes bulged from their sockets as de Silva carefully lined up the lid.

"Down...more...more. Okay. Well done, my good friend!"

The top slotted into its place perfectly with a deep clunk. Compressed air hissed perceptibly from the edges as it settled into position. Lefrage tried to remove his hands but flesh was stuck to the metal. Gently peeling his hands from the supports he rubbed life back into the deep purple grooves cut into his palms.

De Silva removed the ladder clear and took a pair of golden poles, each a yard long and an inch and half in thickness that lay close to the Cross. "They are of acacia wood covered with pure gold," he explained, inserting the poles through the rings on the base. "From now on the Cross can only be moved using these poles."

Lefrage nodded, recovering his breath and massaging his hands.

"Lower the rope from the pulley," de Silva called up.

Lefrage grinned, still breathless, and paced slowly and reverently around the Cross. "My insides have become weightless simply looking at it." He looked over at de Silva, his smile broadening. "I feel as though I've drunk a vat of wine," he laughed, holding his head in his palms, "I'm that light headed."

"You must treat this Cross with the utmost respect, my friend. It has unimaginable power." He looked up. Four gawping faces peered down at them through the trap door. "The Cross must never be touched," he yelled up. "I have made a list of safety rules. They must be followed to the letter. It's absolutely imperative that these rules are passed on to Admiral da Gama. Is that understood?"

There was a murmur from above. Lefrage shot a sceptical glance at de Silva, but then respectfully nodded his agreement under the glare of the goldsmith. De Silva weaved the rope around the protruding ends of the two poles then fastened the end securely above the Cross.

"Lift.... Slowly does it...Careful now! .... Not too fast! ... Hold it there." With the Cross at waist height, de Silva checked that the rope and the knot were secure. "Take it up slowly." They both watched it gradually ascend, the ends of the poles just passing through the frame of the trap-door. "Lift it as high as it will go, men. Whatever you do, do not touch it. It could be the last thing that you do on God's earth."

The four men hauled the Cross until the knot de Silva had tied was pressing against the pulley wheel. The flickering candlelight reflected on the gold and the jewels projecting dappled multicoloured patterns onto the ceiling. De Silva and Lefrage climbed out from the cellar, squeezing between the sea chests and the four men holding the pulley rope.

Lefrage retrieved the ladder as de Silva closed the trap door and dragged an open sea chest underneath the hanging Cross.

"Right men...lower it down gently into the chest."

The chest had been adapted to accommodate the Cross with its wooden carrying poles in place.

The four men stood around the chest speechless.

"It's a masterpiece, Federico!" the short scholarly one declared at last. He searched the faces of his comrades in turn. "I'm feeling...a strange dizziness...and it's not the wine..."

They all felt the warm pulsating sensation coursing through their veins. Grins grew broader as waves of euphoria lifted their spirits to heights they had forgotten existed. Their bodies become weightless, as if floating on air. They were overwhelmed by an extraordinary feeling that had been dormant within each of them... an eternal truth that was instantly recognisable. It was a deep feeling of omnipresent love. Each man gazed at the other their eyes blurred with tears... all speechless... their hearts pounding in their chests...their spirits co-joining to become part of the greater divine spirit that is everything that is.

De Silva had felt it too, only this time it was stronger than at any other time since starting the project. He saw their almost childlike ex-pressions of joy, as if the Cross had spoken to them of an undying uni-versal truth that they had instantly remembered. The joy of seeing the same reaction in each of the men brought tears to his eyes.

"You're all good men..." he said nodding slowly holding back a surge of emotion "...*all* of you. Now you can all feel and know God, as I do, living deep within you." He clasped Lefrage's shoulder...more for support than affection. "The Cross...will always give out....this energy," he managed to utter, his throat tightening like a vice. "This is an undying energy. It's God's.... undying love.... for mankind." His quivering lips stretched into a broad smile as he nodded in certain affirmation. Tears cascaded freely down his cheeks.

They watched the great man stand quietly before his creation, his magnificent work complete.

"The base of the Cross is precisely one third the size and weight of the Ark of the Covenant," De Silva said solemnly, looking at each man in turn. "It is made of identical materials. The King was specific in that regard. The base is of acacia wood lined inside and out with the purest gold. As pure as the gold Bezaleel had used to make the Ark. Part of the King's brief was that I copy the marks on the clay tablets onto the inner gold lining of the base...before they crumble to dust...you understand... This I've accomplished. The secrets will be safe now for generations to come."

De Silva covered the Cross with the lid of the sea chest and fastened the three locks.

"Go now, men," he said handing the keys to Lefrage. "Get this precious load onto the wagon and wait for me in the yard."

De Silva disappeared into the great house as Lefrage's four men carried the chest outside into the yard and carefully placed it onto the back of the wagon, covering it with a canvas.

De Silva returned to the yard with a sealed envelope. "Be sure that the Admiral fully understands the importance of the safety instructions," he said handing Lefrage the envelope. "It is imperative that you do this."

Lefrage thrust the paper deep inside his coat and held de Silva in an embrace.

"I hope all free thinking people of the world will remember you forever for what you have done this night Federico."

De Silva laughed heartily and slapped his friend firmly and affectionately on the back. "I don't think so, my friend. But I remember you telling me something, though. Something about being in a hurry! Go and do God's work for our beloved King! God will keep you!"

De Silva watched Lefrage climb up onto the wagon and take the reins then hurried ahead and opened the gates to the yard. Two of Lefrage's men galloped out on glistening stallions, turning left into the night. Lefrage pulled on the reins and the mares responded instantly. The wagon rumbled out of the yard and accelerated into the street, skidding wide on the cobble, and chased after the horsemen. The other two men kicked their mounts and raced after the wagon.

# CHAPTER 3

Why should we believe this little devil your grace?" hissed one of the six priests encircling the tiny figure. His viper like whisper echoed within the barrel vaulted Lisbon cathedral. "He has made the whole story up. It is overly melodramatic and totally unbelievable. Why all that secrecy for a Cross. He's just after more of those silver coins you promised him."

"Father Dominic, aren't you overlooking one thing," the Bishop's voice erupted, echoing in the cavernous vault. "You can see the truth shining from this boy's eyes. Let me remind you, my son, that it was our Lord and saviour who said 'blessed are the little children', did he not? The boy's done well this night," The Bishop stooped and looked into the angelic face peering up at him. "Tell me again, boy. What was the word the tall man said before they entered the house?"

"I couldn't hear… very…well, sir. It sounded like…'Bafo-me' sir."

"It was probably a password," an older priest exclaimed. "Does it matter?"

"I think it does, Father Francisco," the Bishop's raised voice echoed twice, once within the cavernous nave and then again in the far transept. "I've read a great deal about the Templar trials. Even under the most fiendish methods of torture, no one could extract their secrets. Their secrets went with them to the grave. Many were burned at the stake and others were less fortunate and suffered under horrendous pain." The Bishop grimaced, wringing his hands, as he visualised the torment and agony those men endured. Instantly quashing his feelings of compassion and pity his conviction returned that heresy was a mortal sin against God and the Church and had to be eliminated. Filled with righteous retribution he raised his head haughtily and prayed silently that the Templar's souls would be saved from everlasting damnation.

"They would never talk," he said, at last, full of emotion; his deep admiration and respect for these warrior monks clearly evident. "They would sometimes utter one word. A mysterious word that would fill their hearts with courage and fortitude… to help them withstand the hideous torture they had to endure. The word they would say was 'Baphomet'."

"I have read that," Father Benedict said proudly, unmoved by his Bishop's candidness. "'Baphomet' was the last word that their Grand Master, Jacques de Molay, uttered when he burned at the stake with Geoffroi de Charney," he announced with relish. "It was sorcery. They were all evil men, your grace, depraved sodomites, and murderers. They worshiped a severed head. Even the crucifix of our Lord wasn't sacred to them…they ground it into the earth with their heels. The Church and all Christians were right to condemn them," bitterness erupting from deep within the priest, his voice becoming high pitched and effeminate. "They were the devils spawn," he added cuttingly, his eyes narrowing. "Do you not think it is the language of Satan himself, your Grace?"

The Bishop turned away and faced the altar, disturbed by Father Benedict's venomous outburst. There were too many damaged young men turning to the cloth, their feelings of fear and hate so ingrained he wondered if they could ever learn to dominate them. He faced Father Benedict once more and searched the priest's angry eyes for a hint of mercy or compassion. There was none.

"I do not know, my son," he said sorrowfully. "It's been a mystery for two centuries." The Bishop looked down once more at the boy before him. "It does prove, however, that the men seen by our young friend here are indeed heretics and must be caught and punished. They entered the house of Federico de Silva, the goldsmith," the Bishop turned to face Father Dominic. "Even though Miguel, his apprentice did not confess, we have evidence against de Silva and proof that he is linked not only with these evil doers and sorcerers but is receiving instructions from…. our *King!*"

"Where did you say they were taking this Cross, boy?" Father Francisco asked in a kindly voice.

"To Admiral da Gama's flag ship, sir..."

"This unfortunate country has a King who not only condones the Knights of Christ, my brothers, but collaborates with them," the Bishop proclaimed, shaking his head in despair. "I suspect that Admiral da Gama is sympathetic to the cause. He's been given twenty ships to spread their heresy deeper into the wildernesses of Africa and India. We must get someone of the cloth aboard one of these ships and find out exactly what they have planned for this Cross. We must know their methods of spreading their distorted and blasphemous brand of Christianity to these new lands." The Bishop looked at each of the clergymen in turn. "Father Benedict, I think you will be perfect for this Holy task."

"I would be honoured your Grace," Father Benedict bowed.

"Good. Then we have not a moment to lose. Pack your bag immediately. I want you on board one of the ships before this Cross is loaded on board da Gama's flag ship."

Father Benedict returned a few minutes later carrying a small travelling bag containing fresh cloths, prayer books and his Bible.

"You must avoid arousing suspicion at all costs. I want you to establish a Catholic mission in Cochin. It's on the southern tip of India and da Gama's last port of call. Here is my signed commission," the

Bishop handed the priest a parchment and a bag of gold coins. "There should be enough in the bag to pay your passage and keep you fed. Trust no one, Father. These heretics will stop at nothing to protect their secrets."

Father Benedict took the gold and stowed it with the Bishop's authorisation deep within his bag and bade them all farewell. As he walked briskly down the hill towards the docks the boy ran past, bare feet slapping on the cobblestones, eager to get home and show his mother the five silver coins he had accumulated that night.

Soon the vista of the harbour and Vasco da Gama's fleet spread out before him. The moon had unravelled a narrowing carpet of yellow light that crossed the calm water; the flickering lanterns of the fleet cast long shimmering reflections turning the black water, either side of the yellow carpet, into a fairy land of glimmering lights. The southwesterly breeze fanned the burning torches lighting the bustling dockside.

Father Benedict stopped before one of the ships being loaded up with provisions for the long sea voyage. Sacks of groats, beans, dried peas, almonds, flour, ships biscuits, salt, dried apples and prunes; cases of salt beef, salted fish; barrels of wine, fresh water and beer were being hoisted over the ships gunwale onto the deck or were being carried by an endless stream of porters. A thick cocktail of smells permeated the air and excited the senses. It was a hive of activity with overseeing officers bellowing orders to the crew who were either stowing goods or climbing the shrouds and masts in preparation for the voyage ahead.

The windows of the ship's towering stern were lit up like a three story tavern. Above the rudder a newly varnished plaque gave the name of the vessel. It was the 'Sao Gabriel'. Father Benedict recalled the name. It had been Vasco da Gama's flagship when he first sailed for India in 1497.

"Ahoy there," he called to a bearded officer on the poop deck. "Who is the Captain-General of the 'Sao Gabriel'?"

"I am he. Alfonso de Albuquerque at your service, Father," he replied jovially, leaning over the handrail sixteen feet above the cleric.

When the priest heard the name his knees buckled.

"*The* Alfonso de Albuquerque..! The actual 'Lion of the Seas'..?"

"That I am," he chuckled.

"This is a great honour for me. I've read so much about you. Could I purchase a passage to India, sir? I have an instruction signed by the Bishop of Alhandra to set up a Catholic mission in the new territories."

"The honour is all mine. Come aboard, Father. I'll meet you on the main deck."

Albuquerque emptied half the bag of gold coins into his palm then checked the cleric's signed paper.

Alfonso de Albuquerque was a tall, well built and a fearsomely good-looking man of fifty years. He wore a long greying beard that hung the entire length of his black waistcoat. On his head sat a black hexagonal velvet hat with a cluster of small golden coloured cotton balls on the crown; his thick overcoat had extended drooping shoulders with flamboyantly embroidered sleeves that billowed out to the elbow. A wide bright blue, white and black fabric sash covered his abdomen, his sword and dagger hung from a separate silver studded leather belt. Over his white seaman tights he wore light brown leather boots, which covered his knees.

His sharp eyes darted back and forth from the Bishop's commission to the cleric. He disliked all priests. Only garlic could take away the bitter taste they left in his mouth. But it was necessary to endure their hypocritical self righteous ways. They played a vital role maintaining the peace with the natives. Albuquerque shared his Admiral's conviction that they could not hope to hold control and govern any part of the new world without first winning the hearts and minds of the aboriginals.

Satisfied, he handed the paper back to the priest. "I'll let the Admiral know that I have acquired an additional passenger during the voyage. My first mate will take you to your quarters. Nunes," he bellowed.

Instantly a black bearded middle-aged seaman wearing a blue bandanna appeared from a door beneath the aft castle. He wore thick pantaloons to the knee, stockings and black brass buckled shoes. His sweat stained grimy white blouse was open at the front revealing a shining muscular torso, the thick hair on his chest soaked and matted with perspiration.

"Father Benedict will be a passenger, Nunes. Take him to the cabin Gonzales used. My crew will be at your disposal should you need anything once we are under way. Then we'll have time to talk. Good night, Father."

Nunes escorted Father Benedict back through the aft door and down two flights of steps to the cabin allocated to the priest at the rear of the lower deck. It was a yard wide and two yards deep with a small port side window. Built against one wall were two wooden bunks and under the window was a chest for stowing his belongings.

"It's a bit small, Father," he apologised, bowing respectfully and pulling off his bandanna to reveal a head of thick curly black locks. Then he smiled affably, "but you'll get used to it. The Captain-General's cabin is right above you. You will eat with the crew amidships, if that is all right with you Father. Bread and groat porridge at first light…ships biscuit and dried fruit at noon and a salt beef or salt fish dinner at dusk. Call me if you need anything." He closed the door behind him, leaving the priest to settle in.

From the moment they set sail Father Benedict was stricken by seasickness. For nine days he barely ventured out of his cabin. On the morning of the eleventh day the ship sat dead in the water, becalmed in the doldrums. The priest staggered weakly to the steps and climbed to the main deck. The whole ship was alive with activity: scores of crewmen were climbing or descending the shrouds that extended from each of the three mast heads to the port and starboard sides, others were working along the yards of each mast adjusting the sails whilst men on the ground pulled on the halliards and sheets; top sails, gallants and royals were unfurled; men on the bowsprit, with just the netting between them and the ocean below, pulling on the jib-guys; every man endeavouring to make use of any breath of air that fluttered the canvas.

Nunes spotted the pathetic, emaciated figure in the black habit standing by the port side gunwale looking out over the smooth, windless ocean. The sun beat directly down mercilessly upon them all. On deck the air was as hot as a furnace.

Nunes draped a tarpaulin shelter from the main mast to a nearby hatch and arranged for a special meal to be brought up on deck. He stayed with the clergyman until he had finished. Benedict spoke freely to Nunes under the watchful eye of the Captain-General who peered down occasionally from poop deck.

At dusk the Captain-General summoned Nunes to his cabin.

"Well Nunes…what do you make of him..?" Albuquerque's eyes searched his old friend's face.

"He asked a lot of queer questions, sir."

"Did he now? What sort of queer questions were they?"

"When I asked him about his mission he kept on asking me if I knew anything about the Admiral's flag ship, sir."

"The 'Flor de la Marr' eh? What else?"

"He asked me if I knew anything about her cargo."

"I see." Albuquerque stood up abruptly; stooping his head to avoid the low beams in his cabin and began pacing the floor. "Did he mention what it was he was interested in?"

"He said that there was something of great importance to the church being transported to India. He wanted to know if I knew about it."

He stopped pacing and faced Nunes. "Well! Do you know anything about a special shipment for the church in the 'Flor de la Marr'?"

"No sir."

"Well, neither do I," he quickly added. "Bring Father Benedict to me. I'd like to know a little more about this cargo our Admiral should be carrying."

Two minutes later Nunes had returned with the priest.

"That will be all, Nunes, thank you," Albuquerque smiled amiably. "Please be seated, Father," gesturing with his hand to the leather chair and sat behind his polished mahogany desk. As the cabin door closed he leaned forward across the desk and began: "I'm sorry to hear that the sickness had taken you, Father. I'm pleased to see that you are over the worst. I can expect you to attend dinner in my cabin with my officers very soon. I dare say you are looking forward to reaching India, Father?"

"Yes." Father Benedict managed a wan smile. "I'm not a good sea-man."

"It will take eight months before you reach Cochin." Albuquerque noticed the cloud of gloom descend over the priest's face. "You can get to know a person very well in that length of time…. within the confines of a ship."

"I suppose so," the priest's nerves suddenly tightened and his stomach began to flutter.

"There is nowhere to hide on a ship!" He looked the priest in the eye. "I want to be perfectly frank with you, Father. Alhandra is where I was born. Not much happens there without me hearing about it. I know that the new Bishop elect is not Portuguese. He is Spanish and, I suspect, the Dominican order were involved with his appointment."

"I'm but a humble priest, Captain-General. I do what I'm told."

"But you are Portuguese none the less. How do you feel having a foreigner as your Bishop?"

"He is a man of the cloth. The nationality of my Bishop is not relevant."

"He is Spanish, Father. I think it matters a great deal. Do you con-done the ways of the Inquisition?"

"Heretics must be brought to trial, Captain-General," he snapped in a high-pitched and effeminate tone. "They are subverting the very word of God…" his mouth twisting strangely "…and all our souls are in deep jeopardy," the pitch of his voice escalating with every word. His eyes had a fanatical, almost manic, look. "Do you not agree, Captain-General?"

Albuquerque looked down at his polished desk, his eyes following the grain of the wood, sickened by the priest's outburst. To him the priest had all the hallmarks of the ruthless and sadistic Dominican order behind the Spanish Inquisition. He gazed into the priest's eyes and saw only hate. Shrewdly taking measure of the man before him, acutely aware that one misplaced word said to a priest of his ilk could lead to excommunication or even worse, he needed to defuse the situation urgently.

"You are our guide, Father, when it comes to saving souls," he said calmly. "I trust the church implicitly in these matters." Albuquerque's eyes bore into the clergyman. Before him he could see only an enemy to his King and country. "Do you have any plans for your mission in India, Father? How do you think you can benefit the people there? It's such a radical, lonely and daunting task for someone as young and inexperi-enced as yourself."

"My plan is written in the scriptures and I have God to comfort me and show me how I can best preach His word to the people."

"Have you always wanted to be a missionary, Father?"

"I consider it an honour to have been chosen."

"That's not what I asked. You don't seem to be the missionary type. Is this the life you chose?"

"No. But I'm honoured to…."

"Yes. Yes. Then the Bishop of Alhandra ordered you to set up this mission at very short notice, did he not?"

"Yes," admitted the priest, his expression remaining calm although his heart was racing and his stomach began to twist.

"So you will set up your mission in Cochin. But for what purpose?"

"What do you mean? What other purpose could there be?" he sneered, bridling against Albuquerque's hostility.

"What is it you think the Admiral is carrying in his ship?"

"Ah! Francisco…erm…Nunes has been talking. He gave me his word he would keep our conversation confidential."

"Nunes is my first mate. It's his duty to report everything unusual to me. I am Captain-General…and the law on this ship," he said slapping his hand on the desk. He glared at the priest icily. "Well! I'm waiting for your answer, Father."

"I don't really know myself. I heard that there was something being carried in the flagship that might be of great interest to me. I thought that if I could discover what it was… I was just curious. That's all."

"I see." Albuquerque scowled, seething inside at the young priest's audacity. He let his anger dissipate; certain the cleric knew exactly what was in the Admirals ship but let the priest think that he had outsmarted him for the present. The moments passed. "Thank you for seeing me, Father," pulling a congenial smile. "I hope you find the remainder of the voyage more agreeable. That will be all."

The moment his cabin door closed the Captain-General stood and paced the floor. Satisfied that neither Father Benedict nor the church knew anything substantial about the Cross he decided to wait until an opportunity presented itself during the voyage before troubling the Admiral with this obnoxious spy.

The fleet had taken 87 days to reach the southern tip of Africa, taking a looping, wide route into the Atlantic. They took on fresh water and fruit at a port on Africa's southern cape then continued up the east coast of Africa to a settlement north of the island of Madagascar called Mombasa.

Albuquerque had confined the cleric to the ship during the fleet's two stops along the African coast.

Before leaving Lisbon, Father Benedict had believed fervently and wholeheartedly in his adventurous and courageous countrymen; that they were spreading Christianity across the globe in a manner befitting the civilized nation he had been born into; that they could never dishonour the name of his King and his Pope; that the savage natives he had heard and read about were being peacefully and willingly introduced to the path of God and to righteousness.

This illusion was to be tested when the priest heard from the crew shortly after each stop that Admiral da Gama employed ruthless and bloody methods to restrain and control the natives. Father Benedict was to learn that massacre and butchery perpetrated upon the African native people by the Admiral was commonplace.

In September 1502 the fleet sailed west-northwest to a group of uninhabited tropical islands known as the Seven Sisters. All twenty ships weighed anchor within the shelter of the islands. Albuquerque took the opportunity to arrange a meeting with Admiral da Gama. His long boat collected Admiral da Gama from the 'Flor de la Marr' and the two great men of the sea were taken ashore.

"I have a spy aboard my ship Admiral," Albuquerque announced with a grin as the two men strolled alone along the white coral sand. Cotton-wool clouds raced across an otherwise beautifully clear blue sky, the occasional one crossing the sun momentarily, giving a short respite from its furious heat. The shore to their left was flanked by Coconut palms that waved and bowed in the stiff breeze. "He is Father Benedict. His cover is to set up a mission in Cochin."

"What's he after?" The Admiral stuck out his boot and pushed a giant Coco-de-mer, a jumbo-sized double coconut that bears an uncanny resemblance to the well-proportioned features of the female form from waist to thigh.

"He's been sent by the Church to find out about the Cross."

"What! Did he admit that?"

"No sir. All he knows is that you're carrying 'something interesting', to quote his words." The two men stood beside the coconut. "He probably knows it's a cross, but nothing more." Albuquerque squatted to examine the nut more closely. "It's extremely lifelike, isn't it? Look! It even has pubic hairs."

A wave washed over their boots and lifted the nut two paces up the beach.

"I am yet to be invested as one of the brotherhood," admitted the Admiral as they moved slowly to where the nut had rested. "What I do know is that the Knights of Christ can be trusted implicitly. The secret of the Cross will always be safe. It's impossible for him to know anything damaging." They stood over the intriguing coconut once more. "The church has caught wind that we have something…that is all. If they knew anything more it would be common knowledge by now. There's no danger, Alfonso. We will watch him, then feed him gradually with snippets of disinformation and then, when the time is ripe, we will use him."

"We should take this back for the men to see," Albuquerque suggested grinning at the coconut, then noticing da Gama's reproachful glance, he quickly added, "...well maybe not."

"Their imaginations can do without this sort of stimulation, Alfonso."

The two men chuckled together as they both marvelled at nature's inventiveness.

"This is paradise, Alfonso. Don't you think? A man can repair his soul here. I think they should be Portuguese forever." He lifted his arms dramatically to shoulder height and faced the shore. Looking up at the towering cliffs of grey granite, eroded into beautifully smooth, rounded and surreal sculptures, he proclaimed: "I claim these islands for King Manuel. I name them 'Ilhas do Almirante' (Admiral Islands)... And thanks be to God there are no wretched natives to subdue!"

"Congratulations, Admiral. I'll wager that any man stranded here would never want to be rescued!"

The two men laughed and returned to the waiting long boat.

The fleet arrived at Calicut on the18th October 1502.

For Father Benedict the full horror of Admiral da Gama's brutality was about to become known to him. What had occurred in Africa did little to prepare him for what was to follow in India. His naïve illusions about his illustrious countrymen were quashed forever. To avenge the massacre of Cabral's men at Calicut, the Admiral had captured a ship carrying Muslim pilgrims travelling to Mecca, which included hundreds of women and children, also the lame, the infirmed and the elderly. First he looted it, then fired it...keeping the fire fed for four days until every living soul on board had been burned to death. Their screams were to haunt Father Benedict practically every night for the rest of his days.

The 'Sao Gabriel' docked at Cochin on 21st November 1502.

Alfonso de Albuquerque clasped the priest's arm before he went ashore.

"Listen to me Father. I know how you abhor the Admiral's methods of controlling these people but ask yourself this question: If your family and friends were to settle out here to live, wouldn't you expect the governing forces to be strong enough to ensure their safety and prosperity?"

"The price is too high!" His eyes were alight with rage and he struggled to free himself. But Albuquerque's grip tightened. "What right does da Gama have to massacre those innocent people?" he screamed effeminately.

"It was not only to avenge the murder of Cabral's men that the Admiral fired that ship! These people must be taught that killing Christians is in violation of the Papal Bull. The harsher the methods; the more effective will be the deterrent."

"If we murder them, how can we preach to them that the word of God is *Love*?" he screamed, struggling to control his suppressed emotions, tears trickling down his cheeks. "We have taken their land," he cried. "We should respect their beliefs and customs and have a more civilised way of dealing with troublemakers."

A crowd of fascinated natives had gathered at the foot of the gangplank to watch the two foreigners from far off lands locked in bitter argument.

"Control by the use of fear and suppression," the priest continued, "fuels nothing but hostility. You will never win their hearts that way. I can never understand the mentality of people who adopt those methods and claim them to be in the name of Christianity!"

"You are a long way from home, Father. You will have plenty of time to think. If you have anything in you at all, you might search your own…hypocritical soul… and discover for yourself what the right way actually is."

Albuquerque let go of his arm and watched the black robed figure with his small bag of belongings walk the gangplank and jostle through the sizeable crowd that had gathered on the quay.

The air was heavy with the scent of spices, perfumes and incense; the humidity was stifling and the scorching sun burned Father Benedict's face. He weaved his way through the throng of bustling natives and porters carrying boxes and sacks containing all kinds of exotic merchandise, rolls of fabrics and earthenware jugs.

Before he turned down a side street, Father Benedict looked back at the 'Sao Gabriel' and Alfonso de Albuquerque, the 'Lion of the Seas', his one- time hero. His lips twisted into a grimace of loathing and disgust. With a contemptuous twist of his shoulders he strode on and vanished from sight.

The harrowing screams of the dying pilgrims wracked Father Benedict's nights and Albuquerque's last stinging words tormented him by day.

'How could a man of the cloth be accused of hypocrisy?…' he would reason, '..The Church had used fear, it was true, but it was used justly and righteously for man's own salvation. The Church would never use terror and mass slaughter as mercilessly and as ruthlessly as those damned adventurous countryman of mine!'

Over the next seven years Father Benedict's nightmares progressively increased in severity. His hatred for Albuquerque and da Gama mounted adding impetus to his purpose of uncovering the Cross' secret powers and possibly discrediting or better disgracing his countrymen at the same time.

Many of the guards at the fort in Cochin had given him, over the years, sufficient damning information for him to conclude that the mysterious Cross was a definite threat to the Church.

He had found vindication and solace from perpetual torment and habitual soul searching in the Church leaders of the past: Pope Julius II, who repeatedly proclaimed the infallibility of the Church and Pope Zachary whose discovery of the 'Constitutum Constanti' gave the Church unlimited authority.

Father Benedict began drafting his letter to the Bishop of Alhandra.

The morning after finishing the first draft of his letter, his face dripping with sweat and his head still reeling from the screams in his nightmare, he received an invitation from the Viceroy of Cochin, Conde de Alvor requesting him to attend a banquet to celebrate the recapture of Goa.

Puzzled by the unwelcome intrusion but honoured by the invitation he climbed aboard the Viceroy's carriage on the day of the banquet. A nurse and several of his children from the mission had come to see him off. Two of the boys chased after the carriage as it climbed the slight incline into town.

Leaving the crowded streets the carriage turned under a stone arch dedicated to Vasco da Gama and through the main gateway into the Viceroy's estate. The carriage moved more swiftly up the long, curving driveway, the horse's hooves clipping the cobbles in a cheerful trot. A cooling breeze entered the open window making a welcome respite from the still, sultry air. He glimpsed beautifully manicured undulating lawns surrounded by ornate gardens through the tall cypresses and palm trees that lined the driveway. Taking the final curve the Viceroy's palatial mansion, a replica of the home he had left behind in Portugal, spread out majestically before him.

A young native boy dressed in a green silk suit and an orange silk turban ushered him through the main entrance to the lounge and announced his arrival to the host and the hundred other guests.

The women were dressed in long gowns of satin or silk in strikingly vibrant colours of reds, greens, blues and whites or with oriental floral patterns upon more neutral shades of pale yellow or ochre. The men wore fashionable braded tunics and three quarter pantaloons and coloured stockings. The myriad of colours was a feast for the cleric's eyes.

The Viceroy greeted him warmly, introduced him hurriedly to four naval officers who had just arrived from Goa. An announcement bellowed from the far end of the lounge that the guests were to take their places at the great one hundred and thirty foot long dining table.

With his young voluptuous wife's arm linked into his, the Viceroy led the procession of guests into the dining room and took their places at the head of the table. Four bunches of exotic native, sweet smelling flowers had been carefully arranged and placed at even intervals along its centre. Huge bowls filled with fruit were placed between the flower arrangements, white and gold braided plates were framed by golden cutlery and the crystal wine glasses looked dazzlingly beautiful upon the white linen tablecloth embroidered with orchids and roses.

Father Benedict was seated next to the four officers and listened politely to their endless tales of their campaign in Goa. They described, too graphically for the priest's ears, how the Portuguese forces had been initially defeated then counterattacked leading to the eventual victory of Alfonso de Albuquerque, at an enormous cost of human life on both sides.

Finally the seemingly continuous courses of exquisite and exotic foods had ceased being placed before him by an army of native servants. The young boy rang a small bell and called for silence. He then introduced the Viceroy, who slowly rose from his throne like chair and looked regally down upon his guests.

"I am especially happy and privileged to convey great news from our illustrious mariner, the 'Lion of the Seas' Alfonso de Albuquerque. In alliance with the Hindu sea captain Timmaya of the Vijayanagar he has defeated the Muslim fleet and conquered the area called Goa." The banqueting hall erupted into resounding cheers and applause. "The Captain-General has said…," the Viceroy continued above the excited chatter and laughter, raising a hand to lull their excitement, "…he has said in his communiqué to me that he considered the island in the Mandovi River to be a perfect base from which the entire Indian continent could be governed in the name of his majesty, King John." The guests applauded and cheered again.

His speech continued by giving tributes to the four officers seated with the priest, who were to receive honours from the King for bravery in the field of combat. He then went on to predict that in the very near future Goa would become the centre for all trade between Europe, Asia and China.

The Viceroy concluded his speech by recognising the contributions and efforts of the dignitaries seated at the table and then announced: "Father Benedict's work here at the mission has been an inspiration to us all, seeking new and imaginative ways to overcome the barriers that divide our communities. Alfonso de Albuquerque has specifically requested that Father Benedict should join him immediately in Goa with the object of choosing a site for the new Cathedral. I can think of no better person to perform this task."

The Viceroy beckoned the amazed priest to stand up and accept the acclaim and applause from the guests. "Your ship leaves Cochin in two hours."

At the mission Father Benedict hastily scribbled instructions to the nurse for the running of the mission in his absence and hid the letter to the Bishop under loose stones beneath the chapel altar. With a small bag packed he hurried to the docks.

The cleric was seasick during the entire three-day voyage, his tiny ship having to battle four hundred miles up the coast against the monsoon winds.

"Welcome to Goa, Father," Albuquerque shouted from the quay-side. "I'm sorry to inform you, Father, that I have received information that could jeopardise your assignment. Kamal Khan, Regent for the infant Ismail 'Adil Shah, has organised a massive army to recapture Goa. Their attack is imminent."

"As you know, Captain-General, my assignment has been sanctioned by His Holiness Pope Julius. There is no way of stopping God's work. I will find a suitable site for our Cathedral," Father Benedict proclaimed as he climbed out of the long boat, clipping his words self-importantly.

Albuquerque sighed sadly realising that age had not mellowed nor humbled the cleric.

"And that is exactly what I intend to do. I then want to return quickly to my mission in Cochin." He turned haughtily from the seaman adding as he strode down the quay, "there's still much work to be done."

"I know, Father. You have ploughed the young souls and planted many good seeds." Albuquerque moved quickly to overtake the cleric and fixed him with his gaze. "Seriously Father, it is the wet season, but the rains this year are heavier than ever before. I can't defend a Muslim attack in this weather. I have withdrawn my forces to our ships moored in deep water to wait out the rains. It could take six or seven months before we can make another counter attack."

"It's not raining today, Captain-General!"

"That makes the risk even greater. It will suit the enemy too."

"I must go. It's a risk I have to take."

"I've always thought you were foolhardy, Father, but it will be certain suicide if you go inland." Albuquerque was firm, but not insistent, sure that the priest would not head his warning. 'Your time has come,' he thought. "I have a small garrison here in the Customs Building. I'll order a squadron of my men to escort you. You are right. It's better not to delay." Albuquerque handed one of the guards outside the Customs House a hastily scrawled signed order. "Go with God, Father." The seaman returned to the quayside and boarded his longboat.

Six troopers, armed with matchlock muskets, accompanied Father Benedict up the gentle slope to the summit of the hill, about 800 yards from the river. The troopers immediately formed a defensive line, kneeling in front of the clergyman, facing southwest towards the area where the enemy had last been seen. Forked rests supported the barrels of their 6 foot long guns and each gun was primed and ready to fire.

Father Benedict looked back towards the river. From the spot where he stood he had a spectacular panoramic view across the estuary to Albuquerque's ships moored in the distance. The Captain –General's longboat had still more than a mile to cover before reaching the fleet. With a self-satisfied smile the priest took out his prayer book.

Hoards of natives charged towards the hill from the east.

"Run for your life, Father," a trooper yelled, pulling at the priest's habit.

"Retreat!" shouted the sergeant.

Father Benedict was oblivious of the approaching danger. He had never felt closer to his God. He continued praying and making the sign of the cross to each point of the compass,

"Come on, Father!" the soldier screamed again.

"This is God's work. They will not harm me."

"Then say a prayer for all of us, Father."

The soldiers bravely formed a protective semi circle around the cleric, aimed their muskets and fired at the advancing army. Within seconds they were all hacked to pieces by the scimitar brandishing enemy thirsty for Portuguese blood. The butchered corpses were left to rot where they lay.

The rains that year had persisted for eight months holding Alfonso de Albuquerque's fleet at their moorings until 25th November 1510. Albuquerque embarked on his counter offensive, mercilessly slaughtering all Arab civilians and children and raised every house and mosque to the ground.

Immediately after the battle the Captain-General climbed the small hill with two of his officers to the spot where his squadron of sailors and Father Benedict had perished. From the hilltop he wirily looked across the battlefield, thousands of dead strewn amongst the smouldering fires as far as he could see, then he turned seaward to view his victorious fleet, gloriously lit by the sun with all colours flying resplendently in the hot wind.

Bloated with pride he squatted and studied the grass at his feet. Broken and crushed bones protruded from the soft ground, their bodies long since eaten and their clothing rotted and torn by eight months of rain and wind. He lifted a fragment of Father Benedict's crucifix from the muddy ground. It had the head and neck of Christ, carved in ivory, upon ebony. He kissed it and said in a soft reverent voice: "Mark this spot! This shall be the site for our new Cathedral."

The first stones of the Cathedral were laid in 1562 but the great building took ninety years to complete. In 1610, with construction still in progress, the Sé Cathedral was officially dedicated to St. Catherine. The Cross, which had been secretly transported from the fort in Cochin and held in the Viceroy's palace, was ceremoniously carried up the nave.

The Cross dominated the nave for more than a century. It glowed like a beacon from within the Cathedral's tenebrous barrel vault. Its gold reflected the dim light with a constant, almost eternal, warm intensity coalescing with the multicoloured seductive gleam of its innumerable jewels. Its mesmerising aura hinted at a hidden power of inconceivable strength; it exuded an energy that touched the soul of all who came near to it. Pilgrims journeyed from all regions of the sub continent and from the distant Orient, Arabia and Africa and beyond to witness and feel the Cross's rejuvenating and soul enriching properties. The legend of the 'Fiery' Cross of Goa was born.

'Golden Goa' became a thriving, vibrant cosmopolitan city and was at the heart of European trade with the Sub Continent and beyond to the Orient. But during the latter years of the seventeenth century its artery, the Mandovi River, began to clog with silt preventing merchantman from reaching its docks. By 1721 a new port, Panjim, was emerging at the mouth of the Mandovi River built with the salvaged stones and materials from the abandoned buildings of the old city.

# CHAPTER 4

The Archbishop of Goa, Don Sebastian de Andrado, had been summoned by King John V to return to Lisbon and to bring with him the Cross of Goa.

He purchased a passage on the majestic Man o' War 'Vierge du Cap'. The great vessel, the pride of the Portuguese fleet was to sail on the noontide on Friday 13th April 1721. But it was the day he was to marry Maria de la Luz de Valdema, the nineteen year old daughter of the wealthiest landowner in the province Sanchez de Valdema, to the Englishman Robert Radclyffe.

When Maria de la Luz learned from her father that the Archbishop had cancelled the ceremony she was devastated. Her life-long dream of being married in the Sé Cathedral before the 'Fiery' Cross of Goa had been shattered at the last moment.

Sanchez de Valdema made an offer to the Archbishop of Goa that he knew he could not refuse. Ten bags of gold for the new orphanage in Panjim if the Archbishop would perform the ceremony before the ship sailed.

The Archbishop was overwhelmed. Having wrung the wealthy landowners hand with heartfelt gratitude he then needed every ounce of his guile and prodigious powers of persuasion to convince the Captain-General of the 'Vierge du Cap' to delay the sailing of the great ship for one hour.

The Captain-General reluctantly agreed on condition that he and the squad of sailors assigned to transport the Cross of Goa to the vessel would be on board ship before one o'clock.

On hearing the Captain-General's condition de Valdema promised the Archbishop that his daughter would be at the Sé Cathedral for the wedding ceremony no later than 10.00 a.m.

But Robert Radclyffe watched the flickering hour candle beside the Cross of Goa melt halfway down to the 'XII' marker. The young groom looked forlornly at his best man, Philip Campbell a fellow merchant navy-man, and then glanced anxiously back for the hundredth time towards the entrance of the Sé Cathedral. Both doors were fully open.

From where Radclyffe stood the entrance reminded him of a glaring, gaping mouth that sucked in the sun baked hot air into its cavernous belly. There was no sign of life on the gravel beyond the doors, which reflected brilliant white in the blazing sun. Angular parallel beams of sunlight as robust as marble pillars burst onto the stone floor through the five windows above and around the entrance on the east wall. The light rebounded on the white painted walls and permeated deeper into the heart of the barrel-vaulted interior reaching the massive beautifully carved wooden rederos that towered over the main altar, its gold leaf glistening, depicting scenes from the life of Saint Catherine.

Robert William Radclyffe, a young Englishman of twenty-one years, smiled nervously at nearby guests sitting restlessly either side of the aisle. Seeing the red leather bound gilded diary laying on the pew he picked up the weighty book. It fell open at the pages where he had placed his two passages on the 'Vierge du Cap'. He read again the departure time written on the two square pieces of paper above the signature of the Captain-General Rodriguez:

*'Sailing Noon-High Tide on the 13th day of April in the year of our Lord 1721'.*

He then turned to the inside front cover and reread the comforting inscription:

*To my dear brother Robert,*
*I was delighted to learn of your engagement yesterday and send you this diary on the 'Margarita' sailing for Bombay today.*
*I am sorry I cannot be with you on your wedding day but ask you to record all the events of your day in this diary. I would dearly love to read it.*
*I wish you both a lifetime of happiness together and pray that God will keep you both safe during your journey home.*
*I will arrange for you to meet me here in France next year.*
*Your ever loving brother,*
*Charles.*
*Paris, 28th May 1720*

Radclyffe snapped the diary shut.

"You're not to worry, Robert," his best man consoled, his strong highland accent resounding within the cavernous space. "She's sure to be along any minute now."

Radclyffe nodded. "I hope you're right Phil," Radclyffe's border accent was less pronounced. "We canny miss this voyage. It would take me a whole year," he lowered his voice to a whisper, "to save up enough for another passage home on the pittance Maria's father pays."

"Heck. You're worry yoosel' t'death...that you will. Listen. If she doesny get here within the next quarter of an hour I'll go search for her me sel'. How's tha'?"

"I'm not too sure I can bear to wait another quarter of an hour…"

"Will yer stop it now, man. She'll be here I tell ye."

Robert Radclyffe put down the heavy book and bowed his head in prayer. He looked older than his years and cut a dashing figure. He wore a three quarter length claret velvet coat, with a high collar and flared cuffs; the lace frill of his shirt bubbled up under his clean-shaven chin and fell from under the cuffs to partially cover his hands, his white knee length britches were fashionably baggy at the thigh and tucked into high leather boots.

The Archbishop appeared from his cloisters and mounted the dais in the centre of the nave looking harassed and dishevelled. His round ruddy face, which usually glowed more from the fruit of the vine than from righteous thoughts, was drawn with anxiety and worry.

Word had reached the clergyman that the bride's carriage had broken an axel on debris littering the main road from Panjim to Goa and a replacement carriage had been rushed to the stranded couple.

The Archbishop leaned over to groom and best man, perspiration dripping from his brow and chin and whispered hoarsely: "The bride and her father are expected at any moment." He dabbed his face nervously with a large white silk handkerchief.

Two minutes later they all heard the crunch of horses' hooves and the grinding of cart wheels on the gravel outside. Every head turned; hushed murmurings and sighs of relief wafted through the vaulted interior as the two shapes approached the entrance. The silhouettes of the bride and her father, she slightly taller than him, were sharp against the glaring brightness filling the doorway. The organist proclaimed their arrival with gusto, pounding the opening chords of Radclyffe's choice of popular music, 'Well Hail Wayfairing Stranger'. As they moved down the aisle the congregation hummed approvingly at the beauty of the bride's dress lit by the shafts of sunlight from the windows.

The bride's dress was of white satin, fashionably layered, belling out at the hem that hung just above the floor, with nine feet of train brushing the stone slabs of the aisle. She held a large posy of bright tropical flowers in her right hand, her slender dusky right arm protruded the three quarter length puffed sleeve of her dress; her left arm was tucked loosely inside her father's.

The easy tempo of the organist suddenly increased urging the bride's father to hurry.

Sanchez de Valdema was dapper, his head tilted proudly, wearing a dark green suit with gold braid around the high collar and white lace frills on the cuffs. A white silk shirt billowed out from his cream and beige waistcoat fastened at the neck by a matching dark green neckerchief with a golden pin. A flawless diamond, the size of an almond, sparkled from the pinhead. His dress sword swung freely from his left hip, the bejewelled golden hilt glinting in the reflected light.

Radclyffe's heart was pounding in his chest. Centuries of mixed marriages with Arab, African, Turkish and Portuguese settlers and traders had made Goan women arguably the most beautiful in the world. Her gossamer veil, crowned with yellow and orange blossom, did little to conceal her dusky sensual radiance. But this enchanting apparition was approaching him with unusual rapidity. The sight took his breath away.

The organist continued increasing the tempo until the individual notes of the tune were indistinguishable, blending together to form variations of one augmented chord. Bemused guests on both sides of the aisle smiled and bowed as the couple glided quickly by.

The instant they reached the dais the music ceased although the vault of the cathedral continued to reverberate with the cacophony for several seconds more.

The father smiled at the bride, gently took her hand and kissed it. The moment had come when Sanchez de Valdema had to give his daughter away. She had grown so fast. The little girl, his 'pumpkin', was no more. He clung onto that sweet faded memory of her waving to him as a child. He wanted more time. He smiled at that beautiful women before him and realised it was too late. His tearful eyes were drawn inexplicably to the Cross of Goa. Its invisible radiation affected his mind and body, the lustre of the gold and its dazzling jewels intensified the sensation it exuded. An extraordinary wave of peace enveloped him. He bowed his head and backed away from his daughter and joined the other guests.

The Archbishop opened his arms and welcomed the couple and the congregation. He read hastily from the Bible then recited a litany at such a fast pace that the confused congregation were completely lost with their responses.

The bride and groom stood transfixed before the radiant Cross of Goa. It was positioned on a rectangular four-foot high marble plinth behind the Archbishop. The reflected sun light from the Cross cast dappled patterns of reds, blues, greens and turquoise onto the bride's dress and veil and also upon the Archbishop's white and gold cassock and mitre. A surge of pleasure and warmth passed through the bride and groom, their bodies weightless and tingling. Then the Cross spoke to them telepathically with a certainty and truth that reached the depths of their souls. The spiritual experience was enriched by the sweet sound of the choir, their voices echoing with a warm resonance that pulsated within the vault of the Cathedral.

Radclyffe stood statuesque, his tricorne hat held under his right arm, looking into the loving veiled eyes of his bride. They had been both swept up into their own glorious world, oblivious of the ceremony taking place, conscious only of the incredible feelings they were both experiencing. The Archbishop had been reciting the vows, to which Radclyffe, mesmerised by his bride's eyes, unconsciously answered up to a point. Then there had been a long silence.

"With this ring I thee wed," the cleric repeated once more, raising his voice with growing impatience.

Radclyffe jumped to attention, dropped his hat then fumbled through his pockets for the ring. All eyes of the hushed congregation were upon him.

Philip Campbell nudged Radclyffe's right arm. He turned to see the ring held tightly between his best man's fingers.

Radclyffe took the ring with an embarrassed smile and retrieved his hat. He offered the ring to the Archbishop.

"Not to me, sir," the Archbishop's eyes rolled upwards with exasperation. "Say after me, 'With this ring I thee wed' and put it on your bride's finger."

Radclyffe looked down into the smiling orbs that twinkled before him. She held out her tiny finger. He was transfixed. Her beauty was so breathtaking.

"Say the words, my love," she whispered.

"Wi--th this r-ing I th-e-e wed," he stammered.

The Archbishop continued on with the vows then gabbled another incoherent litany that ended suddenly with him staring expectantly at the groom once more.

She gazed amorously up at her husband, who was completely lost in her eyes.

"You may kiss the bride," the Archbishop repeated loudly.

Neither could believe it was over. They saw perspiration dripping from the Archbishop's chin, his bulbous eyes darting from one to other waiting for them to kiss.

"Well, come on!" his patience at an end. "Come on! Hurry it up lad!"

As they kissed with growing passion, the Archbishop snapped the Bible shut, turned on his heels, his cassock billowing out, and made off to his cloisters.

Six armed seamen advanced at quick march from the back of the Cathedral, three along each side wall, then turned at the nave and ushered the congregation out, with the bride and groom at the head of the alarmed but submissive crowd.

They all gushed out of the Cathedral into the mid-day sun. The heavy oak doors slammed shut behind them.

Only the newly-weds were unperturbed by their abrupt ejection from the house of God. The driver of the carriage helped them both inside, climbed up to his seat and took them out of the cathedral grounds and onward to the docks.

Four of the sailors removed their shoes, following the Archbishop's earlier instructions, inserted the golden poles into the rings on the base of the Cross, lifted it slowly from the marble plinth and lowered it carefully. Marching quickly down the aisle, their bare feet slapping on the stone floor, they waited by the door.

Outside, amid the confused, slowly dispersing crowd, an open backed wagon drew up with five saddled horses tied to the back. The driver knocked a prearranged sequence of raps on the door.

The doors flew open and the four sailors emerged carrying the Cross. They climbed onto the wagon and lowered the Cross carefully into a wooden crate, hammered down the lid and covered it with a tarpaulin. Moments later the remaining sailors ran out of the Cathedral carrying a great sea chest followed by the Archbishop, his travelling robes blustering out, clutching a bulging cloth bag in one hand and carrying Radclyffe's diary in the other.

He climbed up beside the driver of the wagon. One of the sailors joined them with a cocked musket in his hand. Two mounted sailors galloped ahead of the wagon, which was accelerating up the driveway. Clusters of wedding guests jumped out of their path. The remaining three horsemen followed as a rear guard.

Turning left at the Cathedral's main gate the wagon with its escort speeded down Rua Direita towards the jetty and the Mandovi River. The wagon bumped and jolted over stones and debris littering the road lined by derelict, decaying houses and shops.

The Archbishop clung firmly onto his cloth bag and Radclyffe's diary, looking sadly upon the old, deserted city of Goa. He reminded himself of how 'Golden Goa' used to be only ten years before: the streets thronged with people of all nationalities, the shops and warehouses bustling with activity; at the docks ships offloading merchandise from the Japans, China and Africa; cosmopolitan Goa was at the hub of world trade and was growing into the busiest trading centre in the world.

As the wagon rumbled under the Viceroy's Archway the Archbishop was sadly aware that it was time…time for him and the Cross of Goa to go home. Golden Goa was no more.

The wagon and its escort arrived at the jetty where two long boats waited. The Archbishop spied the newly-weds at the front of the nearest boat and joined them. Once the Cross and the six sailors were aboard the oarsmen pulled hard, taking them all towards the resplendent 'Vierge du Cap' at anchor a mile out in the silted Mandovi.

The mighty Portuguese Man o' War 'Vierge du Cap' had finally got under way at 1.30 p.m. on Friday 13th April 1721. Her harbour mooring ropes were hauled and the anchor weighed, her mainsail billowed in the sun and her topsails unfurled and cracked in the northwest monsoon. Crowds of spectators lined the riverbank to witness the great ship leave port for her final voyage home.

But the cheering and the shouting were quieter than was usual for such an occasion. The crowd was abnormally subdued. Experienced mariners and ordinary land dwellers alike looked on in disbelief. Some onlookers stared in silence pondering the sheer folly of the Captain-General whilst others were more verbal with their criticism.

They spoke incredulously and anxiously to each another: 'how could he put to sea on an ebb tide when she's so low in the water?' and 'how's he going to negotiate the treacherous southern headland of Cabo Raj Niwas?' and 'she'll be heading for the bottom if a cyclone catches her. If not, she's going to be manna from heaven for any pirate 'round these waters'.

The delay in missing the high tide could not, for once, be blamed upon the accumulation of silt at the docks or upon the sluggishness of the lighters. Many heard of the vast treasures being loaded aboard the great ship in countless sea chests and wooden crates of every shape and size and were quick to assume that the Captain-General's greed had got the better of him.

The 'Vierge du Cap' was the pride of King John's fleet, a carrack of traditional design with high fore and aft castles; fitted with 72 cannon and with a deep draught and a broad beam. She was a war galleon but equally well suited for transporting goods and passengers.

The heavy vessel slowly gathered speed along the Mandovi estuary. The heat haze had blurred her beautiful, graceful lines and her sails. It was indistinct: ghostly and mystical, a levitating phantom, a mirage above the choppy surface of the estuary. Imperceptibly the great ship made her way towards the ocean. Flags of all sizes and colours blazed up the main stay, over its three great masts and down to the stern, some long and thin streamers of vermilion and gold and blue waving ten to fifteen feet out over the port side; the hot afternoon sun glinting on its towering gilded stern like a giant golden jewel. Despite any misgivings the crowd may have held that afternoon, she was an awe-inspiring sight firing the imaginations of adventurous souls that watched her departure.

Within her belly she carried the greatest quantity of treasure ever to have been transported in one ship. She was a floating treasure house of gold and silver bullion, chests of gold and silver coins, diamonds, rubies, sapphires and emeralds, and priceless ecclesiastical treasures. She carried additionally fifty fare-paying passengers, all their possessions and valuables.

Laboriously she made her way out from the protection of the estuary into the Arabian Sea where it met the full force of the monsoon blasting down the west coast of India. The fully stretched sails swung on the yards to face the prow heeling the creaking vessel dangerously over by thirty degrees; the portside gunwales close to being swamped by the swell of the foaming deep ultramarine ocean.

The wind brought some relief from the suffocating humidity and heat. For Captain-General Alfonso Antonio Rodriguez, after twenty years sailing the southern oceans, this was to be his last voyage. He leaned against the sloping quarterdeck, his hands firmly and resolutely clasped behind his back, wisps of greying black hair had been tugged free from his tight queue and waved across his wide sloping forehead, over his cheek and across his clean shaven jutting chin.

It was the freedom of the open sea that always exhilarated Rodriguez. The responsibility of carrying the most valuable treasure cargo ever to be loaded in one ship filled him with pride and excitement. He stole one last brief look over his shoulder at the Mandovi estuary and the distant towers of old Goa. He promised himself that after bringing his ship safely home he would buy that vineyard in southwest Portugal and live in luxury for the rest of his days.

His idyllic dream was soon to be shattered by the events that were to unfold during the last voyage of the ill fated 'Vierge du Cap'.

Rodriguez's officers and crew feared the worst. Missing the noon high tide had meant that they were all at the mercy of the treacherous Cabo Raj Niwas. Whispers wormed through the crew that catastrophe was imminent and that the Captain-General had callously gambled with all their lives to line his own pockets.

It would require all of Rodriguez's seafaring skills, intuition and courage to safely navigate and skirt the rocks and reefs that lurked just beneath the surface. Razor sharp living rocks were waiting to rip the ship's hull to matchwood.

He used an old fort and Franciscan monastery that stood proudly and enduringly on the promontory as a marker. Holding a westerly course for twelve miles his ship was broadside to the ever-strengthening monsoon wind. She was heeling perilously, groaning and creaking under the strain. The port side gunwales were submerged, water cascaded onto the lower gun decks.

The situation measured the nerve of his crew as much as it tested his ship. He gave the order to man the pumps. The remainder of the crew waited, their eyes riveted upon their captain, some were praying out loud but two, leaning against the gunwale holding the shroud ropes, were openly critical:

"He's waiting too long" one grizzled old seaman cried out revealing four rotting, scurvy ravaged teeth.

"We'll turn turtle or be ripped to pieces," the other shouted, turning to the others for support. "If he don't go now we're all shark bait furr sure!"

Another closed his ears to their words but muttered, between clenched teeth: "Come on you harlot! Turn! *Turn*!"

The first mate, Juan Ramerez, snarled at the two men and growled: "Curse your treacherous souls to hell." He turned his back on them and watched the bows of the listing ship smash through the swell, silently praying to God that Rodriguez would turn the creaking, groaning vessel soon.

Rodriguez checked the distance, the monastery just a dot on the horizon. He held course for another five silent nerve-racking minutes. The topsail on the foremast broke loose of the yardarm and began to flap. Ramerez sent two men up to secure it. She was heeling by forty degrees. One of the men lost his footing and there was a gasp from the crowd below. He clung to the rope by one arm, his swinging body hanging directly over the ocean. The crew watched with baited breath as the topsail broke completely free, cracking like a whip and flapping wildly. The sailor hauled himself to safety and joined his mate to complete the repairs.

The waiting continued. The minutes passed like hours. Then Rodriguez gave the order:

"Hard to port coxswain...fly with the wind..." Rodriguez felt the surge of relief from all the crew on deck. He knew he had not only consolidated the respect of his old hands but also made a lasting impression upon new members of the crew. With his hands clasped behind him, he slapped a clenched fist firmly into the palm of his other hand twice; his chin jutted resolutely high and his gaze remained inscrutably fixed straight ahead.

His old friend, Miguel Fernandez, grinned, revealing a solitary tooth. He knew the satisfaction and delight that was coursing though his captain's veins.

"Hard to port it is, sir." Then, still grinning, he shook his old head. "But fly with the wind, you say? Not in this old tub you won't. I'll do what I can wi' 'er, and that's a promise." The coxswain pulled on the wheel feeling the excitement and exhilaration exuding from Rodriguez.

"Hoist the gallants and the royals," Rodriguez bellowed to the crew, noticing with hidden delight that his order had already been anticipated. "Two men for the topsails...if you please...Señor Ramerez".

"Yes sir, Captain-General." The first mate jabbed a bony finger in the direction of the two sailors that had openly doubted his Captain-General. Within minutes the canvases were unfurled and she was under full sail.

The heavy vessel was hauled up by the wind like an over-laden beast, surging with a lumbering momentum, crashing and ploughing her way through the swell. Explosions of spray shot upwards from the bows, rainbows flashing in the mist over the portside. The timber creaked and the stays, shrouds and ropes were as taut as the acres of canvas billowing on the three great masts. Rodriguez looked out over the stern. His escort of four frigates with only main sails and cross jacks unfurled bounced with restrained eagerness in his wake.

The sickening rolling of the ship across the swell had been replaced by a constant up and down motion as they ran with the wind and waves. He was amused to see one of his passengers, the Archbishop of Goa, braced against the gunwale. Saturated by the spray from the bows, oblivious to anyone or anything, heaving up whatever fluid remained in his corpulent stomach.

Mr. Robert Radclyffe and his new wife, Maria, appeared on deck and went to his aid. Then he saw His Excellency d'Ericeira, the Viceroy of Goa, shakily venturing out, filling his lungs with sea air. Other passengers gradually came up from their cabins, clustering in groups on the main deck below Rodriguez, slowly reviving themselves. The women still looked resplendent in their full bright coloured satin dresses, fashionable hair-does of tumbling curls and sparkling jewellery.

All the passengers had begun to regain their spirits; the women laughed and chattered with excitement; the men, equally well dressed but more dishevelled, adopted more nonchalant postures and pretentiously tried to explain the art of seamanship to their womenfolk.

But they had seen the handsome Captain-General gazing down at them from the quarterdeck railing and each one was surreptitiously vying for his eye.

Rodriguez continued to watch the Archbishop stagger about the deck with Maria Radclyffe's arm about his bulky waist.

The Archbishop peered up and saw Rodriguez on the towering structure of the aft castle, which rose and fell with sickening consistency against the hazy blue sky. The forlorn round figure turned comically and dashed for the side.

Rodriguez was gripped with amused compassion and affection for this little man once more. As he gazed at the ecclesiastical torso hanging limply over the gunwale he recalled their extraordinary conversation an hour before, just after weighing anchor in the Mandovi River. They had been heading slowly towards the mouth of the estuary when the boson had rapped on Rodriguez's cabin door:

"The Archbishop of Goa, sir." The boson's deep voice had reverberated within the Captain-General's luxurious wide low cabin. Rodriguez had stood, with hands clasped behind his back, facing the massive window that spanned the entire width of the stern. The four foot high window sloped inward from the ceiling. It was divided into ten sections two feet wide, each section having eighteen eight-inch square frames; the top frames were finished with elaborate gilded curves and carvings. The mahogany and teak furniture glistened and shone in the sun light flooding through the window; the highly polished floorboards glared blindingly. Rodriguez's massive mahogany desk, intricately decorated with inlaid designs, separated the two men.

"Thank you. That will be all, boson." Rodriguez continued staring at the two towers of the distant Sé Cathedral. It stood high on the slope behind the Customs building, its shabby pealing white paint reflecting in the sun.

The boson towered over the Archbishop. He winked an eye encouragingly at the short corpulent robed figure then turned and left, quietly closing the heavy oak door behind him.

During the awkward silence that followed, the Archbishop nervously fingered his large silver crucifix and chain that hung from his neck. He glanced around the cabin admiring the beautifully inlaid woods of every shade and colour. The opulent luxury enhanced the regal aura of the Captain-General. The only sound was of the great ship's creaking timbers. The endless quiet unnerved the cleric.

"We had an agreement, your Grace, if you recall," Rodriguez said finally with quiet firmness, still facing the window.

The Archbishop's heart skipped a beat and he dropped his crucifix. Rodriguez turned quickly to face the small round shape before him. The Archbishop felt his stomach churn and his knees buckle.

"Let me remind you," Rodriguez's gaze fastened onto the Archbishop, who quickly nodded agreeably, boldly forcing a tentative smile. "You were to be on board my ship at one o'clock, were you not?"

The Archbishop continued to nod, his wan smile stiffening into a grimace.

"It was vital that I caught what remained of the high tide today. I gave you special permission to conduct your last service in the Sé Cathedral on the strict understanding that you would be on board this ship before one."

The clergyman's contrite expression seized Rodriguez with a surge of amused compassion, which he fought to conceal. "It was almost thirty minutes past one o' clock when we finally stowed your Cross away. Kindly explain yourself, your Grace."

"A thousand apologies, Captain-General..." The Archbishop had turned visibly to jelly. "It was a wonderful thing that you did for me Captain-General." His expression changed magically into one of benevolence and joy, throwing his arms out wide. "It was because of you alone that the young couple were joined together this morning. God bless you my son. You will be rewarded in heaven a thousand.........."

"Yes. *Yes*. Yes your Grace!" Rodriguez barked in mock exasperation. "Do you see my point, sir? I missed the tide and with it a most favourable wind. All because of your infernal wedding ceremony," his voice raised more for effect than in anger. "Need I remind you that there are other passengers aboard this ship besides your good-self? Fifty to be precise! I have a responsibility to get them to Lisbon as fast and as safely as possible."

"We are under way are we not?" The Archbishop's large brown wise eyes sparkled. His smile broadened, becoming a warm, kindly glow. "God bless you, my son," he said once more holding his arms out towards Rodriguez. "These two beautiful people were joined together under the glorious ' Fiery' Cross of Goa... Thanks to you! They were the last couple to do so. You have given them a perfect start along that uncertain but glorious road called matrimony. And I have gold for the orphanage!"

Sensing defeat, Rodriguez turned and faced the window. Had avarice got the better of him, he wondered. His ship had been dangerously over-loaded when he agreed to take on board an extra thirty cases of gold and silver that the Viceroy had insisted on bringing with him, in addition to the Cross of Goa. 'Had he risked too much?' he asked himself. His anger began to dissipate only to be replaced by guilt.

The ensuing silence intimidated the Archbishop once more.

"I have your Cross safely locked in the bows," Rodriguez said after several minutes. "Tell me about this Cross of yours," he faced the cleric once more and smiled, his tone mellowing considerably.

"It was the priceless gift of King Manuel. Our great and illustrious pioneer Vasco da Gama brought it to India," the Archbishop proclaimed proudly, sensing that the Cross was the real reason why he had been summoned to the Captain-General's cabin. "It was kept in the fort at Cochin before ….."

"Yes. *Yes*. I *know* its history." Rodriguez snapped impatiently. "What of its secret powers?" He smiled quizzically, arching his eyebrows, his forehead folding into several deep ripples. "I've heard tell that it has an extraordinary effect on many who have approached it."

"You have heard correctly, Captain–General. The righteous will feel it immediately. God's spirit will pulsate in their hearts and through their veins and arteries." He proclaimed with confidence, now fearless of the Captain-General. "You must have absolute faith. Only then will the power of the Cross reach you in the manner you desire. For non-believers who venture too close, or touch it," he paused, "the consequences would be fatal."

Rodriguez fixed the cleric with a wide-eyed stare. The success of the voyage depended upon reaching Ile de France ahead of any cyclones. Years as a mariner had taught him that the only thing to fear was the sea. He was positive that it was his own resourcefulness, skill and judgment pitted against the wild, powerful forces of nature that brought him safely into port. He had seen too many good men lost to the fickle whims of the ocean. God did not always help those who tried to help themselves.

"These are dangerous times, your Grace," he said quietly and very slowly. "I'm not about to open my soul to you. I want to know what is so special about this Cross, apart from its shape...of course."

"It is the shape that makes it special, my son. The base, and what it holds, is the secret behind its power; a power so incredible that it is beyond, with respect, your wildest imagination." The Archbishop watched scepticism build in the Captain-General's eyes.

"What's in the base?" Rodriguez asked incredulously, arching one eyebrow. He was beginning to wonder how this sorcerer of an Archbishop had escaped the Inquisition.

"An ancient knowledge had been bestowed upon the Knights of Christ. Vasco da Gama, who was to become a Knight himself, knew the reason for building the Cross and what was inside its base." The Archbishop chose his words carefully. Four hundred years had elapsed since the demise of the Knights Templar but the Inquisition was still as rampant as ever. "I swore an oath on the day of my appointment as Archbishop and as custodian of the Cross never to reveal the Cross's secrets."

"Will this Cross help us make Lisbon safely? Will its power help this ship...should we encounter a cyclone? Can you and your Cross ensure the safety of this ship, your Grace?" Rodriguez asked placing his cards firmly upon the table.

"The Cross of Goa is not a good luck charm, my son," he said indignantly, although he dearly wanted the Captain-General to know and feel the real power of the Cross's energy for himself. "We are all God's children, my son. It is within your own power to safeguard this voyage by taking every precaution not to endanger the lives of those in your care. Your ship appears to be very low in the water. But," he quickly added, raising his shoulders sympathetically, "I dare say you have a very good reason for taking such a risk."

"Yes I do." Rodriguez's eyes had turned to stone. "I must remind you that it is you who has made my task all the more difficult...because of your failure to get on board with your Cross at the agreed time...you have cost me a favourable wind and tide. I must now navigate the Cabo Raj Niwas on an ebb tide which adds to the risk and will result in additional sailing time."

Rodriguez peered down at the forlorn shape from the quarterdeck. The heaving Archbishop had not moved from the gunwale, leaning helplessly over the side. Rodriguez could feel guilt rising once more from the pit of his stomach. Overloading his ship had been the first real risk he had taken during all his years at sea. Rodriguez turned towards the helm, the Archbishop's words repeating in his ears-'you have a very good reason for taking such a risk---taking such a risk--taking such a risk.' He rubbed his face. "How does she blow, coxswain?"

"She'll be dragging her feet all the way, Captain sir. We'll need to shed some of this load before she'll ever be dancing the waves again. I've never felt a ship so heavy on the rudder." He looked across at

Rodriguez, his eyes determined and resolute, and sensed the torment his friend was under, but he also knew that there was neither arguing nor reasoning when he was in that kind of mood. "With God's help we shall make Calicut by the morning, sir."

At Calicut, 300 miles south of Goa, the small fleet struck a south-west course with the southern monsoon.

On the ninth day at sea, at a position two thousand five hundred miles from Calicut and five hundred and thirty miles north east of Ile de France, the cyclone struck.

Rodriguez ordered colours to be hoisted up the fore stay in a pre-arranged sequence, instructing the nearest frigate to bring the other frigates into tight formation. But the cyclone came upon them with swift ferocity. A curtain of rain descended reducing visibility to zero before he could read the escort's acknowledgement to his signal.

The winds ripped down shrouds and yard arms then changed direction with even greater force, the mountainous seas tearing down rigging and stays. The foremast snapped like a twig under a huge wave that broke over her bows. The volume of water cascading below decks outweighed the amount that could be expelled by the pumps. The 'Vierge du Cap' was sinking. The over laden ship was doomed to the merciless sea unless Rodriguez could make a decision to shed some of its load.

The decision had to be made immediately. Although it was early afternoon the sky was as dark as night. Rodriguez clasped the doorframe of his cabin as the floundering ship rolled violently in every direction. The Archbishop's words haunted him.... distracting his mind: 'It is within your own power to safeguard this voyage'... 'It is within your own power'... 'within your own power'.

'If the treasure and the cargo were to go overboard,' he reasoned, 'it would all be lost forever.' But his instincts were screaming at him: 'No one could possibly expect him to actually dump all of that treasure!' The alternative, however, seamed suicidal and therefore just as difficult to contemplate.

Rodriguez went back onto the aft castle and rang the ship's bell. The remnants of his crew assembled on deck, soaked and exhausted from exposure to the hurricane force winds and the tearing ferocity of the driven rain.

Of the original 285 crew only 217 were left huddled on the deck below him. Eleven officers clustered around Rodriguez. Ten men had been lost that afternoon and forty three of the sixty five injured were too seriously hurt to be moved and remained below decks with the ship's surgeon and his assistant.

"Men..." Rodriguez bellowed through a loud hailer "...in the interests of safety for the ship and the passengers and to keep our cargo intact, I have decided to reduce the draught weight of the ship. You will proceed to the gun decks and jettison every cannon, every cannon ball and keg of powder over the side. *At the double...!*"

The crew disappeared below. Each of the ship's 72 cannon were dismantled and heaved through the gun ports followed by 3500 cannon-balls and over two hundred of barrels of powder.

The ship's buoyancy was restored, but this posed another potentially disastrous dilemma for Rodriguez. The coxswain and two of the crew were struggling desperately at the helm to keep the lightened ship with the wind and prevent it from turning broadside onto the gigantic seas. The wind's direction had veered ninety degrees, north by north east and had strengthened. The main mast crashed over the port side like a felled tree. Foaming plumes were whipped up from the tops of the mountainous waves, the sea spray mixed with horizontally driven rain that smashed against the towering wooden hull of the stricken vessel.

The giant 'Vierge du Cap' pitched and rolled helplessly at the mercy of the sea. The grotesque stumps of the lower fore and lower main masts protruded above the fore deck. Ragged canvas from the comparatively undamaged mizzen flapped and lashed from the yards. Sea and rain-water slopped the decks. The crew battled to clear away the piles of rigging, stays and spars. The broken masts and yards, with shrouds and sails still attached, were draped over both sides of the ship.

The crew worked all night and the following day clearing away as much of the debris as they could to give the helmsmen greater control of the ship.

On the second night of the cyclone, two hours after Rodriguez had ordered 130 of his exhausted crew below, only the coxswain with an assistant at the wheel and 80 men remained on deck to keep the great ship afloat.

The two men clung grimly to the huge wheel. It was positioned on the aft castle behind the mizzenmast and before the door leading to the Captain-General's cabin. The coxswain had woven his old sinewy limbs into its spokes whilst his assistant held the clamps and ropes securing the wheel against the incredible forces exerted against the rudder. Between them and the other crew they kept a straight course running with the waves. These rolling monsters lifted the stern almost vertically thrusting the bows deep into the trough then the wave broke over the aft castle onto the two men. Seawater surged over the submerged bows swamping the decks, covering the stumps of the fore and main masts. The coxswain rubbed his inflamed eyes on his bare arm. Grimacing he squeezed them shut and cursed between clenched teeth to avoid seeing the bows plunging sickeningly and terrifyingly into the pitch darkness. Somehow the bows rose up once more as the wave passed under the keel. He let his head drop onto his chest and prayed silently to his God.

The door swung open behind the helm and a warm wedge of light lit the soaked deck about his feet. The coxswain's mate turned to see the silhouette of the Captain-General gripping the doorframe as the ship began to dive once more. A sheet of water cascaded in front of Rodriguez, falling from the castle above and onto the backs of the exhausted men at the wheel.

With the bows rising Rodriguez lunged for the safety rope tied betweenthe aft castle steps and the mizzenmast and hauled himself up to the two men. They had been at the helm for eight hours. Five more men had died or had been washed overboard that night. Rodriguez clung to the safety rope as the ship began another dive deep into a trough. He jammed his foot against the mizzen to withstand the impact.

"How goes it, Miguel?" He hollered as the bows began to rise up, his voice just audible above the howling wind.

"What a bitch! This ol' tub won't give in. She keeps on coming up for more. We'll make it, sir…God willin'!"

They braced themselves as the ship began another fearful plunge. When the bows began rising the coxswain yelled at his Captain against the noise of the wind and sea: "Jettisoning her cannon has definitely saved her, Capt'n."

"Let me take a turn on the …," Rodriguez's voice was smothered by the torrent of seawater falling from behind them.

Rodriguez watched his old friend slowly untangle himself from the spokes as the bows rose then, grasping his arm, the coxswain staggered clear taking hold of the safety rope.

"Release the ropes and clamps," Rodriguez hollered to the mate. "Get below both of you. Tell Alvarez to report to me."

The mate pulled himself up the safety rope as the stern began to lift with the oncoming wave. The force of the sea against the rudder wrenched Rodriguez's arms against their sockets. Screaming with pain he held on to the great wheel. He continued bracing against the incredible force as the ship dived once more and then water cascaded onto his back. The wheel jerked hard to starboard and the handle of the wheel cracked Rodriguez a stunning blow on the left cheek. With Herculean strength he held on again, pushing the wheel against the force of the wave. The pain numbed his senses and blotted out the din of the tempest. The bows steadied and rose up once more.

Preparing for the next dive he glanced at his old friend.

The coxswain was waiting to be sure his skipper had control. Rodriguez felt a surge of affection and admiration for this stoic old man of the sea. Without him, he thought, they would all be food for the sharks. He had always been there, like a rock. The coxswain stiffly pulled himself hand over hand along the safety rope towards the swinging aft door. Rodriguez watched the exhausted man ascend the rising stern, using up the last vestiges of his strength. The ship shuddered unnervingly before diving more viciously than at any time before, the deck perpendicular to the trough it was about to sink into.

The wiry old bird lost his footing. He clung onto the rope, his legs dangling in mid air. His exhausted aching body smacked onto the vast girth of the mast knocking the wind from his lungs and tearing his left hand from the wet rope. The ship bounced like a cork deep into the trough then the deluge of seawater fell onto them from the stern.

The Captain reached out and grabbed his right hand just as Miguel fell. The ship began to rise as the huge wave passed under the keel; the force on the rudder wrenched the wheel from Rodriguez's grip. He was flung away, still holding the coxswain. The wheel spun anti-clockwise and the ship veered hard to port.

The two men slid across the flooded quarterdeck and smashed against the starboard side of the castle. The vessel shuddered, hovering on a wave crest and broadside to the next approaching monster. They both scrambled single-mindedly up the inclining deck to the wheel and heaved on the spokes in unison turning the rudder to starboard. As the ship descended she surfed back into the trough, with the giant wave looming above the stern, her bows straightened up just before the wave smashed onto the aft castle, much of its force dissipated as they were propelled forward by the breaking wave. Rodriguez braced his full weight against the wheel, seawater smashing onto his back, as the cox-swain grabbed for the safety rope.

Miguel turned, his red eyes sparkling, "Are you getting the feel of her, sir?" he yelled above the din. "She's a vixen and no mistake. It's like a tumble with my wife. You must ride her out."

"You can keep your wife to yourself if she's anything like this." The wind, rain and sea slashed into his face. "Get below you old devil and get some rest. Just keep a firm grip or you'll never get another tumble with that wife of yours."

Miguel wanted to bellow with laughter but his battered body, stiff with exhaustion, could not respond. But the gleam in his eye and his toothless grin was enough to warm Rodriguez.

The mysterious and unpredictable Indian Ocean had tried to claim both men many times before. Each time one had denied the sea from taking the other. Together they were invincible. Rodriguez felt youth and fearlessness coursing through his veins once more. A feeling, he feared, he might never experience again. It was then he realised that it was the sea that gave him life. No amount of wealth could buy that.

Alvarez reported for duty. Together they held course for the next hour and half. The waves had ceased breaking over the stern. Gradually the wind and rain eased. A dagger of grey light could be seen cutting across the horizon. It filled Rodriguez with renewed hope that he still might get his ship and its vast treasure home safely.

With the dawn he saw the full extent of the damage. The bowsprit had gone. Stays, shrouds, broken timber and other debris dragged over her bows. He sent Alvarez to check on the damage.

"Two long boats lashed between the fore and main are smashed by broken yards, sir." Alvarez reported. "The two pinnaces stacked between the mizzen and main are untouched. There're fallen shrouds and miles of twisted rope still littering the decks. It's a death trap, sir."

"She's a very sorry sight indeed. But we're afloat, Mr. Alvarez! Thank you. Go below and send up the next watch and help the rest of the crew attend to what rigging we have left."

"Aye...aye, sir."

As the ship pitched on the high swell Rodriguez could feel the rudder responding sweetly to the slightest movement on the wheel. Content to wait for better light and rest his crew longer before pitching them into the hazardous task of clearing the decks, he continued to let his mind wonder as he gazed across her bows, headless of the clutter and debris before him.

At midday the sun was breaking through the racing, thinning clouds. He lashed the wheel tight and doused his face with rainwater caught in the canvas covering a pinnace. He winced when his left hand smacked onto the large swelling on his cheek. Suddenly burning once more he tenderly pressed around the bone for a possible break. There was none. Taking the wheel, keeping the bow straight, he gazed into the brightening horizon.

Miguel joined him at the wheel. "How's she blowing, skipper?" The coxswain looked gaunt and weary.

"She feels good, old friend..." slapping him firmly on the back "...ring the ship's bell, if you will. It's time I get these decks cleared of debris. It's slowing her way."

"She's in a terrible shape, Captain, but she stayed afloat!"

"Aye...she's afloat; with all her treasure intact. I think we'll make it home. Don't you agree, coxswain?"

"Aye, its very possible, sir. Things could get very awkward if we run into any pirates, though," he added facetiously as he rang the bell. "We've nothin' to shoot and nothin' to shoot with!" He noticed Rodriguez's smile broaden. "Except a few hundred onions and a lump of worm infested dough!"

"Any maggot of a privateer caught in that tempest will now be food for Neptune and his mermaids. The seas'll be free of 'em for a while, I'm sure of that!"

The coxswain leaned against the quarterdeck railing and sniffed the air. "There's land not too far over the horizon," he called out.

Back at his Captain's side he asked: "Do you have any idea of our position, sir?"

"At a guess…," pointing up at the thinning cloud in the northwest, "…judging from where the sun appears to be…," he made a quick mental assessment "…the storm would have driven us east… we cannot be far from Ile de France. Take the wheel, please coxswain. I'll get someone aloft."

"Right you are, Cap'n..," his calloused hands gripping the helm "… she's feeling good, skipper! As light as a feather! Just like my wife after a wild night!"

"I've seen your wife, you old devil, an' she's never looked like a feather to me!"

"Not after a wild night, you 'aint," he chuckled under his breath as Rodriguez gave orders for his bedraggled crew to clear the decks.

By late afternoon the decks were reasonably clear, the mizzen had full canvas, except for topsails and gallants and the cloud had broken to reveal patches of blue sky.

Dazed and ill looking passengers were venturing out on the main deck. Most had bandages on their legs, arms or heads. They said very little, the women hanging onto their men's arms, stopping frequently to keep their balance in the strong swell, some watched the crew mending canvas and scrubbing the decks.

The Viceroy and his wife stood beneath the aft castle. He pointed up to one of the crew strapped high up on the swaying mizzen scouring the horizon with a telescope. Miguel was off duty at the prow deep in conversation with Robert Radclyffe.

At a quarter after six Captain-General Rodriguez emerged from his cabin in a clean uniform, looking as resplendent as the day they had left Goa. He passed an eagle eye over his ship: 'She's recovered some of her elegance,' he thought 'her dignity intact and her crew and the passengers were coming back to life. Soon we'll be docking at Ile de France. After repairs we shall be homeward bound. We have survived' he chuckled triumphantly to himself, looking over her storm ravaged bows. Rolling cumulous sat like a billowing grey forest on the western horizon.

The crew continued with repairs, making good the shrouds on the mizzen and unfurling new canvas on the yards. Passengers milled about the main deck, some lending a hand with replacement ropes and lashings. Rodriguez stared down at his coxswain and pondered the old seaman affectionately: 'Where would we be without you, dear old friend?' he asked himself.

Miguel looked up, as Robert Radclyffe searched the pages of his diary, and saw his Captain smiling down from the quarterdeck. Their bond strengthened when their eyes met. 'You're a lucky bastard. I hope your luck holds, you old devil,' he thought to himself turning back to Radclyffe and the diary, his old craggy face creasing up into a broad grin.

"This is my sketch of the 'Fiery' Cross of Goa," Radclyffe said slowly in broken Portuguese, his Scottish accent affecting the meaning he was trying to convey.

"There is no disagreement," Miguel said shaking his head vigorously. "Your 'Fairy' Cross of Goa is very excellent indeed! It is a 'Fairy' looking drawing, Señor." stabbing his finger on the diary. "It is very ......."

"*Land on the port bow*!" the lookout yelled from above.

Passengers and crew scuttled to the port side, straining their eyes at the distant horizon, chattering and laughing with relief and excitement.

"Reef ahead..! *Reef Ahead*..!" the same voice screamed out urgently from the mizzen. All the crew broke away from the gunwale and dashed to their stations.

Passengers were pointing towards the grey shape on the horizon, oblivious of impending peril that lay directly ahead.

Rodriguez knew the topography of the landfall. It was unmistakable. But from the distance and angle of the twin volcanoes of Bourbon Island he was immediately aware of the peril that lay before them. Fear chilled his spine and tingled the nape of his neck. A more treacherous reef rose up from the ocean depths peeking just beneath the surface of the water one hundred yards ahead. But the ship was already over the reef.

"*Sixty degrees to starboard*!" he yelled.

"Sixty degrees to starboard it is, sir," answered Carlos Esculdia, his relief coxswain, spinning the great wheel clockwise. The ship responded too sluggishly.

"Look lively lads…this is not Ile de France. We are heading for Dead Man's Reef."

"*Harder…Harder to starboard…*!" Rodriguez roared.

The bows of the great ship lifted high on a wave. As it sank into the trough it veered to starboard heeling broadside on the swell. Light sea spray broke over the starboard prow soaking Radclyffe and Miguel.

The crew pulled on the mizzen halliards.

"*More sail*… Mr Ramerez…if you please."

"Aye, aye..."

Men scampered up the shrouds of the mizzen and extended the sail on the top, gallant and royal yards. The men below busily adjusted the halliards to accommodate the fresh rig.

The ship rolled sickeningly on the swell, the reef looming closer on the port side. The going was slow. The ship was broadside to the reef, a deadly black shadow lurked just beneath the surface thirty feet away. The shattered ship was making no way and each wave pushed them closer to the razor edged rocks.

Then, with wind in her few remaining sails, she began to cut the water to starboard and the threat receded.

"Look, Jakes Knob," Esculdia pointed to the pinnacle of reef breaking the surface 400 yards on the port side. "We are as good as in St. Denis, Captain-General."

Rodriguez nodded, but a look of foreboding had crossed his face. He waited until they were beyond Jakes Knob, a protruding clump of rock marking the end of the reef: "Come about if you please, coxswain," he commanded sombrely and uneasily.

"Coming about Cap'n…." The coxswain spun the wheel anti clockwise.

"Let go the halliards," he bellowed then pointed towards the island. "Steer a course directly at that nearest mountain."

The crew let go the ropes and the sails swung on their yards.

"We'll make it to St. Denis, alright. I only pray that we can get her repaired before every pirate in the Indian Ocean hears about us. They'll be swarming like flies round a pile of horse shit when they get wind that the pride of the King's fleet is moored helpless in this God forsaken hell hole carrying a cargo of treasure, the like that has never been seen nor heard of before!"

"I put into St. Denis last July, sir. It was very peaceable, then," Esculdia added reassuringly.

"I'd choose Ile de France any day," retorted Rodriguez. "It's only 110 nautical miles to the east-northeast. St. Denis is a den of iniquity. Every public house has become a disease-infested brothel serving all forms of slime, vermin and lice that ply the Oceans for booty."

It was dusk when Rodriguez guided the battered, lumbering 'Vierge du Cap' into harbour. Her solitary mast proudly carrying her colours aloft, victorious over the might of the ocean.

There were two other ships in the harbour, moored close together, their silhouettes black against the fiery shades of reds, violet, orange and yellows of a south sea sunset.

Rodriguez scanned the harbour through his glass, focussing upon the two suspicious looking ships. The coxswain and first mate were at his side.

"They have no colours flying and they look in a bad state of repair." he lowered the lens a fraction. "There are men in a long boat ….they are rowing fast for the shore….they are from the nearest ship" He lifted the lens. "The light's too bad…I can't read the names of the ships".

"It doesn't look good, Captain," the coxswain glanced at the first mate. The boson joined them and squinted into the fading light.

"Well, we have little choice," Rodriguez sighed in resignation; he gazed thoughtfully at the three men. "I think we should prepare for the worst, gentlemen. Let go the anchor and ring the ship's bell. Boson," withdrawing a large key from his waistcoat pocket, "as I address the crew unlock the doors to the armoury."

The next moment he heard the mighty anchor smack the water and the bell ring out over the still air of the evening.

Rodriguez waited for all his men to assemble on the main deck under the ship's lanterns.

"As you are all aware, there are two ships keeping us company in St. Denis this night." He leaned heavily on the quarter deck hand rail. "I believe them to be privateers. In any event, I'm not prepared to take any chances." He paused. "I'm sorry men…but shore leave is cancelled."

The groan was followed by shouts of protest from men on the fore-castle.

"I have you all to thank for helping to save this ship. I had hoped that tonight we could all celebrate deliverance from the forces of the ocean. This will have to wait for another time…."

The men's jeering and shouting escalated.

Rodriguez raised a hand and the din gradually died down.

"I am sending ten men ashore in a pinnace to reconnoitre. We need to know the strength of our seafaring neighbours."

Rodriguez called out the names of the ten men chosen for the mission.

"Those men's names I have called out will go to my cabin at once. Every man will be armed with a musket, swords and daggers. The rest of you will remain on deck until the pinnace is launched then you may choose your weapons from the armoury. I'm in your debt, gentlemen… each and every one of you. I can solemnly promise that you ALL will be rewarded handsomely when we reach home."

"*If* we reach home, more like…" came a voice from the forecastle.

"We must stand together. If we do we are unbeatable. These men on this island may outnumber us, but every one of you here is worth ten of them. I am a man of my word. After we have defeated these lice …"

A cannon boomed from one of the two ships moored in the harbour. There was an instant of shock. Nobody moved. There was silence on deck. Only the creek of the timbers and the rigging could be heard.

Then, as if from nowhere, swarms of human rodents climbed over the gunwales and up the shrouds of the mizzenmast. The filthy diseased creatures, their eyes full of lust and greed, had surrounded and over-whelmed the crew before anyone could fully grasp what was happening. The cutthroats were looking down from every vantage point, waving cutlasses and muskets in the air, jeering, shouting, taunting and laugh-ing.

Rodriguez gazed down helplessly at his crew. They were outnum-bered three to one and unarmed. He saw their reactions change from rage to humiliated resignation, their heads hung low. His heart sank when the mob began goading and taunting them. No blood had been spilled, which compounded his sense of betrayal. His ship with all its treasure had been taken without having fired a shot in their defence. He felt sick with shame, failure and dishonour.

Two men in dishevelled navy uniforms appeared out of the mass of shouting, laughing and stinking bodies and approached Rodriguez on the quarterdeck. One was tall and thin and clean-shaven. The shorter one wore a grimy ragged sweat stained French naval uniform. Fleas and lice were causing him considerable discomfort. The din from the hoards was deafening. He looked up at his men and raised his hand. Instantly there was silence. Thick stubble covered his face and surrounded a thin cruel mouth that twisted up into a sneer as he studied Rodriguez.

"That was a very nice speech," he said slowly in broken Portuguese, his French accent thick and heavy. "Unbeatable eh..?" His men shrieked with laughter. "Do you...err....speak English, Monsieur?" The resonance in his voice was menacing.

"Yes...a little." Rodriguez's back had stiffened noticeably. He looked squarely at the two men before him.

"Good. It's for the benefit of my friend 'ere." He turned to towards the taller man on his right, gesturing with his arm. "This is my associate Lieutenant John Taylor. My name is Olivier le Vasseur," he announced grandly, one eyebrow raised as he looked down on the defeated faces staring blankly back at him.

There was a commotion at the bow end of the main deck. Men hanging in the shrouds of the mizzen cheered as the frightened passengers were brought up on deck.

"Mr. Taylor and myself have commandeered this ship and everything in it," he shouted above the noise. "Your passengers will hand over all their valuables to my men moving amongst you. You will come to no harm if you do as I say. My men will then take you to our boats and you'll be taken ashore."

He looked at Rodriguez. "Translate, if you will, for all your Portuguese passengers."

Rodriguez finished his translation and le Vasseur's men gathered up the watches, jewellery and wallets and herded them to a rope ladder hung over the side of the ship.

Four men came forward, grinning and laughing. One spoke up excitedly to Taylor and le Vasseur. "The rumours are true, Cap.n! The ship's brim full of treasure, sir."

A wave of excited chatter passed through the pirates, some drooling and staring with manic expressions, barely able to contain their lust.

"Tell me what you have seen," asked the taller man.

"There're gold bars, hundreds of chests of coins and jewels and such like. I've never seen so much..." he burst out into hysterical laughter, igniting the others into even louder cheering and raucous laughter.

Le Vasseur raised his hand once more. It took several seconds for the excitement to subside. Then a man pushed his way forward, his face ashen.

"What is it?" Le Vasseur asked.

"We found forw'd a mysterious looking cross, Cap'n. It were in a wooden crate. Pure gold it is. Some men broke open the crate and touched it. It… it…it sort of exploded in a flash of white light, sir. It was brighter than any lightning. I was standin' far away an' it sent the men flyin'. All the men close by…they'll all be dead, sir. At least sixteen men…all burned to a cinder, they be."

The Archbishop fearlessly pushed his way through the crowds, climbed the steps to the quaterdeck and faced le Vasseur. "You will- er- have no need, my son, for the- er- Cross stowed in the bows," his English faltering slightly. "It's an old relic… from the Sé Cathedral, you understand? It's the property of King John and very dangerous. Anyone who touches it is cursed into damnation. It will be safer with me."

"The relic that he speaks of is bewitched," Rodriguez spoke up in support. "It will bring a curse on you as it did for us. Let the Archbishop keep his Godforsaken relic."

"Relic indeed..!" Le Vasseur fixed the clergyman with his sabre sharp eyes. "I've heard of this magic Cross you have stowed in the bows." He leaned towards Taylor and whispered.

"Do not go near it, I warn you." The Archbishop cursed himself the moment he blurted out the words.

"You warn me!" Le Vasseur, snarled, pulling a pistol from his belt and took aim at the small round figure before him.

Rodriguez stepped sideways putting himself protectively in front of the clergyman. As quick as lightning, a man leapt down from the mizzenmast and cracked Rodriguez on the skull with the hilt of his cutlass. Rodriguez slumped to the floor.

"I know its powers" Le Vasseur stepped over Rodriguez's inert body inconsequentially and scowled at the Archbishop. "Do you think I'm a fool? I have attended the Grand Lodge in Paris where I heard the legend of the Cross of Goa."

He scratched his stubbly chin, looking slowly around at all the beaming, expectant and excited faces of his men. Then he turned in a full circle with his arms outstretched mockingly, and shouted up to them, "We'll be very careful with your Cross, I can assure you, your Grace." They all shrieked with delight. Taylor joined in the laughter, slapping Le Vasseur heartily on the back.

Le Vasseur pointed to the coxswain with a long, bony figure. "You there...take your Captain and put him in one of the boats. He may travel with the women. The rest of you can use your two pinnaces to get ashore. But first," he looked down at the crew, "who among you has knowledge of how to transport this famous Cross, eh? Anyone joining me will become richer than you can possibly imagine."

The crew waited silently whilst the first mate and four others removed the tarpaulins from the pinnaces. Then two men approached the aft castle. They had been part of the squad that had collected the Cross from Sé Cathedral.

The boson grabbed one by the arm. "What the hell do you think you are doing? He'll slit your throats once he gets what he wants. If he spares you then you'll be outlaws, outcasts for the rest of your lives….."

"Get your hands off me, Boson."

"Think carefully, lads. You'll never again be able to set foot on your homeland…."

"We were promised a fortune when we came on this voyage….. there's no hope of that now with you lot. We are going to get our share, one way or the other." He shrugged free of the big man.

It had taken two hours for all the crew and passengers to get ashore. The night was cooled by a northeasterly sea breeze. Rodriguez, the cox-swain and some of the crew had gone into St. Denis to find shelter for the passengers who were hanging around the docks or walking in dejected clusters along the shore.

The Archbishop, Robert Radclyffe and his wife Maria sat on the quayside, their legs dangling over the edge, with the Viceroy and his wife sitting nearby. They were all silent.

Shanty music, clapping and singing and the beet of feet stamping and dancing on the 'Vierge du Cap' deck filled the night. Whenever the music stopped it was replaced by shouts and whistling and raucous laughter punctuated occasionally by a pistol shot followed by resounding cheers. During the celebrations long boats plied back and forth between the pirate ships and the 'Vierge du Cap'.

Rodriguez and the coxswain found the small sad group at the dock-side and stood behind them looking out at their battered ship. Rodriguez drew his telescope from his inside coat pocket.

"Look!" Rodriguez pointed in the direction of the two pirate hulks, offering his glass to the coxswain. The others, not having heard them return, turned and looked up at Rodriguez in startled surprise.

"One of their ships has weighed anchor and broken sail."

Everyone on the dockside peered into the pitch darkness, but the lights from the town made the blackness dense and impenetrable.

"She's moving closer to the 'Vierge du Cap'."

One of the crew, dripping wet, approached Miguel Fernandez and said something in a low voice and ran off quickly towards the town.

Miguel announced to the others what he had been told: "A few of the crew have swum out to spy on those beggars. They wanted to see what they are up to. Those little pieces of French dog's turd…erm… beggin' yer pardon me lady…" he bowed his head to the Viceroy's wife

"…they've renamed our ship 'Victory'!"

"What!" Rodriguez's exclaimed, his back straightening with contempt as he continued following the path of the slow moving ship with his glass.

"It sure rubs salt into the wound." Miguel squinted into the darkness.

"There will be many deaths when they attempt to move the Cross," the Archbishop said in a ghostly tone. Rodriguez stared silently at the short fat priest for a moment, his scepticism had vanished having heard the fate of the vermin who had touched the Cross. The cleric's remark hung in the night air for seconds and they all looked in the direction of their ship.

A ball of fire billowed up from the other pirate ship at anchor. The flames quickly took hold of her rotting, tar soaked timbers and climbed the rigging to engulf her completely. The fire illuminated the entire harbour, the inferno reflecting in the still water and lighting up the sails of the other pirate ship nearing the 'Vierge du Cap'.

Thick oily smoke obscured the flames until a fresh explosion shook the doomed vessel and the foremast slowly collapsed with its rigging, its tattered sails and shrouds ablaze, and fell back onto the main mast.

Rodriguez fixed his gaze on the burning ship. "She was the 'Victory' …they've fired her!" he exclaimed with an exasperated lilt to his voice.

"That's Taylor's ship," said Miguel. "Then the other ship'll be the 'Cassandra'. The 'Tube's' ship…"

"What's the 'Tube'?" asked the Viceroy indignantly.

"Olivier le Vasseur," Miguel replied quickly. "He's called the 'Tube' 'cause he melts down the gold and silver he takes real fast like."

"Olivier le Vasseur?" Rodriguez queried. "I thought he was called 'The Buzzard' or 'La Buze'."

"Either way," said the Viceroy quickly. "If I catch the little bugger, sorry dear," he gave a fleeting smile to his wife, "when I get hold of him………"

"You say that now, dear," his wife said, clutching his arm. "Everyone knows you couldn't hurt a fly. We all know what he deserves, but I don't think a woman should be subjected to hearing such language, especially in such distinguished company as the Captain-General."

The Viceroy looked uncomfortably down into the black water below, the tops of the swirling ripples touched with orange light from the burning hulk. The others watched in silence as the fire engulfed the sad vessel, once a proud vessel of the British naval fleet.

No one spoke for several hours.

Rodriguez watched the dawn breaking as he had a thousand times before. The band of turquoise that lit the horizon began to widen. It was underscored with a line of scarlet and orange that brightened with each passing second.

But the new day would be like no other for him. With daybreak would come the dreaded affirmation that the events of the previous night actually took place. He had lost his ship. His greed had destroyed a lifetime of dutiful and honourable service to his King and country. He fooled himself that wealth would bring contentment in his retirement when, at the brink of disaster, he realised that it was the sea and his knowledge of the sea that could only bring him lasting peace and happiness.

He gazed at the three forlorn figures at the dockside with him, Miguel having escorted the Viceroy and his wife into the town an hour before. Maria Radclyffe was leaning against her husband's chest in a deep sleep, whilst Robert waited for the Archbishop to finish reading his diary.

"They've unfurled the main sail on the mizzen mast," Rodriguez announced. Maria awoke with a start. They all looked out into the half-light. "They're turning her round and preparing to get under way. Yes... the 'Cassandra' is putting about also."

They silently watched the ships complete their slow pirouette. As the pirate ship's starboard side drew parallel to their vessel they saw a puff of smoke billow from the port side, then another and another. Then the reports from the cannon fire reached them as three more smoke plumes belched from the ship.

"Where will they go?" asked the Archbishop.

"They'll be bound for Ile Ste. Marie. That's where they'll divide the spoils. These slime will be sharing out the greatest treasure they're ever likely to see." Rodriguez's shrewd eyes narrowed then he looked across at the clergyman. "It's a strange thing, your Grace, but all I see is my ship going away from me. The wealth suddenly means nothing to me. It's like a great burden has been lifted from my shoulders."

"Not so strange, my son..." The Archbishop lifted a left buttock and let wind.

"Your Grace..!" Rodriguez waved the air whilst pegging his nose with his fore finger and thumb. "...what the devil have you been eating?"

"Apologies Captain...but what will happen to my Cross? Will this man called the 'Tube' really melt it down? Will it ever be recovered? Will Robert and Maria be the last to ever have the joy of standing before the Cross of Goa? Will anyone else ever feel that extraordinary uplift of spirit; receive that incredible experience that enriches belief in God?"

The Archbishop wrapped an arm affectionately around Radclyffe's shoulder.

"The Cross could be found; maybe centuries from now. Your diary could even avert a catastrophe. It'll be your duty and responsibility my young friend to make sure that each succeeding generation of your

family is made aware of the Cross of Goa, its powers and of its importance." The Archbishop smiled warmly. "I will help you my son in this
great endeavour."

# PART TWO

# CHAPTER 5

This first Tuesday of 2007 was, as most New Years begin, cold, murky and wet. Weather conditions were deteriorating by the minute as the London evening rush hour got under way. A gusting, bitter east wind tested the resolution of the most hardened city commuter. It whipped sleet and icy rain through the concrete canyons; it cut into the homeward bound travellers hunched behind taught, straining and bending umbrellas. They flowed like tributaries merging into wider, faster moving rivers that hurried to overland main line train terminuses or eddying into clusters at bus stops, or being swept down the subways and drawn into the warm protective caverns of the London Underground.

People cascaded to the lower levels on escalators, surged along tunnels and flooded onto packed platforms. Those that managed to squeeze onto the southbound Northern line platform resembled so many penguins balancing on an island of pack ice, manoeuvring and jostling for position, melting sleet and snow still evident on their coats.

A stooping flamboyant old gentleman was teetering on the edge of the platform. Clive Norton-Smythe, art advisor to Royalty and the aristocracy and also celebrated art dealer wore a black velvet cape fastened under the chin by a mystical gold broche and a matching wide brimmed floppy hat. He was in the front line of the throng close to the tunnel entrance stinking with expensive sickly cologne popular with certain men east of the Bosporus. He leaned heavily onto his cane with one arm his bony fingers protruding beneath lace shirt cuffs, causing his shoulder to jut upward parting his thick, white hair which flowed down his back and down the front of his cape; his head protruded forward, pivoting on a thin scrawny neck, like that of a vulture. Commuters in close proximity withdrew from him, pressing back against the force of the crowd.

The platform P.A. system announced in an alien monotone that the next train was for London Bridge. Nervously the old man's beady deep-set eyes searched up and down the platform and darted from face to face.

A commotion broke out at the back of the platform. The old man stretched and craned his neck to see over the mass of heads behind him but could see nothing. He resumed searching the gloom of the tunnel for a sign of the train, tapping the platform impatiently with his cane and muttering furiously and incoherently to himself.

Norton-Smythe was on his way to see his principal client, the millionaire artist Alex Radcliff, who resided in East Sussex. In early December Radcliff had been found on a deserted island in the Indian Ocean. He had been missing for over seven years and presumed drowned at sea. Norton-Smythe, who had accumulated great wealth from the sale of Radcliff's paintings, was as embarrassed and confounded as the rest of the art world by Radcliff's untimely rescue. A death threat had been delivered to Norton-Smythe's Bayswater flat early that morning. Stricken by fear and indecision he delayed contacting the artist until that afternoon. The words exchanged between the two men were fiercer than he had anticipated. It was Radcliff who suggested they meet and speak face to face.

Peering once more into the blackness of the tunnel a draft of dank air wafted into the station and lifted a few white hairs hanging over the old man's shoulder. With relief he stepped back from the platform edge as the faint clatter of the approaching train could be heard in the tunnel. There was a scuffle in the crowd a few yards behind him. A tall hooded man in a light blue anorak, wisps of greying ginger hair protruding from under the hood, charged through the crowd. Shouts of indignation and outrage were drowned by the train's thunderous clatter building to a crescendo as it burst out of the tunnel.

In that instant a sledgehammer blow hit Norton-Smythe between the shoulder blades. His head reeled back, his arms rising up to billow out his cape like the wings of a giant bat. His cane flew up, circling slowly, as his body was propelled helplessly straight into the path of the oncoming train. The body was crushed upon impact with the glass of the driver's cab then vanished beneath the train wheels. The train continued on into the platform, its emergency breaking system bringing it screeching to a halt over two hundred feet further into the station. His cane had flicked off the train's roof and landed amongst the crowd.

A strange stillness descended upon the platform as if time had actually stopped. People gaped open mouthed, their minds grappling with the horror that had just occurred. All were stunned into an acute awareness of their own mortality, the uncertainty and fragility of life and how quickly the candle of life can be snuffed out.

The eerie silence was broken by a collective murmur from the crowd, like the groaning of the wind through telegraph wires, as individuals passed on, in quiet reverent voices, to neighbouring commuters their interpretation of what had occurred.

The assailant, using the confusion and shock of the crowd, had scuttled on his hands and knees through the legs of the commuters to the rear of the platform, ascended the escalator unchallenged and had vanished into the night.

Transport police identified Norton-Smythe's remains from details found in his wallet. When the news of his death reached Whitehall panic echoed through the corridors of MI5 and the Home Office. Norton-Smythe had been linked, during his under graduate years at Cambridge, with the three notorious traitors of the Cold War and had been under surveillance since the early 1960's. Fearing that his murder might trigger another spate of embarrassing espionage investigations, the Home Office had given Scotland Yard two weeks to solve the crime and apprehend the murderer.

Chief Inspector Charles Hawkins of Scotland Yard had commandeered the control room at Bank Underground Station as his Incident Headquarters. Hawkins and three Detective Constables were huddled in the corner of the small dimly lit room.

Hawkins assigned D.C. Dixon and D.C. Anderton to commence preliminary investigations at the deceased address and make inquiries into Norton-Smythe's contacts and associates.

Hawkins turned and peered up at his giant Ghanaian colleague.

"You know…it always amazes me, Omollo!" he complained, emptying the remains of a bag of peanuts into his mouth. Hawkins spoke well but with a slight London accent. "Out of all those eye witnesses only four could give us something…," Omollo stooped to try and comprehend what his boss was saying "… substantial to work with." Hawkins began pacing the twelve-foot long room. "One of them was right beside the victim…" Omollo listened keenly, waiting for Hawkins to finish. He continued pacing in deep thought. "All their descriptions were sketchy …next to useless….It's always the way, Omollo. The greater the panic to solve a murder the least possible clues there are to catch the criminal." He stopped pacing.

Hawkins was of medium height and build with closely cropped fair hair brushed flat on the scalp. He was still in excellent physical condition. His fiftieth birthday was only months away and with it retirement from the force. Hawkins was the traditional hardy copper, beginning his career at Hendon, then two years on the beat. He had passed the Criminal Investigations Department examinations with distinction and by dint of hard, dedicated work he had slowly but surely climbed through the ranks. He had been shot three times in the line of duty and decorated for valour beyond the call of duty on two occasions. His loathing for computers was common knowledge amongst his colleagues. He considered the new generation of coppers as little more than button pushers with 'no stomach for proper field-work'. Nevertheless the youngsters in the force revered him. Their knick name for him was…'Bullitt'. It was attributed more to the speed he went into action than to his striking resemblance to Steve McQueen.

"You mentioned earlier that two witnesses had smelt something on the assailant?" He asked testily, trying to dislodge a peanut wedged between his teeth.

"Yes sir."

"Read me those last two reports of yours again," Hawkins ordered, pushing hard with his tongue against the peanut.

John Omollo was a Ghanaian Moslem, 6ft 4 ins tall and weighed 19 stone. His ready smile showed a mouth full of gleaming white teeth and his skin had the sheen of ebony. He was the brightest of Hawkins' new group of detectives. Omollo flipped rapidly through his notepad.

"Mrs. Pilgrim, sir. She said that the assailant wore jeans and a blue anorak. The hood was up. She could not see his face." Omollo spoke slowly and precisely, his deep voice having become even deeper in deference to the seriousness of the crime. "She said that he was about 6ft tall and noticed tufts of greying ginger hair sticking out from beneath the hood. When he had pushed passed her she said that she could definitely smell the Gauloises brand of cigarettes on him. She said that she had just returned from a weekend in Paris, sir, and recognised the br…"

"Whereabouts was she standing?"

"Right at the back of the crowd, sir..."

"Okay." He spat out the piece of peanut. "What about the other one?"

Omollo flipped a couple of pages. "A Mr. Arnold, sir. He had been standing right behind the victim. He said that someone shoulder charged him, pushing him to the right. He said that the person was a tall hooded man in a blue coat. He saw the assailant push the victim into the path of the train. He was also sure he could smell Gauloises cigarettes on the man. He said that he occasionally smoked them himself."

"When I saw the victim's remains I got a whiff of his perfume. It was very strong…believe me! If he was so close to the victim how could he be so sure it was Gauloises? You'd have a job to smell raw sewage above that cologne!"

"The assailant had pushed right into him, sir...almost knocking him down. He said that his face had brushed against his anorak."

"Okay." He moved closer to Omollo. "Lets consider the facts," his voice almost a whisper. He looked up thoughtfully over Omollo's left shoulder towards the grimy corner of the ceiling. "We have received a report from Southern Trains at London Bridge Station that a man matching the description of the assailant caught the 5.40 p.m. Brighton train from platform fourteen."

Hawkins began pacing again, his eyes concentrated on the floor just ahead of his feet and his hands dug deep into his raincoat pockets.

"The same person was seen getting off the train at Wivelsfield," he added in the same low voice. "Norton-Smythe, the victim, was Alex Radcliff's agent…a neighbour had overheard him screaming at someone called Alex at about 3.30 this afternoon…this Alex Radcliff lives close to Wivelsfield… in some sort of castle?" He looked up at his junior colleague. "*An artist*…with his own castle…? He's done very well for himself, eh…!" his lips pursed thoughtfully "…we'll have to check this one out."

Hawkins paced silently for a moment then stopped, dwarfed beneath his assistant.

"Norton-Smythe had just taken out a new Life Insurance Policy. The beneficiary….?"

Omollo searched his note pad.

Hawkins did not wait for an answer. "… is none other than Mr. Radcliff." He spun on his heels and marched towards the door beckoning Omollo to follow with a wave of his arm. "Come on, young man. I think we ought to go and have a little chat with this Mr. Radcliff."

# CHAPTER 6

The first news reports of Alex Radcliff's rescue instantly captivated people's imaginations worldwide. Every living soul on the planet who could read or could watch a television set or sit close to a radio watched or learned how this bearded, bronzed, naked and emaciated figure was rescued from a tropical beach and led towards a helicopter. It had been the helicopter pilot who had taken that first film of Radcliff before whisking him away from the uncharted island in the Indian Ocean on 7$^{th}$ December 2006 back to Mahé in the Seychelles.

Then the media arrived at Victoria, the small capital of Mahé, bringing with them chaos and frenzied activity. The island buzzed with hoards of reporters, technicians and camera crews; satellite dishes sprouted up like mushrooms; sightseers and treasure hunters flocked to the island for glimpses of the rescued Englishman.

Desperate methods and unethical devices were being employed by journalists of both the press and television to sustain world attention in Radcliff's story: they tried bribing the helicopter pilot, even employing unsavoury tactics and coercion to persuade him to take them to Radcliff's island; one reporter, to satisfy the demands of his editor, had resorted to taking video footage of Bird Island, north of Mahé, claiming it to be the actual island on which Radcliff had survived for seven years; the tabloids paid bearded actors to be filmed being lifted off a nearby island and fabricated interviews that had them telling of hidden treasure.

It was in the early hours of the 7$^{th}$ December in the penthouse suite of the Lakeside Leisure Hotel, Chicago, Illinois. The king of the under-world, Don Angelo Cinisi, had stabbed his index finger onto his cell phone.

"Yeh, boss..?" Toni Ramaliche had answered from two floors below.

"Get your butt up here fast."

"Sure thing boss..." He threw five hundred dollar bills onto the bed and began pulling on some clothes.

A nude woman slithered snake like from the silk sheets and crumpled the bank notes between her scarlet painted fingers. Ramaliche struggled with his pants, heaving them on as he hopped on alternate feet towards the private elevator. He fell into it, rolling hard against the back wall like a sack of potatoes; the doors closed giving him time to finish dressing before they opened again at the penthouse lounge.

"Take a good look at this," Cinisi had shouted from the far side of the room pointing at the giant plasma T.V. screen fixed to the wall. "I'd been watching the big fight from Vegas when I switched onto some news program…"

Cinisi's recording of the report of Radcliff's rescue appeared on the screen. It had shown a short interview with Radcliff at Victoria Hospital surrounded by medical staff; then superimposed were pictures of Radcliff before his accident seven years before.

"What about that?"

"It's that artist feller ain't it?" Ramaliche was thinking fast desperately trying to anticipate Cinisi's next question.

"Who the hell do yer think it is? Tom Hanks? I've bought all this guy's paintings! He was supposed to be dead!" Cinisi was choking himself with rage. "Now he's back….*alive, for fuck's sake*!!!" He threw up his arms in exasperation. "I stand to lose millions here because of this son of a bitch. What the hell am I going to do?"

"Sell the paintings, boss," Ramaliche answered quickly, the idea having suddenly sprung into his head. But he was too quick. He saw Cinisi's reaction and wished he had kept his mouth shut.

"*What*! You're testing my patience. Your prick has more brains than your brains. I'd make a loss, you idiot…"

"Yeh, but you could put the squeeze on these limeys and force 'em to pay up," Ramaliche had watched with growing confidence as Cinisi contemplated this suggestion.

"Get to London. Take Carlo and Pauli. Meet with this British guy… that faggot who sold me the paintings two years ago. Scare the shit out of him until he pays. If he doesn't pay get those limey mercenaries to do the hit…make sure you tell 'em to take out the artist first." Cinisi prodded Ramaliche in the chest with one of his short fat fingers. "Then I want you to meet with the guy you have at the Pentagon. Tell him I want those top secret cannons pronto."

"Sure thing boss…" Ramaliche had left Cinisi staring furiously at the T.V. screen. The recording had been held on an old photograph of Radcliff's face.

# CHAPTER 7

A man lay sprawled across a sofa, his skinny frame stretching its entire length, his right arm hanging limply to the floor, a Gauloises cigarette burning within his cupped hand. He had black hair, plastered flat to his scalp, which accentuated his sickly pallor. Several smoke rings rose up in quick succession from his mouth as he watched the news on T.V.

The morning cacophony rose from the Marseilles streets to the fifth floor apartment, entering through the balcony windows with a sea breeze that moved the long net curtains.

Jean-Claude Narbonne sat bolt upright and turned up the volume with the remote control.

Moments later he heard the key turn in the front door. He switched off the TV.

"Pierre," he had called out in a high-pitched effeminate tone. "Get in here…there's some great news."

Pierre Droux had returned from his morning coffee. He stood at the door to the lounge. He was stocky, his round face craggy and weather beaten. His thinning fair hair just covered his scalp and a stubble of grey whiskers stood out from leathery ruddy skin. He was wearing a thick blue fleece and jeans.

"What is it, you seedy little cretin," his gravel voice grated. "Have you caught something terminal?"

"Mind your mouth old man. You're pushing me too far."

"Is that so! Well it was to your grandfather that I made my vow. I promised Louis…my best friend…on his deathbed that I would help you to find your family's treasure. You need me Jean-Claude. Don't you ever forget *that*!"

Jean-Claude drew deeply on his cigarette and opened the glazed door to the balcony. The noise from the busy street below burst in with the chilly sea air.

"Do you remember that British artist who went missing…" He coughed after inhaling the cool air. He slammed the door shut. "He has been found on an uncharted island in the Indian Ocean." Jean-Claude paused. "He'd been there for over seven years…!" Pierre's face was inscrutable, "….it was on the news."

"What uncharted island!" Pierre snapped. "There isn't one in the Indian Ocean. Me and your grandfather searched that ocean for the best part of twenty years."

"Well there *is* one now. And you two ancient mariners missed it!" Jean-Claude sneered.

"Did they happen to mention where it might be….?" Pierre asked sheepishly, moving slowly into the room. "….Roughly?"

"They're not likely to do that are they? This Radcliff said in an interview that he proposes to claim that island for himself."

Pierre sat on the edge of the armchair searching the morning paper. "Here it is," Pierre looked up at Jean-Claude then proceeded to read the article to himself. "You're right!" He folded the paper deep in thought. He tossed it onto the coffee table between him and the sofa. "The Indian Ocean's a vast place," he said slowly, "and I know it like the back of my hand."

He sat opposite Jean-Claude. Staring him straight in the eye he grunted: "An uncharted island, eh! I wish your grandfather were here, now. If it exists then that's where your treasure'll be. We've searched everywhere else! All I need is a few clues, Jean-Claude. Get those for me and I'll get you that treasure."

"During that news interview the reporters asked Radcliff if he had found treasure. The camera picked up something in his eyes. He wants that island for himself. There's treasure…I'm sure of it! Later they interviewed Radcliff's art agent in London. He's one of those mouthy queers…."

"What. Like you?"

"They asked him the same question. He knew something. I'm going to find out what it is."

"Well get to it and do something useful for once in your life. This is the breakthrough we've been waiting for. Oh! By the way, what did that private detective want?"

"His snooping days are over," Jean-Claude had announced proudly.

"What!" Pierre gazed at him contemptuously. "You did him in! You idiot! You psycho! What the hell's wrong with you?"

"He was asking too many questions about my mother. He wanted to know how she died! I knifed him and shoved him off the cliff. It'll be months before they find the body." He watched Pierre's anger grow, narrowing his eyes like a fiery demon. "Don't worry…" he laughed, "…you're getting more like an old woman with each passing day."

"The last thing we want on this treasure hunt is Interpol on our tail."

"I'll be in England. And no one will suspect you."

In a room at Hotel Magdelene in Sainte Victorete, close to Marseilles airport Carmen Burgos sat at the end of her bed. She had been brushing her hair listening to the television news. She heard the name Alex Radcliff mentioned. She dropped her hand mirror. It lay face upward, unbroken, on the thick pile carpet.

Previously, on the 13th June 1999, when she had heard news that Radcliff had been lost at sea, the mirror she had been holding had smashed into tiny fragments on the stone floor.

Carmen immediately turned up the volume with the remote control.

She watched in stunned amazement as a thin bearded man attempted to answer the reporter's multitude of questions. It was his voice. He was hoarse and his speech was hesitant and slow but it was him. Tears welled up in her eyes as she listened to her fiancé for the first time in over seven years.

When the report was over she had switched off the television and sat dazed, elated and confused on the bed. Remembering suddenly why she was in Marseilles she dabbed away the streaks of mascara running down her cheeks.

Carmen had recently learned from her dying mother that she had been adopted as a baby from an orphanage in Seville. She had hired a private detective to find her mother. His investigations had brought her to Marseilles. The detective had called her at the Hotel the day before, giving her an address of an apartment in the centre of the city and arranged to meet with her that evening. He had failed to show up.

At the address the detective had given her Carmen pressed the button numbered 52 at the main door.

"Oui?" said the elderly voice from the security speaker.

"Is that Jean–Claude Narbonne?" Carmen asked cautiously in English.

"Non." There was a pause. "But come on up," a heavily accented voice had said. "He will be back in a few minutes."

The front door unlocked. Carmen took the lift to the fifth floor. Pierre had been standing by the front door to the apartment.

"Entre," Pierre beckoned her inside. As she passed by him he savoured her perfume, studied her shapely legs and watched the sway of her hips. He congratulated himself on this second piece of good fortune that morning. "Would you like a coffee?"

She span on her heals, feeling his eyes undressing her. "No, thank you."

"May I take your coat? Please take a seat Miss...erm..." Pierre smiled ushering her into the lounge.

"Carmen Burgos." She handed him her white trench coat. "Thank you."

She had worn a light brown roll neck jumper and a figure hugging red skirt. Pierre watched her settle gracefully onto the sofa and sat in the armchair opposite. She was the most exciting and intoxicating woman he had seen in years.

Carmen was in her mid fifties but looked twenty years younger. Her thick wavy auburn hair bounced upon her shoulders framing a classic heart shaped face with wide set eyes. Her curving gypsy nose had a slight, beautifully chiselled line which complemented her small cleft chin and gave her full lips greater sensuality.

She listened to Pierre's slow, softly resonating seductive voice apologising for the traffic congestion, the noise of Marseilles and the weather.

Pierre could feel her warming to him. Soon she was drinking cognac and answering all of Pierre's cleverly thought out questions.

Jean-Claude burst into the apartment waving an airline ticket in the air. He saw Carmen seated on the sofa opposite Pierre and eyed her suspiciously.

"This is Carmen Burgos, Jean-Claude," Pierre said standing to vacate his seat for Jean-Claude. "She wishes to talk to you about her mother. She has come from Seville. Carmen was given this address by a…detective she had hired," Pierre winked as Jean-Claude went around him to the armchair. "She claims that you might be her half brother."

Jean-Claude fixed her with a hypnotic stare. "Really? So you must be the gypsy bastard my mother had bragged about."

Carmen's mouth had dropped open. Regaining her composure she stammered: "I… was born…in Seville." Her tone did little to disguise her dislike for his manners.

Jean-Claude had lit a cigarette and cocked his head mockingly to one side. "I can see her in you," he said with an obsequious sickly grin. He looked away only for an instant. Carmen detected a deep sadness suddenly cross his face.

"She only came home," he sneered, "because my father fooled her into believing she had inherited some money. I was eight years old," he looked directly at her once more, his eyes wider, assuming the look of an angelic innocent child, "when my mother arrived home at the flat. It was a Sunday evening. She had looked lovely. I ran into her arms."

The Frenchman's speech had slowed to a hypnotic monotone. Carmen could feel her mind being overpowered by the force of his will. "My father stormed into the room, drunk with rage, and tore me from her arms and threw me out of the room. I could see him through the open door dragging my mother, screaming, to the window." His eyes had narrowed demonically. He held her in his gaze. Time stood still. In that instant she had received something from the Frenchman telepathically. A command….but she could not identify exactly what she had to do.

Sensing that something sinister had occurred she fought to break free from his power and look away. But he was too strong. Then suddenly the force and the tension vanished.

But unbeknown to her the Frenchman had successfully embedded a seed in her subconscious mind. That seed could be germinated at any moment he chose.

"He pushed her from the balcony," Jean-Claude said icily, his eyes reliving that terrible moment.

Carmen sat stunned. Her inability to move horrified her even more.

Pierre shook Jean-Claude's shoulder. "What are doing, you fool! Why did you tell her that?"

Jean- Claude shrugged free of Pierre's grip.

"She was our mother," he said coldly, his eyes narrowing once more "and you are my half sister, Carmen. She had to die. You *do* understand that *don't you?*"

"Si," she heard herself say. But she wanted to scream out and escape from the monster before her.

"You are a friend of Alex Radcliff aren't you?"

There was silence. Pierre could only stand by, open mouthed. He remembered witnessing power of that magnitude once before in his life. It had been in Jamaica. A voodoo ceremony had been linked with the death of a farmer. He knew that Jean-Claude indulged in black magic rituals. Then he realised for the first time the depths of depravity the man before him had sunk.

"I know all about you, Carmen," Jean-Claude continued, his voice was soft and coaxing. "I am your brother. You can trust me. I'll ask you again. What is your relationship with Alex Radcliff?"

"We were to be married," Carmen heard herself answer dreamily. "It was a long time ago. Now he has come back to me."

"You're certainly full of surprises today, Jean-Claude," Pierre said, rubbing his stubbly chin. "What are you going to do?"

"She'll prove to be a very useful card to play. We'll keep her here until the time is right. I'm going to London as planned. When I get back I'll have the location of the island and we'll have this trump card up our sleeve when we negotiate with Mr. Radcliff."

"You're already into drug dealing, you're a cold blooded murderer, you've got five whores working for you and now you're adding kidnapping to your list?"

"Think for once...you old fool. With her under our control we'll have a longer breathing space before anyone can connect the detective's disappearance with her." His grin sent a chill up Pierre's spine. "Watch this!"

Jean-Claude had looked straight into Carmen's deep brown eyes. "When I click my figures once and say your name you will see Pierre as an old trusted friend and you will be happy to do anything he asks you to do." He turned to Pierre. "Sedate her with some powerful sleeping pills or something."

Jean-Claude had clicked his fingers. "Carmen," he said softly.

Carmen looked at Pierre and smiled warmly.

Jean-Claude chuckled. "She'll climb into bed with you if you ask her."

"You sick bastard! Just make sure you get your arse back here fast. Don't do anything stupid." Pierre raised his eyes to the heavens with foreboding. "That is….if you do really want to see that treasure. Try and keep a low profile, eh!

# CHAPTER 8

Alex James Radcliff was born on the day of peace, 8th May 1945. For Radcliff life had been a battle since the death of his parents, killed in separate incidents, when he five years old. William his elder brother took charge of his orphaned sibling's upbringing but in doing so sacrificed a scholarship to Cambridge University.

Radcliff possessed an extraordinary gift. Proclaimed a prodigy by his art teacher, Radcliff was taken under his wing to nurture his outstanding talent.

Sure in his mind that his younger brother's future was secure William paid the £10 emigration fee to Australia High Commission. On the 23rd February 1961 he boarded the Greek ship 'Australis' bound for Melbourne

Alex Radcliff embarked on his own voyage of discovery. She was sixteen, one year younger. But after eighteen months of bliss their relationship ended.

Then one fateful evening, his heart in shreds from the breakup, his land lady had called him downstairs to answer a telephone call.

"Alex, there has been accident…" an old woman's voice had said. There was bitterness in her tone. "William is dead…" her voice was remote, cold "…he was killed…in a car crash…at Wangaratta."

The receiver fell from his hand.

Slowly he climbed the stairs to his room. Alone on his bed he searched the cracks in the ceiling, following them round and round the solitary bare light bulb. But the lines he followed had no answers to his question.

"Will...Will…" he repeated, his head rolling from side to side on the pillow. He sobbed uncontrollably.

Unbeknown to him the shock had somehow connected with a dormant harrowing memory secretly locked away by the traumatised innocent mind of an eight year old boy. It had exacerbated a guilt that had embedded itself deep within his subconscious mind.

Radcliff retreated from the world, immersed in his art work financed by a substantial inheritance that included his mother's Devon farm. Among the few items that he kept was Robert Radclyffe's old diary.

He worked at a fanatical pace, within a zone of high excitement and deep emotion for days often without sustenance until eventually collapsing with exhaustion. Inner demons would erupt from the caldron that boiled within him, leading him to bouts of binge drinking followed by long periods of deep depression. His subtle choice and application of vibrantly contrasting colours delighted the eye and elevated the senses. There were suggestions of Van Gogh's passion in his work, his radical style was inspired and his natural technical ability compared favourably with all the great masters. His brush strokes were fast and purposeful.

During this period of self imposed solitary confinement he produced vast quantities of canvases. He was acclaimed to be the greatest British artist of the twentieth century.

A woman did not enter his life again until old age was looming. When it did he was smitten. But soon after meeting the beautiful and voluptuous Carmen Burgos however, Radcliff had been swept over-board from a catamaran and lost for seven years stranded on an island in the Indian Ocean.

Radcliff rescue became global news.

His six foot frame had become lithe and deeply tanned belying his advancing years. The mane of matted and greying ginger hair had been trimmed and the long bushy beard that reached his chest had been sheared off. Bushy eyebrows hung over wide set grey-green piercing, intelligent eyes that reflected his love of life but also conveyed a strange, compelling sadness; his sunken, gaunt cheeks accentuated a strong jaw line, his leathery weathered flesh pulled tight across his cheekbones; his nose was straight and pointed; his compassionate but sensual mouth was relatively small stretching readily into a beaming smile. He had rounded, slightly cleft chin that turned upward.

Disturbed and confused by Norton-Smythe's telephone call that afternoon, Radcliff had taken a long walk in the snow. It was dark when he reached the short cut from Wivelsfield to his home. Entering the huge clearing that surrounded his home he leaned into a stiff east wind blast-ing huge snowflakes into his eyes.

A beacon of yellow light shone through the heavy murk, casting its warm glow across the carpet of new snow. A few strides nearer and the bluish grey shadows of the octagonal twin towers were discernable, a huge cold mystical shape warmed by the main entrance light. His pace increased as he crossed the fixed drawbridge of his home...Muirhurst Castle...expecting Norton-Smythe to be waiting for him at the door.

Radcliff had sealed up the castle's main entrance eight years before. Snow had drifted high against this newly rendered stonework and half-way up the right hand tower.

Radcliff unlocked the double mortise of the oak door to the opposite tower. He pushed hard against the stiff hinges. Once inside he passed through the tower's double archway and into the cavernous hallway lit by a solitary light on the right wall next to the lounge door. Opposite a wide, magnificent wooden staircase curved serenely to the upper floor; to the right of the staircase stood a grandfather clock. High up on the left wall four latticed windows, each five feet high with gothic arches, had been strategically positioned just below the battlements overlooking the clearing in front of the castle.

The clock's Westminster chimes rang out the three quarter hour.

Radcliff hung his light blue anorak in the hallway next to the wall light, entered the long rectangular lounge and switched on the nearest of the two seventeenth century chandeliers. He turned on an antique radio placed at one end of the huge oak dining table. The notes from a piano filled the empty room.

Crossing the room he stoked the fire and placed a log on the embers. Soon it was blazing in the stone Tudor fireplace.

The gentle rhythm of Chopin's weaving notes lifted Radcliff's spirits.

He poured himself a large whiskey from the well stocked liquor trolley he had set within the recess of an expansive rectangular bay window overlooking the snow covered central courtyard.

The fluid warmed him. He poured another as he watched snowflakes falling and swirling in the space outside. Looking out to his left he could depict the grey, forbidding battlements and his thoughts returned to Clive's shattering revelations earlier that afternoon.

The 8 o'clock news was announced on the radio. He stooped over the curving wood frame of the wireless and turned up the volume.

The reporter described Norton-Smythe's murder adding the police description of the killer: '…he was a white male, about 6 feet tall, approximately fifty or sixty years of age with greying ginger hair, wearing jeans and a light blue anorak with the hood up….' He then reported how Radcliff was associated with the deceased. Radcliff's heart skipped another beat.

The announcer continued: 'Alex Radcliff is the famous artist whose sensational rescue had become world news only a month ago. He had been stranded on an island in the Indian Ocean for seven years. Since his dramatic rescue Sotheby's have announced today that Radcliff's work has been devalued by 90 percent. Nevertheless his estate, which was managed entirely by Mr. Norton-Smythe, is still estimated to be worth in excess of 1 billion pounds. Radcliff is said to be living alone in his East Sussex home.'

Radcliff switched off the radio. The sudden silence was unnerving. Then he remembered the death note that he had received that morning. For the first time since leaving the island he feared for his life. The stone walls had the oppressive weightiness of a tomb which chilled him to the bone; the unlit areas of the vast lounge seamed to conceal something sinister, the flickering fire bringing life to the shadows. The green wood hissed.

There was a sharp crack.

He ducked behind an armchair.

Peering over the top, he smiled at his own foolishness.

Skirting the armchair he warmed himself beside the fire.

The castle had been built in a quadrangle design with a central grass area the size of two tennis courts, now completely enclosed by the blocked off the main entrance. The lounge and the banqueting hall, with bedrooms above, made up the left side of the quadrangle; the twenty-foot high battlements towered over the top end with the sealed off main entrance at the opposite end; the chapel and the music room on the right side completed the enclosure. At each corner and at strategic intervals along the walls jutted smaller octagonal and semi octagonal towers.

All the rooms excluding the lounge, the main bedroom directly above it, the chapel and the music room were locked.

Having mentally gone through all of his safety precautions he began to feel reassured.

Carmen's silver framed photograph caught his eye. She was smiling at him from the mantelpiece. The picture had been taken with her standing on the central lawn, with the lounge French windows in the background. The afternoon sun glinted on her long, wavy auburn hair and full sensuous lips; her face was lit perfectly capturing her beauty and caught the sparkle in her dark brown Spanish eyes. Her shoulder length wavy auburn hair, ablaze with different shades of reds and browns, framed her classic heart shaped face. A cluster of daffodils bloomed close to her feet.

He kissed the cool, smooth glass longing for the day they would be reunited. His smile was clouded by uncharacteristic pessimism.

Outside, twenty yards along the battlement wall from the tower in far corner beyond the chapel, an assassin, camouflaged in white overalls, had rested the barrel of a high-powered rifle on the stonework. He focussed the telescopic sights onto his target whilst constantly wiping snow from the lens. The height and angle of the shot meant that the top of the bay window obscured the view of Radcliff's head and shoulders. The hunter watched his prey, waiting for him to move nearer to the windows that would give an uninterrupted view of his head.

Radcliff gulped the rest of his whiskey and returned to the trolley for another. As he poured his drink his thoughts drifted to the Cross of Goa; how he saw the Cross through the crevice in the mountain. Only its top section had been visible, sparkling with a thousand gems, protruding from a massive mountain of treasure; then noticing that more than half the treasure was beneath a subterranean lake the refracting light magnifying the intensity of each glittering jewel and gold coin.

On the battlements the gunman had his target in full view. His finger eased on the trigger to brush away several large snowflakes from the sights.

Radcliff returned to the fireplace. Feeling warmed by the drink he remembered his success the previous day at the British Library. It was the culmination of three weeks solid research. The history book had an engraving identical to the one his ancestor had meticulously sketched in his diary which proved unequivocally to him that what he had seen was the actual Cross of Goa.

The assassin took aim once more but his target had moved. Raising the cross hairs a fraction he saw his prey returning to the fireplace.

Radcliff stood before Carmen's picture, sipping his drink, imagining them both, as he had a million times before, on the island digging out the Cross and the treasure from the mountain. He took the picture with him to the armchair nearest the door to the hall. The old, red leather bound diary of Robert William Radclyffe, lay open face down on the arm of the chair.

Seated before the blazing fire he lifted the diary, balancing his whiskey glass on an arm of the chair, he held Carmen's photograph against the exquisite sketch of the Cross of Goa. As he studied the two pictures side by side the fiery liquid warmed and soothed his insides. He resolved to ponder Norton-Smythe's murder later and let the reassuring and relaxing warmth of the fire fuel another dream of Carmen.

A sudden sharp double rap on the heavy doorknocker reverberated inside the hall. Radcliff leapt to his feet, the nape of his neck tingling and his heart pounding in his chest. The diary, the tumbler and the picture fell to the floor.

He stood erect beside the fire, motionless, barely breathing, listening and waiting, his senses on full alert. He was back on his island, his chin and nose pointed skyward smelling the wind, assessing and estimating the danger.

The gunman saw the book fall and the tumbler bounce on the rug and roll towards the fireplace. He watched and waited with the cross hairs of his telescopic sight fixed on Radcliff's legs. Then his target turned away and was gone. He rested the gun on the snow and rubbed his hands together, breathing and sucking life back into on his frozen fingers.

In the dim light of the hall, Radcliff nervously approached the oak door. A second double rap on the knocker echoed inside the base of the tower.

"Who is it?" He called out, pressing his ear against the ancient, iron studded door.

"Mr. Alex Radcliff?" A man answered, his voice muffled by the thickness of the wood.

"Yes. What do you want?" Radcliff demanded.

"It's the Police, Mr. Radcliff," the same voice replied.

Relieved, Radcliff released the double mortise lock and swung open the door. Snowflakes flurried inside with a freezing draft.

"I'm Chief Inspector Hawkins and this is Detective Constable Omollo. We are from Scotland Yard." Radcliff quickly glanced at the identity cards they offered up to him. Snow eddied and swirled around the two men. "May we come in? I would like to ask you a few questions."

Radcliff ushered them inside, through the hall and into relative warmth of the lounge.

Hawkins went straight to the fireplace. Omollo remained respectfully behind the armchair.

"You have quite a place here, Mr. Radcliff," Hawkins said, holding his hands up to the blazing logs. "Log fire; smells good!" He turned on his heels and warmed his rear. "Tapestries!" he beamed, looking across at the wall opposite. "Magnificent!"

"Yes. Thank you," Radcliff nodded, managing a congenial half smile. "Yes they are. Yes they are." Radcliff's strange double affirmative had developed on the island in times of extreme anxiety or danger… meticulously checking out the threat until he felt safe...then double-checking his findings. "They need restoring." Radcliff waved his arm towards the armchair. "Please sit down."

Hawkins stooped and picked up the tumbler, then reached across and lifted the old diary and the photograph and handed them to Radcliff.

"Thank you. An accident…" Radcliff said awkwardly, replacing Carmen's photograph on the mantelpiece, "…. just now. The knock on the door…"

Hawkins smiled amiably. "I'd be jumpy living in a place like this, sir." He sat in the armchair nearest to the bay windows. "Do you live alone?"

"Yes. Yes, I do."

"It's a magnificent place, Mr. Radcliff. How did you come by it?"

"We…my fiancé and me…bought it at auction about eight years ago," Radcliff explained as he strode to the great dining table under the tapestries and returned with one of the chairs and sat between the two men, facing the fire. "Yes. Yes, we bought it about eight years ago at auction."

"Are you married, Mr. Radcliff?"

"No." Radcliff looked up at Carmen's photograph.

Hawkins followed Radcliff's gaze then fixed Radcliff with his sharp eyes. "What would you pay for a place like this? If you don't mind me asking…?"

"No. Not at all," he lied, hoping that conversation would ease his nerves. "We were very fortunate. The vendor had gone into receivership …the administrators accepted my winning bid of £5 million. An absolute fluke…. you might say!"

Hawkins whistled, glanced at Omollo and chuckled. "Well done!" He said with genuine admiration "I've seen most of the castles in the south. This is a new one to me. It's very similar to the one at Herstmonceux, isn't it?"

"They were built at the same time. It's two thirds the size of Herstmonceux, but you're correct, Chief Inspector. They are both built of the same French brick and the architecture and designs are very similar. They were both gifts from King Henry V to two of his knights who fought at Agincourt."

"Does it have a name?"

"Muirhurst...it's called Muirhurst," he smiled proudly.

Hawkins looked around the lounge. "It must cost a pretty penny to keep a place like this going!" He smiled enviously.

"I've closed most of it," Radcliff answered, tiring of the questions. "I only use the bedroom upstairs, directly above this room." their eyes following Radcliff's gaze up at the frescoed ceiling. "It has an en-suit bathroom. I've just had a kitchen fitted here in the corner of the lounge… behind that partition," pointing to the corner of the room behind Omollo.

"How far do the grounds extend?" Hawkins pressed on testily.

"It has 550 acres and a lake," Radcliff answered quickly. "The lake is fed by a spring which is also the source of the Eldar River, a tributary to the River Ouse. It runs east through West Chailey. There's a wonderful pub called the King and Queen…" Radcliff paused in deep thought, his eyes lost in the flames, remembering those blissful spring days with Carmen. "It sits on the river bank…" He added dreamily glancing at her picture.

Hawkins silently admired the woman in the picture whilst waiting for Radcliff to continue.

The rifleman on the battlements raised the rifle, the cross hairs of the sights moved from the head of a man seated in the nearest armchair across to his target, who was partially hidden by the man seated. He could see the legs of another person seated in the farthest armchair. He prepared himself for a long wait.

"Is that a picture of… your fiancé?" Hawkins asked, feeling Radcliff's sadness.

"Carmen…? Yes…yes it is."

"Have you seen her recently...?"

"No," Radcliff snapped, shaking his head. "No, I haven't, Chief Inspector," his patience exhausted. "I shall be seeing her soon…I hope so anyway. Inspector…sorry Chief Inspector…I'm sure you haven't come all this way to talk about my home and my personal life."

"No. I apologise. You are quite right, Mr. Radcliff." Hawkins looked across at Omollo and the big man opened his note pad "I have some bad news, Mr. Radcliff. Mr. Clive Norton-Smythe…your art agent I believe…was murdered this evening."

"Yes, I know. I heard it on the news. It was on the news."

"I see. I have some routine questions for you, Mr. Radcliff," Hawkins' said congenially. "The initial steps of these enquiries follow a laborious and methodical pattern, I'm afraid." Hawkins half smiled, his eyes riveted on Radcliff, watching his every move and reaction. "I wonder if you wouldn't mind telling me where you were between the hours of 5 and 7 o'clock this evening, Mr. Radcliff."

"No, of course...I was out walking."

"Do you normally go for a walk in this type of weather, Mr. Radcliff?"

"Well I love the snow. Today I needed to clear my head and think some things through."

"What time did you leave for your walk and when did you return?"

"Clive phoned me at about 3.30, therefore it must have been about half an hour later when I went out. I got back just before the 8 o'clock news. Yes, that's right. That's right. The clock in the hall was chiming. It was 7.45. Yes it was."

"Four hours! In this blizzard! Where did you go?"

"West Chailey," he answered calmly. "I went on to North Chailey and beyond before turning back."

"Can anyone substantiate that, Mr. Radcliff?"

"No. I didn't see a soul. I had the peace and quiet I needed. I always think more clearly when I'm walking."

"So you had a lot to think about. Did Mr. Norton-Smythe's phone call upset you in any way?"

"Yes. He was on his way down to see me to clear a few things up." Radcliff stared at the flames recalling the voice of his agent then realising that he might never know the meaning behind Clive's incoherent babbling. "I expected Clive to be waiting for me when I returned."

"Is that your blue anorak hanging outside in the hall, Mr. Radcliff?" Hawkins' eyes were piercing and concentrated.

"Yes. Yes, it is. I heard on the radio that the killer was wearing a blue anorak. Many people wear them, you know."

Hawkins got up from the armchair and picked up a ball of partially burnt wrapping from the corner of the huge hearth and carefully straightened it out. It was an empty Gauloises cigarette packet. "Do you smoke, Mr. Radcliff?" Hawkins asked quietly.

"No." Radcliff thought for a moment. "It must have been the plumber's. I had a sink put in over there," he pointed to the kitchen area behind the partition.

"I see." He dropped the cigarette packet in a plastic bag and handed it to Omollo.

"Why did Mr. Norton-Smythe telephone you?" Hawkins returned

97

to the fireplace and leaned on the marble mantle piece.

"He was very upset. He had received a threatening letter this morning. It said that he ..." Radcliff swallowed hard as the reality of his death hit him once again, "...he would die today. Yes. It said that he would die today."

"Do you have any idea who might want to kill him?"

"There are many people out there who disliked my agent, Inspector. I'm still trying to make sense of what he told me on the phone. He sounded frightened and desperate. He mentioned that three Americans attacked him in his flat on Christmas Eve. He seemed positive that these people were the ones that had sent him the death note." Radcliff paused. "Clive become hysterical and blurted out things that were all mixed up.... something about a row with his chauffeur who had left him the night before. Then he suddenly blurted out that WE owed these Americans £10 million!"

Hawkins waited for Omollo to finish writing. The only sound was the crackle and hiss of the green wood burning in the hearth.

"That's a great deal of money, Mr. Radcliff. How could you owe a sum like that without knowing about it beforehand?"

"I didn't have any idea how much money was involved, Chief Inspector. I was absolutely stunned."

"When was the last time you saw Mr. Norton-Smythe alive?"

"Early in December, just after my rescue; he phoned me many times in the last couple of weeks. He'd wanted to arrange a meeting for some time, but I've always been too busy. I've hardly seen a soul, except for my housekeeper."

"When was the last time you travelled to London?"

"Yesterday..."

"Did you meet or contact Mr. Norton-Smythe yesterday?"

"No. I was finishing some research at the British Library. I was there all day."

"That was the last time you travelled to London?"

"Yes. Yes it was."

"What were you researching at the British Library?"

"That's my business," he retorted. "I've a docket in my anorak pocket with the date and time on it if you need proof."

"I advise you not to lose it, Mr. Radcliff!" He tempered his ice-cold glare with a half smile. "I remember the day you were rescued, Mr. Radcliff.... from that island. It was in all the papers.... and on TV. Quite phenomenal! What a test of endurance! You had a long time on your own. Five years, wasn't it?"

"Seven and a half actually..."

"Incredible! Alone for over seven years! Will you be writing a book? People love survival stories. Share your knowledge and experiences with the world! You remember Henri Charriére…'Papillion'?" Hawkins' sharp, penetrating eyes flashed at Radcliff then up at Carmen's picture. "Why isn't your fiancé here with you?"

"She's in Spain, I think."

"Oh. Have you spoken to her since you've been back in England?"

"No. I've tried her home 'phone number but she doesn't answer."

"Does she know you're alive?"

"Listen, Chief Inspector. There's nothing more I want in life than to see her again," he choked, emotion gripping his throat like an iron fist. "She was with me every single moment on that island," forcing a grimacing, quivering smile. "She was there during the long days searching for food and fighting the endless struggle to stay alive; she was there in my dreams during those long lonely nights with only the stars, the moon and a sea breeze…for company." Radcliff gritted his teeth holding back his emotions. He rubbed his head with his hands. "The warmth of her memory staved off the chill of the storms," he blurted with quivering lips, "she was there when I lay in the sun and when I swam." He calmed himself for moment. "Not long before my rescue I saw an image of her when I was trapped in deep water. She led me to safety."

Radcliff's tearful eyes looked directly at Hawkins. "She saved my life, Chief Inspector." He stared into the flames, his shaking hands clenched tightly together.

A few minutes elapsed, both policemen remaining respectfully silent, finding it difficult to imagine the mental and physical anguish that the man before them had endured.

Radcliff looked up, half smiling, and said finally, "Seven years *is* a long time. Things change and people change. Everyone can learn to do without most things. But I'm not sure I would want to carry on if I knew I could never see her again."

Hawkins took a deep breath. Pursing his lips thoughtfully he asked congenially: "What do think are the biggest changes you have noticed since you have been home in England?"

"The pace of life….more cars…..more traffic…more of everything, I suppose," Radcliff stated absently, still gazing into the flames. "I can remember ecologists talking about global warming ten years ago. Nothing has changed there! They are still destroying the rain forests, chemicals and oil are polluting the sea and temperatures continue to rise. Oh yes! There are millions of mobile phones. Everyone has one of those *bloody* things these days."

"Climate change is still one of the biggest issues of the day," Hawkins added looking deeply into the fire. "Quite alarming to think that if this generation cannot solve it, then our children and our children's children will probably pay a fearful price and most definitely never forgive us." He looked at Radcliff and his eyes narrowed. "Many people would give their right arm to have been on your island, alone and away from that sort of responsibility right now. Living your own existence under your own laws…just you and the elements, eh! Do you live by those laws now, Mr. Radcliff?"

"What do mean?" Radcliff glared at Hawkins. The policeman's eyes were as hard and as cold as ball bearings. "What are you driving at?"

"Well, Mr. Radcliff. You've faced life and death situations probably on a daily basis, I'd say. Would you allow your instincts to dictate your actions now that you are back in the civilized world?"

"Did I kill Clive? Is that what you are implying? I don't think your moral code ever leaves you. I was battling against the elements, not human beings. When you forage and hunt for your food, Chief Inspector, you develop a great respect for the forces of nature and especially for all life in all its forms."

"You were angry when Norton-Smythe told you about the debt of £10 million, were you not?"

"Yes, of course. He was on his way to see me and discuss it."

"You had no idea what state your financial position was in?"

"I never got involved with that side of my affairs. That's what I paid Clive to do. He had boasted to me about having quadrupled my fortune since my absence. When Clive told me the exact amount just after my rescue, I did feel quite suspicious. In hindsight, I should have delved deeper into his business dealings but my research was taking up every minute of my time."

"What is it you are researching that's more important…." he nodded towards the picture of Carmen, "…than finding your fiancé?".

"I've finished my research. I have what I was looking for."

"With a woman like that waiting for me, she would have been the first thing I would've been looking for!"

"I have my reasons, Chief Inspector, and they have nothing to do with you."

"Okay." Hawkins drew himself forward to the edge of the armchair and looked Radcliff squarely in the eyes. "How much money *did* Norton-Smythe make whilst you were away?"

"Close to thirty million pounds…. for the sale of my paintings."

Hawkins whistled and raised his eyebrows at Omollo.

"I was amused when Clive said to me that the timing of my disappearance couldn't have been more fortuitous. Demand exceeded supply as it were, and he could more or less name his price."

"Did he sell all your work?"

"All but six of my unfinished works...yes, all but six."

"How many paintings did he sell?"

"One hundred and twenty three…"

"Seven years ago you were already a millionaire. Then you

disappeared." He studied Radcliff's soulful watery eyes. "In the eyes of the art and investment world you were dead. Then, suddenly, you came back to life!"

"That's right," Radcliff looked away absently. "Clive said something about that this afternoon. He blamed me for all his troubles; that he wished I had died on that island. My coming back, he said, was the worst thing anyone had done to him." Radcliff looked away and chuckled. "It's crazy isn't it! I'm worth more dead than alive. What will my work be worth when *I do* eventually kick the bucket?" Radcliff leaned forward, staring into the fire, then ran his fingers through his hair and looked at Hawkins. "And that might not be too far away, Chief Inspector!"

"Really!" he said with indifference. "Why's that?"

"I also received a death note this morning. This one..." Radcliff produced a folded piece of A4 paper from his pocket and handed it to Hawkins.

In lettering cut from newsprint headlines and pasted onto the paper, it read:

'PREPARE TO DIE! YOU WILL BE DEAD BEFORE THE DAY IS OUT'.

Hawkins gaze moved slowly from the note to Radcliff. "Was Norton-Smythe's note the same as this?"

"I don't know," he snapped irritably. "Does that matter now he's dead?"

"What did you and Mr. Norton-Smythe argue about on the phone?"

"I yelled at him and called him a few names. I was very upset. I felt that he had mishandled my affairs and put us both in grave danger."

"Did you know that you were the sole beneficiary of Mr. Norton-Smythe's estate?"

"He had mentioned it years ago, before I..." Radcliff stopped, his eyes meeting Hawkins' fixed, accusative stare.

"Did you know that he had recently increased his life insurance policy?"

"I didn't know that. If you're searching for a motive, Chief Inspector, I have absolutely no money worries."

"You're a very rich man, I grant you. But you must confess that you are much better off with Norton-Smythe out of the way.... and with the £10 million debt to pay off...?" Hawkins stood up and moved towards the fire, letting Radcliff think deeply and thoroughly.

"I did not kill Clive," Radcliff said slowly shaking his head.

Hawkins turned, leaned on the mantelpiece and faced Radcliff. "I have to tell you, Mr. Radcliff," he spoke fast, his eyes drilling into Radcliff's, "a man was seen wearing a blue anorak, about your height and build, at London Bridge station this evening. He caught the Brighton train....he got off at Wivelsfield station. That is the station you use, is it not?"

Radcliff looked straight back at Hawkins. "I've been here all day, Chief Inspector," he said quietly and precisely, a hint of anger and exasperation in his tone. "I've been studying this book," shaking his ancestor's old diary in front of Hawkins' face. "I want you to find the people who wrote that note," pointing to the paper still in Hawkins hand. "My life has been threatened. It looks like I'm next." Radcliff picked up two logs from the hearth and threw them on the fire showering the hearth with sparks and embers.

Hawkins looked down at the hungry flames licking the new fuel. "We have two witnesses. They were standing near Mr. Norton-Smythe on Bank station platform." Hawkins turned slowly to meet Radcliff's gaze. "They said that Norton-Smythe appeared very agitated and scared and mumbled things to himself. He was heard to say that someone wanted to kill him and that your name was mentioned several times."

Radcliff fell silent. His mouth opened and closed, but could say nothing. "I've been here all day," he said finally. "Except for the walk...I swear it."

Hawkins watched the flames licking the logs. The green wood hissed and spat. He looked up.

"I must be honest with you. I was ready to take you in for questioning, Mr. Radcliff. But that will be all for now. I will have a car posted outside. We will be watching your every move. Do you understand Mr. Radcliff?"

"Perfectly well Inspector."

"We shall be in touch. I suggest that you do not make any arrangements to leave the country just yet, Mr. Radcliff. Thank you for your time. We'll see ourselves out. Good night, sir."

"Good night, Mr. Radcliff," Omollo smiled kindly and closed the door quietly behind him. A few moments later he heard the oak door slam shut.

The gunman followed the target's head through the telescopic sights, keeping the cross hairs on him as he threw another log onto the fire. Then the target moved away and out of sight.

In the hall, under the wall light stood an antique candlestick telephone on a small ornate table. The clock struck nine. The Westminster chime echoed majestically within the great hallway. Radcliff pulled a crumpled piece of paper from his trouser pocket. He held the paper up to the light, read the faded numbers Clive had given him and dialled them on the base of his phone. He waited, as he had a hundred times before, until the exchange mechanism cut him off and then redialled. On his seventh attempt Carmen answered.

Momentarily stunned hearing her enchanting Spanish accent after so long, he laughed like a schoolboy 'phoning a sweetheart for the first time. His mouth and lips formed the words he wanted to say, but no sounds came.

'Si' she repeated three times.

"Carmen," he said gently. "It's me….. Alex."

"Alex!" she cried. "It's you…" Her voice trailed off like a long sigh.

Radcliff heard a thud and then the line went dead. He rattled the receiver support for a tone and dialled her number again and again. Calming himself he decided to wait a few minutes, guessing that she needed time to recover from the shock of his call. He returned to the lounge and went straight to the drinks trolley, poured a whiskey and stood by the latticed French doors separating the two huge bay windows.

The gunman drew the breach tight into his shoulder and steadied his aim. He took his time, the target having settled in position, and sucked life back into his frozen fingers then tightened his finger on the trigger.

Radcliff unlocked the French window and looked out over the courtyard trying to see the spot where he had taken her photograph that spring afternoon. Beyond it, barely discernible in the blizzard, the outline of the grey, imposing medieval ramparts and corner tower rose up protectively behind the chapel roof. He squinted into the murk at an odd, dark lump at the far end of the battlement wall. The snow fell more heavily and obscured his view. He closed the window and drank more of his whiskey. He swayed slightly off balance and took a step backwards to steady himself.

He noticed his reflection in the French windows. He imagined seeing Carmen standing beside him, smiling. He raised his glass and toasted aloud: "To us! We'll be together soon!"

He drained his tumbler, the fiery liquid burning his throat and his whole body shuddered. His weight moved slightly to his right side, then, as if tugged sharply at his right elbow, he toppled. At that instant there was a flash of light from the battlement and a pane of lattice shattered onto the floor. Radcliff's head was knocked backwards by the impact of the bullet.

The gunman, Eugene Slaughter once a Sergeant Major in the Royal Marines, scanned the inert body through the telescopic gun sights, focussing on the head. The expanding dark blot on the carpet beneath the target's head was a sufficient indictor that his mission was a success. He methodically dismantled the gun, packed it neatly inside a leather hold-all and dropped it on the snow behind the wall then lowered himself down the rope. He trudged towards the front of the castle, snow crunching underfoot, feeling the circulation returning to his frozen limbs.

He stopped in his tracks and withdrew behind the corner tower of the front wall. A police car, the driver's doors open, stood on the opposite bank of the dry moat close to the drawbridge.

The contingency plan was for his driver to wait at the King and

Queen pub at West Chailey. He retraced his footprints as far as the corner of the battlement wall, then descended the slope to the lake and followed the riverbank for half a mile to the stone road bridge. He climbed the bank and crossed the bridge, crouching below the level of its stone wall, until he could see the pub car park.

The King and Queen was a long thin two-story pub built between the wars in mock Tudor style, the original having burned down in 1917. It was set well back from the riverbank. Snow covered its manicured lawns and gardens that sloped gently to the river. It was a favourite venue for courting couples. An ancient sprawling cedar tree rose up from the centre of the car park, its snow laden branches touching the front wall of the pub and overhanging the lane that led northward over the bridge, spanning the Eldar River, to Wivelsfield.

Several cars were parked outside the King and Queen. The warm yellow glow from the pub's many Georgian style windows cast sparkling golden patches on the freshly fallen snow. A young couple emerged from the pub, the open door casting a carpet of gold across the car park. The couple walked arm in arm southward along the lane.

Slaughter waited until they were well clear then, keeping low and in the shadows, he crossed bridge to the waiting black Ford Galaxy parked beneath the cedar tree.

"Okay boss?" the driver asked as Slaughter climbed into the back.

"Yeh. Get goin', Apeson. I'm bloody frozen," Slaughter rubbed his hands together then switched on his mobile phone. He punched a Chicago number and waited. A voice requested a password. "Octopus", he said, and waited.

Apeson hurtled the black Galaxy north along the narrow country lane, headlights cutting through the falling snow, in the direction of Wivelsfield and ultimately Haywards Heath.

"Yeh?" a voice answered his mobile.

"The ring is repaired," Slaughter announced. "When can I expect settlement?"

"When we hear news that your repairs are satisfactory..." The line went dead.

"*Fuck 'em!*" Slaughter pummelled the back of the seat in front of him.

"What d'e say, boss?"

"The bastards will only pay up once they're satisfied Radcliff's dead. Get back to the hotel," he barked.

The officer stationed outside the castle in the squad car had heard the single shot ring out from the castle grounds and raised the alarm. It had taken a specialist locksmith an hour to open the oak door to the left tower. They found Radcliff lying on his back with his head in a pool of blood.

# CHAPTER 9

Wivelsfield railway station, East Sussex is elevated high upon an embankment. Earlier that same evening a tall, slim man wearing a blue anorak and jeans pushed and jostled through the crowd of commuters filing through the subway. Angry, indignant cries echoed in the confined space of the tunnel under the platforms. A short walkway connected the subway to an old white, feather boarded ticket office nestled amongst snow-covered trees halfway up the embankment.

Two ticket inspectors were at the doorway.

The man in the anorak emerged from the tunnel pushing his way through the crowd. An elderly woman fell screaming to the ground. The inspectors prepared to challenge the man when he reached the ticket office.

But the man scaled a low wall and charged through the snow covered bracken. An inspector gave chase. The tracks in the snow led to a scout hut built into the embankment parallel to the railway line.

Nearing the hut his nerve failed him. Standing thigh deep in bracken and snow he listened, looking back anxiously hoping his colleague was following as back up. Cursing loudly he returned to the ticket office.

Hearing his pursuer retreat, the man bobbed up from behind a pile of logs ripping off his wig and removing his blue anorak. Quickly reversing the anorak he put it back on then stuffed the wig into his pockets. He ran the length of the hut to a snow covered driveway. A ten foot high metal gate and wire fence was lit by the yellow glow of a street lamp. He climbed the link wire, straddled the top steadying himself before the jumping to the road, his breath condensing into a sickly yellow cloud above his head.

Snow cushioned his landing. He trudged along the centre of the street lined with terraced houses and crammed with parked cars. He took the first turning to the left which descended steeply to the main road. Many abandoned cars littered the street. Turning left again into the main road he hurried towards the railway bridge and climbed the wooden steps up the embankment to the white feather boarded ticket office.

A Frenchman, wearing a black anorak, jeans with black hair plastered flat onto his scalp purchased a single ticket to London Bridge.

The man retrieved his French registered black BMW X5 from the multi-story car park in Lower Thames Street and drove north towards

Epping Forest. Nearing the small village of Beachsted he slowed the vehicle to a purring crawl and turned off the lights. The dim glow from the intermittent street lamps was enough to guide him through the village. He took a left turn down a narrow track taking him deep into the forest.

The BMW ploughed through the snow drifts for about a mile. He snatched on the handbrake, opened the rear door and replaced the anorak for a sheepskin overcoat he had stowed in the cargo area. Taking a plastic petrol container he cleared an area several paces from the BMW. Dumping the wig and anorak into the hollow he doused them with petrol and struck several matches together. He watched the flames engulf the small pyre.

Following the road signs back to junction 6 of the M11 he headed east for Felixstowe. A fake European Union passport in the name of Philiepe Boulogne and a ticket for the 7.00 a.m. ferry to Zeebrugge lay on a shelf beneath the glove compartment.

Most of mainland Europe had escaped the heavy snow blanketing the U.K. Once the Frenchman had reached the expressways leading south he made excellent time arriving back at his Marseilles flat in the early hours of the morning.

Pierre had been approaching the front door when Jean-Claude blustered in, tossing his sheepskin coat in the general direction of the hat stand he barged Pierre out of his way to the lounge.

Pierre stopped himself from picking up the sheepskin. Instead he kicked it viciously against the wall.

"Well! What happened in England?" he grunted, following the younger man into the lounge.

Jean-Claude flopped onto the sofa ignoring the question. Pierre poured himself a cognac. "Do you want a coffee?" he asked reluctantly.

"No. Give me one of those."

"What happened?" Pierre asked again pouring him a cognac.

"It all went like clockwork," he laughed cockily. "The old queer told me everything. Radcliff *did* find treasure! His island is south east of the Seychelles. It has to be the place where Bernadin's treasure is hidden. Soon we'll be rich, Pierre!" He looked across at Pierre sitting morosely in the armchair opposite.

"What's wrong? You can drive a man insane! What's the matter with you? You and Grandfather Louis spent all your lives searching for the treasure and all you do is sit there moping and gazing into your glass."

Pierre Anton Droux had been savouring his cognac thinking of better times with his life-long friend, Louis Narbonne.

"Yes, you're right. Louis and me had searched for over forty years for that elusive treasure! But you know nothing of its history…and why? Why…because you couldn't give a tinker's toss for your grandfather. He loved you. He tried a million times to get you interested in the treasure…but you scorned him each time.

"Let me tell you. It was the treasure of the privateer Bernadin Nageon De L'Estang, otherwise known as 'The Loot'. In 1800, from his death-bed on Ile de France, your ancestor bequeathed the triple hoard of buried treasure to his nephew Justin Narbonne to be used to restore your family's status. Justin received all the documentation that Bernadin sent him.

"But there is a cruel twist to the…"

"I know. Why do you think I've never believed the treasure existed? That Justin died searching for it. He died a pauper. Grandad loved the sea. I'm positive he didn't care about the treasure." Jean-Claude's tone rose effeminately. "It was an excuse so he could spend all his time living it up on those desert islands."

"Okay! True…there was no treasure map. None of Bernadin's documents contained a clue to where he had buried it. A sick joke, sure…"

"It was. Our family has wasted almost two hundred years looking for it. I wasn't going to die penniless like all the others. And I won't…I swear to you."

"Louis's last request before he died was that I swear an oath upon the family Bible that I would continue the search for the 'family's' lost treasure with you. Louis gave me all the documentation that the 'The Loot' had sent to Justin."

"Well now I have the missing the vital piece of information…the whereabouts of the treasure!

"Why did you choose to push Norton-Smythe under that train?" Pierre asked slowly, his tone deep and resonant. "I asked you to keep a low profile, you little prick. Why did you have to kill him? Do you want this treasure or not?"

"I won't have you talking to me that way no more. He's dead. I've framed the artist. It's brilliant! It's perfect! We get two birds with one stone, eh? Don't be such an old woman!" He laughed nervously.

Pierre threw his glass at the fireplace and stormed over to Jean-Claude, grabbed him by the lapels and lifted his head up to his. "I'll talk to you how I please. Your Grandfather was the only good thing to come out of your wretched family. Listen to me, you little piece of shit. If they connect you with Norton-Smythe's murder you will not only have Scotland Yard on our backs…but Interpol as well!"

"Alright..! Alright! Calm down old man. I saw an opportunity to get Radcliff out of the way. I had followed him to the British Library and back to his castle several times. He's a creature of habit. It was a walk in the park. I've framed him good and proper! They'll convict Radcliff and throw away the key. Now get your hands off of me." Jean-Claude hissed, his eyes creasing up into vicious slits.

"You have framed him, eh! Enough for a conviction! All of a sudden you are a lawyer now, eh? The only one who'll be slapped behind bars is you! Either that or a mental asylum! Why did you have to kill him? *You stupid idiot..!*" Pierre screamed, with rage, his grip tightening on his throat. "You're putting my head on the block as well. And *I don't like it!*"

"There's nothing…to worry…about," Jean-Claude croaked feeling Pierre's knuckles pressing hard on his larynx. "You are…perfectly safe. Now…let me go. I'm feeling…dizzy."

Pierre tossed Jean-Claude contemptuously onto the sofa. His cognac glass flew across the room.

Jean-Claude rubbed his neck, his eyes narrowing. "Where's that half sister of mine?" he demanded, adjusting his clothing.

"That's another thing." Pierre snapped. "You'd better get more practice with your evil spells and make sure they last. She's gone."

"*What*! You let her go?" he screamed.

"If she gets back together with the artist…and she's surely smitten by that man…. they'll be formidable opponents."

"What happened?" Jean-Claude strutted to the drinks cabinet and poured himself another drink.

"It's done! It's over! So keep your knickers dry. It was New Years Eve and I'd made plans. I gave her a double dose of those sleeping pills. When I got back she'd gone."

"Radcliff's done for," Jean-Claude reassured himself. "There's nothing to worry about there. We're blood relatives and I have her," he clenched his fist in Pierre's face, "…like that!"

"You'd better be sure of that," Pierre scoffed.

"I'm a master at my craft, old man. You should have more respect for me. My powers over this woman have come from a place beyond the imagination of an old goat like you."

Pierre forced a laugh, but a sudden chill run up and down his spine. He poured himself another cognac and gulped it down.

"That artist will be starting a life sentence when we're digging up the treasure," Jean-Claude added with a self-satisfied smirk.

"Oh by the way," Pierre began casually. "That detective you murdered…his body was hauled out of the sea last week…by some fishermen."

"Any other news..?" Jean-Claude asked with exaggerated indifference.

"Who the hell do you think you are? Whatever powers you think you possess you are still accountable to the law. What the devil did you hope to achieve by killing that detective of hers? You're a brainless idiot, Jean-Claude!"

"I'll make you pay one day for the way you talk to me. I'm paying your wages now old man. You show some respect or I'll…"

"You'll what? You need me, Jean-Claude. Your Grandfather was different. He never paid me wages. He was my friend. Friendship is something you know nothing about."

"Friends..! I am my own man. I don't need anyone. Anyway there's no one in this stinking world I would *want* to trust." Jean-Claude drained his glass.

"The pigs have identified the body already. Once they've searched his office files….."

"You worry too much. Files! Bodies! There are million like her, all searching for something. Her file, if such a thing exists, will be nothing more than a scrap of paper."

"You're forgetting something, aren't you? The pigs have had your place marked since your dear old Dad tossed your mother out of the window like a sack of dirty washing. Your tormented twisted soul is corrupted beyond redemption. Whatever you thought of your old man they know you've exceeded your father's evil deeds a thousand times. If that detective had the name Narbonne on his files, your neck will feel the tickle of the guillotine!"

"Listen old man. I forget nothing. You'll do well to remember that!" Pierre retired to his bed.

Jean-Claude swilled several more drinks, sunk into the sofa and slept.

# CHAPTER 10

Carmen had regained consciousness a few minutes after Radcliff's call. Slowly lifting herself from the stone kitchen floor, dazed and confused, she reached for the table to steady herself. Her head pounded. The telephone receiver dangled still from its cable over the front of the pine unit. In an instant she remembered that glorious, delicious moment when she had heard Radcliff's sweet voice. It had been clear and unmistakable.

Heart racing, she gently replaced the receiver. A surge of sheer, exquisite joy passed through her. He was safe! Her prayers had been answered. She forbade herself to dare imagine that they could renew their relationship. It could never be as it was, she told herself... especially after her experience in Marseilles. The memory of her half brother flashed before her. That strange, cold feeling of malevolence began to build deep within her. She tried to banish it but a black cloud of guilt and betrayal descended upon her.

It was dark outside. One solitary light bulb, shielded by an ancient shade, served both the kitchen and living area. It hung from the thick central wooden beam that supported the two small bedrooms above.

She had grown up in that tiny stone house, one of 75 other similar houses all closely huddled together in the remote mountain village of San Sebastian de Garabandal on the edge of the majestic Picos de Europa in northern Spain. A winding, narrow lane over three miles long links the village to its nearest neighbour, Cosio, nestled deep in the valley of the Rio Nansa.

Garabandal's 350 inhabitants are mostly farmers, living simply off the land as they have done for generations. But the incredible events that occurred in the village between 1961 and 1965 changed their lives forever. Four girls from the village experienced the apparitions of the Archangel Michael, Mary and the infant Jesus. Since then pilgrims have flocked to Garabandal from all over the globe to walk in wonder amongst the pine trees where many of the apparitions took place.

The telephone rang.

Carmen jumped to her feet, leaned across the kitchen unit and seized the telephone receiver.

"Alex?" she cried excitedly, her headache vanishing instantly.

"Carmen Burgos?" a deep voice asked in English.

"Si." she answered excitedly, expecting to be connected to Radcliff at any moment.

"Are you acquainted with Mr. Alex Radcliff?"

"Si." she answered anxiously.

"This is the police. Don't be alarmed. I am calling you from England. My name is Detective Constable Omollo. There has been an incident involving Mr. Radcliff...." Carmen slowly sat back in the chair squeezing the receiver hard to her cheek, "...he is alive," the voice attempting to reassure her, ".... but he has been admitted to hospital. We found your telephone number, Miss Burgos, on Mr. Radcliff's person...."

"What happened to him?" she pleaded.

"I'm very sorry but can't tell you very much over the telephone, Miss Burgos. He is in a stable condition."

"He 'phoned me...not long ago...I think I passed out..." Carmen clasped her head trying to pull her thoughts together.

"Mr. Radcliff did phone you earlier this evening. We traced his call." There was a long pause. "Do you think you could come to England and help us with our enquiries, Miss Burgos? We think Mr. Radcliff is in serious trouble and we are sure you can help him. Would it be possible for you to travel to England?"

"When would you want me to come?"

"Immediately please. When you have the flight details give me a call on this number..."

"Wait a moment, please." She opened the first drawer of the unit and found a pen and paper. "Okay. Give me the number."

He did so.

"Once we have your flight number and where it is to land we will send a car to pick you up and take you straight to the hospital."

Carmen replaced the receiver and leaned on the unit, her heart pounding. Her headache had returned with a vengeance. She staggered up the wooden stairs, lit the oil lamp in her bedroom and refilled her small travel bag. The events of her ordeal in France came rushing back to her:

It had taken Carmen over 36 hours to get home from Marseilles. Maria, an old friend and neighbour of her late mother's, had found her on the third evening of the New Year lying prostrate over her parent's snow covered grave, sobbing inconsolably. The wizened eighty three year old woman helped Carmen down the steep cobbled slope from the cemetery to the old woman's house adjacent to the village church.

Maria's stone cottage was almost identical to Carmen's. An open fire and a solitary electric light bulb was the only light source. For Carmen there could not have been a more welcoming place to be. Wrapped in a blanket, with hot broth inside her, Carmen sat on a cushion close to the fire luxuriating in the soothing touch of the old woman's hands stroking her hair, just as her mother had done.

Maria could feel that she had released much of Carmen's anxiety and fear but knew that there was something else much more sinister lurking deeper inside that was tormenting her.

The following morning Carmen was sitting up in Maria's bed drinking a hot herbal infusion with the sharp eyed craggy old woman sitting beside her. Carmen explained why she had gone searching for her real mother and where her journey had taken her. The woman screeched in horror when Carmen had told of her encounter with her half brother and about her abduction.

"How did you escape, my dear?" The old woman had asked.

"This man Pierre sedated me every morning and night. He would always check that I had swallowed the pills before locking me in the room. When he had gone," she had grinned defiantly, "I used my fingers to vomit up some of the dissolved pills to reduce their effect and bided my time. Then, on New Years Eve, my moment came."

The old woman grinned, admiring her spirit.

"My French isn't good but I think any woman can tell when a man is arranging a date. He was very excited that night. He must have been expecting a good time…"

The old woman gave a hearty chuckle.

"He gave me a double dose of pills, but in his hurry he failed to check that I had swallowed the second lot of pills. I drank litres of water then spent two hours picking the lock on the door."

The old woman shrieked with delight. "Oh, excellent my dear!" she exclaimed clasping her hands together over her ample bosom. She leaned over, held Carmen's face in her hands and kissed her forehead. "Your mother and father would have been so proud of you. Well done!"

"Thank you, dear Maria. All I've ever wanted was to make my father proud of me."

"I know that my dear. I knew your father well. Forgive him. He was a proud, stubborn man. He didn't understand the spirit that burned inside you. He thought you had the devil inside you."

"I was too young to understand the apparitions that Conchita Gonzalez and the other three girls were seeing. It was wonderful when all those hundreds of people kept arriving to see the girls experiencing the apparitions. It made me feel very happy to be part of it. Each time was like a great fiesta for me. I just wanted to dance all the time. I couldn't help it if all those boys from the other villages wanted to watch me."

"You hurt more than his pride," Maria said not wanting to expand upon the implications. "He was ashamed. He felt that the whole village was against him."

Carmen's eyes filled with tears. "I feel as though I've done nothing all my life but let people down…" She broke into sobs. "First my father …then Conchita…and now the only man I've ever really loved." She covered her face with her hands.

"Hay…hay! Now stop that!" Maria moved closer holding Carmen in her arms and rocked back and forth. "You mustn't blame yourself… your mother sent you on that journey knowing it would help you. Over time you will feel ready to let the real Carmen shine. The only regret is that she didn't tell you sooner. No doubt she had her reasons."

Carmen had kissed the old woman on the cheek. "Thank you, Maria. You're like my second mother."

"Goodness gracious my girl…how many mothers do you want?"

"Sorry," she laughed, feeling a child again. She looked excitedly into her eyes. "That Englishman's alive, Maria," she said slowly. "Isn't it wonderful…?"

"I know. I saw him on the news. I don't know how anyone can survive all that time alone. It's truly a miracle!" She saw a shadow cross Carmen's face. The old woman's face screwed up into a broad grin which lit up her face. "I know what you're thinking, young woman. Of course he will still be in love with you. You cannot blame yourself for what has happened. You are a healthy woman. He couldn't expect you to be living like a nun? Your life had to go on."

"I know. Thank you, Maria. That's exactly what I've been trying to tell myself. I want to come with you to mass today."

Maria and Carmen attended the small village church several times a day for each of the six remaining days she stayed in the village. Maria's sister had recited the litany on each occasion. Vivid memories had come flooding back with an unexpected clarity of the four girls who had experienced the 'ecstasies'.

With a small travel bag packed Carmen rushed down the cobbled slope to Maria's house and slipped a note under her door. The sound of an approaching taxi made Carmen hurry home for her travel bag. She locked the front door, her stomach churning with apprehension and excitement, and waited. Minutes later the taxi whisked her away down the mountain slope on the first leg of her journey that would take her back into the arms of her lover.

# CHAPTER 11

A short, squat, slightly overweight Afro-Caribbean cleaning woman sat in a ground floor store room at the Princess Grace Hospital, Haywards Heath sipping a piping hot mug of tea. She was watching the 10 o'clock news on an old television set hung high from the ceiling whilst perched on the edge of a wooden box between a stack of plastic drums and a clutter of brooms and other cleaning paraphernalia.

The male announcer stated:

"Alex Radcliff, the heroic British artist who was recently rescued from an island in the Indian Ocean capturing the hearts and minds of the world, was shot this evening at his home in Sussex. He was wounded in the head by a high calibre bullet and admitted to the Princess Grace Hospital in Haywards Heath. A spokesman there stated that he is in intensive care but his condition is stable and not life threatening. Mr. Radcliff's associate Clive Norton-Smythe was brutally murdered earlier today but Scotland Yard cannot confirm if the two incidents are linked in any way."

One of the nurses attending to Radcliff unwound the bloodied towel wrapped around his head. The bullet had gouged a crease in his skull an inch above his left ear. A doctor performing the preliminary examination directed a sharp concentrated beam from an ophthalmoscope onto Radcliff's retinas. He had turned the beam on and off repeatedly many times to assess the severity of Radcliff's concussion. The flashing light had stimulated Radcliff's subconscious brain neurons, reviving a memory that happened during an equally stressful episode in his life. He relived the day he had been washed up on the island in the Indian Ocean:

Radcliff was lying on his back. A rhythmically intermittent powerful glaring light penetrated his closed lids stinging his inflamed eyes. He rolled his head away from the blinding light and attempted to open his eyes, but the glare was too intense. A wave washed over him, the saline liquid aggravating the inflammation burning his eyes. The retreating water cut deep grooves in the white coral sand around his body, sucking at his sodden clothes.

Kicking and twisting his body he rolled onto his left side, away from the flashing light. The glare was still intense. Unable to open his right eye more than a crack he could depict a blurred, hazy dark green strip with intense light either side of it.

Several waves smothered his lower body before his right eye grew accustomed to the light. He focussed upon a tiny translucent crab, standing motionless on the sand a yard from his nose. It held a pile of white sand in one claw. When it was sure there was no immediate danger the tiny creature dumped its load onto a pile of previously excavated sand then darted to the edge of a small hole, eighteen inches away. It waited for a couple of seconds, perched on the edge of its hole, then vanished underground.

The waves continued tumbling over his lower body as Radcliff watched, fascinated by the crab scampering sideways back and forth from its hole, depositing freshly dug sand. As his vision improved he noticed scores of these crabs, all industriously refurbishing their underground habitats before the next incoming tide.

A ribbon of coconut palms, bowing, leaning and jutting at gravity defying angles, followed the line of the narrow beach. He estimated its length to be about two hundred yards long. At its far end it curved out to a palm-covered foreland. Cliffs of grey granite rose steeply up from behind the foreland and the rest of the bay, looming over the palm trees like a giant wave. The cliffs were at their highest behind the foreland, gradually reducing in height to their lowest point directly behind him. Here they were only about twenty feet high.

Laying on his back once more the sunlight flashed onto him with dazzling brilliance and unceasing regularity. One moment he was exposed to the sun's searing heat then the next he was sheltered in the cool shade. It was this flashing light that had aroused him.

A solitary towering palm leaned out over him, its fronds partially sheltering him like a huge sun umbrella. The sea breeze caught its thick leaves, moving them slowly and evenly across the late morning sun.

He rolled to his right side and propped himself up on his elbow he saw that the bay ended just twenty yards behind him. Shielding his eyes from the glare he followed the rocky shore line. A steep tree covered headland jutted eighty yards out to sea. The headland climbed inland for as far as he could see. The cliffs behind him sloped gradually to a ledge, behind which the gradient merged with the headland. Rocks and boulders littered the base of the cliff and the corner of the beach.

Another wave washed over his legs. He forced himself up with both arms into a sitting position and watched the sea advance and retreat, washing over his lower limbs. His throat burned with every breath and his parched swollen tongue protruded from between his cracked rubbery lips.

The crystal clear, cool liquid came sweeping up to greet him. He was overwhelmed with a desperate desire to bury his head into it and suck up the fluid. Somehow he resisted the temptation although unsure exactly why. Thirst gripped his mind. He looked back towards the cliff, his eyes plotting a course to the ledge then feasted on the lush foliage of the forest above.

Stiffly he had removed the bright yellow life jacket and let it fall beside him. The name "JINX IV", stencilled in bold black letters on the jacket, jolted his memory: The catamaran; the meeting with his cousin, Frank Cockspur, in Durban; the cyclone and then the giant waves that had loomed from nowhere.

The first wave had been like a rolling black mountain of water terrifyingly gathering height as it bore down upon him from the port bow. In an instant the small boat had been lifted vertical sending Radcliff tumbling backwards. He reached out and grabbed the stern handrail and clung on, his body twisting in mid air. A sudden downdraft sucked on his body stretching every sinew in his arms, the bones on his fingers pulled from their sockets until their grip failed and he fell into the blackness of the trough sixty feet below.

Three more of these monsters had followed in succession. When they had passed the catamaran was out of sight. He was alone in the middle of the Ocean. Kicking off his trainers and then his jeans he tied knots in the end of the legs, filled the trousers with air then tied up the waist. Radcliff then surrendered himself to the mercy of the currents.

Hauling himself to his feet Radcliff staggered to the corner of the beach, tossed the life jacket onto the rocks at the foot of the cliff, peeled off his anorak and sodden white Fair Isle roll neck jumper and stood naked before the cliff readying himself for the ascent.

With each breath rasping at his raw throat the relatively straight-foward twenty-foot climb to the ledge drained him of energy. He sagged to his knees then collapsed prostrate on the ledge, his bear skin frying on the hot rocks and the sun's searing heat burning his back. Suddenly there was no pain, only an overwhelming desire to sleep. Fighting to stay awake, he raised his head up a few inches.

He saw paradise.

The whole curving bay lay before him, its two headlands turning inward like a horseshoe. Beyond it was the deep aquamarine ocean, vast and frighteningly beautiful spreading out to a seemingly infinite, hazy horizon. Closer to the island the water had a greenish tinge cut by sharply defined waves, growing darker and more knife edged as they approached the island, curving scimitar like, with the general outline of the shore. The crest continued rising, becoming top heavy and translucent as it advanced. The break of the wave moved along its length like a zipper, the sun reflecting on the white foam frothing up before it. As the wave pushed on inexorably towards the white sand it laid out behind it a lace work pattern in foam. The wave broke four more times on its journey, each time proportionately smaller than the last, the shade of the water turning a lighter turquoise until it was finally absolutely clear water sweeping onto the beach.

With Herculean effort he raised himself onto his knees, his mouth and tongue swollen and sticky with a saline froth bubbling up with every breath, he crawled up the gradient into the blissful shade of the trees.

Revived by the cool, damp conditions under the forest canopy he ascended higher, battling through the dense undergrowth, every breath rasping and burning his lungs and throat, for over a hundred yards. There the tree cover ended abruptly. A grassy plateau opened up before him. The heat radiating from it took his breath away. He retreated back into the shade.

Radcliff leaned back against a tree trunk, gasping for breath, giddy and nauseous from dehydration. His mouth swollen and cracked, his heaving chest was on fire and all he could hear was his own wheezing gasps for breath. Slowly he sunk to the base of the trunk. Exhausted, he lay quite still amongst the leaves of the undergrowth.

The thick, succulent leaves dangling above his face looked cool and moist. He grabbed at them, picking a handful and chewed the thick, bitter tasting leathery substance. The cellulose congealed unto a glutinous mass inside his mouth. He rolled onto his stomach but, devoid of saliva, he was unable to vomit. Frantically he pulled the slime out from his mouth, gagging as he did so then collapsed face down in absolute despair.

Then he heard it.

It was distant but very distinct: the sound of water falling from a great height. That glorious noise came from the far side of the plateau. He clawed at the tree trunk, heaving himself up he searched the scorched grass and shrunken bushes covering the plateau. At the far side, approximately a quarter of a mile away, a dome shaped mountain rose up from a rock face skirting the rim of the plateau. The rock face protruded shoreward away from the slopes of the dome shaped mountain.

Close to the end of the rock face Radcliff saw the thin, glistening white column cutting a vertical line down the rock.

Wild with thirst and excitement he ran out onto the plateau. He wilted under the sun's searing heat and sagged to his knees. With the sound of the cascading water he gathered enough energy to dash for the nearest bush. Resting in its shade he ran, crouching to the next. Continuing in this fashion he crossed two thirds of the plateau. At the last patch of shade, gasping for each breath, his lungs and body on fire, his mind crazed by the sound of falling water he held himself back.

He bobbed up, standing erect for a second, with manic tormented eyes he examined the terrain.

It was over a hundred yards between him and that cool, crystal clear liquid crashing over the rocks. Mad with thirst he made a final effort, staggering through the tall grass, falling over rocks, scurrying crab like and finally crawling on all fours over the final twenty feet he reached the edge of an oval shaped lake. He rolled over the bank and let himself slide into the clear, cool, fresh water.

# CHAPTER 12

Slaughter emerged from the Gatwick Hilton Hotel, crossed the driveway and hurried to the end of the approach road far from the prying CCTV lenses. A clear starry night had chilled the air. Most of the snow had thawed, but the heavy frost glistened around white snow patches and shrunken stacks against hedgerows and walls. A black Ford Galaxy was parked in the shadows.

Slaughter opened the rear door of the Galaxy and climbed in.

"How d' it go, boss?" Apeson asked nervously.

"Couldn't be worse," Slaughter barked. "If we don't finish him tonight we can say goodbye to our three million quid. Ferring!" He snapped, "What 'ave you sussed out about this bugger?"

"Radcliff's been transferred to intensive care, sir."

"Don't 'sir' me, son," Slaughter growled. "You're not in the Queen's Army now, thank God. Call me either 'Boss' or 'Mr. Slaughter'...understood?"

"Yes..s...s boss."

Apeson started up the Ford's engine and switched on the heater.

"Well? Go on."

"Yes..s...s ..er....boss?"

"Give me a full report, you idiot!"

"Sorry, b..b..boss. He's on the third floor of the east wing. There're four coppers guarding him night and day, all wearing heavy body armour and carrying automatic weapons. Two are positioned on the ward and two are at the main entrance by the stairwell."

"Times of change over..?"

"The two with Radcliff change every four hours, the other two every seven hours."

"Complicated..! When's the next one?"

"Which one, sir...I mean...boss?" Ferring glimpsed the fury building in Slaughter's eyes. "The two with Radcliff came on duty at 9.00 p.m. boss. The other two aren't due to be replaced until 4.00 a.m."

"Did you find a way in?"

"I've unlocked a window to a store room in the east wing. All the wards and theatres are served by the central stairwell and lifts."

"Okay! Now you and Apeson will go in and finish the bleeder off. You will be using new handguns with special ammunition. Both of you will be disguised as doctors, so get yourselves some white coats. Now listen carefully you two…. especially you Ferring. I don't care how you do it…. just make sure you get Radcliff tonight. Is that understood?"

"Yes boss," they answered in unison.

"Get him and we'll all be rich. If he gets away," Slaughter stared straight at Ferring, "and I find out you've messed up, you're dead meat." He expected Ferring to wilt under the intensity of his gaze. Instead a fire ignited from within the young ex-soldier. Slaughter congratulated himself on his recruitment skill. "Don't you disappoint me either, Apeson. Okay," he slapped Apeson's thigh. "Round up the others and pick me up here at midnight. I'll tell ya all of me plan then. We'll go into position before the next changeover."

# CHAPTER 13

That Friday evening Carmen Burgos was dozing at Radcliff's bedside, her hand in his. She had remained at his side since her arrival at the Hospital on the Wednesday agreeing only to use the rest room adjacent to reception if the night nurse would call her immediately there was a change in Radcliff's condition.

A drip feed bottle hung from a high gantry on the other side of the bed; wires were attached to his arms, chest and abdomen feeding data to computers. An array of VDU screens faced down from their fixtures behind Radcliff's bed.

The night nurse was doing her rounds at the start of her shift. She quietly entered Radcliff's room renewed the drip feed bottle, checked the wires and tubes attached to Radcliff's upper body and arms and noted down the data.

These noises aroused Carmen. She raised her head sleepily.

The nurse squeezed Carmen comfortingly. "You look exhausted. Why don't you go back to the rest room for a while and get some good rest. I'll let you know…," she smiled warmly.

Carmen nodded submissively. Slowly standing and stretching her stiff limbs she reached over and kissed Radcliff softly on the lips. She walked the length of the ward to the rest room. Two uniformed policemen wearing full body armour were on guard at reception clutching submachine guns. One of them smiled at her as she passed.

Radcliff had sensed Carmen's presence. Her kiss, as sweet as spring rain and as warm and reassuring as an embrace, immediately stirred his senses. It set off a surge of chemical and electrical impulses through his mind unlocking an event stored in a special recess of his memory. The event had occurred on the island just before his rescue. He relived that extraordinary episode in his life in a vivid dream:

He had awoken with the dawn lighting the roof of his cave. The cave was no more than a narrowing hole in the cliff eight feet deep, seven feet across at its mouth and fifteen feet above the lake very close to the waterfall.

A few minutes after these first morning rays of light hit the roof of his home the tropical sun would burst over the tree-covered ridge opposite and shine directly into his cave.

Radcliff reached for his sharpened rock and began to etch another line onto the wall of the cave.

He had devised a reusable calendar, twelve rectangles carved into the roof and the walls of his cave. At the end of each completed year he chiselled out the marks in the rectangles and scratched a vertical line over the cave entrance. There were seven of these lines, his New Year commencing on 14th June, the anniversary of his arrival on the island in 1999.

They had set sail from Durban on 7th June 1999. Four days out the storm hit blowing them deep into the Southern Ocean. The following day the wind reversed south-westerly whipping them back up into the Indian Ocean. It was the day that the giant wave had loomed up from nowhere and washed him overboard. He had spent two days drifting in the ocean, at the mercy of the currents and the winds, before being washed up on the island.

The granite was difficult to cut. Gripping a sharpened rock in his palm he hacked at the rock to mark the 30th line in the November box on the ceiling. Increasing the power of the blows, sharp fragments flew into his face. His temper began to fray. Clenching his teeth he hit the rock harder and harder. The final blow missed the target; his stone tool glanced off the rock scraping skin from his knuckles.

He cursed and screamed in a fit of rage fuelled by every repressed emotion, deep frustration and extreme fatigue. With a final exasperated wail he hurled the stone out of the cave.

Hearing the splash of the rock hitting the lake's surface he lay on the floor of his cave, his head hanging from the entrance, and watched the ripples radiate out to the surrounding banks of the lake.

He imagined his island to be where the stone had broken the surface and the ripples were his prayers for help radiating out to the distant world.

In all the years he had been on the island there had been no sign of ship or aircraft, nothing to put an end to the interminable monotony and intolerable loneliness. Hopelessness had been seeping deep into his mind for some time, eroding his spirit, weakening his resolve and will to survive.

Despair had visited him many times before but on each occasion thoughts of Carmen had lifted him out of despondency and depression. He had carved her head and torso from a tree stump. He would spend days talking to her image and caressing its smooth contours until hope had been regenerated and restored.

But this time he had sunk to a lower level. Years of complete and utter solitude had caused deep emotions to build up. These feelings surged into his mind like a tidal wave. Nothing could hold it back.

Looking up he could see the black silhouette of the ridge beyond the plateau crowned by halo of blazing light. Moments later the sun would burst over the top. But for Radcliff the new day promised only more despair and hopelessness. He had come to the end.

He could not endure another day.

Lowering himself down to the lake he swam in its cool, clear waters feeling its silky sensuousness on his skin for the last time. He sat on a rock beneath the waterfall letting the full force of the crystal clear liquid cascade upon his skull, over his shoulders and down his back. From this position he watched the sun rise well above the ridge opposite, its blinding glare reflecting on the lake.

Closing his eyes he waited for a hazy image of Carmen to appear in his tormented mind and then dived deep into the lake and touched the bottom, twelve feet below. He wedged his leg between two rocks then rammed another over the top to hold his feet fast should his resolve falter.

He waited.

His lungs ached for air. In concentrating to keep his jaws clenched he lost the image of Carmen. Praying that they would meet again in the next life he pursed his lips lighter and pushed his tongue against the roof of his mouth.

At the height of his struggle to give up his life he felt a wave of utter tranquillity and peace wash over his mind and soul. Everything seemed unbelievably clear. A bright light appeared before him and he yearned to be consumed by it.

It was then that Carmen swam to him out of the light. She was naked and smiling warmly, beckoning to him to an area surrounded by rocks about nine feet from him. It was a corner of the depths normally in permanent darkness. Somehow that morning the sun's rays had penetrated into it. Carmen was pointing to a spot now lit up in a blaze of colours glistening and shining with such brilliance that Radcliff was compelled to investigate.

With bursting lungs he found a rock to smash his leg free of the trap. Blindly and frantically he hit at the rock but it held fast. With his strength ebbing away he hit repeatedly but the rock was jammed tight. After one final blow on the rock he began to pull frantically on his leg, tearing his skin raw. With one last tug his leg came free. With his lungs collapsing around his rib cage like cling-film, his tired arms pulled for the shimmering sunlight glinting on the seemingly unreachable surface, his legs hanging limply behind him.

His first gasp of air choked him. In a fit of coughing he hauled himself out of the lake and rolled over the rocks onto the bank. Lying prostrate on grass he lost consciousness.

When he came to the sun was high in the sky.

He dived back into the lake searching for the place where he had seen Carmen and the coloured stones. But pitch darkness had returned to that part of the lakebed. Blindly he felt and grabbed for anything loose that was on the lake bottom and surfaced.

Standing in the shallows of the lake he opened his cupped hands. There were diamonds, rubies and other gems lit by the sun, their beauty and mesmerising lustre dazzled him. Ecstatic, he screamed and shouted for joy.

Radcliff returned to his cave, placed the jewels reverently and carefully into a recess close to the spot where he kept his tools and fed ravenously on a meal of roots, mango and bananas from his food store. Sure there were more jewels in the lake he made a small container from bending bamboo shoots into shape and weaving sapling bark in and out of the skeleton. He dived until dusk and filled up his basket.

He sat leaning against the cave wall, the firelight glinting and sparkling on clusters of diamonds, rubies, sapphires and other jewels and coins spread out before him. The light from the flames played on the knobs, protrusions and indentations of the ceiling and walls, animating them with dancing shadowy shapes.

The reflected colours of the jewels mingled with the warm glow from the fire. Laying on the floor he dreamily recalled the night of the Spring Ball at the Palace Hotel in Brighton.

He saw himself in his tuxedo dancing with Carmen. She was gliding and swaying in her beautiful cream and gold evening gown, her dazzling jewellery gleaming and sparkling under the blaze of crystal chandeliers. It had been one of the best evenings of his life. He lay watching the shadowy shapes continue their dance until he fell into a blissful sleep.

The following morning he had awoken with a new heart. He felt reborn. The experience of seeing Carmen again made him feel part of the whole cosmos and everything that exists and had ever existed. For him it was a spiritual revival and a promise of deliverance.

The jewels and coins lay sprawled on the floor of his cave, his back and legs indented with the shape of the gems. He chewed on a root he had cooked the night before, his mind inexorably drawn to finding where the jewels had come from.

Swimming to the centre of the lake he scrutinised the source of the waterfall. The water spouted from a yard wide gash in the rock about forty feet up the rock face. From there bare rock rose more gradually for the next thirty feet. Above that the tree cover and vegetation grew thicker and more varied, continuing upward to the summit of the dome shaped mountain.

He climbed to where the waterfall spouted. The force of the water was fierce. He searched the fissure with one hand as he clung on to the rock face. The fissure had been worn smooth over the aeons giving away no clues as to the origin of the jewels.

He continued climbing, the footholds taking him diagonally onto the escarpment that fell sheer to the beach. He looked down. His insides turned to jelly. Squeezing his body against the rock he cleared his mind. Looking up the bare rock face rose almost perpendicular for one hundred feet then the slope was a more gradual incline where trees and other vegetation managed to take root. Ascending fifteen feet along this diagonal line he spotted a vertical crevice nine feet above him.

The handholds were few and far between. He clung on; not daring to look down, he worked his way inch by inch, his body thrust hard against the bare granite. Finally he stretched up and gripped the base of the crevice and lifted himself up.

With one foot securely wedged against a protruding rock he peered inside. The crevice was over twelve inches wide at its widest point and about 6 feet in height. The suns rays shone directly into the fissure lighting up a huge cavern. The widening shaft of light touched a mountain of colour. Diamonds, rubies and a multitude of other precious stones, jewels, gold coins and bars sparkled and gleamed from the tenebrous depths of the cave.

Cramp in his right leg forced him to break away from this mesmerising and dazzling sight. Resting his foot and adjusting his grip he peered again into the cave. The sun had moved a fraction illuminating more of the magical mountain of jewels and gold. He could see that a greater proportion of treasure was hidden beneath the surface of a subterranean lake. The refraction of light gave these submerged gems a different and spectacular shimmering lustre.

He noticed a strange, but very familiar looking cross protruding from the top of the mountain. Only the top section of it was visible, and slightly askew, but he knew instantly that it was the Cross his ancestor had drawn in his diary.

Then, as if a light switch had been turned off, the cave was in pitch darkness. But he remaining transfixed at the crevice unable to believe what his eyes had just seen.

Lightning lit up the sky around him followed by a deluge of rain, which bombarded his naked limbs and cascaded down the cliff face. Taking a longer but less dangerous route back, the hand and footholds more frequent, he worked his way over the bare rock to the waterfall.

Back inside his cave the rain had cooled his euphoria. He gathered up the jewels from the floor, held them in his open hands and smiled ironically. It had been Carmen who had led him to the treasure but what he had discovered in the cave had far greater significance. He had seen the Cross of Goa. His desperation to get off the island was greater than it had ever been before.

He threw the jewels into the depths of his cave and pounded the rock wall with his bare fists, howling at the bitter joke that had been played on him. His anger and frustration intensified with each blow of his knuckles against the bare rock. He cursed Carmen for having led him to the jewels, for not letting him die and put an end to the torment he suffered.

He sagged to the floor, his hands dripping blood and sobbed, calling out repeatedly to her, begging her for forgiveness.

Radcliff's streaming tears were unseen by the night-nurse, too busy watching the monitor screens and noting down data on a chart. She returned to the reception desk where the police officers sat guarding the ward and updated her computer files.

# CHAPTER 14

In the early hours of Saturday morning, just after mid-night, a black Ford Galaxy, its road lights extinguished, moved imperceptibly along the hospital driveway. The driveway ran parallel to the east wing of the Princess Grace Hospital. It was lined on both sides with Douglas firs.

The design of the new east wing followed the latest trend of 'toy-town' architecture, having a central entrance section with a great gabled pointed roof separating the two long flat roofed sections either side. Its lights cast long golden carpets between the gaps in the trees which sparkled on the frosty grass.

The Ford Galaxy veered off the drive onto the verge nearest the building and trundled beetle like over the frozen grass. It slowed to a stop under the cover of a fir tree opposite the entrance, its double doors and awning lit brightly by fluorescent lighting.

Two men in black dropped silently from the side of the vehicle and sprinted to the right side of the entrance. Ferring prised open the unlocked window and they both tumbled inside. Stripping off their black overalls they donned doctor's white coats, attached forged I.D. cards to their breast pockets and stuffed the new silenced handguns into the top of their trousers and casually stepped out of the store room in apparent earnest conversation.

They walked slowly, their discussion well rehearsed, towards the lifts adjacent to the stairwell. The two police officers guarding the entrance and the stairwell watched the doctors suspiciously. The lift doors opened. Wanting to appear engrossed in an important debate they let the lift doors start to close before jumping to hold the lift.

At the third floor the two men waited by the stairwell window overlooking the driveway for a pre-arranged signal.

A police squad car turned into the hospital driveway. Unhurriedly it purred by the concealed Galaxy, wisps of white exhaust smoke lingering in its wake. Four black shapes spewed from the Galaxy and hid under cover of the firs. They watched the squad car reach the main hospital entrance, turn sharp left and double back up the drive towards the east wing entrance. Keeping low and in the shadows they assembled behind the slowing squad car crouching beneath its rear window.

The driver brought the car to a halt and two policemen got out from the rear and walked towards the east wing entrance, their heavy boots crunching on the frozen gravel. Three of the black shapes fanned out like wolves stalking a prey whilst the forth bobbed up by the driver's window and discharged one bullet from his silenced weapon into the driver's head.

Hearing the glass of the door shatter both police officers turned but before they could act a burst of deadly crossfire thudded into their heads. They crumpled to the ground. Quickly and efficiently the four assassins carried the bodies back to the macabre squad car, its exhaust smoke curling up in the chilled air and its headlights eerily bathing the hospital wall with light. They piled the bodies onto the back seat. One of the four leaned through the driver's broken window, switched off the lights and turned off the ignition.

It was deathly quiet.

They returned silently and stealthily to the waiting Galaxy.

A voice called out eerily over the car radio. It repeated the message several times with increasing urgency.

The Galaxy driver flashed the headlights giving the signal for the two men on the third floor to go into action.

They burst through the swing doors to the ward in heated debate. One of the guards looked up hoping it was the relief crew. He checked his watch. The other guard continued admiring the nurse's thighs. The nurse looked up. The two men in white coats drew out their weapons. A look of terror seized the nurse's eyes as a handgun was raised directly at her forehead.

A succession of dull thuds from the two weapons ended all three lives.

Carmen had heard the thuds from the rest room. They had sounded like heavy boxes being stacked rapidly one on top of one another. But her senses were on full alert. She peered nervously around the rest room door fearing that it was her half brother looking for her.

Two men dressed as doctors were checking each of the patients' faces. Then she saw the guns. Her thoughts turned immediately to Radcliff.

"Alex!" she shouted.

One of the gunmen skidded on the polished floor and aimed his gun at her. "*Alex*! *Alex*..!" She screamed out.

Apeson pulled on Ferring's arm. "Come on you idiot! Don't waist time on her."

But Ferring's body was charged with adrenaline. He fought free and squeezed the trigger at the instant Apeson grabbed the gun. The discharged bullet exploded inside a computer monitor cascading glass and hot debris onto a patient below.

"Come on you crazy bastard." Apeson yelled dragging him down the ward. Ferring turned the gun on Apeson, his eyes bulging manically.

"*Search those beds*," Apeson yelled at him. "*Now*...!"

Jolted from his madness the two men continued their frantic hunt through the ward for Radcliff, and then began searching the six private rooms at the far end of the ward.

Radcliff had drifted in and out of consciousness several times after Carmen had left him. He had heard her screams and then the explosion at the far end of the ward.

"*Carmen!*" he yelled out, sitting bolt upright in the bed and reached out with both arms and pulling on the drip tube. The gantry toppled onto his head wound, the pain arousing him completely.

He could hear the sounds of running feet and doors being opened. They were getting closer. Sensing danger he fought free of the tubes and untangled himself from the wires.

Weakly wriggling to the edge of the bed he swung his legs onto the floor. Levering himself up and using the curtain for support he staggered from the bed, treading jerkily, half falling, for the door. He grabbed onto the door handle and rested. Checking that the narrow corridor was clear he lunged for the swing doors six feet away. He half fell half staggered through them, his arms flailing and his rubbery legs somehow moving fast enough to keep pace with his toppling body.

Grasping a cupboard door handle with his left hand it opened inward and he fell sprawling onto piles of cleaning materials stacked inside. Quickly donning some green overalls and a green elasticised head cover, he picked up a bucket and mop.

The stairwell was ten feet away, directly opposite the cupboard door. He propelled himself forward out of the cupboard towards the stairs. His legs collapsed from under him and he fell headlong across the corridor. The plastic bucket bounced and clattered down the stairs. Above the din he could hear running feet approaching him from behind the swing doors.

The two police officers guarding the entrance on the ground floor heard the commotion and were climbing the stairs to investigate.

Radcliff reached for the first step with the one hand and pulled himself to the edge whilst using the mop in his other hand to propel himself forward. He slid headlong down the first flight of stairs rolling to the feet of a nurse, who had been climbing the stairs from the floor below.

The two white-coated men burst through the swing doors as the nurse stooped to help the cleaner up. The men bounded past them, taking three steps at a time, not giving the cleaner or the nurse a second glance.

Their footfalls echoed in the stairwell. They stopped abruptly when the police officers below challenged them. Several thuds were heard followed by rapid footfalls.

Radcliff dropped the mop, clasped the handrail and hurled himself down the stairs leaving the nurse gaping in amazement. At the basement he staggered, dizzily along an endless warren of corridors, his bare feet slapping on the smooth floor surface. Spotting an emergency exit to his right he pushed on the release bar and fell out onto the frozen grass.

The grass area, the size of a tennis court, separated the east wing from smaller clinics and treatment houses. He lay prostrate gasping for breath on the frosty ground. With the chill penetrating through his thin clothing he lifted himself wearily to his feet.

"Don't move!" A voice bellowed from a loud speaker. "Stay exactly where you are." He was caught in the cross beams of several torches.

Radcliff froze on the spot. A squad of armour-clad policemen surrounded him pointing automatic weapons and handguns at him. Two others were holding back salivating Alsatian dogs, straining and choking on tight leashes. Above them clouds of condensed breath were mystically illuminated by the powerful torch lights.

"Mr. Radcliff?" the silhouetted figure asked in astonishment.

"Yes. Yes." Radcliff shuddered, immediately recognizing the voice.

"Well, well, well! Mr. Radcliff!" The officer glanced back at his men with an amused expression. Their stance relaxed slightly although their weapons remained pointed straight at Radcliff. Hawkins smirked at the barefooted figure in the undersized green smock and elasticised hat before him.

"You look like Nell Gwinn!"

Amused grunts emanated from the group of policemen.

"Did you…" Radcliff coughed his throat raw and parched. "Did you catch them?" He croaked hoarsely.

"Who..?"

"Those two blokes...the ones...the ones in the white coats?"

"White coats…!" Hawkins exclaimed sarcastically. "…You ought to be taken away by someone in a white coat!" His men savoured the joke. Hawkins half turned towards the officer beside him.

"Driscall...give Mr. Radcliff your coat and take him inside." Driscall helped Radcliff on with the heavy-duty yellow and black anorak. "When you're feeling better, Mr. Radcliff, we shall want a statement from you. See that our intrepid Mr. Radcliff gets some hot soup or something inside him."

As Radcliff turned to leave, Hawkins grabbed him by the arm and looked him straight in the eye. "Those men got away. But they will pay for what they have done tonight! I can assure you of that. I've lost seven good men, Mr. Radcliff. I knew them all...and their families." Hawkins released his arm.

Radcliff bowed his head solemnly as Driscall guided him back through the emergency exit into the warmth of the hospital.

"I *will* get these scum bags…!" Hawkins pledged as Radcliff disappeared inside the building. "…even if it means doing a deal with the devil himself…they will be brought to justice!" He turned quickly on his heals and marched head down through his men.

His men drew respectfully back then followed him to the squad cars, the dog handlers following up in the rear.

Hawkins climbed into his car and flipped open his cell phone. Driscall answered his call.

"As soon you have a statement from Radcliff, take him and the woman, Carmen Burgos, to my sisters. Whoever's responsible for that carnage tonight will stop at nothing to finish what they have started. Make sure you send at least one dummy vehicle before they leave the hospital. Clear?"

"Yes sir."

During the journey back to London, Hawkins sifted his memory for perpetrators of similar operations. But he could think of no group, faction or organisation that possessed the weaponry and professionalism to execute an attack on the scale that had just occurred.

# CHAPTER 15

Radcliff was escorted by one of the nurses to a private room on the ground floor. He shuffled through the open door in outsized slippers clutching a mug of hot coffee close to his chest. He had a fresh dressing around his head and a blanket draped over his shoulders. The clock above the bed showed the time as 3.15.a.m.

A woman sat in the armchair beside the bed. Between her legs sat a small travel bag. The auburn haired beauty wore a black roll necked jumper and bright red trousers. She rose very slowly from the chair and approached him, her tearful, smiling eyes searching Radcliff's face with excitement and longing.

"Alex…," she said his name with a lengthy sigh, her seven year wait was over. She shook her head, tossing the hair from her eyes and rushed at Radcliff, her lips quivering, her arms held out wide.

Radcliff's shuffling quickened in pace as he tried to hurry around the bed to meet her, his mouth opening and closing dumbly. He was about to envelope her within his blanket when the nurse managed to snatch the mug of hot coffee from his hand. Radcliff embraced her tight, his head pressing hard against hers.

"You have come back to me," he whispered hoarsely. "Thank God!" He squeezed her tightly. "Carmen…. Carmen," he repeated. He pulled back his head to see her face.

"Alex, Cariño," she cried as tears of joy cascaded down her cheeks. She caressed the back of his head as she looked up, her lips moving in prayers of thanks. "It's a miracle!" she laughed through her tears.

Radcliff saw her trembling mouth open. Parched for her kisses, he cupped his hands around her cheeks and slowly brought his lips onto hers.

They fused themselves together, each soul thirstily drinking from the other.

P.C. Driscall had entered the room. He coughed tactfully.

Locked in each other's arms they turned their heads to face him.

"Excuse me, Mr. Radcliff…. Miss…but I've orders from the Chief Inspector to take you both to a place of safe custody immediately," P.C. Driscall said forcefully.

"I've given you a statement…the doctors have discharged me," Radcliff stated amiably. "I want to go home, if you don't mind, officer?"

"These people who are…. erm…" Driscall began clumsily then, glancing at Carmen, began searching for the right words, "…. who are after you, Mr. Radcliff, will be desperate to finish… their…. erm… work. They're watching us now…. waiting for an opportunity to strike. We've organised two decoy cars with our people inside dressed to look like you. When I hear that we've successfully lured these people away we'll take you and Miss Burgos to the safe house."

"I'll need some money, clothes and things," Radcliff stated irritably, impatient to be alone with Carmen but aware that resistance was futile.

Driscall lifted up the holdall. "I've got your clothes." He handed the bag to Radcliff. "We'll collect any other personal items you might need from your home tomorrow."

"Looks like we have to go with the nice policeman, sweetheart…" Noticing the confusion and alarm in her eyes he demanded: "Where is this house?"

"Purley…in Surrey…it'll take about twenty minutes." His intercom bleeped. "Right…okay," he answered. "We've heard from one of the decoy cars. They're being followed. They've taken the bait, sir!" he announced, his voice rising as if to prove his point. "If you please, sir, our car is waiting."

They followed P.C. Driscoll to the waiting police car.

At the safe house a handsome middle-aged woman greeted them, wearing a pink dressing gown, her blond hair in rollers. She introduced herself as Louise, Chief Inspector Hawkins' sister. Louise was a year older than her brother, with identical features except that her nose had a wider bridge and was hooked slightly. She led them upstairs to the first floor bedroom overlooking the small front garden.

"Sleep well, both of you. I'll see you in the morning." She closed the door and locked it from the outside. "Sorry…," she called out. "… my brother's instructions."

They both sagged onto the double bed and lay in each other's arms, alone for the first time in over seven years. Neither believed that their waiting was over. He hugged her tighter. Carmen was the first to break the silence.

"They told me you had severe concussion and that you might never recover." She propped herself up on one arm and carefully lifted Radcliff's bandage. She gasped. "Cariño! It's like a great dent in your skull!" She replaced the bandage and consoled him with kisses. "Can you remember anything…"

"I had…had spoken to you." He thought a moment. "The line had gone dead…."

"I think I fainted… or something," she laughed.

"I remember looking through the French windows," Radcliff said gazing into her huge watery brown eyes. "I was thinking of you…I felt something tugging at my right arm. I lost my balance!"

"Too much alcohol..!" She chuckled.

"Whatever happened…it saved my life!"

"Who are these people, Alex?" she asked caressing his cheek with her hand.

"This is Clive's doing. I'm sure of it! He's got himself…us… involved in some dirty dealings…"

"Selling your paintings?"

"I wouldn't put anything past Clive. The unscrupulous sod! He said that my work had been selling like hot cakes…"

"Hot cakes..?" She said, utterly confused.

Radcliff chuckled. "I'll try and explain quickly. He…Clive… mentioned something about three yanks…sorry, Americans. These blokes evidently walked into Clive's office and bought all my remaining canvases. At his prices, too…!" Radcliff shook his head.

"It sounds very…how you say…fishy!"

"It stinks, doesn't it?" He sighed deeply. "Anyway, on the day of my rescue the price of my painting dropped like a stone…"

"How many canvases did they buy?"

"All of them…the finished ones anyway…one hundred and twenty three!"

"How much did Clive get for them?"

"Thirty million pounds sterling..."

"What did they lose?"

"These types do not lose…at anything! Clive said they wanted ten million."

"Make a deal with them…."

"Clive's dead, sweetheart," he interrupted softly. "They had wanted cash…but now?" He paused, shaking his head. "Time for talking is definitely over."

She rested her head on his chest. They lay silently in each other's arms for a few moments.

"What're we going to do?" she asked finally.

"I'm taking you to my island."

"When..?" She chuckled.

"Now..." He kissed her. "I'll have to get my passport, some ready cash and a few things…. I've got a bag ready. It's been packed for some time…."

"Yes but…how?"

"Easy…just leave it to me." He cupped her face in his palms and looked her tenderly in the eyes. "Listen, sweetheart. I've got some incredible news! I've found the Cross of Goa!"

"The Cross of Goa?" she looked away struggling to remember its significance. She stared excitedly back at him. "Your ancestor drew that wonderful picture…yes... I remember that old diary…"

"It's on the island, Carmen. I knew it was the Cross the moment I saw it. It looked just like the drawing! I could only see the top half ……but that was enough…" Radcliff sat up, looking excitedly down at Carmen. "As a small boy I used to imagine finding the Cross. Discovering that Cross…you've no idea what it means to me…!" He paused for a moment, his eyes brimming with excitement, wonder and joy.

"It was in a deep cavern, Carmen …," cupping her face in his hands and reliving the moment his eyes first saw the mountain of jewels crowned with the Cross of Goa. He kissed her tenderly. "…it looked as beautiful as you….it was incredible…indescribable!"

Carmen smiled, amused by his boyish exuberance, but wanting him to stop. "Yes, but the Cross cannot be that important?"

"There's more, sweetheart!" wanting to tell her everything. "There's treasure! More treasure than you can imagine! It was all buried inside the mountain with the Cross."

A cloud crossed her face and she turned away.

"What is it? What's wrong?"

"It's nothing, cariño. When you mentioned treasure…. it made me think of someone, that's all." Memories of her incarceration in Marseilles flooded back to her like a forgotten, terrifying nightmare. She had heard and understood enough French to know that both her abductors were obsessed about treasure. "It's all in the past." She smiled, her eyes drawing him to her. "All that matters is us."

"I can't believe you are here… with me." He pulled her on top of him and squeezed her.

"I'm scared, Alex," she whispered in his ear.

"Everything's okay…we are together. Nothing…nothing can happen to us. Believe me. If we can get back to the island, no one will find us… it's uncharted…. a tiny unknown speck in the Indian Ocean. For seven years I lived there…alone…. without seeing a single being…no ships… no planes. Nothing! It's the Cross I want, Carmen. The treasure is unimportant. We must get this Cross. .it is more than just a Cross…!"

"I remember you telling me…." She stroked his hair then played with one of his curls. "…that it possesses…. mysterious powers."

"That's right! The Knights of Christ used an ancient arcane knowledge to build it. Robert Radclyffe has written about it all in his diary. I'll read it to you when we are basking in the sun on the coral sands of our own island."

"I…. I don't want to let you down," she said suddenly, the shadow of fear crossing her face.

"You'll never let me down," he said slowly, stunned by her change of expression. Her eyes were wide and had taken on a haunted, mysterious look. He held her chin, lifted it and kissed her gently. "You'll *never* do that! Do you hear me?"

"That's all I've done in my life, cariño. I seem to always let the ones I love down," she cried. "First it was my father, then the girls of my village and now you."

"Me?" he rolled her onto her side and held her tearful face in his hands. "How have you let me down?"

"I've been unfaithful to you, Alex," she confessed, holding back her tears. "I'm so sorry, my love. I never gave up on you …please believe me! It's just that…" she broke down and sobbed. "I didn't believe…that I'd ever see…. you again."

"Seven years is a long time," he stoked her greying auburn hair. "You've never lost your faith in me. I know that. I could never expect someone as attractive as you to remain alone …"

"But there's something else I must tell you………"

"You are here with me now," holding her firmly, her sobs subsiding. "I don't want to know. It's all in the past."

"No. You don't understand, Alex. There's something…"

"You're not in love with someone else, are you?"

"No. It's nothing like that."

"You've not murdered anyone?"

"No," she chuckled through her tears.

"Then there's nothing I need to know. We are together. That's all that matters."

"Yes, but…"

"It doesn't matter. You're here…with me. It's enough for me."

"You forgive me?" she looked up at him incredulously, wiping her eyes with her open hands.

"There's nothing to forgive. The sooner I get you to that island the better we'll both feel."

"Wait, Alex. Think for a minute. These people who are after you…. they're assassins! They're hired killers!"

"They've been chasing the wrong car. We're safe here. If we can break free and get a flight from Gatwick…get out of this country……….."

"They'll be determined to get you this time. That policeman…Driscall… said. They'll have people watching for you at the airports, Alex!" she said, her eyes tearful and imploring. "If we do manage to get on a plane we'll lead them straight to the Cross…and the treasure!"

"You're right!" he kissed her forehead. "Why didn't I think of that! We'll have to lead them up the proverbial garden path…"

"¿Que?"

"Lose them…. send them on a wild goose chase!"

"Ah! That's up the path of the garden?" her eyes glowing once more.

"Yes," he laughed. "Where can we lead them…"

"Get them as far away from the Cross of Goa as possible," she suggested excitedly.

"That's right." He sat bolt upright. "Got it! How would you like to see the Australian outback?"

"The outback..? What's this outback place?"

"The bush... nobody lives there except for a few cattle ranchers and the aborigines. It's flat, dry and barren."

"What kind of bush is that?"

"No," he chuckled. "That's its name. It's the real Australia. Most Aussies live along the coast...where it's more.... comfortable. My cousin Frank lives in Melbourne. We'll contact him. He'll provide us with some transportation."

"Australia." She touched her lips with her forefinger, deep in thought.

Radcliff waited.

"What do you think?" he asked, impatient for her response.

"Could you lose these people in Australia?"

"We'll follow the exact same route I took 30 years ago.... I could loose them... I'm sure of it! I almost got lost myself."

Carmen smiled.

"Whatever we do, we must take the initiative. Any trouble we encounter will be on our terms. The odds will be more in our favour."

"Okay." She looked at him, her eyes full of trust. "Yes. Come on. Let's do it."

They sealed it with a kiss.

"First we need to buy some airline tickets. Let me borrow your mobile and credit card, sweetheart."

Carmen delved deep into her travel bag and handed them to Radcliff. He switched her mobile phone on. It showed the time as 5.10 a.m. He called a specially allocated number at Gatwick Airport for V.I.P.s and reserved two first class seats on the 10.30 a.m. BA/Qantas Flight Q657 to Melbourne, he had Carmen send a text message to his cousin Frank in Australia asking for a car to meet them at the airport then arranged for a taxi to meet them in five minutes outside the cinema in Purley High Street.

"Come on...," he said. "...out through the window." He struggled into another sweeter, pulling it over the one he was wearing; he opened the sash window and threw his holdall out. The next moment he was hanging from the frost-covered windowsill. Swinging his body he grabbed a drainpipe with his right hand then, with both legs gripping the pipe, he let go of the sill. He slid a few feet down the icy pipe until a wall bracket stopped his fall then jumped from the pipe to the ground. He waved to Carmen to follow from the small front garden.

Carmen looked down at Radcliff in stunned admiration. The street light behind the high privet hedge shone on his upper body. Her head began to spin. She recalled the time, as a young girl of twelve…she had climbed to the top of her parent's barn to rescue her kitten. Placing the kitten inside her blouse, its head poking from the top, she inched her way back across the rooftop. Stricken suddenly by vertigo it had taken her mother over an hour to talk her down.

Hearing again her mother's endless words of encouragement she threw her travel bag down to Radcliff then turned and lowered herself out of the window. Hanging, petrified, she glimpsed the drainpipe and gingerly reached out for it, but it was too far away. Her fingers began to slip on the icy sill. With both hands on the sill she edged nearer to the pipe. She stretched out her right arm again, her fingers touching the pipe, but her left hand was slipping. She tried to get her right hand back to the sill, but her grip had gone. In that split of a second, hurtling through space, thoughts raced through her mind as fast as the house bricks flashed before her eyes. It was an experience that she had always dreaded: the horror of falling and being seriously hurt or worse.

Radcliff caught her. He stumbled backwards under their combined weights flattening their luggage and the thick privet hedge bordering the lawn. Broken branches dug into Radcliff's back and legs and powdery frozen snow fell down his neck. Carmen lay spread-eagled on top of him, with her back on his face.

"¡Madre mia..!" She exclaimed loudly with elation and relief, disentangling herself from Radcliff and the hedge.

As she rose to her feet Radcliff grunted then yelped with pain. He held up his arms for assistance muttering incoherently to himself.

"What's the matter?" she asked pulling him to his feet.

He continued groaning under his breath as he brushed the snow from his sweater.

"You are so grumpy! Why is this?" Her voice echoed in the cold silence of the early morning.

He glared at her, pressing a rigid finger hard against his lips. "*Shh-hhhhh..!*"

"It's not every day you have someone really falling for you!" she laughed, brushing the snow from her coat.

"Quiet! Come on," he whispered retrieving their flattened bags. "Let's get out of here."

They ran up the road and turned into the High Street, relieved to see the taxi waiting outside the cinema as arranged.

"Gatwick Airport," he directed the driver as they climbed into the back. "But first we need to take a bit of a detour. Okay?"

"Where would that be, guv?"

"Wivelsfield."

The driver was stocky, bald headed and middle-aged. He had a round, battered face and broken nose, a large gold earring adorned one ear. They watched him set his satellite navigation. He turned and studied them for a moment. The silence was un-nerving. "You're that artist-feller, 'aint yer?" His broad smile revealed a missing front tooth.

"You're very observant!" Radcliff said, retaining his composure and dispelling his sudden misgivings. "Can we get going, please..."

"Sure. I remember seeing you on the Tele...when you were found on that there island. Your face has been in all the papers lately. What with that murder and then you being shot at.... I never forget a face, guv. Anyway it's an honour to have you my cab, sir," he said jovially.

"Thanks," Radcliff said, concealing the alarm and disappointment of being recognised so quickly. "There'll be an extra tip if you step on it."

They sped off in a westerly direction towards Chipstead and Wood-mansterne.

"There's not much traffic, guv. Once we get on to the M23 we'll make good time."

Radcliff, still feeling uneasy, pillowed Carmen's head on his chest and dozed spasmodically throughout the journey, saying nothing.

At Wivelsfield Radcliff directed the cab driver along the narrow lanes to Muirhurst castle. Piles of drifted snow were still visible in the woods. A police squad car was parked on the grass verge just before the drawbridge. "*Stop..*! Turn back... quickly please."

The taxi skidded, slewing on the ice and returned back up the lane.

"Head for West Chailey. Drop us at the King and Queen car park."

The cab driver reset his navigation system. Within minutes the cab stopped in the empty car park beneath the great cedar tree.

"Wait here," he handed the driver five twenty pound notes Carmen had given him.

"How long will yer be, guv?"

"What's the time?"

"Five fifteen."

"Are you sure?"

The driver pointed to his clock.

Radcliff closed the rear door of the cab baffled and turned to Carmen, who was getting out the taxi. "When I rang Gatwick it was ten past five."

There was a silence as she stared at him for a moment. "My mobile! It has Spanish time...you inglés!" Carmen laughed.

"We'll be back in about half an hour." Radcliff said as the driver's window descended with a hum.

"I'll give you until five. Okay guv?"

They crossed the road bridge. The night was full of stars, their magical but dim light reflecting on the frost and remnants of old snow.

They slid down the riverbank and followed the right shore of the Eldar River westward to the lake. At the boathouse they climbed the steep frozen slope to the castle wall. Inset in the stone wall was an old oak door. It was just as he had left it over seven years before when he and Carmen used the old secret escape tunnel to get down to the lake for midnight swims. Radcliff removed a loose stone from one side of the ancient, cracked and weathered doorframe. He groped inside the hole. There was nothing. He reached deeper into the hole.

"It's gone. The key has gone." He pushed his weight against the oak door but it held fast.

"Is there another way in?" Carmen asked him anxiously.

He shook his head feeling each stone of the wall surrounding the door frame. "Look!" he pointed at the twisted doorframe and a deep crack in the wall. "Subsidence..! It has moved the whole structure."

Using a slither of wood he prized out another larger stone. Brushing away the loose cement he reached down with his fingers deeper into the crack. His index finger touched the top of the key. Clasping it between his finger tips he carefully extracted the six-inch skeleton key and inserted it into the lock.

The mechanism was jammed fast.

"What's the time," he asked as he waggled the key in the hole He tried turning it again.

"Half past five...sorry...four," Carmen said closing her mobile.

"I've an idea." Radcliff stopped battling with the lock. "Wait here." He ran off towards the boathouse. He slipped on the icy slope and slid the remaining few feet. He crashed feet first into the rickety timbers of the old building. A large slab of frozen snow fell from the roof onto him, covering his whole body under a mound of snow.

Carmen shrieked with laughter. When his arms burst out of the snow and began flailing around helplessly her hysteria intensified. With his legs free he pushed and kicked to free himself but his efforts were as ineffectual as an upturned turtle's. Carmen was doubled up, helplessly groaning and shrieking on her knees holding her sides.

Radcliff's embarrassment turned to anger hearing her laughter. In a desperate bid to save himself from further humiliation he summoned up all is strength and somehow levered himself into a position to crawl out of the avalanche.

Radcliff returned and leaned exhausted against the stone wall by the oak door, holding a tin of grease. His stern, perplexed expression was enough to send Carmen into further convulsions of laughter, her tears glistening in the half light as they rolled down her cheeks.

He handed her the tin and proceeded to press the glutinous black substance into the lock. She tried desperately to stop laughing but Radcliff's expression of obvious displeasure and confusion exacerbated her plight. She sagged against the wall in a breathless wheeze.

Radcliff turned the key and pushed on the door. It opened.

"Come on," he pulled on her elbow. "We haven't much time."

Carmen entered the tunnel with Radcliff right behind her. The blue light from her mobile lit the way up the narrow passage carved through the rock. The dank air chilled them to the bone. Water dripped onto them as they splashed through the half frozen puddles. The dim light struck two moss covered steps. They led upward, the light from the mobile 'phone unable to penetrate the pitch darkness above them.

"What's the time now?" Radcliff asked as they ascended the steps leading up to the trapdoor within the chapel vestry.

Carmen checked her mobile. "It's twenty to five."

They crawled out onto the vestry floor. Carmen hurried from the chapel across the lawn leaving Radcliff to close the trap door. She reached the French windows and waited for Radcliff.

"Go in," he called to her. "The window's unlocked."

Carmen shuddered, finding it colder inside the lounge than it was outside. Powdery snow had penetrated the broken lattice in the French window. It covered the drinks trolley, the stone floor and was stuck to the heavy curtains. In the half light she saw the shape of a body drawn in chalk… around the head the outline was more vivid, contrasting with the dark stain on the carpet.

Radcliff saw Carmen standing transfixed before the spot where he had been found and guided her towards the fireplace.

"Wait here sweetheart," he said kindly. "I'll be a couple of moments. I've a bag ready upstairs and some cash in the safe."

"Don't leave me here," Carmen pleaded.

"You'll be okay. Look!" He picked up the diary from the chair and gave it to Carmen. "It's the diary, darling. Hold on to it for me. I'll be back before you can say… Cross of Goa."

Within a few minutes Radcliff returned through the lounge door with a carrier bag containing his passport, £20,0000 in £20 notes, and a change of clothes. Carmen rushed to meet him and handed him the heavy book.

"This dairy contains everything about the Cross of Goa," he said stuffing it into the bag. He fastened the zip. "Come on. Let's get going."

Radcliff took her hand and led her back the way they had come. He locked the oak door, replacing the key and the stones and retraced their steps back around the lake, along the riverbank over the bridge to pub car park. The taxi driver saw them approaching, flicked a cigarette into the snow and started the engine.

# CHAPTER 16

Hawkins' deep sleep was shattered by his pager bleeping. Irritably he switched on the light and squinted at the small screen. It instructed him to report to SO8 on his immediate return to headquarters.

Arriving back at New Scotland Yard at about 7.30 a.m. he took the lift to the fourth floor then followed the centre corridor until he found the door marked: 'Arthur J. Brickman, Head of Forensic Science Laboratory'. He rapped and opened the door.

Brickman rose up as Hawkins entered, his huge frame towering over an undersized desk, and held out his arms warmly.

"It's good to see you Charlie." He spoke as if suffering from a permanent head cold; his thick lips stretching into a wide charismatic smile, swelling crab apple cheeks which almost swallowed up his deeply set small, sharp brown eyes beneath greying bushy eyebrows.

Brickman's massive, square shaped head was crowned with thick black, wavy hair that came to a widow's peek above a broad furrowed forehead. His nose was a lumpy mass of pulverised flesh, a legacy of years playing rugby for the force. It was devoid of any supporting bone, bending slightly to the right ending with a knobbly mound that had two red spots at the tip. Below it was a proud and determined chin jutting defiantly bringing a charismatic symmetry to his face.

He slapped a great hand on Hawkins' shoulders affectionately, his whole face creasing up with pleasure.

"How are you Art?" Hawkins said pumping his other hand vigorously.

"Good…you're looking tired young man."

"It's been one of those..."

"I know. I've got two bits of news for you Charlie. The first is this…."

He turned off the light and flicked a switch. The images of three cartridge cases appeared on a white screen.

"I've received confirmation from the F.B.I. just half an hour ago by fax that the weapons and the bullets these buggers used last night are classified!" Brickman handed Hawkins the single sheet of paper. "They are top secret, Charlie! So secret, in fact, that only a handful of US Government personnel are supposed to know of their existence."

Hawkins studied the facsimile.

The US Government F.B.I. seal was on the top right side and the sender's name-'Agent Arnold Fitzpatrick'- on the left side; there were pictures of the handguns and machine guns with a brief description under each one. At the foot of the page Fitzpatrick had included photographs of the marks these weapons had made on cartridge cases. There was an explanatory note that the cases had been retrieved from a ballistics test done for the Pentagon on November 28, 2006. They matched exactly the photos projected on the screen.

Fitzpatrick had summarised:

'There were twenty five semi-automatic hand-guns and twenty five automatic machine guns, all newly invented prototypes, each class of weapon having specially designed ammunition. The manufacturer released the prototypes to the Pentagon for testing. The identity of the signatory on the receipt docket is under investigation. This is classified information and due diligence, discretion and care must be observed in divulging the contents of this message.'

"These yanks and their *bloody* weapons..!" Hawkins sighed.

"I spoke to Fitzpatrick a few minutes ago," Brickman stated. "It must have been 1.30 a.m. their time.... which would account for his attitude.... he was very abrasive and that's a fact.... telling me that the 'President himself had brought in the *bloody C.I.A.*!' And that us '*bloody limeys*' had better 'get our act together before every criminal and terrorist hears about it!'

"He did admit that the US was as mystified as everyone else. These 'top secret' weapons have laser sighting, of course, but the major break-through is that they can be programmed to control the velocity of the specially designed bullets. These are wonderful little devils that explode a split second after entry into the victim causing a massive haemorrhage; like a miniature depth charge. A 'dumb dumb' without an exit wound! The blood is retained in the body leaving very little mess. You can bet that a major investigation will ensue in the States. Heads will roll... that's for sure! This will put you under great pressure, Charlie. Both M.I.5 and M.I.6 will be there in the background watching your every move."

"That explains why there's little or no blood near the bodies at the hospital."

"Fitzpatrick said he will get back to me later today. Keep this under your hat, Charlie. You can be sure that M.I.6 and M.I.5, not to mention the P.M., will be hot on our arses from now on. Oh! By the way, Fitz-patrick did mention that the 'Mob' are probably involved."

"Just to knock off Alex Radcliff...? How could an artist upset the 'Mafia'?"

"Beats me..! Oh yes! The other thing I must tell you...your sister called me just before you arrived. She said that Radcliff and the woman had escaped from her house and had been seen at Gatwick Airport."

"*What!*" Hawkins punched one hand into the palm of the other. "They've gone to Gatwick! Why didn't you tell me?"

"Sorry Charlie. I had to show you these slides first. Everything's okay...?"

"Okay, he says!"

"They're in the V.I.P lounge waiting for their flight," Brickman chuckled.

"Where in God's name is he off to?"

"Australia. He's bought two tickets to Melbourne."

Hawkins snapped his fingers. "Of course...he's got a cousin down under. He's a sailor. Did you know about Radcliff...his accident at sea... that he was stranded on an island?"

The big man nodded his great head. "I think the whole world knows about that, Charlie! Your people are there...they're keeping an eye on things with airport security. Don't worry!"

"Don't worry...don't worry...you say!" He looked at his watch. It was 8.00 a.m. "Damn! I have an appointment with the Super at 9.00 a.m."

"Well then! Now you have a *bloody* good reason not to be there, haven't you?" Brickman chortled.

Hawkins smiled, loving his attitude to superiors in the force.

"Well! You know that I've little time for these ambitious types. They spend all their hours scratching their arses, planning and scheming for their next promotion, rather than getting down to the nitty-gritty of doing what they are actually paid to do. It means that the likes of you and me have to pick up the crap they can't handle. And we get abused in the process! Got time for a quick bacon sandwich?"

"Show me the way."

The small sandwich bar was a stone's throw from New Scotland Yard. It was warm with steam bellowing from the tall shiny chrome earn of boiling water, the aroma of coffee mingled with sent of hot tea and fried bacon.

They sat on stools set against the window. Brickman wiped a hole in the glass fogged with condensation and peered out. Office workers, wrapped up against the cold, slipped and skidded on the frozen pavements.

"Well what do you think, Charlie? Did this artist feller knock off that Norton-Smythe or not?" Brickman said quietly, biting a chunk out of his smoking sandwich.

"He's a strange bloke."

"I recon I'd be too. Seven years alone on an island would change anyone's personality a tad!"

"He was very on edge during the interview. He lives on his own... in a castle! If he did murder his agent he's definitely not the type to wait around for the police to question him." He sipped his piping hot tea. "He's hiding something... I know it."

"Could be trying to outwit you on that one..."

"Last night's episode has vindicated him, I think. He's the altruistic type, anyway, very talented too."

"Well who's your prime suspect? Any clues yet?"

"There's the Mob, of course. They would've contracted out...maybe ex military, mercenaries...it was professionally done. Then there's Norton-Smythe's French chauffeur. He's disappeared. They were shacked up together.... very cosy."

"Oh yeh...there's a lot of it about...."

"They had some sort of 'lovers' quarrel the day before. Other than that there's no obvious motive...nothing missing from the flat. I have one of my team tracking him down."

"Your artist is about to leave the country, Charlie. Can you let him escape with all the eyes of the world watching your every move?" The big man gulped his tea, his eyes on his young friend.

"I'll get one of my men on the same flight," he answered indifferently. "At least I'll know where they'll be for the next twenty-four hours or so. It suits me down to the ground if those two want to be heroes...they'll lure those buggers out there. All I have to do is wait."

"Charlie!" he snapped in rebuke. "What about the woman?"

"Don't worry. The Aussie police owe me a favour or two. They'll keep an eye on them."

"Oh Yea!"

# CHAPTER 17

Slaughter and Apeson were seated in the breakfast room of the Hilton Hotel, Gatwick. Apeson had arrived as Slaughter was finishing his full English breakfast and coffee. He listened to Apeson's report on Radcliff's movements and eased back in his seat and glared at the man opposite him.

"He's going to Australia!" Slaughter barked. "What makes you so *fucking* sure they're here…at Gatwick? Why not Heathrow, eh..?"

"There's a bloke I know in security," Apeson stated confidently. "The buzz is going round that Radcliff and his woman will be intercepted before they board the flight to Melbourne."

"What time's his flight again?"

"About 10.30," he shrugged.

"Let's get one thing quite clear," Slaughter growled, leaning across the table. "There are no more 'abouts' and 'maybes'. There can be no more mistakes. Understood?"

"Yes, boss." Apeson poured a glass of water and drank thirstily.

"One more mistake and you'll be joining Ferring. One swipe with the chain saw was all it took to separate his head from his body. He's now part of a consignment of scraps that will eventually be sold as dog food."

Apeson choked up some water.

"We're going to assume that Radcliff will make the flight. But we'll wait for the last minute just in case they nab them. Okay? I've got some good news for you. I'll be coming with you. I want to make sure we get the bugger this time. These yanks will 'ave got wind of our latest botch up by now. If we can knobble the little shit just after he lands in Australia we might still get our money."

He leaned back in his chair and signalled to a waiter for service.

"I'll have another coffee."

As the waiter strode off to the kitchen he said to Apeson: "Get a couple of tickets on that flight and then contact Mombasa and get four men to meet us in Melbourne."

"Okay, boss,"

Apeson waited for more instructions.

"Like *now!*"

# CHAPTER 18

The last three passengers shuffled through Gate 48 as security staff inspected their passports and boarding cards for flight Q657 to Melbourne. Hawkins stood unobtrusively behind the airline personnel.

Two heavily built men wearing pin striped suits and camel hair overcoats hurried towards the gate. The bright florescent lights reflected on their tanned shaven heads and heavy gold earrings adorning both men's ear lobes.

They eyed Hawkins suspiciously.

Hawkins had already grabbed a handful of boarding cards and was assiduously counting them. The moment they were clear of the gate Hawkins flipped open his mobile phone, arranged for his call to be put through to the flight deck and described the two men to the pilot, also advising him that one of his detectives would be joining the flight.

He checked the time. It was 10.26 a.m. He punched another sequence of numbers.

"Booth..?"

Detective Constable Booth answered.

"Get on flight Q657, now. The pilot is expecting you. Two suspects have just boarded, dressed as businessmen. Definitely ex-army, bald heads the lot. Once you have sighted them give their seat positions to the pilot. Do not approach them. Watch and report their movements to Airport Security in Melbourne. Understood?"

Booth replied in the affirmative.

"I'm positive they'll not make their move during the flight. But if you suspect anything…anything at all…report it first to the pilot. Keep a low profile, Booth. *And* keep an eye on Radcliff and the woman, will you? Make sure that the Aussie security takes charge of them. And Booth…get the return flight home..."

Radcliff and Carmen had settled themselves into their first class seats at the forward end of the aircraft. The thundering thrust of the four Pratt & Whitney engines accelerated the heavy bird down the runway until the airflow tilted its nose skyward and it gracefully lifted off the ground. Within minutes they were breaking through the thick cloud and were bathed in morning sunshine. A television monitor above them displayed the flight data and showed the time as 10.35 a.m.

An electronic gong signalled the passengers that seat belts could be unfastened.

"We've done it!" She cried, releasing her seat belt and flinging her arms around Radcliff's neck, kissing him passionately.

"Australia here we come!" Radcliff laughed, concealing the apprehension building up within. He had expected to be challenged by the police or airport security but everything had gone very smoothly...too smoothly. "And then... the island and the Cross of Goa!"

"Tell me again how you found it?" Carmen asked, sunshine flooding into the cabin to add golden highlights to her auburn hair. She nestled back into her own seat, but yearning to be enveloped in his arms.

"It was at a time when my spirits were at their lowest. Strangely it was just before I was rescued. I had decided to end it...I'd had enough.... I swam to the bottom of a lake.... and wedged my foot between some rocks at ......"

Carmen sat up suddenly. "That's incredible!"

"What is?"

"I had a vivid dream of you one night. It was...November.... the end of November last year. You were trapped.... just as you said. You saw me. I watched you struggling to get free...I knew that I had to guide you to some jewels.... I could see your life ebbing away. It was terrible. I was sure you were going to die but there was nothing else that I could do. I awoke in a cold sweet. It seemed so real, Alex. I tried to get back to sleep...I needed to know if you were safe."

"That's exactly what happened. I wouldn't be here if you hadn't come to me!"

"Then it was...more than a dream!" She said incredulously, her voice as soft as silk.

"You saved my life! You were as real to me as you are now. Later I did bring most of those stones to the surface." He remembered that moment when he first saw the jewels and his face glowed with wonder and amazement. "They were beautiful, Carmen.... the rubies were huge and cut exquisitely! As too were the diamonds! Each one glittered and sparkled in the sun."

She turned away and gazed reflectively out of the window. The night of the dream she had been with Miguel Navelgas, who owned a small holding in Casio, three miles from Garabandal. That morning, guilt ridden, she had broken off the relationship. She climbed the steep mountain road for home. Maria spotted her as she turned the final curve and waved frantically at her. She had called out to her:

"Come quickly... Carmen...it's your mother.... she's been taken ill...come quickly."

She had died that afternoon.

Her relationship with Miguel and the shame she felt brought back the harrowing memory of her half brother. She wanted to tell Radcliff everything. She looked down on the bank of cloud thirty thousand feet below. The jet's progress across the nobly, wavy white sea was imperceptible. The winter sun lit the eastern faces and peeks of the bubbly surface with an intense silvery white light casting long deep shadows.

The high brightly lit peeks and dark troughs of the clouds beneath her, she mused, were an excellent representation of how her life had been.

Maria's words came softly into her mind: 'You are a healthy woman. He couldn't expect you to be living like a nun? Your life had to go on!'

She snapped herself out of her malaise and turned to Radcliff giving him the warmest smile she could manage.

"Will you read from that diary?" she asked. "I want to know more about this Cross of Goa."

"Okay," he said breezily, relieved her mood had changed but his concern remained.

He removed the diary from the bag and commenced reading. A few minutes later Radcliff noticed her gazing reflectively out of the window once more.

"There is something…" she turned to face Radcliff "…something I don't quite understand: since Federico knew, from the secret formulae in the tablets, how to build an Ark why go to all that trouble to design a cross as well? Simply reproducing something as potent as an Ark would be enough to impress the natives and convert them to Christianity."

"Their aim was to keep the secrets of the tablets safe. It was the King's ingenious idea. It was a disguise. No one outside the brotherhood knew exactly…."

"The brotherhood..? Do you mean…the Templars?"

"Well the Portuguese arm of it. They're called the Knights of Christ. The secrets they've preserved are hidden in the Cross; secrets that the church had coveted for so long and eluded even the probing tentacles of the Inquisition. Federico's flamboyant, strange looking design worked… it was the perfect disguise. A Cross of pure solid gold, encrusted with jewels which would appear to be just another over embellished work of art, an artefact dedicated to the glory of God."

She reclined in her seat, sighing deeply, luxuriating in its softness. "Now we're going to bring the Cross back to life." She turned to him, her eyes ablaze. "If we could bring it home, we could do…so much…so much good with it, Alex."

"One thing at a time sweetheart…we need to escape from these buggers first…which we will…of course." Radcliff's smile of confidence covered his apprehension, knowing that the first 24 hours on Australian soil would be crucial. He added as reassuringly as possible: "With

Frank's wheels we'll get clear of Melbourne and be on our way north. We'll lose them in the bush. We'll be okay, sweetheart."

Carmen gazed out of the window in quiet thought.

She turned and leaned over to stroke his face and hair. "Did you see any sign of human life on your island?"

"There were some rock carvings along the shore and at the top of the mountain…probably made by the pirates. I was its sole inhabitant," he chuckled "…for hundreds of years probably."

"Tell me about this helicopter pilot! The man you'd trust with your life. I'd like to meet this hombré!"

"Kurt Van der Koche. You'll love him. Since my rescue I've spoken to him several times on the phone. Five times now Kurt has ferried Seychelles' government officials to the island. He was convinced they were out to steal the island from me… so he used to take evasive action! He took them on a zigzag course, often overshooting it, to keep its whereabouts a secret. It's because of him I've still got an island to go back to."

"It's *your* island…*you* actually own it…?"

"Just about…; Kurt confirmed it over the phone just before Christmas. My island is beyond the territorial waters of the Seychelles and too far out from the Chagos islands."

"Your own deserted island..!" She sighed, luxuriating in the thought. "It's everyone's dream!"

Radcliff began describing his island when her head sagged sideways onto her headrest. He studied her peaceful, sleeping face leisurely for the first time since his rescue. A few grey hairs flecked her thick auburn waves, her face was a little thinner and her cheeks had lost some of their bloom but she was still to him one of the most beautiful women he had ever seen. He leaned across and softly kissed her cheek then settled back into his seat and quickly followed her into a long dreamy sleep.

A stewardess awoke them at 1.30 p.m. with a tray of hot food.

After lunch they exercised, climbing the stairs to the lounge and then took it in turns to walk the length of the aircraft.

Slaughter was first to recognise Radcliff as he passed by his seat. "That's 'im!" shaking Apeson out of a doze. "Take a good look."

Apeson lifted himself above the seat level and waited for Radcliff to turn back. "There's a copper three rows back," he whispered to Slaughter. "He's watching us and Radcliff."

"I know. He followed us on. Our blokes will take care of 'im after we land."

Radcliff turned at the rear of the plane. A shaven headed heavily set man in a business suit was staring menacingly at him. A few seats behind a lighter built man in more dishevelled cloths scrutinized him openly whilst keeping a watch on the larger man in front. Radcliff returned as casually as possible back up the aisle, stealing a glance at the two bald headed men seated together.

Back in the first class area he lowered himself back into his seat, his face ashen, letting his head fall back onto the rest. He tried to control his breathing and slow his racing heart. Closing his eyes he look long deep breaths.

Sure in his mind that the two bald headed characters wouldn't attempt anything until they arrived at Melbourne he tried to work out who the third man was and what role he would be playing.

Carmen awoke.

"I haven't told you, Alex, about my trip to Seville," Carmen began. "I was born in Seville. It was like returning. ....." She noticed that Radcliff's eyes were closed. She picked up an in-flight magazine and began flipping through the pages.

"Sorry, darling...," banishing the third man from his mind. "...what were you saying?"

"I was saying that I visited the place where I was born. Seville."

"Oh!" Radcliff looked across at her, immersing himself into the warmth of her brown eyes that glowed back at him. He smiled. "I thought you came from the north...you're a mountain village girl, aren't you?"

"That was my home. But I had been adopted as a baby. My mother told me that before she died. I've always loved to dance, especially Flamenco, but never really understood why. Now I know...I was born in Andalusia in the south. It must have been my gypsy blood. Have you seen the gypsies perform?"

"On TV a long time ago." Radcliff said vaguely, puzzling over the third man once more.

"It has everything, Alex" Carmen continued. "Rhythm, sensuality, sexuality, excitement, emotion, passion, skill...and dedication...all portrayed by the singer...or the guitarist, or the dancer. The singer is called 'El Cante'. The dancer expresses passion through skilful foot tapping...castanet clicking...or with just the beat of a stick or the clapping of hands. It begins with slow sensual movements full of grace and loveliness building to a crescendo of noise, rapid rhythm and wild abandonment. Every loving couple can relate to it... the performers relive their passion in every dance."

"Wasn't it the gypsies who invented the guitar?" he asked indifferently.

"It was born in Seville although it probably evolved from the Indian sitar," she answered proudly, failing to notice Radcliff's unease, relishing this opportunity to tell him about Flamenco. "The original gypsies came from India and North Africa. They settled in Andalusia during the 15th century assimilating the local Moorish and Jewish folk laws into their culture. After these races were banished the gypsies were left alone to develop this mixture of cultural folk dancing."

Her sweet voice and delightful accent soothed his fears and cleared his mind as the sun's warmth would lift a sea mist.

"In the 1860's it became known as Flamenco, but it didn't grow into the style we recognize today until the early 1900's."

"How did you know you've got gypsy blood?" He asked with smile.

She raised her eyes to the ceiling. "You weren't listening, Mr. Alex Radcliff! I said that my mother had died..."

"I'm sorry..."

"She told me I'd been adopted...."

"Sorry...I didn't hear that..."

"Shhh...!" She touched his lips with her finger. "It's okay. It was her dying wish that I locate my real mother. I had traced her to Marseilles. I was about to go to her apartment one morning when..." she smiled radiantly, "...when I saw you...on the television news. You were covered in hair and being helped aboard a helicopter."

"So you were in France! I tried a thousand times to reach you. Did you find her.... your real mother?"

"Si...pero..., sorry," she shook her head, her auburn hair flowing from side to side across her face, "she was..," she turned to face the window, her hands fiddling with buttons on her blouse, " ... she had been dead for many years."

Radcliff touched her hands. "Then you lost two mothers..." She turned her head to face him. He saw fear in her grieving eyes. "Was she Spanish?" he asked hoping to dispel her anguish.

"No," she said nervously, the memory of her abduction and her half brother's evil smile very vivid in her mind. "She was French...and already married. It was her lover who was the gypsy. Quite a sordid little story, really" she added, rubbing her brow. She smiled warmly, leaning over to kiss him on the cheek. "Let me go on telling you about Flamenco," she said cheerily.

"Okay. You're determined to finish your lecture...."

"You want me to stop...?"

"Not a chance," he smiled.

She examined his grey-green eyes, testing his sincerity.

"Come on, get on with it, woman!" He snapped with mock impatience. "This is all very interesting. You were saying ...how the Flamenco started."

"Yes...well...Flamenco began in Andalusia," she began picking up her train of thought. "A Gypsy is poor and his life is very hard. It's that toughness that brings out that special quality....the excitement, vitality and passion that is in their music: the rhythm of their guitars; their soulful songs of love, passion and betrayal; their dancing, clapping and stamping. These are the ingredients that revitalise the gypsy's soul."

Radcliff watched her as he listened, mesmerised by the way she brought it all to life by her passionate gesticulations and darting, flaming eyes.

"Each district has its own dynasty although the most famous area is Triana in Seville. The songs and dances have been handed down from generation to generation. Each performer never wavers from the original words or dance steps although they add his or her personality and interpretation to them.

"There's a male dancer named 'El Farruco' who instinctively knew the 'Solea' and a singer called 'Tragapanes' who was taught his song by 'Cagancho', his father. It was all he had to pass on to his son...but his song made him famous throughout Seville.

"They're a very proud people. They know that anyone can sing and dance their Soleares and Bulerias...they call such people 'Payos'...but anyone would agree that a performance by a gypsy is more profound... it retains the originality of the dance. The female singers are equally legendary...with names like 'La Concepccion' and 'Maria la Morena'.

"My father...," she turned and faced him, her eyes welling up with tears of pride, "...was a singer and a real gypsy. His given name was 'El Pajarito'."

Radcliff leaned across the gap between their seats and squeezed her tightly. "That was delightful." He held her chin and kissed her softly. "Your father must've been quite a man!"

"Si."

They sat in silence for a moment.

"Do you want to hear more about the Cross of Goa."

"No! Not now," she answered quickly. "Tell me about the things you did and what went through your mind when you were on that island," she said as if the thought had just popped into her head. The question had burned in the back of her mind since her vigil at his bedside. "How did you handle being alone?" she asked pulling herself back into her listening position once more with her legs curled under her. "I want to know everything. No secrets!" She teased, wrinkling up her nose. "What did you get up to?" she asked with one of her delicious throaty chuckles.

"Okay," he smiled then made her chuckle more with an expression of extreme guilt. "Whatever happened you were never far from my thoughts............I'd dream of our long nights at the castle...the moonlight swims...making love in the long grass beside the lake." He looked into the deep brown pools that were her eyes and immersed himself in them.

"It went in stages. My feelings I mean. At first it was very difficult to come to terms with what had happened to me. All I heard was the sound of the wind, the surf or the squeal of the occasional bird. It was quite frightening. I thought I was going to die there. It was the thought of a long lingering death that scared the shit out of me."

"I can imagine," she reached across and caressed his arm. "Nothing can prepare you for an experience like that."

"Hunger takes over your mind. I had fresh water in abundance but two weeks without a substantial meal and believe me your whole being is geared to perfecting skills with bows and arrows, traps and any other means of getting food. Anything that moves becomes fair game! Even ants larva!" He chuckled at her grimace.

"¡Por favor! Insects! Madre mia! Forget the diet. Just tell me what went on in your mind."

"Some insects are very nutritious," he laughed. "Alright! The nitty-gritty, eh! During the first weeks I hovered between panic, nausea and sheer depression. I became very introspective. I know this might sound like a cliché, but I didn't realise the extent my life was reliant upon the comforts of modern living! I took it all for granted. I had, like most people, a roof over my head; I shopped at the supermarket and had instant entertainment by switching on the radio or watching T.V. I could buy materials for my work…or buy anything I wanted."

"We don't know how lucky we are until it's gone," she agreed emphatically shaking her head. "When you compare the lives of people in...say Fiji...we are all spoiled brats!"

"All the time we wonder where it all goes wrong! Why we can't get it right. What's it all about? Our behaviour is seduced by the comforting assumption that very little will happen to us if we indulge ourselves in small temptations. These indulgences turn into habits, which become difficult to break. During the initial period I found that living without these seductions was the main cause of my fear. Feeling very vulnerable …inadequate…I became guilt ridden and neurotic. Deep feelings of insignificance were magnified by the fact that I was surrounded by ocean… there was a fairly large mountain towering over me…. and at night…a ceiling of trillions of stars…I felt very alone."

"Does size really matter?" she asked in mock earnestness.

"Well I…" he began, but then saw the twinkle in her eyes. "Thank goodness for that, eh! Keeping a stiff upper lip could have a new meaning…."

They chuckled happily together.

"But soon these feelings of insignificance were to disappear. What I experienced after the first few months on the island was astounding! It was uncanny! I put it down to this: living in the modern civilized world offers us many opportunities, perhaps too many! Life gets too complicated. We are often prone to making the wrong choices. By having these choices stripped away; down to the simple fundamental needs of keeping alive, I became at one with the elements. The mountain, the ocean and the night skies became my friends and allies."

"How? Whenever I look at the stars...the vastness of space...and the universe ...it makes me feel very small and insignificant."

"You'll see what I mean. It was very hard at first: but learning to hunt and fish to survive; no longer being afraid of being completely on my own, I began to feel in tune with my surroundings. I was in harmony with my island, at peace with the solitude. I began to feel really alive. It was like being reborn. I was still afraid and apprehensive about my situation but by acting on these stimuli in hunting, searching for food and herbs and protecting myself from the elements...boosted my moral and feelings of self reliance. The only major problem was being there without you." He looked into her eyes. "I craved for you...you have no idea how much."

"¡Qué hombre..!" She covered her mouth with her hands in mock horror.

"I wanted to see you...to be with you...to feel you...to hear you! So I sculptured an image of you out of a tree stump," lowering his head with embarrassment.

Her tearful nut-brown eyes, glistening like deep pools, were ready to devour him. "Oh, Alex!" was all she could say, shaking her head submissively. She reached across the gap between the seats and flung her arms around his neck and kissed him passionately. "You carved *me* in wood?"

"I saw you immediately inside the tree stump. It was my first attempt at sculpture. I remembered that time back at the castle...when you carved that dolphin. I watched your technique and tried to copy it. It's not a bad likeness.... I think you'll like it."

"When did you start it...to sculpt me, I mean?" Her eyes welled up with tears.

"I must have been there about three years...yes, three years. Until then I had been working on ways of escaping. I had built two rafts; both were smashed to pieces on the rocks. I hit my head on a rock and was knocked unconscious on my last attempt. Luckily some of the raft stayed together and carried me back to shore. After that I resigned myself to being alone for many more years. In preparation for this, although always hoping someday I'd be rescued, I needed to keep your image fresh in my mind; finding the tree stump was the answer to my prayers.

"I would go to you practically every day of those four and half remaining years," he admitted, squeezing her to him. "But there's irony in this story."

Carmen slid back in her seat and adopted her listening position

"It was after finding the Cross of Goa and all that treasure. I was spurred into building a new and better raft. Instead of using logs bound together with vines and sapling bark, I used ten equal lengths of thick, dried bamboo. I cut a hole through each end of the bamboo and threaded saplings through the holes making the raft rigid and very strong. It was nearly ready for launching when a cyclone hit the island. It raged for two days and nights.

"I had spent that last night of the storm sitting beside you. By morning the wind had abated. Returning to my cave I stopped on cliff top above horseshoe bay…"

She chuckled.

"Well, it looks like one from above…" he answered, laughing with her. "Looking down, I couldn't believe my eyes…." He paused thoughtfully, looking dreamily at the ceiling of the aircraft. "It was rocking on the heavy swell like a beautiful, white apparition. I kept rubbing my eyes and face with my hands expecting to awake from a dream."

"What was it?" she asked impatiently.

"A yacht! She looked immense…with a white and red hull and white and blue superstructure. It terrified me for a moment. I ducked quickly back into the trees. I was also suddenly conscious of my nudity. I sat there on the cliff top, hardly able to move, building up the courage to swim out to it.

"I'd prayed virtually every morning to be rescued and to be back in your arms. Sometimes I'd just look out across the ocean from the top of the mountain and imagine you, in Garabandal, climbing the hill to the pine trees… as we did that Easter……"

"I'll always remember that Easter we spent together in my village. Whenever I wanted to feel you close to me I'd walk up to the pine trees. Which was practically every day until……." her head dropped sadly, then she peered up at him with her watery eyes and gave him one of her beautiful broad smiles. "I'm so sorry…"

"Listen sweetheart! Your spirit never did give up on me; I'm living proof of that. You saved my life on that island. Whatever happened… happened. Don't dwell on it, darling. All of my prayers have been answered. I was rescued, I've got you back again and pretty soon we'll be digging up the Cross of Goa!"

"Oh, Alex! Do you really think so?"

"Yes I do." He yawned. "There's something else too. I think we could use some shut eye."

She nodded, making herself more comfortable in her seat. "Mmm… mmm," she yawned and stretched her legs. Within minutes they were both asleep.

The stewardess shook his shoulder gently.

"Where are we?" Radcliff he asked.

"We are approaching Singapore Airport, sir."

# CHAPTER 19

In the early hours of that Saturday morning a brand new black Cadillac CTS was parked outside an office building on Westchester Avenue, its twin exhausts smoking menacingly. F.B.I Agents Fitzpatrick and Forbes were positioned 100 yards behind in a Chevrolet Impala watching and waiting for the three occupants to make their move. Two other vehicles separated them from the Cadillac.

It had been just after midnight when the New York Bureau received an anonymous tip-off that a heist was imminent at the address given them and that one of the robbers in the Cadillac would be carrying one of the missing secret weapons.

Forbes and Fitzpatrick were in their mid thirties, their boyish good looks belying the considerable experience these two men had accumulated during their short time in the field. They had been partners for only five years and were rated the most successful team in the Bureau. Both men new the joys of being fathers of young families and retained a youthful belief in their own invincibility. Each possessed sharp laser like intelligent eyes that revealed also an underlying conviction and integrity. Acutely aware of the imperfections within and without the Bureau, their mission was to try and make a difference and change things for the better.

Heavy snowfall was settling on the sidewalks and on the road surface.

A group of people emerged from the building. As they ran for the other two vehicles one of them signalled the Cadillac. When they sped off the open space exposed the Chevrolet.

The driver of the Cadillac put the vehicle into a screaming wheelspin, spray and smoke enveloping the car and made a 'U' turn, heading north back along Westchester Avenue.

Forbes rammed the lever into 'Drive' and the SUV responded instantly. Their vehicle sprung from the kerb, tyres squealing as it spun around, narrowly missing two motorists in the process, and set off in hot pursuit.

The black vehicle had taken a left turn at high speed towards East

167th Street and on to East 169th Street then right into Boston Road. It veered right before the Cross Bronx Expressway flyover and darted in and out the smaller city streets reaching speeds of over eighty miles an hour, the two agents keeping close on their tail. The narrow street opened up onto the Expressway interchange. It accelerated over the Hudson River on the New Jersey Bridge and skidded off a slip road and burst through a crash barrier attempting to double back to the Expressway.

The Cadillac hit a ditch and veered right smashing into one of the pillars supporting the overpass. The three men got out and opened fire with automatic weapons, fanning out as they advanced. Bullets smashed the windshield and peppered the bodywork. Forbes radioed for assistance before they both ran for cover behind the concrete pillars under the overpass.

Protected from the worst of the blizzard, the temperature below minus 15 degrees Celsius, a hail of bullets hit Fitzpatrick three times in his right side. He sank to the ground.

Forbes squeezed himself against the pillar, stretching his lithe frame as thin he could as bullets zinged and buzzed around him, caught in relentless triangular crossfire.

Blindly emptying his handgun into the darkness he was hit in the left arm.

Strangely he felt no pain. It hung limp and useless at his side. He rammed his gun into the palm of his left hand. Blood trickled over the weapon as he fumbled to reload his pistol.

The snow had partially covered his partner's body, but his staring eyes and gaping mouth were still visible in the murky light. Fitzpatrick's life had seeped away, its warmth cutting deep into the snow around his right side soaking the area crimson.

Another burst of gunfire smashed into the pillar baring the steel reinforcement above his head and close to his shoulder. He heard sirens howling and screaming from the city side of New Jersey Bridge. But Forbes had no time to wait for back up. He needed to attack or die.

He eased off his overcoat and removed his trilby hat. Bullets continued to rain on him with deadly accuracy cutting into the concrete pillar just inches from his head. He stuck the hat on the end of the gun barrel. Holding out his hat to the left he peered around the right side of the pillar. Twenty rounds smacked into his hat sending it flying into the air.

With a mental fix on two gun positions Forbes threw his overcoat to the right and dived left blasting the two gunmen to hell as he fell onto the snow. He rolled onto his back oblivious of the cold, his left arm still numb and lifeless.

Red flashing lights lit up the area.

Forbes aimed his gun at the escaping gunman but the magazine was empty.

He got to his feet, picked up his bullet-riddled hat and overcoat and went to his partner. Kneeling beside him he gently pulled the lids over his friends staring lifeless eyes. His thoughts went out to his widow, Carol, and their two kids Toby and little Josh.

His partner and friend was no more. His training had taught him how to deal with this type of shock. It was his friend's wife and children who would feel the full impact of his death, they would probably never get over their grief, it was they who were to pay the ultimate price.

Forbes was gripped suddenly with thoughts of his own mortality. He felt vulnerable for the first time. No longer invincible, Forbes was struck with the realisation that there was a high probability that his own family would be faced with the same devastating loss some day.

He looked at his own shattered body and shuddered.

An officer of the NYPD helped him to his feet.

Arthur Brickman received the following e-mail message from the New York Headquarters of the F.B.I.:

'Agent Fitzpatrick and Agent Forbes were in pursuit of three suspects in the early hours of this morning. A gunfight ensued in New Jersey beneath an underpass. Two suspects were shot dead and identified as Sergio Griezale and Mark Cabbo from Chicago, both known members of the notorious Cinisi family. Both Agents were fired upon, Agent Fitzpatrick died from his wounds and Agent Forbes is recovering in hospital. The ballistics check found that one of the bullets recovered from Fitzpatrick had been fired from the same type of weapon used in the English hospital incident. Neither Griezale nor Cabbo were using the classified weaponry. By State Department exigent all US Intelligence forces are to identify and apprehend the third gunman immediately. We will keep you informed of developments.'

# CHAPTER 20

Takeoff from Singapore Airport was smooth, the aircraft climbing rapidly to its cruising altitude of 39,000 feet. Carmen puffed up her pillow curled herself up into a foetal position and sighed peacefully.

Radcliff, with apprehension churning in the pit of his stomach, watched enviously as she drifted into a restful sleep. Her mouth dropped open slightly to expose some of her teeth, like pearls nestled within the delicious fleshiness of her full red lips. Her breathing was deep and even.

He switched on the movie channel and watched the 'Da Vinci Code' whilst alternating with in-flight data screen.

The small aircraft shape was slowly moving across the map of Indonesia, nearing the island of Borneo. He leaned across Carmen and peered out of her window. A sharp crescent moon hung from a star filled sky. He squinted into the blackness but there was no trace of scarlet on the horizon.

By the end of the film the aircraft on the screen had nudged forward to a point between Borneo and New Guinea.

Radcliff removed the headphones and slowly slipped into a restless doze.

A cramp in his calf muscle awoke him. Carmen was beginning to stir.

"Good morning, sweetheart!" Radcliff said cheerily, stroking her hair, wanting to continue reading from the diary to help take his mind off the trouble that lay ahead. "We are almost at the end of the story. This last part describes Robert's wedding and how the Cross of Goa was captured by pirates!"

"¡Qué hombré! Alex!" she objected, rubbing her eyes. "You're an obsessive!"

"Maybe a little obsessed," he corrected jovially. "I want you to know and understand everything about the Cross before we reach Australia. We might not get another chance once we've landed."

"We'll still have the flight to the Seychelles."

"True. But there's a million other things I want you to know as well!"

"Okay. You win. Let's hear about Roberto's wedding."

Radcliff cleared his throat as Carmen adopted her listening position once more. He began:

"It was Friday 13th April 1721; the day of Robert's wedding…,"

Carmen struggled to stay awake. She chuckled when he came to the part where Captain-General Rodriguez of the 'Vierge du Cap' reprimanded the Archbishop of Goa, Don Sebastian de Andrado, in his cabin for being late and startled the rotund cleric out of his wits causing him to drop his crucifix.

He was reading how Rodriguez took his stricken, battered ship into the harbour of St.Denis when Radcliff noticed Carmen's eyes sagging.

"Try to stay with it, sweetheart. This is part where the pirates take the ship..."

"Sorry…I've been listening…I promise. But why did Robert write so much about the voyage? It doesn't have much to do with the Cross, does it?"

"Bear with me…this is history, darling! It's an accurate record of what actually occurred. It *will* liven up soon."

At that moment the stewardess served them with a hot breakfast, a glass of orange juice and coffee.

Refreshed they prepared to continue with the diary.

"How far away is your island from this….Bourbon Island?" Carmen asked.

"Bourbon …it's about a thousand miles to the south."

"Where were you when those waves struck your catamaran?"

"Further east I'd say…we'd been blown up from the Southern Ocean. I must have drifted with the currents for about a thousand miles, though…." Radcliff's voice trailed off as he recalled those horrific days floating alone in the Ocean.

"Let's hear about these pirates!" Carmen said cheerily

Radcliff finished reading.

He glanced over at Carmen. She was sitting with her body wedged rigid against the seat. Her eyes were filled with horror.

Snapping the diary shut he leaned across to her. "What is it…?" He touched her tightly clenched hands then lifted up her chin with the tips of his fingers.

"There's something I must tell you, Alex," her lips were trembling. "You will hate me after I've told you. I'm sorry, Alex. I think I've ruined everything for you."

"How…how could you ruin…" Radcliff tried to laugh cheerily but her contorted face squeezed into expressions of extreme anguish and torment.

"It's the treasure, Alex," She said slowly then babbled out: "I know that there are some people looking for it."

161

"Who?"

"People that I know..."

"You know! Who...who can you know...?"

"The people who abducted me..."

"*What*! Radcliff shouted. He looked around at the other passengers. "Abducted you!" he exclaimed in hushed amazement. "Who. . .who abducted you?"

"There are two of them...they were French. They know about you, Alex. they know about us! I've let you down, haven't I?" She began to cry.

He kneeled by her seat and held her tight. "It's okay.... It's okay."

She clenched him tight, her fingers pressing hard into his shoulders.

"I sensed something had happened." He drew back and waited for her tears to subside. "Who were they? Why did they abduct you?"

"They thought I would be useful." Shame stopped her from telling him about her relationship with one of the Frenchman. "They drugged me and locked me in a bedroom for weeks. But I got away and found my way back home."

"Did this happen in Marseilles?"

"Si. The detective I hired found my real mother's address."

"But how did they know about the treasure?"

"His family...the Frenchmen's family...have been searching for treasure for hundreds of years. He knew a great deal about you, Alex! My French isn't good but I understood most of what was being said. They talked about treasure...many times...on the telephone. Then on New Years Eve they were making arrangements to travel to the Seychelles."

Radcliff's blood ran cold. "The Indian Ocean is a very big place."

"I'm scared, Alex." Her watery eyes looked desperately into his. "They still have power over me, I know it! I don't want to let you down again," she said, wringing her hands anxiously. "Can you forgive me?" Her pleading eyes searched his.

"There's nothing to forgive! We're a pair...you and I! Together we can do anything. How can I lose when I've got a real live gypsy queen by my side?"

"Yes!" She laughed. "I am a gypsy, aren't I," she said proudly, wiping away the tears from her cheeks with her palms.

"That's right! That's right!" he said in his strange double affirmative. "You are my gypsy queen, who is going to help me unearth the Cross of Goa."

"Si, si!" she exclaimed clasping her hands around Radcliff's neck. "We must never be apart again, Alex. I couldn't stand it. I'll never let you down again, Alex. I promise."

"No more of this nonsense. Come on, Carmen. You're tired out, that's all."

Radcliff called the stewardess.

"When do we land in Melbourne?"

"In half an hour, sir."

# CHAPTER 21

Radcliff and Carmen were one of the first to be cleared through customs and immigration. He glanced back over his shoulder.

Two bald headed men clutching camel hair overcoats fought their way through the queue at passport control, knocking luggage and passengers aside, and were closing in on them fast.

Radcliff glimpsed the third man leaning against a distant pillar with a cell phone pressed to his ear watching the commotion unfold.

"Come on, sweetheart," Radcliff took Carmen's hand, completely mystified by this third man, and strode briskly across the arrivals area... through the milling passengers...to the information desk.

"What's the hurry?" She asked.

"I have to collect Frank's car keys. Without them we'll be in real trouble."

The woman at the information desk handed Radcliff back his ID with the keys. He peered anxiously over his shoulder. The two men were clear of immigration and were about to give chase.

An armed Airport Security officer approached them. Radcliff had the keys in his hand. He considered taking Carmen's arm and making a dash for it but realised that he had no idea where Frank's car was parked. His heart sank deeper with every stride the officer took toward them. Convinced they were about to be marched off to the departure lounge and extradited back to the U.K., Radcliff prepared to tell Carmen that their dream was over before it had really begun.

"Mr. Alex Radcliff?" he asked in a whining, nasal accent.

Radcliff nodded.

"Gooday! Will you both follow me, please?"

"What's wrong officer?" Carmen asked with a simpering smile. Her alarm having turned to cold fear when she saw the compact machine gun the officer was carrying. "What do you want with us?" Fearing they were about to be imprisoned inside one of the horrific detention camps she had seen on TV. She turned to Radcliff with a desperate pleading expression. "What does he want with us, Alex?"

He shrugged his shoulders despondently, but filled with anger and frustration he silently cursed Clive for bringing all this trouble down upon them. He was going to lose Carmen just when they were so close to escaping.

The security man led them through the melee of passengers with the two bald men close behind.

"Where are you taking us?" Radcliff asked as they approached the exit.

"To your car sir... It's parked just outside."

They both stopped for an instant and looked at each other. With beaming broadening smiles Carmen skipped, her hand in his, as they hurried to catch the security man waiting outside the huge revolving doors.

Carmen and Radcliff recoiled back for an instant when the heat from outside struck them. The overcast sky had caused an oppressively high temperature with humidity at saturation point.

The security man escorted the couple to a pale green Citroën Xsara Picasso parked beyond the taxi rank.

"Thank you." Radcliff shook the man's hand vigorously, blessing Frank's thoroughness and forethought as they threw their luggage onto the back seat and climbed into the car. "Thank you very much, officer."

"She's right. Take it easy, Mr. Radcliff, and good luck to both of you."

Accelerating away Radcliff's eyes were glued to the rear vision mirror. The two bald headed men were climbing into a waiting taxi.

The mysterious third man was standing with the security man at the exit doors to the terminal.

Radcliff switched on the radio, mainly to hide his unease, keeping a close watch on the taxi in the mirror. The Sunday evening traffic was light through the sprawling Melbourne suburbs, with the taxi keeping two or three cars behind them throughout the numerous stops at road intersections.

Carmen settled back in her seat, excited and relieved to be on the road. She gave him one of her gorgeous smiles each time he looked across at her.

"Is your Aunt still alive?" she asked suddenly.

"Frank's mother?" he answered, as they stopped at yet another set of traffic lights. He saw the taxi pull in behind a van.

"Yes. She lives on Phillip Island, south of Melbourne. She'll live forever!"

"What happened to your brother William?"

"Will? He was on his way to visit Frank's mum…with some friends. They were travelling down from Sydney…. just before reaching Wangaratta…it was dark, the driver dozed off and the car hit a tree. Will had been in the front passenger seat…he'd just unfastened his seat belt to get more comfortable. He was hurled through the windscreen." He looked slowly across at Carmen and smiled. "He's buried in Wangaratta."

"I'm so sorry, Alex. It must have been very hard on you."

"It devastated the whole family. I still miss him. But I have many, many happy memories of him to treasure. Will left me Robert's diary." His eyes were glued to the mirror as the taxi overtook two cars and slipped in behind a Toyota 4 X 4 stuck to the Citroën's bumper. "We should reach Wangaratta tonight."

Radcliff accelerated the moment they reached the road north and the open country. He glanced across at Carmen. She was sleeping. When he checked the mirror the taxi had gone. He watched the mirror for several minutes hoping the taxi would reappear. With the enemy out of sight his imagination went wild. He glanced at the digital speed counter and decelerated to 100 k.p.h.

Radcliff was still trying to work out where the taxi could have gone when they drove through Yea, 56 miles north of Melbourne. Carmen awoke and looked sleepily around her.

"What time is it?" she asked drowsily.

Radcliff checked the car clock. "Five past eight. We've done quite well. It's only taken us an hour and ten minutes to get here."

She looked out on the yellow and ochre sea of undulating pastures of burnt grass broken only by intermittent splashes of dark green; gums perched upon the wave crests and dotted on the slopes and in the troughs.

"Everything's so burnt and dry," she commented sorrowfully. "It reminds me of Andalusia…although there are less trees in the south of Spain. Does it ever rain here?"

"In the winter and spring usually," he laughed. "September and October…spring time…. are the best months to see Victoria. This is the dairy farming state, believe it or not! These rolling hills are green and lush then…or should be!"

"It's climate change! Global warming is …"

"Yeh! I've heard nothing else since I got back!"

"It's very real, Alex! There're desperate water shortages in Spain."

"Thirty eight years ago, when I was in Queensland, at a place called Alpha on the Tropic of Capricorn, a cyclone hit. I was on my own, sitting it out in my car. The rain was horizontal; the wind bent giant gums like saplings and my car, a Ford Falcon…a huge American job… was tossed around like a toy. I thought I was going to die! When it was over I found the locals dancing in the streets! They hadn't seen rain for over five years. Then I came along… "

She laughed.

Radcliff pulled the car off the road and turned so they faced the sunset. "Look at that, sweetheart! Australia's gift! Feast your eyes upon it…"

Carmen looked up and gave out a groaning sigh.

The low cloud had cleared from the western horizon leaving a backdrop of high cirrus that had turned a fiery orange and yellow. The underside of the nearer clouds had turned to a bubbling sea of crimson and orange, of every hue and intensity. Above the cirrus, away from the red ball of the sinking sun, a light turquoise lagoon receded into infinity. The sky had a vastness not experienced anywhere else in the world and it seamed to echo the immensity and emptiness of the country.

"...Australia has some of the most mysterious and extraordinarily beautiful sunsets you're ever likely to see."

Later, with the light fading, Carmen leapt with excitement, clasping the dashboard like a child, as several wallabies hopped across the road in front of them. Then a few minutes later a pair of grey kangaroo skipped on the grass verge beside them for about a hundred yards.

At Wangaratta, 75 miles north of Yea, Radcliff checked them into the Hotel. After freshening up they dined then relaxed at the bar for a while telling her more about the island and the Cross of Goa.

It was then he realised why the taxi had ceased chasing them.

Passing the reception desk, on their way to their room, Radcliff asked the clerk for a wake-up call at 6.30 a.m.

Jet lagged and fatigued they both sagged into bed.

But they slept too soundly, missing their wakeup call.

He leaned across the bed and kissed her shoulder gently. "Wake up, darling!" She looked ravishing laying face down. Her thick auburn hair spread over the pillow, a white sheet barely covering and her voluptuous body. The mark of her bikini bottom was just visible across her wide hips. He noticed some bruises on her thigh and arms. He ran his hand over the soft, smooth skin of her back.

She turned and pulled him to her. Her back arched stretching her full, shapely breasts seductively, her large nipples growing to the size of ripe cherries.

"Its half past nine!" Radcliff laughed. "We've overslept! We must make a move. Come on, darling."

"¡Hombré! I need some breakfast first." She gripped his waist between her legs and pulled him to her.

"Later my gypsy queen..!" Reluctantly freeing himself from her hold. She rolled onto her side. "We must go," flicking her rump with the tips of his fingers.

"Ahhh!" she yelped. "Why? What's the hurry? We've escaped... you almost said as much yourself last night at the bar. We are safe here." Her lips were like moist strawberries. She half turned enticingly onto her back, stretching her arms above her head into a glorious pose, her nipples standing erect on her ample breasts. She groaned when he kissed one of them.

"I want to take you to lunch at a terrific Spanish restaurant just over the border in New South Wales," he told her, hurriedly pulling on his jeans. "But we must leave now," escaping to the bathroom.

Drying himself he could hear no sign of movement from the bedroom.

"Come on, darling," he called out, "I really want to do this!" He carefully applied a new dressing to his head wound and brushed hair over it. He emerged from the bathroom cleaning his teeth.

"Let's get going…" returning to spit out the frothing paste into the basin, "…or we'll be too late."

She sleepily trudged nude to the bathroom, pouting playfully. He flicked her bottom as she passed by him. She turned on him, deftly unfastened his jeans and fly and whisked his jeans down with one swift movement.

"What do I have hear…?" She chuckled, squeezing his manhood with both her hands.

Radcliff moaned as she pushed hard against him. He was squashed between her and the doorframe. They kissed.

"Not now…." somehow managing to extract himself from the situation and hoist up his jeans. "Later…I promise…" he said breathlessly.

The bathroom door slammed shut in his face.

"I'm going to take a shower!" she yelled. "Do we have time for that?"

"Okay! But hurry," He shouted above the noise of the shower. "I'll find us some breakfast. I'll meet you in the foyer in ten minutes."

It was a perfectly clear morning, the sun was searing hot and the humidity level was bearable. Radcliff drove fast and hard north on the straight Hume Highway. Most of the traffic was heading south. He said very little on the journey, only to point out the Snowy Mountains on the eastern horizon.

Sensing that something was wrong Carmen had said nothing, letting Radcliff deal with the situation his way. They reached the Murray River, the state border between Victoria and New South Wales, just before noon.

Reaching the river Carmen noticed that Radcliff had become perceptively more relaxed. Before crossing the bridge Radcliff turned right off the highway and followed a narrow stony track for a quarter of a mile. Wisps of high cirrus did little to screen the blazing sun. They reached the riverbank, shaded by gum, and continued along the track for another 100 yards.

"So what happened about that Spanish restaurant?" She asked raising her left eyebrow with a deliciously inviting look in her eye.

"I thought you'd prefer this…" he smiled, hastily taking their bags from the rear seat.

"Why do we need our things?" she asked, her puzzled expression vanishing the moment she heard bottles clanking.

"Well…" he shrugged, stacking the bags against a rock "just a little something to wash down the sandwiches…"

They slowly undressed each other on the small pebbly beach, piling their cloths neatly on the bags, then stepped into the river hand in hand and wallowed in the cool fast running water. They splashed, swam and laughed blissfully. They felt completely safe and untroubled.

It had been too long since they had enjoyed a moment together as much. Carmen studied Radcliff's lithe body, bronzed by years in the tropical sun. It glistened in the patches of sunlight breaking through the gum leaves.

She swam to him. He took her waist and pulled her high up out of the water. He kissed her hard on the mouth as he let her slowly slide down his skin. Holding her against him, Radcliff braced himself firmly against the full force of the torrent. It washed up against her ample and shapely bottom and up the small of her back. She curled her legs around his whilst, gripping him tightly. She felt him rigid and manoeuvred herself deftly until she held the tip of him just within her. The rush of water about them heightened their feelings of sensuality. Passion and joy gripped her body and she moaned with the pleasure. They looked into each other eyes gasping, kissing, holding and pulling, gripping and thrusting, with increasing tempo.

They slowed their movements, both wanting to prolong these feelings of ecstasy to their absolute limit. The force of the water squeezed her tight against him. She let go of him and flung her arms up in complete abandon to the forces of their passion, of nature and of the river. She screamed. Throwing her head back and arching her spine her hair touched the water. He supported her at the waist, kissing and running his teeth over her ample breasts.

Their locked and entwined bodies were a mesmerizing, beautifully pulsating and rhythmically writhing sculpture that withstood the surge of the river like a magnificent buttress. Her convulsing exquisite body, held firmly against his, moved in spasms of rapid and slow grinding movements. Radcliff had dreamed of a moment like this a thousand times alone on the island. He squeezed her to him. Her body had become weightless. It was part of him. Carmen shuddered and screamed with delight, as his thrusts lifted her.

They kissed, their tongues pressing and searching their mouths, as he frequently ran one hand over and over her upper body. Their eyes wide open, neither believing they could experience such absolute splendour…at one with God and the universe. Radcliff began thrusting deeper and faster. Her body stretched and tingled; waves of head numbing pulses flowed up her spine; her pelvis demanding that she pressed harder and clasp stronger onto him. Then they were both seized by that exquisite sensation, their actions uncontrollable as they squeezed harder together to increase the pleasurable friction of their writhing, rubbing bodies.

Carmen held his face with both hands and shrieked with joy as her orgasm continued to intensify. They both groaned and laughed as their bodies were seized by their intense climax. He lifted her higher out of the water as they continued climaxing together. The speed and strength of his thrusts sent her eyes rolling backwards as thrilling shudders ran up her body and numbed her skull.

Laughing and exhausted Carmen unwound her legs from him. Radcliff, breathless and still thrusting, griped her tightly to him. His head was nestled between her breasts as he tried to prolong the sensations and hold the memory forever. It was more fulfilling and glorious than his wildest dreams alone under that waterfall.

He stood holding her for several seconds as they laughed and kissed and squeezed each other, Carmen loving him still firm within her. They breathlessly spoke of the joy each was feeling. She linked her hands behind his head and pulled his head towards her lips.

A blinding flash of light followed by an ear splitting explosion blasted through the air, the concussion blasting the loving pair off their feet and into the river. Ghalahs, rosellas, rainbow lorikeets, cockatoos and finches and other birds of all colours and sizes shrieked from every bush and gum tree in the vicinity.

Carmen and Radcliff were blasted backwards into the surging current and were carried down river. Red hot debris plummeted around them. A smoking jagged, twisted piece of metal fell next to Radcliff. He glimpsed on the scorched green paintwork the name 'Picasso' before it disappeared beneath the surface of the water.

The dry bush ignited immediately, tongues of hungry flame reached up to the leaves quickly engulfing the gum trees, which exploded into balls of fire. The westerly breeze fanned the inferno up river.

They drifted thirty yards before Radcliff could find a foothold on the riverbed. He grabbed Carmen's arms and pulled her to him, shielding her from the blaze.

"Are you hurt?"

She shook her head.

Seeing the alarm in her eyes he held her firmly, enveloping her in his wing like shoulders.

The searing heat singed his hair and scorched his back. Dipping beneath the surface of the water they swam for the left bank and clung onto protruding tree roots.

Protected a little from the heat Radcliff gestured to her to wait. He pulled himself out of the river and fleetingly glimpsed a white open back pick-up truck parked off the road beside the bridge. Four armed figures were running down the track towards them.

"I'm going back for our things. Go with the current down river… keep close to the bank," he called after her as the current swiftly took her away. "I'll see you at the bridge," he yelled.

Radcliff took three steps towards the inferno but was forced back into the river. He pulled himself along the bank against the current, keeping his body below the surface until he reached the shallower water at the elbow. The water had warmed considerably despite the strong current. Keeping below the surface as much as possible he slithered over the riverbed like an indecisive salamander. Lifting his head he saw their clothes. Although protected by a rock they were smouldering.

Backing into deeper water he took a long deep breath and prepared himself. He exploded out of the river into the searing furnace. His surge lifted a covering of water over his back. He grabbed their pile of scorching clothes and stuffed them into the bags. The plastic handles had melted exposing the wire reinforcement. With his face and body roasting and his hair starting to burn he ripped the sleeves from his shirt and dived back into the river.

Looking back from the river he saw the cover of the top bag ignite. He dashed up the beach once more, the heat penetrating his scorched skin as if he was being skinned alive. As he wrapped the soaked shirt-sleeves around the handles the cloth hissed on the bare wire. He could feel himself withering, his lungs collapsing, as he grabbed the bags and dived into the river letting the current take him away from the furnace.

Within seconds he passed the spot where he and Carmen had separated. He kicked towards the left bank, pushing himself against the reeds and roots to break his speed. Nearing the girders supporting the bridge he saw Carmen's head popping up above the long drooping dry grass.

She wrapped her arms around his neck, clinging onto him with a grip of iron, as he tossed the bags up the bank. Her frightened eyes darted between Radcliff, the truck and the blazing bush. "There's a man up there…and four by the river…they've got guns Alex!"

"Okay, sweetheart," he said soothingly, gently removing her arms. "Let me take a look."

He hauled himself out of the river and peered around one of the girders.

The white open back truck was parked off the road close to the bridge. The driver was wearing desert combat trousers and a white tee shirt. He was looking down in Radcliff's direction relieving himself between the truck and the bridge. Radcliff lowered himself back into the river and whispered his plan to Carmen.

Using the reeds and roots to pull himself twenty feet back up river he climbed the bank and, keeping low, he ran in a wide arc up the slope and hid behind the rear of the truck. A few cars slowed as they approached the bridge then continued on. Swarms of flies descended upon him, clustering around his mouth and eyes. He looked under the truck waving the flies away constantly from his eyes. There was no sign of the driver. He crawled to the front of the truck and looked around it.

The driver was descending the slope towards Carmen.

Arming himself with a large rock he strode stealthily down the slope. He came up behind the man and smashed the rock repeatedly on his bald scull. The man slumped to his knees. Radcliff hit him again and he collapsed motionless at his feet.

Seeing the driver fall, Carmen lifted herself out of the river, took hold of the bags and ran up the bank. She opened the driver's door, threw the bags inside the cab and climbed up to sit behind the wheel of the truck.

Radcliff had already jumped into the open back, falling amongst a rocket launcher and three rockets. He loaded the weapon and took aim at the men searching the bush close to the blaze. Flies crawled around his eyes, nostrils and mouth. Hearing the starter motor cranking the truck's engine he gripped the launcher with both hands, squinting through the layers of insects around his eyes, and fired the rocket.

The engine ignited. Carmen grated first gear before engaging it with a jolt. Swinging the truck on full right lock, the rear wheels spinning on the bone dry, rocky ground, great thick clouds of dust rose up around them. Radcliff was sent crashing backwards against the left side of the truck and then tossed in the air as they bounced over the rocks. Gripping the side Radcliff looked back to see the rocket explode, sending two of the men flying into the air.

Reaching the road Radcliff heard the squeal of tyres as a car swerved to avoid the truck. Bullets whistled overhead then a second later the report of machine gun fire was heard above the roar of the engine. More bullets smashed into the road and clanged onto the rear bodywork of the truck.

Carmen opened up the throttle, but the diesel engine was sluggish. She battled to find second gear. With the clutch engaged the truck was rolling to a virtual standstill.

The two armed men had reached the road. They took careful aim at the cab. Carmen pulled the gear lever with both hands. The selector slipped the cog into place with a loud clunk. At that instant Carmen's foot slipped off the clutch peddle. The truck lurched forward as she ducked below the level of the dashboard. Bullets thudded into the cab door and down the side of the truck. The truck accelerated away with bullets whining through the open window and peppering the roof. She used the side mirror to guide them over the bridge and out of range of the guns.

Carmen's small delicate hands gripped the steering wheel like a vice, her tiny knuckles protruding white under her skin and her face taught with a determined stare. Every muscle and sinew in her tender shimmering naked body was rigid, her torso leaning forward over the wheel, her eyes wide and bulging with concentration. She followed the

Hume Highway through the town of Albury, on the New South Wales side of the river, and on where the highway cut a straight line through a stand of red stringybark and blue gum trees.

Radcliff had been laying flat on his back clinging onto the side as they weaved through the local Albury traffic. Carmen accelerated out of town and drove as fast and as far as her nerves allowed. Suddenly Carmen broke hard, sending Radcliff crashing against the cab and then swerved left down a narrow track heading deep into the forest of gums.

Radcliff was flung to the right with everything else in the back including the launcher and rockets. The left rear wheel mounted a rock lifting Radcliff and all the hardware high into the air. He landed beside the launcher only to be propelled into the cab once more when she stamped hard on the brake. A cloud of dust enveloped the truck as it skidding to a halt. The engine stalled.

There was absolute silence for a moment. The only sound was the rustle of gum leaves and the dust settling around them.

She leaned on the wheel and sobbed. Hearing the cab door open, she looked down to see Radcliff looking up at her. He was battered, bloodied and white with dust. Her sobs turned to laughter. He climbed up beside her and she threw her arms around him, gripping him with all her might.

"Hold me, Alex. Hold me tight." Gradually her tense, rigid body softened and relaxed. Her skin warmed against him. They felt again that glorious oneness they had experienced at the river.

"We've done it, cariño? We've beaten them?" she said, gazing searchingly into his eyes. She gently brushed away the dust and flies from his face.

"They'll be back. You can be sure about that."

She turned away with a look of bitter gloom.

"It's a war, isn't it!" she muttered after a long pause.

Radcliff told her about the men he had seen on the plane.

"The third man was keeping an eye on us and the two bald headed guys. He watched them as they got into a taxi and follow us for a while. They wanted to be certain which direction we were headed. I thought… if we could make it to the river we'd be safe."

"Now I understand. There's no Spanish restaurant, is there?"

"I'm sorry, sweetheart."

"You inglese! Well…what do we do now?"

"Let's get dressed and get away from these damn flies."

"Well, we've out-witted them so far,"

"What the flies?" He jumped to the ground loving her optimism.

She hurled herself from the cab onto his back. "Win or lose, mi cariño, we have to stay together," she laughed, sliding down his back. "I couldn't face losing you again."

"That feels nice!" He turned and drew her to him and kissed her. "I couldn't go through that agony again either." They embraced warmly. "Okay…. we'll need the odd miracle or two, granted, but I feel we can do it!"

"We've won another battle, cariño! I feel very elated suddenly. I haven't felt quite as good as this since I was a child. All my life I've always felt as though I've let people down. For the very first time I don't. It is a fantastic feeling, Alex! I feel alive." She felt him move against her. "I want you, Alex." She held his face in her hands and kissed him hungrily, her tongue stroking his as she drew from him his love and passion. Her hands clasped him and began rubbing him. She groaned with pleasure as his erection grew and jumped up into his arms with her legs wrapped about his waist.

Her eyes were on fire. He had never seen her this wild before.

"Love in the dust..?" Radcliff chuckled; his hands gripping the cheeks of her beautiful rump, his fingers embedded into her soft, ripe flesh. Their bodies moved and rubbed, fusing into a single pulsating entity of flesh on two legs.

Radcliff moved towards the truck and supported her weight against the driver's seat.

She laughed between her gasps, feeling him penetrate deep into her, and threw her head back ecstatically, pushing her breasts harder into his face. "I don't like dust," she groaned, and then giggled. "I prefer mud. Did you ever wallow in mud?" As she inhaled her breath hissed between her stretched lips. "It's nice, isn't it?"

"With you," he laughed, loving this new side to her, "everything is nice."

She groaned, close to orgasm. "Don't ever leave me, Alex," she gasped. "Oh…Oh…OOh!" her body convulsing faster.

Radcliff was still a long way from climax but he kept ahead of her. Her legs were squeezing on his sides and back, restricting his breathing. But there could be no stopping. This was for her. She was quivering and grinding simultaneously as the rhythm of her movements intensified. Then, gripping him to her with all her might, her body stretched. Numb with passion, she burst into uncontrolled gyrations.

Radcliff felt and heard her squeals of ecstasy. "Maybe miracles run in threes?" he laughed.

She kissed him breathlessly. "Come on, cariño," she purred. "Its your turn."

"We could be here all day," he kissed her back. "I can wait." She unwound herself from him and he lowered her to the ground. "There's another famous river just north of Bourke."

"We'll make love there then."

"It's called the 'Darling'," he chuckled.

"Sounds perfect!" she cried excitedly, her shimmering dusty breasts bouncing as she laughed.

"It does, doesn't it! There's one problem, though."

She searched his eyes for the answer. "What's that, inglese?"

"It's dried up this time of the year!"

"You fool!" she punched him playfully on the arm. "Come on you dustman. Get your clothes on."

They dressed into their soaked clothes. Carmen's white shorts were scorched down one side and her green and yellow top revealed her lower spine and hip. Radcliff squeezed into his waterlogged jeans and sleeveless safari shirt.

"Maybe we should check the bags…," Carmen began.

Radcliff was about to drive off when he suddenly hurled himself across Carmen. He seized his burned bag and began frantically searching inside. He pulled out a bundle wrapped in a denim coat and peeled off the soaked material to reveal a large box shape inside a plastic bag. He opened the bag and breathed a sigh of relief.

"The diary…it's okay!"

They checked their other belongings then Radcliff drove the truck back onto the highway and continued north along the Hume Highway with Carmen nestled close up beside him.

"This road would take us to Sydney. We're going to turn west about seventy-five miles further up and head for Wagga Wagga along the Stuart highway. After Wagga Wagga we'll head northeast up the Newell highway, crossing the Murrumbidgee River…."

"These Australian names are very curious," she chuckled.

"It's a very curious country! We'll head towards Bourke along the route I took years ago. With a bit of luck those buggers will think we're making for Sydney."

Carmen slept throughout the journey, passing Wagga Wagga and Narrandera, where they crossed the Murrumbidgee and travelled north along Newell Highway.

As they neared the small town of Ardlethan, 45 miles south of West Wyalong, Radcliff was forced off the road by a lorry train speeding south. She awoke with his shouting and swearing, the truck skidding and fish tailing, dust billowing up around them. He looked anxiously across at Carmen as he fought to get the vehicle back up the steep camber and onto the metalled road surface.

"Australia's so very dry," she said with complete composure.

"Yes," he laughed. "I think we deserve some food and drink!"

"You're driving!"

"There's a bottle of water and some wet sandwiches in the bag."

They ate ravenously and continued on their journey.

"When can we stop?" she asked wearily, tired of looking at the burnt undulating slopes dotted with gums with the occasional small town flash by mile after mile.

"This truck isn't quite up to the standard of a Citroën, is it? Don't worry, sweetheart. I'll trade this in for a faster car at the next big town."

"I'm not so worried. I've got you. But I could use a bath and some new clothes. And you!"

The country north of the Murrumbidgee was flatter and drier. The cluster of gums became more sporadic and the towns became smaller and less frequent. There was little wild life for Carmen to see. When they finally reached a wooded stretch of highway after the town of Alleena, Carmen thrilled at the sight of wild budgerigars, many rainbow lorikeets, pink and white galahs and some white cockatoos. Later she heard a strange crow-like squawking, laughing sound as they approached the town of West Wyalong.

"A kookaburra…!" Radcliff yelled, pointing up to the top of a telegraph pole.

She looked up and watched the strange bird with a long thick beak fly off across a dry, burnt paddock towards a large farmhouse with a red painted corrugated roof.

A few moments later they entered West Wyalong.

# CHAPTER 22

Slaughter and Apeson had waved down the first vehicle to cross the bridge. It was an articulated lorry approaching from the south. The lorry's air brakes hissed and squealed, the driver bringing the vehicle to a shuddering halt. Apeson climbed up to the cab, shot the driver and hauled him out. Slaughter climbed up beside him, Apeson drove the lorry north over the bridge into New South Wales.

Slaughter furiously punched some numbers into his cell phone and waited. "Get me Holland," he shouted into the device, which looked minute pressed against his huge bull like head. "I'll wait. Just get a fucking move on."

Apeson said nothing, keeping his eyes glued to the road ahead.

"Holland? Listen. We've got major problems. Yeh! It's this fucking artist bloke. Yeh....Yeh...Listen will ya?...Yeh, he got away....*listen for fuck's sake*! I need you in a chopper....I don't care, find one.... you know I'm good for the money. I want you to take three men...I don't care who....choose who you like. Listen to me for fuck's sake! I'll tell you where to search in minute...I want you to nail this son of a bitch... and the woman. Take whatever weapons you need to do the job. Just do it! Got it? Right! They're in a white open back truck heading north. They're probably making for Sydney. What...you're breaking up," Slaughter stuck his head out of the open window for better reception, "What! If they've ditched the truck you'll have to do a bit of detective work, wont ya'. How the 'ell should I know...just use your bloody brains. The quicker you get that chopper the less distance they'll cover. Right! Get moving! Just make sure you get 'em."

# CHAPTER 23

A banner had been strung across the West Wyalong main street which read:

'RODEO- SATURDAY 21st JANUARY & SUNDAY 22nd JANUARY'

Wide, cool sloping verandas covered the raised boardwalks. Cars and trucks were parked, front on, in the wide, busy main street in the place of horses tethered to rails. Either side of the main street were wooden two story nineteenth century buildings all with red painted corrugated iron roofs. The hoardings fixed to the front of most shops, cafés, restaurants, banks and stores were all brightly painted in a profusion of colours.

"It's like one of those old wild-west theme parks!" she beamed excitedly. "Why do all the houses have red metal roofs?"

"Metal dissipates heat very effectively. It keeps the interiors cool during the day…and at night time it retains enough heat to keep you warm."

"Pretty clever..!"

"I need to change some sterling for Aussie dollars."

He parked the truck in the only available space, opposite the bank, took £6,000.00 worth of soggy twenty pound notes and his passport from the bag and crossed the road to the bank.

He was gone for over half an hour. She raised a half smile as Radcliff climbed into the cab. Perspiration had run down her cheeks cutting shiny lines through the dust.

"Sorry, darling. These bankers drive you mad!"

"It's okay. You're here now. There's a garage selling second hand cars at the crossroad. Get the fastest one they have. I'll go and do some shopping. Can I have some dollars?"

"Travellers cheques!"

He signed five $20 cheques and handed them to her as she got out of the truck. He watched her, admiring her body as she dashed towards the covered walkway and out of the searing heat of the sun.

178

Radcliff found the garage selling second hand cars. On the fore-court stood a gleaming red 1970 model Ford Gran Torino with the famous white stripe down the sides. Paying with traveller's cheques the dealer accepted the truck in an exchange deal.

Radcliff offloaded the rocket launcher and two rockets from the truck and stowed them in the boot of the car then nonchalantly tossed their burned bags onto the back seat. The salesman looked on in amaze-ment.

Turning the ignition key the engine fired first time.

Radcliff throttled hard, the rear wheel spinning dust at the salesman as he fish tailed out of the forecourt. Its menacing deep-throated growl turned a few heads as he drove back up the main street of the small town.

Radcliff swerved the car up to the boardwalk and skidded to a halt enveloping Carmen in a cloud of dust as she emerged from 'Eleanor's Boutique'.

"What do you think...? Fast and stylish, eh?" He called out through the dust cloud. "Like it?"

"Wow!" she squealed, her beaming face emerging out of the dusty murk. "I Love it!" She threw the bags and boxes onto the rear set and climbed in.

"Did you ever watch that T.V. series 'Starsky and Hutch'?" Radcliff asked jovially.

"I remember seeing it a few times...at a friend's house. It was dubbed with Spanish actors...there was this funny little character..."

"You mean Huggy Bear?"

"Si. He used to make me laugh. I want you to be my 'Huggy Bear'. That'll do for me," she said, smiling warmly at him.

"Right on, sister!" he started the engine with a roar. "Let's get washed and get some food inside us. I want to see you in those new things."

It was 3.30 p.m. when they finally got back on the road for Bourke, the next large town before the Queensland border and the Darling River. The further north they travelled the flatter and more burnt and barren the landscape became, any trees that appeared traced the courses of the meandering creeks.

"This is the outback," Radcliff commented.

"You can keep it."

"It does have its own unique quality. It's like looking up at the stars...it makes you think."

"All I want to think about is getting away from this place and these killers, Alex! I want to get to your island and see this Cross of Goa. Tell me more about your island."

The hot wind from the open window billowed and pulled on her new yellow top and her gleaming, shampooed auburn hair. She had on a pair of red trousers that were cut just below the knee. He was wearing the new safari shirt she had bought him but could not abandon his old jeans.

Radcliff described the island's shape; the dome like mountain that rose up like a tortoise shell; the different species of trees and palms; the types of birds and other wildlife. When he turned to see the impression he had stamped on her mind she was sound asleep with her head slumped forward on her chest.

With the Torino cruising comfortably but feeling alone, the memory of his trip thirty years before came flooding back. The road was absolutely straight, cutting a narrowing black line to the horizon. Distance and perspective appeared to have a different dimension; the vibrant ochre's, reds, browns and yellows seemed to retain their vivid colours even to the horizon instead of fading into a bluish haze; the horizon, undistorted by humidity, appeared to stretch away far deeper than anywhere else. Radcliff felt its unique magic and desolation once again.

They had been travelling for nearly three hours. Radcliff battled against fatigue by playing mind games. Then he heard a distant whirring coming from behind. Leaning out the window he caught sight of a helicopter, like a small black mosquito, about two miles away but gaining rapidly.

He rammed his foot on the accelerator pedal. The Gran Torino responded instantly, the roaring crescendo awaking Carmen. She saw the tension in his face and his eyes fixed dead ahead. She looked over her shoulder and saw the helicopter advancing, now less than a mile from them. She searched the flat, burnt and barren countryside ahead for cover.

"Look!" She screamed above the din, pointing to the left.

In the distance a line of gums ran parallel to the road. The helicopter was growing in size by the second in the rear vision mirror. He willed more speed from the growling V-8 engine.

There was a turning ahead that led directly to the line of trees. The helicopter was almost upon them; armed men were crouching by the side door taking aim.

Waiting until the last possible moment, he released the accelerator and stamped his foot on the brake pedal. All wheels locked into a straight skid. Clouds of dust and burning rubber enveloped them. They were about to overshoot the turning. Radcliff removed his foot from the brake pedal and heaved on the handbrake. Tweaking the wheels left the rear slew out into the centre of the road. Instantly he turned into the skid and the car went into the sideways slide. With dust billowing over the car he prepared to accelerate when the road came into view.

The helicopter continued travelling forward, the pilot performing a mid air pirouette. With its nose pointed toward the ground it resumed the chase. The Torino was completely hidden in a dust cloud. A burst of gunfire exploded plumes of dirt several feet wide of the car. Radcliff throttled hard, straightening the front wheels.

He missed the road by 5 yards. The Torino crashed into rocks and smashed up against anthills, sending the vehicle leaping into the air. The car hit the ground, its suspension crunched onto the framework, crashed into more rocks and then smacked into a termite mound sending a cloud of red dirt and dust billowing up over the bonnet.

Miraculously the Torino continued on, bouncing and leaping, as bursts of gunfire rained down smashing the rear window. Radcliff fought for control, spinning the steering wheel right and then left.

The Torino found the flat road surface with the helicopter hovering directly above them. The car rocketed forward towards the tree cover, leaving a dust cloud swirling up in its wake.

Carmen's horrified eyes were riveted upon the charging helicopter, its nose pointing straight towards Radcliff's side of the car. Two men were crouched at the side door taking careful aim.

The trees were too widely spaced to offer sufficient cover. Radcliff swerved off the road just as the gunmen opened fire. The car plunged down the bank of a dried up creek with a trail of bullets striking the mud road behind them. Swinging the Torino on hard right lock they leaped and jumped over the rounded rocks and stones of the creek bed towards a wooden bridge.

Radcliff and Carmen squeezed themselves against their door pillars as the Torino bounded onwards. With the bridge just 2 yards away, a hail of bullets rained down from the helicopter peppering holes in the roof and thudding into the upholstery and the floor. They reached the shelter of the bridge as a final burst of bullets thudded into the wooden planks and hit the boot lid, which flew open.

"!Que hombre!" Carmen screamed above the noise of the helicopter.

Radcliff dashed for the boot as the rapidly descending helicopter was about to land on the riverbank on the far side of the bridge. Two armed men jumped from the open doorway as two others prepared to follow them.

Radcliff loaded the launcher, ran to the front of the car, took aim and fired, diving for cover behind the car. Flames from the explosion licked the underside of the bridge and blistered the Torino's bonnet and front fenders.

The blast had killed all on board and enveloped one of the men on the ground. The other had been blown into the creek. He lay ten feet in front of the car. The man got to his knees and fired a burst of bullets at the Torino. Radcliff crawled to the rear and reloaded the launcher.

Carmen had already run from the car and climbed the riverbank.

The man staggered towards the bridge raking automatic gunfire as he advanced. Carmen had positioned herself on the bridge directly above the gunman holding a massive rock above her head. She was straining to hold it steady as she took careful aim. Flies covered her eyes and mouth. She toppled slightly as she hurled the rock down onto the man. It caught him a glancing blow on the head and left shoulder and he collapsed to the ground. The gun clattered on the stones.

Radcliff ran forward and grabbed the gun. But before he could use it, the man, with blood oozing from the side of his head, rolled onto his back. He pulled a pistol from inside his body armour. Radcliff dodged behind the car as two shots clipped the rear wing of the Torino. Radcliff peered over the boot to see him fire two more shots towards the smoking wreckage of the helicopter. A scream cut through the air.

Radcliff ran forward and opened fire, riddling the man with bullets. Instantly the body sagged lifelessly. Radcliff dropped his weapon and sprinted to the bank and clawed his way up to Carmen. Blood pulsated from a wound in the right leg, above the knee. He tore a sleeve from his new shirt and stemmed the bleeding with a tourniquet. The flies swarmed around the blood.

He gently stroked her hair and she gave him one of her magical smiles. It was then he noticed the ground under her right shoulder. It was soaked with her blood. A bullet had entered just above her right breast shattering her shoulder.

He felt her hands. They were cold. He smiled encouragingly. "It'll be okay. Everything will be alright, sweetheart," His throat choked so he barely could speak. He rubbed her hands comfortingly as he tried to think. "Don't worry, darling. Keep still."

She nodded and weakly squeezed his hand. "I feel cold, Alex." Her voice was distant and barely audible. He ripped off what was left of his new safari shirt and covered her.

"I have to get the car here, sweetheart. I'll be as quick as I can."

She smiled and gripped his hand tighter.

"Whatever happens to me, you *must* carry on. You must get to your island and get that Cross. Promise me, Alex." Her eyes were piercing with a fiery determination. "Promise me," she pleaded hoarsely, try-ing to raise her head. The effort was too much and it sagged back to the ground. "Promise me, Alex, that you will get that Cross of Goa." She paused gasping for breath. "Nothing must stop you. Do this for me. Promise me, Alex."

"Save your strength. Let me get you out of here."

"Promise me, Alex. Please say it. Say that you will leave me at the hospital, no matter what, and return to your island." Her imploring eyes burned into his.

"Okay sweetheart…I promise."

She released her grip. "I will come to you later…" she said in a whispering sigh "…as soon as I'm…better…my love."

He kissed her hand tenderly, tears spilling through his closed lids.

"I'll be back…." He stood, barely able to see and hurtled, stumbling and reeling down the slope to the car.

Radcliff fought with the ignition and the throttle until the battered Torino finally spluttered into life. He drove back to where they had descended into the river but the bank was too steep. Franticly he struggled in various places along the river, the car either sliding or getting stuck on the angle of the bank.

With precious seconds ticking away he reversed into the creek, cursing and praying as went. Finally, by running at the bank at an oblique angle, the Torino launched itself over the crest of the bank like a lifeboat breaking over heavy surf.

Reversing the car carefully beside Carmen's unconscious body, he brushed away broken glass and bags from the back seat and gently placed her broken body onto it. Covering her with floor carpet he scrambled to the driver's seat and throttled the screaming, steaming engine to breaking point down the track. A dust trail twenty feet high rose up in his wake.

An hour later Radcliff following the road signs for Bourke District Hospital he turned the overheating, battered, bullet riddled car right, off the highway into Tarcoon Street and screeched to a halt outside the Casualty Centre.

After examination Carmen was taken by aero-ambulance to Sydney General Hospital for emergency surgery. Radcliff watched the sad, small aircraft take her out of his life once more.

He turned away, trance like, and fired up the crumpled, burned wreck and drove it to a garage for repairs to the cooling system. A large crowd had gathered around the Torino by the time the welding was completed. They all cheered Radcliff off as he turned back onto the Mitchell Highway.

Just outside Bourke he stopped the car before the Darling River and walked slowly to the middle of the bridge. He looked down at the dusty, dried up river bed, strewn with rounded boulders and rocks. Radcliff clenched his fists and let out a wailing scream that pierced the still afternoon air. Unstoppable tears flowed down his cheeks as he hammered the bridge with his fists.

"You okay mate?" came a voice from behind.

Radcliff turned around slowly. A white taxi idled, its stocky driver leaning from the window. Radcliff nodded, wiping his face. "A bit tired, that's all. Just tired."

"That can be a killer! Take it easy mate." The electric window hummed closed and the cab continued on over the bridge.

Radcliff pressed on northward, driving the Torino relentlessly for two hours. It was dusk as he descended the hills into the small Queensland town of Cunnamulla. It sparkled and glowed like a golden jewel against the blackness of the hills beyond. A flash of lightened lit up the northern sky.

He parked the Torino outside the Hotel, untied the string securing the boot, pulled his bag from under the rocket launcher and refastened the boot. Huge drops of rain thudded and splattered onto the bullet-holed roof.

Paying for a room he used the clerk's telephone to call the hospital in Sydney. 'She was stable and in recovery,' was all they said.

He retreated to the seclusion of his room with a bottle of whiskey and switched on the television. People were cheering at the winner of an inane game show. Letting the fiery liquid anaesthetise his mind he settled back on the double bed to read from the diary. But all he could see was Carmen's face and her blood soaked shirt.

A reporter on the television news jolted him from his melancholy. The reporter was standing beside the road bridge: "I am at the scene of a terrorist attack near Albury, on the Murray River. It occurred about midday." The camera panned down the river to the blaze. "Fire crews are still fighting the inferno." The picture then showed a close up of a piece of a rocket. "This was found nearby." The camera zoomed in to show the French manufacturers name. "The rocket is similar to the type used by the Mahujahadin in their guerrilla war against the Russians back in the 1980s." The reporter dropped it to the ground and picked up another piece of twisted, burnt metal. "This is the number plate of a Citroën 'Picasso'. The police have still to identify the occupants. Four bodies have been found. Three are thought to be the terrorists; two have been badly burned and one was found with blows to the head close to where I'm standing. A body lay in ditch beside the road. He is thought to be a truck driver, killed by the two terrorists who are thought to have hijacked the truck to make their getaway. This is Mike Dressler for Channel 9 news at the State border."

Radcliff switched off the television and took a long swig from his whiskey bottle.

# CHAPTER 24

Jean-Claude Narbonne and Pierre Droux had, in the meantime, arrived on Mahé, the main island in the Seychelles archipelago and had located the 'Island Hopper' helicopter hire company.

Kurt Van der Koche was the proprietor. It was little more than a glass fronted hut at the far side of the airport runway.

"We are friends of Alex Radcliff." Pierre Droux said in French taking a bundle of Rupees from his wallet and placing them enticingly on the counter. "He said that you would be willing to take us to the island."

"If you are friends of Messier Radcliff, you would not need money. Can you tell me why he gave you my name?"

Kurt Van der Koche was a stocky Dutchman of medium height, in his late forties, his pink scalp shinning through thinning fair hair. His heavily set face was full of humour with lively intelligent eyes and a bulbous nose. When he laughed, his thick lips revealed a set of perfect teeth. He glanced at the other Frenchman. His smile quickly faded.

"You are the only person that knows the island's whereabouts," Pierre shrugged lifting his arms from his sides congenially. "He said that he was very busy with his artwork and could not come himself."

The Frenchmen had researched back issues of the island newspaper at the library the day before. They found several articles on Alex Radcliff. On the day of his rescue, the 7th December 2006, the front pages had for several days been dedicated to the sensational event. Standing proudly beside him in one of the 'photos was the helicopter pilot Kurt Van der Koche who had taken him off the island.

"I'm sorry messieurs but I am not permitted to take you."

Pierre took more notes from his wallet and waved them in his face.

"No. I'm very sorry. Why don't you charter a yacht? I'm sure, in time, you will find the island."

"What do you know about the treasure?" Jean-Claude demanded. Pierre kicked him hard on the shin.

Kurt noticed the other Frenchman wince. "I'm a conservationist and do not get involved with treasure hunting. Now, please excuse me, I am very busy."

Pierre could feel Jean-Claude's temper rising. He smiled quickly and thanked Van der Koche for his time. He took Jean-Claude by the arm and steered him out the door.

"*You idiot*! Why did you have to mention the treasure? We must keep a low profile you fool! We'll hire a yacht like he suggested. We'll be able to take our time loading the treasure aboard."

Kurt watched them talking outside the hut. Treasure hunters and curious tourists had been coming to his hut on a daily basis over the past month, some begging; many willing to pay vast sums of money to be taken to the island.

Then Jean-Claude turned and glared at Kurt. The eyes of the Frenchman bore into Kurt's, chilling his blood and sending a shiver up his spine. Kurt quickly dismissed an ugly premonition that flashed into his mind, shrugged his shoulders and concentrated upon his booking schedule before him.

# CHAPTER 25

Chief Inspector Charles Hawkins slapped the morning paper down on the breakfast table. "This man is starting World War III," he shouted in exasperation, looking skyward for divine guidance.

His wife gently placed a plate of two smoking bacon sandwiches next to the newspaper. The headline read:-

'TERROR ATTACK SETS AUSTRALIAN BUSH ABLAZE'

"What does it mean?" his wife, Susan, asked returning to the sink and the washing up.

"It's this artist feller, Alex Radcliff."

"You didn't tell me he was in Australia. Is he a terrorist?"

"No," he answered irritably, taking a large bite from the sandwich. "I can't say too much. In fact the less you know, my angel, the better. Radcliff and a woman escaped protective custody and got on flight to Melbourne. Some people are after him. Radcliff's a very unusual person ...'danger' is his middle name"

"It seems like it."

He went to her and put his arms around her tiny waist. She melted in his arms. She was small, blonde and gorgeous but tough, manipulative and resourceful. They had recently got back together, after a two years separation, on condition that Charles took early retirement. She had been adamant. She could no longer go on living in constant fear for her husband's life. Her weapon had been to leave him...until he promised her that the 'Radcliff' case would be his last and that he would leave any heroics to younger members of his team. Her victory had meant that she was able to dream and make plans for their retirement.

"I will have to go out there, darling." He whispered in her ear.

She pulled away. A glass smashed on the floor.

"You bastard! You promised me! You just have to be the great *I am*! What about *our* future? You never keep your word, Charlie!" her voice broke and tears welled up in her eyes. "All our dreams have gone up in smoke--the Bed and Breakfast place...the new car...trips abroad... everything! You promised me. How could you do this? Didn't you realize that I meant what I said? " She burst into tears.

"Take it easy, Sue." She recoiled away from him. "I want all of this as much as you do…I love you, for Christ's sake. I have to finish this case. It's very important. I must see this through. Many of my men, good men, have been killed. I have pledged…to bring them to justice."

"You have *pledged*! You *idiot*! Don't I *mean* anything to *you* at all? What about the *promise* you made to me?" She screamed through her sobs.

He moved forward to take her in his arms.

"Don't touch me. Get *out*! *Get out*!" She ran up stairs and slammed the bedroom door.

He leaned heavily against the worktop; head bowed gazing at the broken glass. Every emotion came welling up, as they had done a thousand times before. He handled it the same way. By mechanically getting on with what had to be done. The first thing was to brush up the mess on the floor, then put on his overcoat. He quietly closed the front door of his Selsdon home on the Surrey Downs and returned to work.

Susan heard the front door close and punched the tear soaked pillow, her head buried deep into its feathers, and screamed with rage, frustration and despair.

On reaching the office Hawkins found two messages on his e-mail:

One from his duty officer advising that two tickets had been booked for the 10.00 a.m. BA/Qantas flight 678 from London Heathrow to Sydney and that Detective Constable John Omollo had been assigned to accompany him; the other was from Arthur Brickman advising that the F.B.I. had provided irrefutable proof that the Mafia were behind the attacks on the hospital and on Radcliff.

Chief Inspector Hawkins and Detective Constable John Omollo arrived at Sydney Airport just after 5.00 p.m. on the Wednesday evening. The two detectives from Scotland Yard were immediately whisked by police helicopter to the smouldering site at the Murray River, then on to West Wyalong where Hawkins interviewed the used car salesman and on again to the battle scene at the bridge over the dried creek and from there to Bourke District Hospital.

They were standing on the exact spot Alex Radcliff had stood 48 hours earlier watching the helicopter fade into a speck in the cobalt eastern sky. The evening sun burned their backs and necks and the incessant small darting flies swarmed around their faces.

Two New South Wales state patrol vehicles approached from behind the hospital and drew up alongside Hawkins and Omollo. Recent rains had encouraged new shoots in the burnt grass between the airfield and the hospital giving it a tinge of light green.

The two detectives checked over a new green Range Rover loaned to them for assisting the state police in apprehending the 'terrorists'. It was fully equipped with the latest surveillance aids and satellite navigation, food, drinking water and Gerry-cans of fuel.

Wasting no time Hawkins started up the Rover and, with a plume of dust trailing in their wake, they sped north for the Queensland border.

Two emus joined in the race, their legs pounding the ground, their haughty beaks held high, until they sensed certain defeat and feigned disinterest, veering off in a wide arc towards the setting sun.

"Excuse me, sir…," Omollo's deep voice resonated inside the vehicle, "…but couldn't we cover much more ground searching for Radcliff from the air?" He swung the sun-visor over the passenger's window. "How do you know that he went north, sir?"

"Well I'll tell you, young man," Hawkins sighed, unaccustomed to this kind of insubordination. But he was strangely drawn to his amiable and eager to please young colleague. "We are getting very close and the people chasing Radcliff will be even closer. If we buzz around this open country in a chopper it will first scare these devils off and also be like searching for a tick on the back of an elephant. We've gone north because that's the direction he was seen to go by the doctor at the hospital. His bullet riddled, red sports car will be easy to follow and what's more I know that he's driven through this part of Australia before."

"What do you think he's trying to do, sir? Do you think he's drawing these men away from his…erm…fiancé?"

"Could be, young man, but I doubt it. He's smart, this Radcliff. He's been leading them out here hoping to lose them. When he was here before, in the 1970's, he took the exact same route north. Then he veered right, further north, at a town called Tambo and ended up at Cairns by way of Rockhampton."

Omollo checked the map and lifted it to show Hawkins. "This is Tambo," pointing to the spot. "Whereabouts do think these killers are?"

"They aren't far behind Radcliff, that's for certain. We are dealing with mercenaries, ex-military men, here. Failure will not look good on their C.V. They've lost a dozen men, expensive equipment not to mention the helicopter! They'll be all out next time to get the job done. Killing Radcliff is vital. These lice need to recover some credibility within the seedy circles they work in."

"They could have used another helicopter, sir? Maybe a gun ship..?"

"They cost too much. They'll need to economise. They'll be in a 4X4 like us."

Omollo stuck his head out of the window. The hot air blasting into his face took his breath.

"Who are the people that hired these killers?"

"According to the F.B.I. it's the Mafia."

"The Mafia!" Omollo choked in surprise.

"Yep! Don Angelo Cinisi. The Godfather himself! The top banana, no less!" Hawkins chuckled. "I still can't believe that an artist can bring the whole of the American underworld down on him."

"He must have upset them a little bit!"

Both men laughed.

The two men drove on at speed, the sun refracting into a giant scarlet ball hovering over the flat landscape. When they descended into the town of Cunnamulla the remaining embers of sunlight left a deep red line on the western horizon suffusing into darkening shades of mauve and violet. The burring of crickets and the sound of a million croaking frogs filled the night air. Lightning flashed far to the north. Hawkins pulled into a garage. He went up to the kiosk to chat with the owner inside whilst Omollo filled up the tank with diesel.

They found the Hotel on the road junction. It was a brick built, two story building; its flaking green paint revealed cracked sun bleached wood. Wide verandas of rusting corrugated iron, supported by elaborate Victorian wrought iron pillars, sloped out to cover the pavements.

They took a double room for the night. The man at the desk slapped the key to room number 10 on the guest book and asked Hawkins to sign it. Hawkins spotted Radcliff's name.

"Do you remember this man?" holding up a photograph of Radcliff to the clerk.

The thin, balding man squinted at the picture. "Na mate, sorry," he replied congenially with a strong nasal accent. "I've been crook for a couple of days. You a friend o' his, then?"

"Yes. I've something very important to tell him."

"Me Misses told me some pommy took a room a couple of days ago. Hang on a minute." The man stood over a gaping hole in the floor. "*Elsie!*" he hollered down into the cellar. "*What was the name of that pomm that you was tellin' me about?*"

"*R-a-d-c-l-i-f-f,*" came a distant voice.

"That's our friend," Hawkins said. "Can we ask…Elsie…a few questions?"

"She shouldn't be long, she's checking out the grog down there..." he answered smiling amiably, "…I'll show you to 'er rooms and you can settle yersells in."

Later Hawkins and Omollo went down to the bar. It was a smoky small room with a long counter that ran the entire length of one wall. They sat at the counter on high stools. The same man who had been at the desk served them with a beer and an orange squash respectively.

Hawkins studied the small glass no bigger than a sherry schooner glass. Nevertheless he set about quenching his burning thirst by sinking ten glasses in quick succession. They sat for several minutes watching and listening to the animated loud conversations in the brightly lit bar.

The locals talked mainly about the recent rainfalls. A large fellow wearing a checked shirt and wide brimmed hat was telling a tale to a cluster of friends:

"The floods cut off Stringer's station. They had to call in the flying doctor to deliver Maude's baby. Jes' he's a bonsa little feller. They lost a lot of cattle though."

Hawkins looked up and down the bar, feeling suddenly very dizzy. It amused him to see so many tough looking characters, talking and laughing in groups of three or four, sipping from the same small glasses. Some were actually extending a dainty little finger. Hawkins was about make a joke to Omollo when a short, barrel shaped, middle-aged women, stood before them.

"Are you the two blokes that was asking about Mr. Radcliff?" she asked loudly in her high pitched strongly accented voice, her arms akimbo and perspiration dripping from her chin.

They both nodded.

Omollo quickly slid from his high stool and offered it to her.

Climbing up, she shouted above the hubbub and laughter: "Well now, there's not much to tell ya really. I knew he was English just by the look of 'im. Just as I know you're coppers," she announced proudly.

The noise from the pub quietened considerably. Many looked over with distinct admiration at the woman talking to the two men. Her uncanny reputation for making accurate character assessments in an instant had been given another boost. "He took a bottle of whiskey up to his room and made one phone call to Sydney General Hospital," she added with confident aplomb, her back straightening proudly. "I made him a full breakfast in the morning. Like most pomms, he didn't volunteer much by way of conversation. You pomms have jaws like clams, don't yer." A few at the bar cheered and laughed. "He did tell me, though, that he was heading north. I told him how to find the road to Charleville. We had................."

"Charleville..? Hawkins slurred, holding tightly to the edge of the bar. "Elsie, isn't it?" She nodded. "That's the next town north of here... isn't it...Elsie?"

"Sure it is. I warned him, but he wouldn't listen."

Hawkins blinked several times trying to focus on one of the multiple images of Elsie. His lips began to form a word but he couldn't remember what he wanted to say.

"What do you mean? You warned him of what?" Omollo asked, coming to his boss's aid.

"Is your friend alright?" She leaned over to Hawkins. "He looks the worse for the grog, that's for sure." She sat back reproachfully. "There was this terrible storm. It fair bucketed down." She began to laugh, revealing just the one tooth in her upper jaw. " Jes', me chickens were almost swimming down the road like bloody ducks. I said to Fred, I said............"

"Yes, but what about Mr. Radcliff?" Omollo propped Hawkins up as he lurched sideways.

"I warned him. I said the Mitchell Highway would be like a bog after the rains. It goes like concrete with the sun on it, but when it rains! Jes', it becomes like glue, and no mistake. I told him that the mud would be over his axels. But he wouldn't wait for a couple of days. Oh no! Like all you pomms, you think you're going for a blessed drive in the bleedin' English countryside. I told those four other fellers the same thing yesterday."

"Four fellows?" Omollo took the weight of Hawkins unconscious body as it flopped onto his shoulder.

"These blokes said they were friends of his as well! But I knew they weren't. Something mean about 'em. They showed me a picture of this....erm...Mr. Radcliff." She lifted her head haughtily and her mouth contorted as if she had sucked on a lemon. "These were tough characters, make no mistake. Four of them, there were. All dressed in black, black vests, trousers, boots, gold earrings and heavy gold neck-laces. They looked real spooky to me. At least they had one of them big jeep things." She jumped down from the stool. "Well, that's it. You'll be leaving in the morning, I suppose. I'll have some breakfast ready, if you want it....and some black coffee for your friend?" Elsie turned to leave.

"Thank you, Elsie." Omollo held Hawkins steady on the stool. "Will you give us a wake-up call at 8.30?"

"No worries, dear.., " she smiled.

Omollo stooped slightly and hoisted Hawkins over his shoulder and weaved his way through the crowded bar and under the archway to the stairs.

"I'll have the black coffee ready too." She shouted after him, arousing some guffaws from the locals as she squeezed her way back down the bar.

The man in the wide brimmed hat slapped her hard on her ample rear and laughed raucously. "You tell 'em, Elsie," he yelled after her.

She turned on him, punching him hard with both fists. Everyone cheered and roared with laughter. The hilarity increased when the man propped his giant hand on her forehead, keeping her flailing arms out of range. "Come on, you little beauty. Give us a kiss."

"You! I've seen better lookin' apes at Brisbane zoo."

"Yeh! But do they love yer the way I do?"

"Shut up and drink up."

"Is it your shout? Come on lads, Elsie says they're on the house."

"On your bike."

The laughter increased as Elsie escaped to the kitchen.

Hawkins shielded his eyes from the morning sun bursting through the latticed window. He sipped the piping hot coffee Elsie had sent up with the breakfasts.

"Listen, Omollo. I heard some of what that woman…what's her name…. was talking about last night, before I…er…" Hawkins coughed. He squinted with the pain in his head. "Well, she mentioned something about four men in a jeep. The bloke at the garage said that four men dressed in black had filled up a Mitsubishi Pajero yesterday. He told me that the day before these blokes arrived Radcliff's red sports car had slewed off the road into a ditch just outside town. His nephew had apparently winched him out."

"They must have caught up with Radcliff by now!" Omollo looked away dejectedly, his eyes rolled to one side like animated golf balls.

"Well we'll never know if we sit here gossiping. Come on, lad! Finish your egg and bacon. Let's get cracking." Hawkins stood too quickly and gripped the edge of the table for support. "You'd better drive, Omollo," he said sheepishly.

More rain had fallen over night. As predicted the Rover did sink to the axles in the soft, sticky mud. The mud scraped the floor pan, splattered the windscreen and denied grip to all four driven wheels at any one time. Omollo juggled with 1$^{st}$ and 2$^{nd}$ gears, spinning the steering wheel repeatedly from left to right to keep traction and retain their position on the crown of the road where the mud was thinner.

Hawkins talked as Omollo battled to keep the Rover on the road. A signpost showed Charleville to be one hundred miles further down the mud road. Hawkins spoke with emotion and candour mostly about his relationship with his wife. Omollo sensed that the drink was responsible for his need to talk but he felt the intensity of feeling being released and desperately wanted to help him.

Hawkins paused, silently gazing out of the side window.

"There's no understanding a woman's logic sometimes, sir," Omollo said soothingly, tentatively attempting to empathise with his boss. "My parents used to live in Sutton…"

"I know Sutton well."

"They had really bad arguments after my grandfather died. My father had inherited his position as the village Chief but my mother did not want to return to Ghana and live in a mud hut. My father agonised over the decision for days, during which time my mother tried every manipulative ploy possible to influence his choice."

"What did he do?"

"The only honourable thing he could do."

"Good for him. Did your mother stay in England?"

"At the last moment my mother arranged a leaving party. She told the guests that she had always wanted to go back to Ghana and was looking forward to being the Chief's wife. It was the only major problem between my parents that I can remember."

"Women, eh..!" Hawkins prayed that when the Radcliff case was over Susan would have forgiven him and they could enjoy retirement together. A flock of Galahs rose up from the gum forest. He looked across at Omollo, "Is there a woman in your life John?"

"Her name is Sophia. She is from another village...*and* Christian! Her father was the Chief of his village and very much against the relationship. Some things sometimes are just not meant to be." The road dipped down into a flooded creek.

Omollo wrestled with the steering wheel and juggled with gears to keep traction. As he successfully brought the Rover out he grinned the broadest of grins that stretched from ear to ear revealing a mouth full of perfect teeth, lighting up his face. "I've put my heart and soul into the Police Force. My family, and all of the village, are very proud that I have not only overcome all the racial and religious prejudices but also that I have passed my exams to work in the C.I.D."

"Listen, John. God knows what we are up against out here." Hawkins spoke with warmth and sincerity. "I do know that everything that you've learned in your training and your brief time with me will be put to the test over the next day or so." His tone became grave and full of foreboding. "We have to be a strong team. Our survival will depend on it. You will need a sixth, and even a seventh sense...a kind of intuition. Remember we are not just fighting criminals. These men are highly trained soldiers. They are from the very top elite of the English and American armed forces."

Omollo turned to his boss and was surprised by the gravity of his expression, his eyes sharp and piercing. Wrenching his own eyes back onto the road ahead, he could feel the hairs on the nape of his neck tingle and his head began to itch. He prayed to Allah that he would not let this man, his hero, down.

They drove on in silence. Hawkins watched him unobtrusively. Omollo exuded an aura, an inner strength and fortitude that seemed as old as time itself. He remembered his partner, Benny Holden.

"Let me tell you a story, son...Omollo. I had a partner... Benny Holden...you might have heard of him?"

Omollo shook his head.

"It had happened on a summer morning. We had chased five men, suspected of armed robbery to a house in north London. We had them cornered like rats. Then they opened fire with handguns from the bedroom windows. Protected by our squad car we hoped to keep them pinned down until reinforcements arrived. But when they heard the police sirens from the motorway the felons made a break for it out of the front door firing automatic weapons. I was hit in the leg and torso. Benny dived onto me, shielding me...from...." Hawkins winced, feeling again the bullets raking and pounding into Benny's inert body slumped over his chest.

"There were thirteen bullet holes in Benny's back," he said after a short silence. "I want you to know that I have every confidence in you, Omollo," a longer silence added greater weight and sincerity and meaning to Hawkins' words. "You are not reckless and I know that you will think before you take action. I know we can survive this."

Omollo was overwhelmed by his generosity and for his trust. He felt a pride that was similar to the time his father had asked him sit at the head of the table. The whole village had honoured him that night. It had been a wonderful, unforgettable feast.

# CHAPTER 26

Radcliff drove into the small town Alpha in Central Queensland on the Tuesday evening. Thunder rumbled nearby then a flash of lightning cut vertically down into the trees followed by a whip lash like crack that electrified the air overhead.

He parked the battered mud caked Ford Torino outside the Omega Hotel in the main street. An eerie darkness had descended suddenly and a gusting wind lifted the dust from the road. The first weighty drops of rain splattered the bonnet and thudded onto the colander like roof, penetrating the baked ochre crust to reveal patches of its original paint-work then dripped through the bullet holes.

He had climbed the marble steps set between two Greek style white pillars and entered the Hotel through heavy art deco swing doors. Exotic potted plants were scattered about the small lobby which swayed and rustled in the draft. The reception counter was situated on the left wall under the staircase. Behind it sat an overweight balding man in his late fifties wearing a lime green short sleeved shirt. He looked over the top of his newspaper, his smile almost lost under a walrus moustache.

Radcliff sagged against the counter. "Do you have a room for the night?"

"Take yer pick, mate. They all 'ave a shower and television...eighty dollars a night in advance...breakfast's extra."

"I'll take room seven, thanks." Radcliff signed four twenty-dollar traveller's cheques and handed them to the man together with his passport. "I want to make an early start in the morning. Can you give me a wake-up call at seven?"

"Okay. No worries, mate." The man slapped the key to room seven onto the counter then opened a leather bound book the size of a ledger and spun it around to face Radcliff. "Please sign the register, sir."

He watched Radcliff fill in the columns.

"Don't I know you from somewhere? Have you been through these parts before?"

Radcliff was fully concentrated on keeping his writing within the lines. He finished and turned the book around.

"Alex Radcliff, eh?" the big man chuckled with delight as Radcliff picked up his bag. "I knew it was you the moment you walked in. You're that feller who was rescued from that treasure island, 'aint yer? When I saw you on T.V. I said to Marj, me wife, I said 'That's that pomm who was 'ere the night of the cyclone. You don't remember me, do yer? Dick Crofton's the name." He held out his great chubby hand.

Radcliff stood at the foot of the stairs clasping the ornate wooden knob at the end of the banister rail. He shook his head politely.

"It was back in 1970. What a storm that was. Never had one like it since!" Thunder rumbled overhead. "Until now, that is," he laughed.

"I remember that cyclone," Radcliff said wearily returning to the desk. "That night will live with me for the rest of my days. I sheltered in the Rugby Football Club car park. The strength of that wind lifted my Ford Falcon half into the air and the rain was blasted through the doors and windows."

"I was the bloke who saw you the morning after. I took you into the bar and gave you a scotch. Jes' you were in a sorry state. You were quite shaken up…"

"Oh…yes! Of course! I remember you…" his eyes creased up and sparkled with a flash of recognition. "You were all celebrating in the streets…debris all around you…I thought you had all gone mad! I thought I was going to die in that storm!"

"I know," he guffawed. "It's different out here. We hadn't seen rain for five years…. then you came along. It was one hell of a storm, that's for sure! It destroyed the Rugby Football Stand! Fair dinkum! I remember…it came down like a pack of cards…the roof took off and sheered through those gum trees like a sickle cutting through grass. Now you've come back and you've done the same bloody thing!" Noise from thunderclaps reverberated within the building. "Only this time the draught has lasted eight years! They say it's all to do with that 'El Niño'…or whatever…all I know is that we are to expect a bloody big bastard tonight, that's for sure! You must give us warning before you pay us these visits…then we can get our irrigation systems synchronised!"

Crofton laughed.

Radcliff chuckled politely. "Excuse me…er.. Dick, but do you mind if we talk in the morning. I've had rather a long day…."

"I'll bet you came up through Cunnamulla and Charleville again?" Crofton slapped the counter merrily. "No wonder you're covered in mud! You pomms never learn, do yer?"

"That stretch of road is unbelievable," Radcliff retorted. "It's a bog. It was me against the bog! One hundred miles of it! Axle deep in the stuff! I slid off the road a dozen times. I thought I'd never get the car back on the road! It was a nightmare! I didn't see another soul the whole journey!"

"Hardly surprising…you won't find anyone without a Ute or 4 X 4 using that road after the rains," Crofton smiled sympathetically. "You had your Ford Falcon estate wagon last time. You had some good rear tyres on her, I remember. Town and Country. I caught a glimpse of the one you've got now…" he shook his head. "It couldn't be worse for these conditions. You're crazy. It's a miracle you made it through."

"I thought the roads would have improved after thirty years!"

"Well, at least you've got the good sense to head east along the Capricorn Highway. No use trying to go west to Barcaldine. After the rain nothing will get through up there. They're expecting floods again! Everything happens when you're around, eh! Seems as though you've made more than a cyclone happen this time, mate," he added seriously, tossing the newspaper over to Radcliff.

Radcliff read the headline:

'MAN AND WOMAN ATTACKED BY GUNSHIP OUTSIDE BOURKE'.

Underneath were old pictures of Radcliff and Carmen and a close up photograph of the burned out helicopter. He quickly skimmed through the short article describing the battle scene, Carmen's injuries and an extract from a police interview at Barcaldine, which connected the incident with the rocket attack at Albury earlier that day.

Lightning flashed close by followed by a deluge of heavy rain falling on the marble steps then a thunderclap reverberated over and over, fading into the distance.

"Yes. We did run into a bit of trouble," handing the paper back to Crofton.

"How's yer Sheila? Carmen. She right…?"

Radcliff shrugged his shoulders despondently. "The operation on her shoulder is over. They told me that, at least. They don't give much away on the phone. I'll ring the hospital tonight."

"Don't leave it too late. The phone lines are always the first things to go in a storm." There was an ear splitting crack of thunder and the lights went out. "Well, too late! That's our power gone and with it the phone, most likely. Sorry mate." He crossed the foyer and pulled back the curtain. "Yep! The whole town's in darkness." He lifted the telephone receiver on the counter. "Yeh! The phone's gone, too!"

Crofton lit a couple of candles and gave one to Radcliff.

"Thanks. I'll see you in the morning," Radcliff turned and ascended the stairs shielding the flickering flame from the draft. The driven rain pounded on the landing windowpanes, violent lightning flashes projecting eerie animated shadows down the staircase as the thunder rumbled overhead continuously.

"Sleep well, Mr. Radcliff," Crofton called up, slamming the register shut, chuckling heartily to himself.

Radcliff had answered his wake up call, washed, dressed and hastily gathered his things together. At the desk his calls for service had been unanswered and went outside. He stood at the top of the marble steps to see a crowd gathered around his bullet-riddled car. One of the ornamental pillars had toppled onto the driveway landing between the Torino and a Jeep. The street was littered with branches, corrugated iron roofing and other debris. The rain had stopped but the sky was heavy with threatening low cloud.

"You okay, mate?" Crofton emerged from the throng and climbed the marble steps with a large plastic bag in his hand. "You look better for the rest."

"I slept well, thanks, Dick." Radcliff held out his hand. "Well, it was good to meet you again."

"Just a mo'. Let me get yer passport."

He was back within a few seconds and handed it to him.

Radcliff unzipped the holdall and stowed it safely inside. They shook hands firmly.

"You can make your call at Bill Thompson's place just a few hundred yards out of town. He's got a Milk Bar with its own phone line. Yer can't miss it. You'll need this, mate," handing Radcliff a plastic bag. "Your seat's soaked! Good luck, Alex Radcliff…," he smiled as Radcliff closed the door of the Torino, "…something tells be you're goin' to need it…hope yer sheila's right. Oh! One more thing…"

"I know." Radcliff chuckled reading Crofton's thoughts and the twinkle in his eye. "I'll bring you a brolly on my next visit!"

The Ford started up first time.

"That's quite a car!" he shouted above the roar of the spluttering engine. "It's got more holes than Marj's colander!" he laughed, nudging one of the townsfolk in the ribs. Radcliff reversed slowly out into the litter-strewn road. "I think we'll hear a lot more about Mr. Alex Radcliff, George, as time goes by." he said quietly through smiling lips as Radcliff headed out of town.

Thompson's 'Milk Bar' was an isolated two-story house with verandas all round set well back from the highway with ample parking space. The interior was dark and cavernous. A line of tables and chairs were positioned under the four front windows. Radcliff's footfalls echoed on the bare boards as he crossed the empty space to the semi-circular counter at the back of the room. A lean, elderly man with a hooked nose and grey stubble gazed from under bushy brows with indifference as Radcliff approached the counter. His eyes were sunk deep in their sockets, his skin drawn tight over pronounced cheek and jawbones and his dentures stretched his thin lips grotesquely.

"Gooday!" the talking skull greeted him; his accent was heavy. "There's no hot breakfast. The storm brought the power line down. All I have is all you see in front of yer."

"Can you do me a milk shake?"

"I'll 'ave to whisk it by hand. Anything else..?"

"Yes. A bar of chocolate...is your pay phone working?" Radcliff asked, stooping to stroke a grubby white Scotty dog that had appeared from behind the counter, its tail wagging furiously.

"It was half hour ago. It's on the wall mate, by the door."

The dog scampered behind him, its claws clipping and tapping on the wooden floor. It sat looking up hopefully as Radcliff dialled the number for the Sydney General Hospital. He asked for Stevenson Ward and a nurse had put him on hold.

Radcliff squatted and scratched the dog behind its ear. It pressed its head into Radcliff's hand and closed its eyes in ecstasy, sliding its backside nearer, its tail sweeping a rapid rhythm on the floorboards.

The ward sister was the next voice he heard. She spoke to him very softly and slowly. He stood up sensing bad news. After it was said he refused to accept it. He sagged, propping himself limply against the nicotine stained wall.

"*No!*" His cry filled the large room with haunting resonance. The old man dropped a carton of milk. The dog scampered back to the counter and began licking up the spillage. "There must be a mistake..." Radcliff pleaded. "She's not the type to give up. She had too much to live for. Did she regain consciousness?" He shouted at the phone receiver.

"I'm very sorry, Mr. Radcliff. The operation had been successful and her condition was stable. She was in recovery and heavily sedated. She must have deteriorated very rapidly. The post mortem will be held tomorrow, but I think she died from post traumatic shock. Sometimes the body can only take so much. I'm truly sorry, Mr. Radcliff. I can't tell you any more over the phone"

Her words had conflicted with all his instincts. He attempted to speak, his mouth opening ready to form the words he wanted to scream: '*She cannot be dead*!', but all he could breathlessly say was: "I'm in central Queensland! I'll...call you again... when I reach...erm... Rockhampton."

"If you come to the hospital I will arrange for a doctor to see you, Mr. Radcliff and explain everything to you. When you call you could also tell me if you would like to see Carmen in our chapel of rest."

"Thank you sister." He slowly hung up the phone and lifted himself from the wall.

Radcliff paid the old man, picked up the bar of chocolate and left the store. Stunned and fighting off his grief he started up the Torino and continued east along the dirt track called the Capricorn Highway. A road sign just outside Alpha showed 'Boguntungun 72 kms' 'Emerald 174 kms'.

He pulled off the roadside, blinded by tears, infuriated by the obscure town names, the distances and their direction. The Cross of Goa, the treasure and life itself was futile and meaningless without her. He hit the steering wheel repeatedly with the palms of his hands and screamed out her name until tears streamed down his face. He clenched the top of the steering wheel with both hands, let his face drop into his outstretched arms and sobbed.

Minutes elapsed before he could lift his head and gaze through watery eyes at the empty road ahead. The sky had lost most of its heavy cloud cover. With the brighter light he could think more clearly.

He needed to see her for himself and resolved to break his promise and head south from Rockhampton.

This decision boosted his spirits. He started up the Torino and continued east.

He drove through Grange with a few small houses, a general store, a garage and a bar lining the highway. A sign beyond the town indicated: 'Boguntungun 8 kms' 'Emerald 110 kms'.

Boguntungun was a collection of houses built on sections of about an acre cut into the gum forest and connected by a network of dirt tracks. Their bright red painted corrugated roofs contrasted starkly with the dark green foliage of the gum. The desolate houses looked forbidding and sinister with heavy mist hanging on the trees.

About 30 miles east of Boguntungun the dirt highway had a smart, new metalled surface. As he drove the smooth flat stretch of bitumen the sun burst out through a break in the clouds. Radcliff accelerated the Torino.

Five miles along the new road he saw, in the distance, a line of gum trees traversing the shallow valley between the hills to his left. They intersected the highway about a mile ahead of him then continued winding southward. As he approached the line of gums he could see a patch of surface water on the highway reflecting in the sunlight. He decided to open up the throttle of the Torino and burst through the puddle at high speed.

The red car smacked into a flooded creek as if it had hit a brick wall. The back of the Ford reared up perpendicular sending everything inside the car cascading on top of him. The rear splashed down pushing the Ford deeper into a raging flood of water. The gushing torrent was too strong, submerging the front end of the car and forcing it round to the right. Radcliff snatched up his bag, forced open the door and escaped.

Managing to wade back through the torrent he finally found shallower water and safety. Looking back he watched the Torino begin to move, slowly at first, then with increasing speed it hurtled downstream, the current holding it aloft like a trophy. The car listed to one side then flipped over completely before reaching a bend in the creek then disappeared from sight. He castigated himself bitterly for letting recklessness and stupidity cost him another friend.

Radcliff climbed the grass verge, sat in the shade of gum and emptied out the wet contents of his bag beside him. The diary was undamaged and perfectly dry inside the plastic bag. He caressed the shopping bags marked 'Eleanor's Boutique' splashed across both sides in yellow and red.

The sun continued to break through the thinning cloud, when it did it was searing hot. He threw the whiskey and gin bottles into the creek and took a long drink from a half full water bottle.

Propped against the tree trunk, flies and mosquitoes swarming around him he felt despair and hopelessness overwhelming him. He ripped a sleeve from one of his shirts and whisked the insects from his face despondently.

Radcliff remained as motionless as possible conserving his bodily fluids and energy. At dusk he refilled his bag with his dried clothes his passport diary and wallet and finally the melted bar of chocolate. Taking a mouthful of water he stuffed the quarter full water bottle into the bag and took his first step back in the direction of Boguntungun and the scarlet, fiery sunset.

He trudged on throughout the night. The cloudless southern night-sky was packed with a myriad of stars, so clear he could almost touch them. Each one shone with a surreal brightness, their combined effulgence illuminating the highway sufficiently to see his way but dim enough to conceal the deadly wildlife that crept, slithered, crawled and marched across Alex's path often within inches of his feet. A million frogs croaked choruses in and around as many puddles. Other creatures of the night joined in the nocturnal symphony with occasional bursts of eerie sounds.

Radcliff estimated that it would take him eight hours to reach the settlement and rationed himself to one gulp of water and a bite of chocolate each hour. He could have been back on his island with just the stars for company. His thoughts, as always, turned to Carmen. He could not accept her death; her spirit lived too strongly inside him.

Tottering drunkenly on rubbery legs he stopped for a drink. From the slope of a hill he could see dawn breaking on the eastern horizon. Savouring the sweetness of the chocolate in his mouth he continued on. The bottle was almost empty and he had just one piece of chocolate left. As the dawn intensified he could see the road rising and falling ahead of him. Reaching the summit of the next hill the first rays of the sun reflected on red corrugated roofs about a quarter of a mile ahead. He took the final sip of water and let his stride lengthen as he trudged down the slope.

Surmounting the next rise Radcliff saw, in the valley below, the first house of Boguntungun. It had two stories and stood to the left and well back from the highway.

Its roof had the typical red painted corrugated iron which extending as a first floor veranda over the main bedroom that faced the driveway; a wider veranda extended from the level of the first floor and surrounded the whole house.

Radcliff staggered the last few paces of the incline and leaned wirily on the gatepost. A heavily built middle-aged man, in neat navy blue shorts and white short-sleeved shirt, waved from the lower veranda of the house and beckoning him to enter.

Alex sagged, barely able to stand. His feet were swollen and sore and his legs were the weight of lead. Bracing himself by the gatepost he forced himself forward down the hundred-yard drive towards the house. Several dozen chickens clucked and pecked about him as he swayed and staggered towards the house.

The man at the house quickly climbed into the white open-back Toyota truck that was parked under the expansive carport next to the house, and drove up to him.

"You look all tuckered out, mate," lifting Radcliff like a baby onto the truck.

"Thanks," he croaked.

"My name's Rod Napier," he said cheerily climbing into the cab beside him. His heavily jelled jet-black hair glistened in the sunlight. It was brushed flat across his scalp with a clean straight parting. He reeked of cheep aftershave. "You'll be right once my Patsy sees to yer," giving Radcliff a warm smile.

At the house Radcliff lifted his heavy feet up the wooden steps onto the veranda.

"Sit yourself down in that chair over there," he said guiding Radcliff to a high-backed wooden chair.

A deeply tanned blonde woman appeared from the house and softly took Radcliff's other arm and eased him into the chair. She had smallish, sharp eyes set wide apart and a longish nose which had a very slight cleft at the tip.

Radcliff looked up but the glare of the morning sun shone directly into his eyes.

"Thanks very much," Radcliff said hoarsely, pulling his mouth into an appreciative smile.

"This is my wife, Patsy," Rod announced proudly.

She held out her hand. "Pleased to meet you, Mr...er...," her sensual, pink lips opened into a warm gleaming smile, revealing perfect white teeth.

"Alex Radcliff."

Her handshake was soft and warm.

"Get Alex some water, darlin'. Well, I was on my way to Grange," Rod smiled. "It's a bit of an emergency, so if you'll excuse me I'll leave you in my wife's capable hands. See yer later, eh!"

He kissed Patsy, adding, "I'll be back for lunch." Rod climbed into the Toyota and they watched it bounce down the long driveway, striped by the long shadows of the tall stringy bark gums that lined the eastern border of their plot. He waved from the cab as he turned left onto the highway.

"I'll bet you can use a cuppa-tea, Alex," she smiled, the skin under her freckled cheeks were flushed red. "Drink this first," handing him a large glass of cool water and turned back towards the door. Her whole body shimmered under the loose fitting low cut red and yellow flowered frock.

Patsy Napier was ten years younger than her husband. She was in full bloom.

Radcliff gulped down the water. Refreshed, he wiped his mouth with the back of his hand.

Patsy returned and handed Alex a mug of piping hot tea. Her frock fell forward as she leaned toward him. The sun glinted upon a small crucifix. She wore nothing underneath her frock and Radcliff saw the whole curvature of her ripe, freckled breasts that swayed heavily and enticingly with every movement she made. Her fair skin, pink from recent sunburn, had an even golden hue. She welcomed his interest and moved sensuously into her chair.

Politely averting his gaze he took two sugar cubes from the box and stirred his tea.

"Are you from England, Alex?" She raised a hand to shield her eyes from the glare of the sun.

He nodded and sipped his tea. "This…," he coughed to clear his throat, "…tea is excellent. Excellent!"

"What happened to you then, Alex? Are you on a trekking holiday?"

"I was on my way…" he croaked, "to Rockhampton. I crashed into a flooded creek."

"Theresa Creek has claimed many lives when it floods," she sighed waving several flies from her face. The edge of the veranda was just shading her eyes leaving the tip of her nose and full pink lips brilliantly lit by the rapidly rising sun. "It's a very long trek from Theresa creek. You rest up here until Rod gets back. He'll work something out and get you right."

Alex watched with fascination as the line of shadow moved rapidly below her chin. "Have you always lived here in this part of Queensland?"

"No. I'm from New Zealand. I'm a Kiwi through and through. Let me give you a word of advice, right now. Never mistake a Kiwi for an Aussie," she laughed. "Rod's a real Aussie. I met him at a trade fair in Auckland a year ago. He'll be back soon. He's gone to ol' Charlie

Murray's place." she smiled, liking the intensity of the Englishman's interest. "Charlie runs a Milk Bar in Grange. The storm damaged his solar panels. My Rod'll fix it, that's for shore."

She continued talking to Radcliff, her soft, mellow voice soothing his mind. She was telling him a tale of a 'bomb', an intense weather system that hits Wellington from the southern ocean, when his head slumped forward, still clutching his mug of half full of tea. She gently took the mug from him and went inside, preventing the fly door from slamming shut with her hip.

# CHAPTER 27

That Thursday morning, in Barcaldine, Central Queensland, a black Mitsubishi Pajero, with black polarized windows, had turned slowly and menacingly into a garage forecourt and stopped by the furthest pump from the kiosk. The four men got out and stretched their limbs. They were all dressed alike: black combat trousers fastened into the tops of heavy military boots, black vests, an abundance of gold hung from their necks and ears and adorned their fingers and wrists. Their shaven heads reflected the early morning sun.

"Fill 'er up, Apeson. You two come with me," Slaughter commanded with the deep-throated grunt of a silver back gorilla.

Craig Swaine watched the three men approach his kiosk. He was in his late teens and alone at the station. His father and every other able bodied man in Barcaldine had gone to dig out the landslip on the road north of town. Craig's middleweight boxing trophies were proudly displayed in a cabinet next to the CCTV screen above the counter.

"Good-day," Craig greeted the men cheerfully as they swaggered towards him.

"'Ave you seen this person?" Slaughter growled holding a dog-eared picture of Alex Radcliff up to Craig's nose, irritated by the country boy's lack of respect.

Craig pulled back, as if dodging a punch, to focus on the picture. "No. Sorry sir. I haven't."

"You on your own, son?" Slaughter asked mockingly. "This place is like a ghost town."

"Everyone's up the road digging out the landslip."

"What by hand? With picks and shovels?"

"The machines can't get through until it dries out. A bulldozer and two trucks are trapped up there already." Craig switched off the pump. "That will be thirty two dollars fifty, please."

"Is there another road north?" Slaughter barked.

"The only way north is by plane, sir. Or you can go across to Rockhampton and follow the Bruce Highway up."

Slaughter contemptuously slapped thirty-two dollars onto the counter and walked out.

"The road's blocked," Slaughter grunted to Apeson through clenched teeth. The huge man began to pace up and down beside their vehicle.

"I still think we should've got another chopper, boss?"

"I'll do the thinking, Apeson," he yelled stabbing Apeson in the chest with his index finger. "You just listen and do as I tell yer. Get in the motor, all of yer." Slaughter climbed behind the steering wheel. The Pajero burst into life and he furiously floored the throttle. All four wheels span on the tar-mac, screeching and skidding, enveloping the forecourt in blue smoke. The Pajero rocked back onto the highway, turned right, tyres squealing, onto the Capricorn Highway.

"That *fucker* Radcliff will be in Rockhampton by now," Slaughter yelled above the roar of the engine. 'He must 'ave veered off some-where," banging his heavy palms on the steering wheel. "Well, he's lucks goin' to run out soon, and when it does...! He's made fools of ya twice! You three are the most useless piles of shit I've ever come across!" What are ya?" He hollered.

"Useless piles of shit, boss," they answered in unison.

"If you let Radcliff get away again I'll cut off your balls and feed 'em to yer. Do you read me?"

"Loud and clear, boss," they shouted in unison.

# CHAPTER 28

Radcliff was jolted from his sleep by the telephone ringing. Immediately he thought of Carmen: 'the hospital…there's been an error... she is alive.'

A woman's voice answered. What she said was unintelligible to him but he sensed alarm in her tone.

Patsy came out onto the veranda, her face pale and tense. The fly door slammed shut behind her.

"That was Rod. There's been an accident. Someone has smashed into the rear of Rod's truck. He said that he was reversing out of a parking bay onto the highway when a black 4 X 4 hit him…the bugger didn't stop neither." She looked furiously and anxiously at Radcliff.

"Were there any witnesses?" Radcliff asked tentatively.

"No. It happened too fast. Rod said that it was a black Mitsubishi Pajero. It had blackened windows. It was going so fast... he couldn't even get the licence plate number. Rod said that the force of the impact had smashed Rod's wagon around ninety degrees wrecking the nearside rear wheel."

"Is he hurt?"

"He sounds a bit shaken up but no injuries, thank God. He's changing the wheel now."

Hawkins and Omollo had travelled hard and fast, reaching Alpha before midday of that Thursday. Following Radcliff's trail had been easy. After taking a left turn, after Charlieville, they followed the Landsborough Highway to Tambo. Everyone they had asked at road junctions and garages remembered seeing the bullet-holed red and white Torino:

"I seen that car!" an elderly pump attendant had chuckled at a garage in Tambo. "I says to Burt, I says: 'World War Three must a' started!' it was that drilled full o' holes! He seemed to know where he was a headin', that's for sure. After filling up here 'e took the Dawson Development Road. Most of 'em keep on to Barcaldine. He must have known that the roads blocked up there. He'll 'ave kept on goin' at Windeyer, up the Alpha-Tambo Road. Yer can't miss it."

Just after midday, Hawkins was at the wheel heading east along the Capricorn Highway, when a black Mitsubishi Pajero loomed up fast in the side mirror and came out to overtake. Hawkins noticed that the nearside front wing was badly dented and the shiny animal protection bars had been buckled. The black paintwork on the wing had been scraped clean in places with traces of white paint caught in the creases.

"It's them, Omollo!" Hawkins shouted as the black Pajero roared past and faded into the distance. "Let's go get 'em!"

Patsy paced up and down in front of Radcliff, her arms folded biting the nails of her right hand.

"He wants me to get the license plate number of the Pajero as it goes past our place."

"I'll come with you." Radcliff levered his stiff body from the chair and picked up his bag. She waited for him at the base of the steps. Emerging from the protection of the veranda the scorching sun burned the side of his head.

They walked slowly, and in silence, to the end of the plot and stood under a gum next to the wooden fence and waited.

Radcliff could hear the distant roar of an engine being driven hard. Then it appeared fleetingly, like a black bug, on the crest of a hill and then vanished from view. The growling engine was getting louder by the second. Moments later it mounted the next rise and then the sinister looking monster was bounding down the slope towards them. Sensing instinctively who was in the vehicle he turned away and faced the house.

Within a split of second the Pajero was gone. Patsy repeated the licence plate number over and over to herself as they walked back towards the house. Half way down the driveway they both heard the sound of another vehicle approaching. Patsy ran back to the fence, with Radcliff hobbling behind. He got there just as a green Range Rover flashed by. He had seen the driver and passenger distinctly, but could hardly believe his eyes.

"That was the New South Wales police!" She looked incredulously at Radcliff, raising her arms in disbelief. Patsy relaxed considerably as they waited by the fence. Rod eventually appeared in his white Toyota ten minutes later.

Patsy ran to meet him at the gate. Radcliff followed. By the time he had reached them Patsy had finished her résumé of what had occurred.

"The New South Wales police...after hit and run merchants! My arse!" Rod pummelled the steering wheel with the palm of his hand. "There's more to this, darlin'....," Rod shook his head. "I'm going to the creek...," he announced, "...they won't be able to cross...I want to be there when they catch those bastards. I'll take you with me Alex. You've got your bag with yer. You never know we might be able to get you across the creek and on your way to Rockhampton. I'll need me gun. Hop in," pulling Patsy up beside him. Radcliff climbed in beside her.

"Leave your gun, Rod!" she pleaded. "You won't need it with the police there to take care of things."

"Just a precaution, darlin'. Don't worry. I'll be okay. Alex'll be with me." At the house Rod ran indoors, reappearing seconds later with a shotgun and a box of ammunition.

"Thanks for the tea, and…. everything." Radcliff kissed Patsy on the cheek.

"It was good to meet you. Take good care of yourself, Alex Radcliff. And make sure he doesn't do anything stupid!"

She shot Rod an anxious glare.

"He'll he okay," Radcliff smiled reassuringly. He resolved to tell Rod about himself before they reached the creek.

She looked across at Rod. "For God's sake be careful, Rod Napier! Promise me!"

He nodded once and blew her a kiss.

As they turned right out of the driveway Radcliff waved to her but she had already gone indoors.

# CHAPTER 29

On the day Radcliff had telephoned Sydney General Hospital, that Wednesday morning from Bill Thompson's place in Alpha, the Casualty Department had been in complete turmoil and chaos.

A small rest room on the ground floor had been converted into a television news studio. A Channel Nine reporter, clutching a microphone, had been roaming the corridors with her entourage of camera and sound crews and other technicians.

Every available space in the lower floors of the hospital was filled with injured people in beds, stretchers, wheels chairs or lying on the floor. Doctors, nurses and porters weaved around or stepped over the bloody hoards attending to those in a critical condition.

The young dark haired news reporter, her pretty face creased with expressions of compassion and horror from the carnage before her clasped a microphone with a 'Channel 9' tag fixed to the stem. She had positioned herself next to three badly injured people holding loose, blood soaked bandages over lacerations, their clothing splattered and stained with dried blood.

"This is probably the worst accident in the whole of Australia's history," she read in a high-pitched nasal accent from the scripted T.V. monitor. "The scene this bright sunny morning in south Sydney resembles a battle zone. We understand that the Police were pursuing a hi-jacked lorry. The occupants were seen to jump from the cab, abandoning the lorry as is crossed the flyover. It happened at 6 o'clock this morning as people were travelling to work."

A monitor showed an aerial view of the flyover with queues of emergency vehicles lined up on the highway, blue and red lights flashing in the dawn light, the traffic snarled up in every direction.

"The lorry had ploughed across the central reservation," the reporter continued, "and smashed into an oncoming coach. Both vehicles tumbled down the steep embankment onto the railway line."

The injured close to the rest room could see the whole report on TV monitors as it was being broadcast. The editor cut to another camera on the railway embankment. Carriages were piled on top of one another, broken twisted track and burning wreckage covered the area along the railway line, under the flyover and beyond.

"The coach had landed right side up on the track and, miraculously, many of the passengers inside had managed to escape before the Canberra express, which had missed the red light, thundered into the coach and the lorry. The coach and the lorry were shunted a half a mile along the track before everything exploded into a fireball."

The aerial view showed a mangled mess of carriages, locomotives and burned out wreckage plied up a few yards before a road bridge.

"Sixty people have been reported dead so far, including the drivers of the train and the coach. The figure is expected to rise. All the injured have been taken to Sydney General. The number to telephone if you wish to make enquires after relatives and friends will be given a bit later."

A porter, who had been put in charge of ferrying the dead to the mortuary in the lower basement level, punched a number into his mobile phone.

"Sister? This is Cameron. We have a major problem down here. The mortuary is full and I have five bodies lined up in the stairwell and by the lifts! What shall I do?"

"Hold on a moment," the Sister on Stevenson Ward answered and checked her computer. She gave the porter a list of four names and waited for him to repeat them back to her. "All of those people," she directed, "can be moved to the store room. I'll get someone to empty it. The fifth one, Ms. Carmen Burgos, could be prepared for the chapel. I'll get one of my staff to move her up there to the first floor."

It had been ten minutes since the Sister on Stevenson Ward had spoken to Radcliff. She called one of the newly recruited nurses into her office.

"Collect Ms. Burgos from mortuary please nurse and take her to room M170. I will tell them you are on your way."

It was Nurse Carol Dimmock's first day. Eager to escape the blood and carnage surrounding her she gratefully took the lift down to the mortuary. She pushed open the swing doors and entered the long bare room.

Before her, in two neat rows, were twenty beds each bearing a sheet-covered corpse. The swing doors flapped back and forth behind her then there was silence. An eerie quiet unnerved the young nurse.

Seeing death en mass for the first time, Nurse Dimmock moved quickly up the first row checking the nametags tied to each big toe. Turning back down the next row, the second tag had the name 'Carmen Burgos'.

She needed all her strength to start her macabre load moving down the central aisle. The bed quickly gathered momentum. She tried to stop it, her feet skidding on the smooth floor, bringing the bed to a stop just before the swing doors. But, under inertia the corpse continued moving forward, sliding on the sheet, until its feet hit the end of the metal bed frame.

Nurse Dimmock was struggling to get the bed rolling and steer it through the doors when she froze in horror.

The head of the corpse, still covered by a white sheet, rose up slowly.

The nurse was transfixed, her mouth gawping wide and her eyes ready to pop out from their sockets.

The body, supported by one arm, turned onto its left side and the sheet slid to the floor. The right shoulder of the middle aged woman and her right thigh were heavily bandaged.

The woman's eyes opened. She coughed, pointing to the sheet.

The nurse's fortitude abandoned her and she bolted out of the room, bursting through the swing doors, her terrified screams echoing up the stairwell and through the corridors.

Unable to recover the sheet, Carmen lay on her back trying to comprehend where she was and what was happening to her.

Moments later the Sister appeared at the swing doors. She warily approached Carmen, tentatively took her wrist, felt for a pulse then hastily stooped and picked up the sheet and covered Carmen's nudity.

Carmen's confusion intensified when the Sister apologised to her profusely with an expression of utter distress.

Then a porter entered and helped the Sister move Carmen into the bathroom on Stevenson Ward. A bloodied doctor was already inside waiting to examine her. From the cagey answers to her questions Carmen was able to piece together what had occurred.

Twenty-four hours later an elderly, exhausted consultant doctor finally came to see Carmen on the ward.

"I am amazed how well your wounds have healed. Especially after that…erm…bit of confusion yesterday." Doctor Bagshot said with a carefree smile.

"Confusion! Hombré! Incompetence is the correct word, Doctor! *I was amongst dead people…*!"

"I'm very sorry," he humbly wrung his hands. "We've had extreme difficulties here. You must understand…"

"I understand alright. This is gross negligence, doctor! How could this happen. I am recovering perfectly well from an operation and someone in your staff thought I had died. Doesn't anyone check up when a decision like that is made?"

"We are very sorry. I know how angry…"

"Angry! It's hardly the word I would describe how I feel. You must contact my fiancé. You must find him and tell him…"

"Yes. I know Sister is looking into that right now. When he phoned the hospital yesterday he said that he was in central Queensland. It's a very big state…"

"Don't patronise me, Doctor. You have a police force, don't you? My fiancé isn't just an ordinary tourist!" She looked away in disgust and exasperation. "When can I leave?"

"A healthy woman like you. I'd say four to six weeks."

"Qué! Hombré! That's impossible. I'm feeling fine."

"Much of your muscular tissue in your right shoulder has been lost. As I said before, your recovery is exceptional, but you will need regular treatment. It is imperative that you have the right therapy or you could lose the use of that arm completely. There will always be a weakness there..."

"I must be discharged within a week, doctor," Carmen demanded emphatically, her anger growing. She calmed herself, softening the look in her eyes and smiled at him warmly.

"I'm sure you'll be willing to arrange with the Sister that I have a rapid course in therapy and maybe put me on a special muscle building diet? It's very important that I rejoin my fiancé as soon as possible."

Bagshot considered for a second, aware that if the media were to acquire her story it could seriously jeopardise the extra Government funding earmarked for the hospital next year.

"Please doctor," she purred.

"I'll speak to sister on my way out."

# CHAPTER 30

At Theresa Creek later that Thursday afternoon the black Mitsubishi Pajero stood before the gushing waters like a stranded bug. The flooded creek, inundated by further rainfall on the hills north west of Emerald, had evolved into a foaming swirling organic mass of fluid ochre gathering up uprooted trees, branches, dead livestock and other clutter within its bulk as it twisted and snaked across the terrain.

Slaughter leaned against the Pajero, its engine idling throatily, watching the torrent rage before him. The afternoon sun burned down upon his bald scalp. Irritably he waved away the flies swarming about his face.

Hawkins stopped the Range Rover 100 yards before the creek overlooking the Pajero. He disengaged the gears and silently applied the handbrake leaving the engine to tick over. Grabbing a bag from the rear seat he searched urgently for the handguns and boxes of ammunition.

Omollo watched in awe as Hawkins checked and loaded both Browning HP weapons with practiced efficiency and applied the safety catches. A hand gun and several rounds of ammunition were thrust into his lap.

"These are the people we are after…I'm sure of it…" Hawkins stated excitedly, meeting Omollo's searching eyes.

Omollo wanted to speak but his tongue had attached itself to the roof of his mouth.

"Take the wheel…" Hawkins commanded.

As they changed seats Omollo's clammy hands slipped on the steering wheel.

"The old girl at the pub said there were four of 'em…the others must be searching the area. We've got the element of surprise…a great bonus…but we can't take them all in one go…we'll have to take them out one by one. One of 'em will be sent up to smell us out. If I'm right and I'm forced to open fire, you will have to be ready to reverse at top speed the moment he drops."

Hawkins noticed Omollo's huge eyes bulge to the size of golf balls.

"Well, I might miss with my first shot," he added with a wry smile.

Two men emerged from the trees on the northern bank of the creek.

"The current is worse up stream, boss." Apeson yelled running to the Pajero. Brent joined him a moment later. Both stood before their leader, breathless and dripping with sweat waiting for further orders. Apeson spotted the Rover over Slaughter's left shoulder.

"We've got company," nodding his head in the direction of the Rover.

Slaughter slowly turned and raised the high-powered military binoculars hanging around his neck.

Fox emerged from the trees on the south side of the road.

"Boss!" he called out. "There's an upturned red and white sports car lodged in a tree further down-stream…"

Apeson frantically waved his arm at Fox signalling him to keep quiet.

Fox watched Slaughter focusing his glasses on the green vehicle back up the road.

Slaughter recognised both men in the Rover instantly.

"Go and see what they want, Fox," Slaughter grunted with the binoculars held tight against his brows. 'The sacrifice of a pawn to force the coppers to make their play…their last,' he thought.

"If they make a move, nail the one in the passenger seat first," he barked as Fox marched up the slight incline towards the Rover, his automatic weapon aimed at the Rover, the safety catch off. Slaughter waved his arm at Apeson and Brent. "You two…don't just stand there like a couple of spare fucking pricks at a bar mitzvah…get in…at the double."

Slaughter watched and waited.

Fox had covered over half the distance to the Rover when he saw the driver's left shoulder dip. 'He could be engaging a gear,' he reasoned. He waited for the Rover to move forward. It remained stationery. The passenger's head emerged from the window.

"Police…drop your weapon." Hawkins screamed.

Fox levelled his gun.

Next there was a puff of smoke from the side of the Rover. Fox dropped to his knees, his reflexes pulling his finger on the trigger. A burst of gunfire shot harmlessly into the road. Fox fell onto his face, his gun clattering onto the hard surface.

There was an instant of absolute silence.

"Shit!" Slaughter shouted as he clambered into his vehicle. He spun the Pajero around, tyres squealing and accelerated in pursuit of the reversing Rover. Apeson and Brent opened up with continuous fire leaning out of the rear windows.

"Wait until I'm closer, you dumb idiots," he yelled as the Pajero began to narrow the gap.

Omollo was half turned in his seat maintaining a dead straight line along the centre of the road.

The gunfire had ceased but the Pajero had reduced the gap to forty yards. Hawkins considered hanging a hand brake turn when Apeson and

Brent recommenced firing.

Bullets hit the ground, pinged and clunked off the bodywork, peppered the windscreen, thudded into the roof and smashed through the rear window.

Hawkins spotted a white vehicle approaching about a mile back up the road. Several bullets skimmed both detectives' cheeks. Hawkins ducked below the dash board as Omollo remained upright keeping the Rover on a straight line.

The barrage of bullets was unceasing.

Hawkins gingerly raised his head above the level of the dashboard. The Pajero was visible in the right corner of the shattered windscreen. He took careful aim at its offside front tyre and fired two shots. The Pajero immediately veered to its right with Slaughter fighting to keep control, all tyres screeching across the road surface. Blue smoke enveloped them. The gunfire ceased.

"Omollo…can you spin her round?"

He selected neutral for all wheels then pulled on the handbrake whilst simultaneously turning the steering wheel sharply right. The rear wheels locked and the front end skidded 180 degrees to the left. Immediately engaging second gear he released the handbrake and rammed his foot on the accelerator. The rear wheels screeched on the road surface and blue smoke billowed up from under the car.

"Yah—ho-oo-oo-! Yes, indeadee…!" Hawkins slapped the outside of the door. A flock of startled red and yellow rosettes burst from the canopy of gum. "Wow! Well done my friend!" Hawkins slapped Omollo heartily on the back. "How many times have you done that!"?

"You don't want to know the answer to that, sir." Omollo grinned toothily.

Rod Napier had been listening to Radcliff's revelations when they heard gunfire then saw smoke rising up from one of the vehicles ahead. A Range Rover drew alongside their truck, the driver signalling for Rod to stop.

"Radcliff..!" Hawkins shouted in amazement.

Omollo's mouth dropped open.

"You know these men?" Rod asked incredulously.

"Yes…I'm afraid so…," Radcliff's eyes met Rod's. "…I was just about to tell you that they are here because of me." Rod's dumbfounded gaze went back and forth from Hawkins and Radcliff. "I'm supposed to be under their protection," Radcliff explained awkwardly.

"Never mind the introductions, Radcliff," Hawkins snapped. "Get your troublesome arse over here."

Radcliff slammed the door of the truck. He caught Rod's bewildered expression. "I'll explain everything some day. Thanks Rod for everything. Get back to Patsy."

"That's right, sir. We've had serious trouble back there," Hawkins advised. Radcliff climbed onto the Rover, sweeping the broken glass off the back seat with his arm.

"Those buggers smashed into me earlier today," Rod called out. "I've got a shotgun here and I'm prepared to use it."

They all heard the Mitsubishi advancing. It was 600 yards away and accelerating. Bullets smacked into the road then they heard the rattle of machinegun fire.

Rod put the Toyota into a U-turn and chased the Rover with bullets ricocheting and whizzing off the tailgate of his truck.

Hawkins listened as Radcliff shouted above the noise of the engine, giving a brief account of how Rod Napier had become involved.

"We have to get him out of this," Radcliff demanded.

"I agree. Slow up a bit Omollo and wave him past. When he goes by make sure he understands that he must take the first turning off the highway."

Rod gratefully moved to overtake the Rover with the Pajero gaining fast. Slaughter had reducing the gap to 200 yards and the gunfire was unceasing. The Toyota drew level with the Rover.

"Get off the road …at the…next turning," Omollo yelled at Rod.

Rod nodded and sped away. Omollo's zigzagging protective cover was allowing the Pajero to gain ground on them.

Rod took the first right turn, knowing the track through the gum trees, and spun the truck round to face the highway. Hidden by thick bush and with the engine idling Rod rapidly loaded both barrels of his shotgun. His ambush was set.

The Rover passed his hiding place then he heard the Mitsubishi approaching at speed. He rammed the Toyota into second gear and charged between the trees and over the saplings, out onto the highway.

He burst out of the bush like a leaping white knight. Leaning out the driver's window he skilfully fired both barrels single-handed catching the Pajero broadside. He grabbed the wheel as the Toyota smashed into the steep camber. The truck leapt into the air and landed bouncing in the centre of the road. Rod slammed his foot on the brakes locking the four wheels screeching skidding diagonally along the surface. He reloaded his gun.

Two white cockatoos flew out of the gums opposite the Toyota squawking and beating their wings frantically for altitude.

The Pajero had skidded to a halt 15 yards further up the highway.

Slaughter had glimpsed the white truck out the corner of his eye but had no time to take evasive action. His bulletproof window had been raised shielding him from the gunshots but Apeson's head was almost blown off and Brent had been hit in the back. When Slaughter had braked Brent had been tossed onto the floor, groaning in agony.

"Get up and fight you bastard." Slaughter commanded as he wrestled to free the gun from Apeson's dead grip. Brent pulled himself up as Rod prepared to ram the Mitsubishi. Slaughter and Brent fired repeatedly at the driver. Brent collapsed, dying in agony with blood oozing from his torn back.

Rod had been hit three times and slumped onto the steering wheel. The Toyota swerved to the right, careered down the steep camber and crashed into a gum.

Omollo had made a U-turn and was racing back to the ambush scene.

With the Rover 150 yards away Slaughter lowered his window, took aim and fired twenty rounds at the approaching vehicle. The Rover kept coming straight at him. In a desperate bid to escape, Slaughter rammed the Pajero into gear and accelerated at full power emptying the magazine at the Rover as he swerved past.

With bullets slamming into the Rover, Hawkins head crashed against the door window and his limp body slid to the floor. Omollo braked hard and swerved to the left, skidding down the camber in a cloud of dust. The Rover slued to a halt in a cloud of dust just before smashing into a tree.

Omollo leaned over to his friend and held two fingers on a spot under Hawkins' left jaw willing the flesh to pulsate. There was nothing. One bullet had caught him in the forehead. Gently he closed his eyelids.

Radcliff opened the passenger door from the outside to see Omollo's distraught face staring in disbelief at the inert, lifeless body that had been his boss, his hero and his friend.

Radcliff touched Omollo's convulsing shoulders. Tears dripped from Omollo's chin. Radcliff wondered how many more were doomed to die protecting him. Then he remembered Rod Napier. He sprinted the 100 yards separating them from the smoking Toyota.

The windscreen was shattered. Rod's bloody head was slumped on the steering wheel. He was covered in tiny fragments of glass. The right side of Rod's shirt was soaked in blood. He carefully eased his unconscious body onto the passenger seat, then got behind the steering wheel himself and turned the ignition key. The engine fired, engulfing the truck in thick black smoke. He reversed away from the tree, bent the buckled bonnet flat then drove slowly towards the Rover.

"You hurry on," Omollo called out having noticed Napier's condition. "I'll follow you."

Radcliff depressed the accelerator pedal and the Toyota responded readily. He saw the Rover slowly turning in the rear view mirror.

Having seen the battered Pajero hurtle past her house six minutes earlier, Patsy was waiting at the top of the drive fearing the worst when Radcliff arrived.

She cradled her husband bloody torso in her lap as Radcliff raced the Toyota back to Alpha. She directed Radcliff to the Gordon Street District Hospital.

Omollo followed with Hawkins' body laid flat on the back seat.

# CHAPTER 31

Alex Radcliff and John Omollo had taken two rooms at the Grand Hotel on the main street, Barcaldine. It was Thursday night. Radcliff sat at a circular bar staring deeply into a tumbler half full of whiskey. Omollo was in the lobby making several long distance telephone calls. Radcliff gulped the whiskey and ordered another.

The Hotel was four stories high, the Victorian architecture similar to many Bayswater guesthouses in the West End of London. The interior design was lavish, an abundance of white leather furniture with thick, bulging scatter cushions, carefully positioned to optimise comfort for the maximum number of guests; the bar was imitation light oak with gilt trimmings and the décor was light beige with a deep red sumptuous carpets throughout. Crystal chandeliers adorned most of the ceilings. The one under which Radcliff sat covered the whole bar like a sparkling roof of light, its crystal droplets pleasantly tinkling as three giant fans on the ceiling gently aerated the great room.

Omollo entered the bar and sat on the stool next to Radcliff and ordered a tomato juice. He looked about approvingly and reached for his drink. "To the future," he beamed lifting his glass.

"To the future," Radcliff responded raising his glass of whiskey, their glasses clinking firmly together.

They sat in silence for a few minutes.

"Chief Inspector Hawkins and me…" Omollo began, grinning widely, his eyes filling with tears, "…we stayed at the same Hotel as you in Cunnamulla. He…he saw your name…in the register. Do you remember…that woman?" Omollo asked forcing a laugh.

"Yes," Radcliff smiled. "She called me a 'mad pommy bastard'!"

"She didn't think much of Charlie…Chief Inspector Hawkins, either," forcing a laugh, his emotions running deeper than he knew. "Australian beer…it's very strong… apparently …" stretching a taught grin tighter across his teeth, his eye brows unusually high. "These people drink beer from very small glasses." He chuckled with tears falling over his bulging cheeks. "He was very thirsty, you see. …"

"I know." Radcliff gazed into his glass, feeling the big man's pain. "I was initiated into Aussie beer in the same way."

"He drank too many too quickly…" His head sank, tears oozing from tightly clenched eyelids. He sat quietly wiping his eyes with his fingers. "He was a great man, Alex…he was a legend in the force. His wife has taken the news very badly." He paused for a second. "The Yard," he said slowly, "want me to remain with you …to see it through…until these assassins are caught or killed." Omollo looked straight at Radcliff, his expression open and earnest. "I wanted you to know that right away, Alex. As you can see I'm very new to fieldwork. You can object if you want to."

"The Chief Inspector held you in very high esteem, John. I could see that. He was a tough character so it wouldn't have been easy to earn his favour!" Radcliff added with raised eyebrows. Looking into his drink he stated: "I'm in two minds whether to carry on or not. Without Carmen…" he paused shaking his head, "…. I still can't bring myself to believe that she's gone… without her, John…well it all seems so *bloody* futile! I gave her my word that I would go back to the island and get…" He raised his head and faced Omollo. "I've found a very important thing, John, buried on the island. My last promise to her was that I'd go to the island and retrieve it on my own."

"Then you have to go back. You must go back to the island, Alex. I'll help you to get this…thing."

"You'll be risking your life. For what..? To help me win a war! I'm an aging, misguided artist who should know better! Too many people have died because of me. I don't want you on my conscience as well! Go home, John. That's my advice. You've got your whole life in front of you."

"You will go back to the island, then?"

"Probably. I'm going to Sydney first…" he emptied the contents of his glass and ordered another. "If these devils are still after me they'll most likely finish me off on the island. That's my fate, John. Not yours."

"I've a duty to the force. I've also a greater duty to the memory of… my friend…. Charles Hawkins. You forget, Alex. This is my job. Every last one of these people must be brought to justice. I've got to do this for him. You see that, don't you Alex?"

"They'll come in greater strength and numbers. It'll be just the two of us against a well equipped army."

"Davy Crocket and James Bowie..?"

"But that was the Alamo, and they all died, John!"

"Their names live forever, though! In my faith it's the noblest thing a man can do…. to give up his life for another man and for Allah."

"Okay, John. You win," holding up his hands submissively. "It'll be a rough ride, young man! I can promise you that."

"Oh, I believe you, Alex. But Charles Hawkins was an inspiration and I feel his strength inside me now. I'll be fighting as two men!" Omollo grinned, then his face creased up into a magical smile. "You were held under police protection…but now I'll be needing your protection…when we meet and face these devils in battle. I think these killers…Ya!..a..ah…a ah. Eh!.he.he." The big man doubled up with laughter, slapped the bar with his enormous hand.

His infectious, wheezing laugh began to affect Radcliff. He started chuckling.

"They will be the ones needing protection…Eh!.he.he…Protection from *you!*" He screamed out laughing. Tears of sorrow and joy gushed freely from tightly closed eyes and rolled down his ebony cheeks.

Radcliff let the spirit of the moment take him too.

Both men swayed, sagged and shuddered with side splitting laughter.

"I haven't….lost….my temper yet!" Radcliff giggled.

"Heaven…help them…when you do," Omollo spluttered.

The two men stared into their drinks as the laughter abated. Radcliff shrewdly waited a few more seconds before speaking.

"It's only right that I tell you a little of what awaits you when we arrive on the island." He leaned closer to Omollo. "There's treasure..." he whispered "...a mountain of it!"

The whites of Omollo's eyes doubled in size. "Is that the 'object' you mentioned a moment ago?"

"No. The treasure is worth billions of pounds…" his whisper barely audible, "…but that pales into insignificance compared to this 'thing' I'm going back for. It's a Cross John. It's called the Cross of Goa. It could be the most important historical discovery ever made!"

"If it's that important to you, Alex," Omollo said amiably, "then you *must* have someone to help you."

They sat in silence, each reflecting on the events of the previous few days and nursing their wounds.

"Well, John," Radcliff said finally, "I could definitely sink a dozen more of these glasses of fire water but I've made some plans."

"Already..? Where will the field of battle be?"

"Not here!" He chuckled. "I must contact Sydney Hospital first. It all depends upon the outcome of that call…"

"It's about Carmen, isn't it? Why don't you do it now? Get this business laid to rest, Alex, once and for all."

"To be honest, John, I'm scared…I'd sooner have one more night of hope, rather than … She's alive, John. I know it!"

"Then the sooner you find out the better."

"Okay. You're right. I'll do it." Radcliff ordered another whiskey and drank half the contents of the tumbler.

"Good luck!" Omollo's enormous watery eyes glinted in the bright light from the chandelier. He watched him walk away, through the open lounge doors into the foyer.

When Radcliff reappeared he was holding onto the doorframe. He pushed himself into the room. Walking on legs of rubber, swaying and colliding with other hotel guests he staggered to Omollo and leaned gratefully against the bar.

Omollo waited for Radcliff to speak.

Radcliff lifted his half full glass, his gaze concentrated on its contents.

Omollo, fearing the worst, was ready to console his friend. "What happened…? Is she…?"

Radcliff turned and looked Omollo in the eye, his face slowly creasing up into a broad grin. "There was a mix up at the hospital," Radcliff said, barely able to restrain his elation. "She's recovering remarkable well, they said. I'll be able to speak to her tomorrow." He held up his drink clasping Omollo with his other arm wrapped firmly around his great shoulders. "Thank God for her! And thank God for you, John!" He finished his drink and slammed the glass on the counter. "I want to get to Darwin as fast as possible."

"Okay. I'll have a talk with the local constabulary in the morning."

"Good." Radcliff slapped the big man on the back as he stood up. "Well, let's turn in."

Their breakfast table was bathed in morning sunlight that flooded into the long, cheerfully decorated dining room through five sash windows running the length of the wall. Bunches of imitation spring flowers cascaded from hanging baskets positioned between each window. Despite its spaciousness and a high ceiling, the designer had retained a sense of intimacy by skilfully giving it an atmosphere of an English tearoom.

The two men sat next to the French windows overlooking the sun scorched back garden. Omollo listened intently as Radcliff gave a brief account of his exploits since arriving in Australia. He sat gazing into his empty coffee cup, shaking his head incredulously.

A waiter handed Omollo a folded piece of paper.

He looked up at Radcliff, his face lighting up. "The local police have found a witness. They want us over at the police station right now."

Outside the glare of the morning sun was blinding and the air in the main street was already as hot as a furnace. Hurrying under the covered walkways they entered the police station. Constable H.D. Curtis greeted the Englishmen and ushered them into his office.

Craig Swaine had confidently given a full, clear description of Slaughter and his men. The local press were busily taking photographs of the local hero standing beside his proud father and Constable Curtis.

"The burnt out wreck of the Mitsubishi has been found," Curtis stated. "A rancher close to Alpha reported it. He saw a fire on his station. Looking through his binoculars he said that he saw a helicopter land where the fire was raging and pick someone up."

Radcliff waved to Rod Napier and his wife Patsy seated near the entrance and went over to them whilst Omollo took Curtis to one side.

Rod stood up immediately, crimson flecks showed through the bandages around his head and neck, his right arm strapped tightly in a sling.

"My God, Alex!" he shouted, his tone and manner a mixture of betrayal and concern. "What the hell are you mixed up in?" He held out his left hand for Radcliff to shake.

Patsy stood up, stony faced. Omollo strode over to them but remained respectfully at a distance, a few paces behind Radcliff.

Patsy lashed out hysterically and uncontrollably, firing endless questions at Radcliff, none of which he could ever hope to answer. His silence infuriated her still further. She stepped up her verbal attack. Radcliff waited, absorbing the tirade fully aware that whatever he was to say to her would have little effect. She could never understand: Why hit men were out to kill him? Why they had almost killed Carmen? Why he was desperately trying to get back to an island in the Indian Ocean and recover the Cross of Goa and a priceless hoard of treasure? But her harangue was unceasing. With every verbal swipe that she made intensified his feelings of betrayal, duplicity and mendaciousness.

Radcliff held Omollo back as he stepped forward to intercede.

Rod looked on in silence until she finally, broke down, exhausted, into tears of anguish, anger and frustration.

"I'm so sorry." Radcliff bowed his head, choked, also close to tears. 'How many more deaths?' he pleaded silently to God. Was he worth all of this misery, he wondered.

Rod took her in his arms. "She'll be right, Alex. She's had one hell of a fright. You can't blame yourself for what happened, Alex."

Radcliff looked up slowly meeting Rod's apologetic eyes.

"It makes no difference that you came to our house that day...that Pajero would have smashed into my wagon, just the same. I would have blundered into these gunmen and probably got myself killed." He smiled. "You saved my life, in a way."

"That's very kind of you, Rod." Radcliff squeezed Rod's good shoulder warmly. "I'll never forget your kindness and help. I only hope that someday I'll be able to repay you both."

As they were leaving the police station, Curtis confirmed that an aircraft had been provided to take them both to Darwin that afternoon.

"I'm going to phone the hospital, John."

# PART THREE

# CHAPTER 32

It had been eleven days since the Clive Norton-Smythe murder and the first attempt on Radcliff's life. Pierre Droux navigated the luxury yacht for the final time through the reef encompassing Coetivy Island, which was 225 miles south, south east of Mahé and part of the southern Seychelles archipelago

The yacht was one of the latest in the Duchess type. She was just over 75 feet in length, a beam of 18 feet, a draft of 4 feet 3 inches and a displacement of 75 tonnes. The lines of her black hull curved with sensuous elegance; her steeply raked white superstructure was embellished by a sleek black tapering line from the bridge down its starboard and port sides that concealed its tinted windows of the bridge and lounge.

The Frenchmen had secured the purchase on the Tuesday, the day after their arrival on Mahé. From the moment Pierre had heard her twin 2000hp diesel engines growl he was smitten. Their hired crew of three loaded their provisions, weapons and explosives on board whilst Pierre painted the name 'Santa Lucia' on her stern. Jean-Claude supervised the filling of her twin 8,400-litre tanks with diesel fuel.

Safely through the reef Pierre set course at full speed. Her pointed jutting black hull cut through the surf with the menacing deadliness of a great white shark. Sea spray burst high over her lustrous white superstructure leaving Coetivy Island receding fast in its wake; ahead lay the vast Indian Ocean.

Norton-Smythe had given Jean-Claude the first clue where Radcliff's island was located; at Victoria library the Frenchmen found newspaper reports of Radcliff's rescue which reduced the search area to within a 500 square mile block of Indian Ocean, 150 miles east of Coetivy. They divided the area into ten boxes drawn onto a transparent grid, each box represented 2 miles by 25 miles. Eight of the boxes had been cross hatched through.

That Saturday morning the last two boxes marked on Pierre's grid remained to be searched. These were the most distant from Coetivy. Weather conditions were perfect, although a storm was forecast later that evening. Pierre's hopes were running high.

Pierre Droux was in his element. The sea was in his blood. He had traced his lineage, on his mother's side, through a long line of mariners to the Portuguese Captain-General, Alfonso Antonio Rodriguez. The

Portuguese Naval College in Lisbon had been named after his illustrious ancestor in recognition of his dedicated work teaching young men and boys the art of sailing the oceans. The college's coat of arms depicted Rodriguez's last command, the vessel 'The Vierge du Cap'on one side with a strange cross that glowed like a sun; its Latin motto read: 'It is within your own power'.

His craggy face beamed with a grin that grew ever broader reminiscing his golden years with Louis Narbonne, his friend and one time senior officer in the French Navy. For almost fifty years he had helped Louis search for his family's lost treasure. The memories of those glorious years were flooding back to him. His blood filled him with an effervescence and excitement that elevated his spirits to those long forgotten heights when he and Louis scoured every hiding place in the oceans for the lost treasure.

Their first vessel had been a sloop called the 'Sainte Angelique'. Before each voyage they would hire a new crew: all female, all scantily clad and all seeking romance and adventure. They would grace the decks and cabins, each one as enchanting and as beautiful as the oceans and every coral island they visited.

His blissful journey of nostalgia was interrupted by an urgent voice from the radio repeating a weather warning to all shipping travelling south of the main central group of Seychelles islands. He shrugged his solid, square shoulders and smiled ruefully, gripping the helm of his new mistress with greater resolve.

"It looks like we'll finish just before the weather turns," Pierre shouted down to Jean-Claude below deck. "The depression from the south east is deepening faster than they thought and will break early this evening."

Jean-Claude, who had been poring over a tattered sea chart, clambered up to the bridge, the wind pulling at the chart, ripping it along one of the worn creases. "Where the hell are we? I can never make sense of these numbers and markings."

"Here," Pierre snatched the chart before the wind took it and stabbed his finger at the spot. "Hold the wheel steady, will you?" Pierre flattened out the creases carefully on the ledge beside the helm and projected a line from Coetivy east by north east to longitude 56.75 degrees with his index finger. "Give me that grid, Jean- Claude," he snapped.

Laying the transparent grid over the chart he tapped his index finger on one of the boxes. "Look! That's where we were yesterday." Jean-Claude looked on apathetically, infuriating Pierre. Calming his rising temper he continued: "I took a bearing at midday yesterday.... remember?" His finger slid across the chart. "We are about here at the moment... heading on this course. I'll take another bearing at midday..."

"All I want to know is... when we'll we be there?"

"About 2.00 p.m. You'll soon have all that treasure in your sweaty little hands, don't worry!" He shook his head. "My God," he smiled wryly, "your Grandfather and me searched 50 years for that treasure. They were great years with your Grandfather. He knew the ways of the sea. Why can't you take a leaf from his book and at least make an effort to learn?" he searched Jean-Claude's eyes fruitlessly for some sign that he had penetrated the man's dormant soul.

"No need when I've got you! This will be a great year for you and me. Grandpa Louis would've been ........."

"Jean-Claude, you will never know the true meaning of the word 'great' even if you live a thousand years! If you're thinking that all those gold coins, diamonds and rubies will somehow give you everything you have ever craved for then you're in for a bitter disappointment! You have to have something within you...in your soul; you need to love life and you need a woman to share it with. You're like a cripple. You're twisted up inside. Your father should have thrown you out of that window with your mother. It would have been kinder for you and better for the world!"

"Let me tell you this, you sad, bitter old man," he seethed, his eyes narrowing demonically and his mouth twisting grotesquely. "We'll find the treasure because of me! I'll make you rich. You and Grandpa Louis failed. Don't forget that!" his eyes widened manically. "I'll have more power than you can imagine. You forget I'm a master at my craft. You're a pathetic old fool!" He whipped his left hand contemptuously up as if to slap Pierre. "Remember, when I've got the treasure our relationship is at an end," he spat the words venomously. "You'll be grovelling at *my* feet begging for your share of the jewels. That'll put an end to your high and mighty attitude!" Jean- Claude went below and slammed the cabin door petulantly.

Relieved that he was alone once more, Pierre checked his watch. It was half an hour before noon. He settled down at the helm of the 'Santa Lucia' feeling Louis presence close beside him.

"The search will soon be over, old friend," he said aloud. "But your treasure isn't going to be squandered by your Grandson, Louis. I'll make sure of that! My promise to you will be fulfilled once the treasure is unearthed. I will make sure that the treasure is used to restore your family's 'house' just as you and 'The Loot' had wanted.

"Ah! What great times we had, Louis!" He laughed, wallowing in the memories of the women, the parties and the exotic islands they had stayed on. With a beaming smile he sang: 'Thank heaven for little girls', mimicking the voice and mannerisms of Maurice Chevalier to an audience of dolphins leaping and diving before the bows.

# CHAPTER 33

The pilot banked the Air Seychelles Boeing 767 for the final approach to Seychelles International Airport, Victoria. Emerging through thick cloud Radcliff nudged Omollo and pointed down at the runway, a long rectangular concrete strip built on land reclaimed from the sea, a flat stretch of beige and black carpet laid parallel to the shore.

The airport runway was an engineering miracle for the country. The 700 million year old Granite Mountains that rose steeply from Mahe's rugged coastlines, dominating the island from top to bottom had impeded access to the Seychelles. It was the great metal birds that brought tourists in vast numbers bringing with them much needed foreign exchange to boost its ailing economy.

The bloated colourful bird descended gracefully down, like a giant heavily laden pelican, onto the black and pale yellow surface. It used the full length of the runway before turning yards from the sea and slowly made its way back to the small Airport building. The mountain slope rose up with imposing grandeur for little more than one hundred feet. The rest was hidden under low cloud that clung like smoke to the canopy of the tropical rain forest that climbed its steep mountain slopes.

A deluge of warm equatorial rain had the disembarking passengers hurrying for the cover of the airport building.

"What's with all this rain, Mr. Radcliff?" Omollo quipped at passport control with water dripping from his face and puddles accumulating around his feet. "Where's all the sunshine and blue skies you keep telling me about?"

"At least the rain's warm," Radcliff smiled slapping Omollo affectionately on the back.

Outside the building Radcliff went straight to a telephone kiosk on the forecourt.

Omollo waited, watching tourists climbing into taxis whilst the natives, soaked to the skin, crowded onto overloaded, ancient buses. The engines of these vehicles strained laboriously with the demands of the climb, black smoke billowing in its wake, as the driver double-de-clutched to engage second gear, grating away even more metal from ground down cogs. The heavy rain did nothing to impede the easy, relaxed pace of life. It reminded him of his home in Ghana.

Radcliff returned wearing a smile that stretched from ear to ear.

"How is she?" Omollo asked.

"She's really well!" he said ecstatically. "I can't tell you how good it feels to hear her voice. They've arranged special therapy for her. She'll be coming out to the island in about three weeks! What about that!"

"I'm very happy for you, Alex," Omollo grinned joyfully.

"She's planning to invite your boss's wife out to Australia!"

"Really...!" Omollo's eyebrows rose half way up his forehead.

"When I told her about Charles Hawkins...well she wanted to do something for her."

"I met her once," Omollo said sadly. "Hawkins was being awarded his last medal. She was very nervous, but she was kind to me. Not many wives in the force find it easy talking to people like me. She's a blonde lady... Susan, I think her name is."

"We need to get weaving, John," Radcliff moved towards a waiting taxi. "I contacted Chairs Boolean at Government House. I've a meeting with him in twenty minutes."

The taxi splashed its way along the flooded roads, its windscreen wipers just keeping pace with the deluge. Great sprays of water washed over the natives crowding the pavements. Radcliff stopped the taxi at the Clock Tower, in the centre of town, and dropped Omollo off. Within an instant Omollo was soaked to the skin. Radcliff continued on to Government house having arranged to meet him back at the Clock Tower at 2.30 p.m.

Drenched and clutching his single bag of hand luggage Omollo wondered through the narrow streets glancing into the shops and stores, their shelves and window displays sparse and unwelcoming. In the market the natives competed cheerfully trying to eke a meagre living from small piles of fruit, vegetables, nuts, fish and trinkets that were carefully stacked and arranged upon long, rickety tables. Omollo was touched by their great sense of humour and eagerness to please.

His performances to make himself understood using animated gesticulations and extraordinary facial expressions had the women screeching and clutching their sides with laughter and giggling like school children. The men folk cackled and babbled appreciatively in Creole at the big man's pretended attempts to haggle the price of their fruit.

Radcliff's taxi drew up at the Clock Tower. Omollo was waiting, dripping wet, and with a huge toothy grin severing his face from ear to ear. He held four plastic carrier bags bulging with fruit and vegetables.

"You found the market then?" Radcliff laughed throwing open the back door of the taxi.

Omollo climbed in.

They both lurched back as the driver moved swiftly off.

"Yes," he chuckled heartily. "What happened in Government House?"

233

"The island is mine! Officially…!" Radcliff stated proudly as they passed by the Bibliotheque National. "It's beyond the internationally recognised boundary limits of all the surrounding nations," he added quickly. "The Governments of the Seychelles, Sri Lanka, India, Madagascar, Reunion and Mauritius have all unanimously agreed to recognise my island as a sovereign state. I've called it 'Carmen Island'."

"Nice! Very nice, Alex! Well let's not waist any more time. Let's get to *your* island paradise."

They bought more provisions en route to the heli-port: a radio transmitter, a diesel generator, a shovel and pickaxe, sleeping bags and a two-man tent.

Approaching the airport once more, Radcliff leaned over to Omollo. "Charis Boulevant," he whispered, "quietly warned me, strictly off the record, that we must expect trouble. There are moves afoot to take my island, by force if necessary."

"An invasion..!" Omollo exclaimed in a high pitched girlish squeak. "*Already..?*" He said in deep baritone. He grinned broadly and began to giggle.

Radcliff tugged at his wet arm nodding towards the driver.

They watched the driver who appeared oblivious to their conversation.

"We'll have to work fast," Radcliff continued in a whisper. "We must get the Cross out before they invade!"

"I can't believe that these people would invade!" he exclaimed incredulously, his low deep voice resonating in the cab. "What about that guy who got away? He'll be regrouping as we speak."

Radcliff nodded slowly.

The taxi skirted the airport building and stopped outside the small glass fronted wooden hut. A solitary helicopter stood 50 feet away inside a white circle painted on the soaked concrete.

The rain had lessened to a fine drizzle as they unloaded the taxi and stacked the bags, boxes and parcels of provisions and supplies under the hut's awning. It was late afternoon when Radcliff entered the hut leaving Omollo waiting outside with their supplies. Omollo watched the two men talking for several minutes. Then Radcliff signed some papers and they both emerged.

Radcliff introduced the two men: "John Omollo…meet Kurt Van der Koche." They shook hands cordially.

Kurt went straight to the helicopter, threw his bulging attaché case into the cockpit and climbed aboard. Radcliff and Omollo loaded the supplies onto the helicopter and took their seats behind the pilot.

"Kurt is the man who took me off the island," Radcliff explained to Omollo as they fastened their seat belts.

Kurt's face creased up. "Yah! I have to confess to that. For the

234

sake of world peace, I'm not too sure I did the right thing," he chuckled flipping switches overhead and on the dashboard. The engines wined and the blades began to turn slowly. He turned back to face his passengers and handed them headsets. "Put these on and we can talk above the engine noise."

They put on the headsets.

"This man has caused quite a sensation here on these islands," Kurt said over the microphone. "My business has boomed because of him but it's definitely more dangerous!" Kurt raised his voice above the crescendo. "All I've done over the past month is shuttle dignitaries and tourists back and forth to that island of his." The engines roared. "Sit tight and enjoy the ride," he yelled.

The helicopter lifted off and Kurt steered into a right turn. They headed southeast over the airport and the open sea. Kurt flew just below cloud level. The rain smashed in gusts against the glass cockpit. Ten minutes into the flight the weather improved and within no time the cloud and rain were behind them. Climbing to five thousand feet the ocean looked vast and desolate. Its deep ultramarine contrasted with the lighter blue umbrella of a cloudless sky.

They had been in the air almost two hours when Kurt pointed out a speck on the horizon. Radcliff struggled with his seat belt to see over Kurt's shoulder. He took the pair of binoculars Kurt offered him and could depict its unmistakable shape: a recumbent giant. His eyes followed the familiar outline: from its head, a mound at one end of the island; down into a valley, its neck; then steeply up the dome shaped mountain its barrel chest; the mountain sloped more steadily to level out at the marshes at the opposite end of the island completing its body, legs and feet.

Within ten minutes Kurt had descended to three hundred feet and prepared to land.

"That's incredible!" Omollo exclaimed, and then laughed with youthful excitement. "Your island looks just like a turtle swimming through the sea!"

Radcliff winced at the strength of his voice resonating over the intercom'. "A turtle?" He thought for a moment. "I suppose you're right!" Radcliff caught sight of Omollo's excited, animated face and laughed. "I've never seen it quite like that before."

From the air the island was exquisite. An emerald isle lush with tropical vegetation, edged by shades of blue-green to translucent turquoise up to the white coral sand; a small green jewel surrounded by a vast deep ultramarine ocean. It was over a mile and half in length and just over three quarters of a mile at its widest point. The reefs were clearly visible as the aircraft descended. The diverse vegetation covering the island was also easily discernable at low altitude.

Below one hundred feet Radcliff could see the many pathways he had worn along the top of the ridge up to the summit of the mountain.

"It's a paradise," Omollo marvelled.

"Yes," Radcliff agreed absently, as a sequence of nightmare memories flooded back to him.

Kurt turned out to sea, reducing altitude to hundred feet and announced: "The tide is very high. I can't land in that large horseshoe shaped bay. I'm going to try the smaller bay next to it. There's still some dry sand. It'll be tricky but it's our only chance."

Radcliff glanced at the familiar narrow beach that Kurt was entering with high cliffs on one side; a jutting headland opposite separated that beach from horseshoe bay. He noticed the tide was abnormally high but he was totally absorbed by the view he had of the plateau, the lake, the waterfall and his old home: the cave in the cliff face. He wondered if the jewels were still scattered on the floor. Then he recalled the day that he found the treasure.

Kurt skilfully hovered the Gazelle above the small steep beach with one landing ski dug into the coral sand, keeping the craft level with the other ski held above the encroaching waves. The two men jumped into the water and began unloading their supplies. For ten minutes they struggled against the down draft from the rotor blades, crouching low with the bags, boxes and packages, soaked by sea spray and struggling back and forth to the rocks beneath the palm trees at the rear of the beach.

With just the two-way radio, the generator and two food boxes to be offloaded Kurt waved at them frantically, pointing skyward. Radcliff tugged at Omollo's arm and pointed to the landing skis. They had sunk into the sand and were covered by the encroaching tide.

Kurt throttled both engines, sea spray smacked into their faces knocking Radcliff off balance. The right ski was held fast, toppling the aircraft towards the cliffs. Kurt eased off the throttle and the two men dug frantically with their hands to free the buried ski. But the incoming waves and the vibration of the aircraft were causing the ski to bury itself faster than they could free it.

Kurt leaned out from the cockpit to see the two men heaving on the sunken ski. Their muscles in their backs and legs strained with the dead weight, their sinews protruding like knotted string from their arms and necks. Kurt gingerly increased the rotor speed, Omollo continued pulling on the ski whilst Radcliff, knee deep in water, dug ferret like into the sand. Kurt drove the helicopter forwards and right with increased lift leaving no margin for error: thirty feet to the right was a line of coconut palms guarding a granite cliff face; directly ahead were two palms reaching out from the side of the headland, six feet from the rotor blade tips.

Kurt increased the rotor blade speed still further whipping the sea into a dense fog of spray and sending the surrounding palms into a frenzy of bowing and swaying. He then applied lateral direction with the nose of the aircraft dipped. The ski lifted slightly and both men pulled with renewed vigour, thigh deep in water: their muscles tearing and straining and their vertebras about to snap.

"We'll heave together…on the count of three," Omollo wheezed through clenched teeth. "One…two…thre.e..e!"

The sand released its iron grip with unexpected suddenness sending the two men careering backwards into the sea. The helicopter lurched forward, Kurt frantically trying to gain altitude. One of the blades chopped into a swaying palm and the fuselage swung right, the nose of the helicopter rearing up, its tail dipping dangerously towards the two men in the sea.

Both men backed away watching in horror as Kurt wrestled with the controls. The craft had swung around 180 degrees from its starting position and was moving inexorably towards the cliffs, the tail blades scything into the two palm trees showering the two men with debris. Kurt throttled and pulled hard on the controls in a final desperate attempt to lift the craft over the cliff, but the tangled tail blades held him back.

Seizing his chance, Kurt hurled himself from his doomed aircraft. He hit the water beneath and quickly struggled to his feet. As he straddled the waves towards the other two men the helicopter turned over on its left side, almost inverting itself, and drove forward smashing into the cliff and was engulfed in a fireball. A fiery plume of oily black smoke mushroomed skyward. The fuselage and twisted tail slid, screeching down the rocks like a giant dead insect leaving half the cockpit embedded in the cliff. Clouds of steam and smoke billowed up from the wreckage and the sea was ablaze with fuel and oil.

Kurt had been blown off his feet by the explosion. Burning debris fell around him as he stood up.

Omollo and Radcliff waded back to help him.

Radcliff was the first to reach him, hauling him out of the water.

"You okay?"

"Yah! I've really messed up," he spluttered, bending over with his arms on his knees, "…messed up big-time!" Behind him a pall of black smoke had risen higher than the summit of the mountain. He looked up at Radcliff. "I'm so sorry, Alex."

"It's me who's sorry. The tides are treacherous in this bay," Radcliff consoled. "I should've warned you. I was too immersed in my own thoughts."

"*Our supplies!*" Omollo shouted, wading breathlessly past them towards the beach.

"There's a ledge…" Radcliff called out following in Omollo's wake. "It's about twenty feet up the cliff... It'll be wide enough for us to make camp."

The three men ran through the shallower water, littered with ripped and shredded palm leaves and debris from the aircraft, towards the headland to avoid the burning wreckage then followed the beach round to the back of the bay.

Kurt broke away suddenly. "I must look for my attaché case. I'll see what else can be salvaged.....," his voice trailed off, lost in the noise of the surf, as he ran to the burning wreckage.

Radcliff picked up the tent and, with a coil of rope around his neck, he led the way to the cliff. Omollo followed carrying one of the supply boxes. Nimbly ascending his familiar and well-worn zig zagging trail up the side of the cliff, Radcliff reached the seven steps he had hewn from the granite to take them up to the seven-foot wide ledge.

Ten feet along the ledge grew a thick pine tree, which sprouted horizontally from the rocks then bent ninety degrees to rise twenty feet vertically up the rock face. It divided the ledge into two sections: the steps led them to the level part; beyond the pine tree the rock was crumbling and breaking away. The roots of the great tree had levered open a wide fissure between the rock face and the floor of the ledge causing most of that part of the ledge to fall onto the beach.

Omollo found a spot against the pine trunk to stash the box and returned to the beach for another. Radcliff lashed the rope around a protruding rock at one end of the ledge and stretched the line across to the pine trunk. He draped the tent over the line using its guy ropes to hold the shelter secure to the line and the rock face.

Radcliff watched Kurt climbing down the cliff from the wreckage carrying something bulky.

The bay below them and the adjacent horseshoe bay were in complete shadow.

Omollo returned breathless with two carrier bags. He stacked one upon the five boxes he had already brought from the beach.

"We've about half an hour of daylight left," Radcliff stated.

Omollo emptied the other carrier bag and threw it down to Kurt on the beach below.

When Kurt finally joined them on the ledge he opened up the bag and pulled out each item he had recovered: tools, more rope, a jerry can of fuel, a hunting knife, a charred hand-gun a box of ammunition his attaché case and two bottles of gin.

In the fading light Radcliff made a spear from a sapling and descended the cliff to the beach.

Darkness had fallen when Radcliff returned. Kurt and Omollo sat proudly before a blazing fire, the tent roof flapping in the wind, with vegetables bubbling in a billycan hung over the flames. Radcliff threw the spear down in front of them. Impaled on it were four trout sized fish.

Radcliff laid three flat rocks in the centre of the fire; he wrapped the fish tightly inside folded leaves and placed them in a neat line on the rocks. Within minutes the cooking fish added to the exquisite mixture of smells wafting on the strengthening easterly breeze. The flames flattened and flared sending out a shower of sparks onto Kurt's bare legs. He leapt to his feet, rubbing his scorched hairs vigorously, amid raucous banter from his two companions.

"There's a storm brewing," Radcliff announced studying the fast moving clouds. He then sniffed the air instinctively. "A big one. A big one." he repeated strangely. "Any boats out there tonight will be in trouble."

He wove a windbreak from palm fronds and secured it against the protruding rock to where he had tied the guy rope. Omollo and Kurt moved the boxes from the pine tree to support it.

"Aren't we a little exposed up here?" Omollo asked quickly.

"Safe as houses!" Radcliff gave Omollo a hearty slap on the back. "It might get a bit damp though."

"You lived in a cave, didn't you? Why don't we go there?" Omollo asked congenially.

"No way! Sorry, John. There's barely enough room for two. Three…" Radcliff shook his head and threw some dry twigs onto the fire. The three men settled down beside the fire and watched the flames devour the twigs hungrily.

"The Cross of Goa…," Omollo's lips curled up into a broad toothy grin, "…tell us more about it, Alex."

"Okay. Well you remember that old diary, John…the one you saw at my home that time with…with your boss."

Omollo nodded. "It was on the floor…at your home."

"There's a detailed sketch of it in there. I'll show it to you tomorrow. My ancestor…Robert Radclyffe…whose diary it was…had described his wedding day in great detail and he mentioned that he and his bride could feel the Cross' strange, powerful energy.

"It was built to hide a secret knowledge. Vasco da Gama took it to India and it was held in the Sé Cathedral in Goa. The Archbishop of Goa…he wrote about its extraordinary powers…befriended Robert and his wife during the voyage of the 'Vierge du Cap'. They were returning home to England. Pirates took the ship and the passengers and crew were abandoned on Reunion Island.

"Whilst marooned on the island the Archbishop helped Robert make a record in the diary of everything he knew about the Cross. Every detail of Robert's description, and I assume Robert's sketch also, has been scrupulously checked by the Archbishop. Corrections are made in the Archbishop's own hand. For example: he adds in the margin of a page that there's a small box containing white powder hidden within the base of the Cross. Having read the diary many times I presume that the white powder had something to do with the Cross's powers."

"What was this white powder?" Omollo asked, the whites of his eyes were enlarged and lit up by the firelight.

"I'm not too sure. A very weird substance...I can't say what it is. It's probably nothing, John."

"Tell me anyway. I'm sure Kurt would like to hear about this powder?"

"Robert has written in his diary that the powder was the result of heating and cooling gold under special conditions. The Archbishop had added a note in the margin that the ancient Egyptians ingested it; they called it 'mffkzztt'…….. or a name like that."

"That sounds very intriguing," Kurt remarked stirring the vegetables.

# CHAPTER 34

Pierre Droux had called off the search and had turned the 'Santa Lucia' back towards Coetivy. The breeze had strengthened. Heavy purple and black cumulous were piling up on the southeastern horizon, the colour made deeper and more ominous by the setting sun.

Pierre had been adamant that they should turn back, countering all of Jean-Claude's vehement protests. He had said:

"You've never sailed the Indian Ocean before. You have never experienced the ferocity of its winds nor how the gigantic hundred foot waves could appear suddenly from nowhere. They would loom terrifyingly up and crush a small yacht like this into matchwood."

Pierre applied an even, gradual pressure to the chromium throttle loving the throaty growl of the twin engines, listening to them change pitch responsively. He turned his right ear towards the stern, his pleasure intensifying as the yacht increased velocity, listening with a concentrated, reverent stare over the stern on the port side. The foaming wave of the wake grew as the rear of the yacht dug deep lifting its prow, which cut efficiently and effortlessly through the building seas.

But then, looking out over the stern towards the southeastern horizon, just ahead of the storm clouds, he spotted a plume of black smoke. He focussed his powerful marine glasses on the spot.

Pierre immediately turned the vessel about and set course for the pillar of smoke at full throttle.

"Jean-Claude," he yelled. "Get up here you lazy good-for-nothing son of a bitch."

The yacht swayed violently from side to side as it cut across the swell. Jean-Claude staggered up the stairs to the bridge. At the last step he retched, clinging to the handrail. He spat saliva out over the side, the contents of his stomach already emptied a few moments before.

"Look!" Pierre pointed dead ahead. The smoke had thinned and was barely visible.

Jean-Claude put his head out over the side and squinted into the sea spray. "Where? What is it?"

"Smoke, you idiot! It's land!"

"I can't see it. You've changed course! We are heading smack into that storm!"

"It'll only take a couple of hours. There should be enough light to tell if I'm right or not."

"Oh God!" He retched again over the side, saliva dribbling from his gaping mouth. "I can't stand anymore of this…get me back to Coetivy, you bastard. You said yourself that we will die if we're caught up in that storm." He spat into the sea. "That smoke could've been… a ship on fire, a plane crash…. anything!"

A large wave lifted the bows sending Jean-Claude reeling backwards. He reached for the rail but missed and fell backwards, reeling, arms flailing, down the stairs.

Pierre heard a groan then the lounge door slammed. He chuckled. "That's it, you spineless idiot. Get into your bunk and spew your guts out. I'll get you back onto dry land again. You can depend upon your old Uncle Pierre."

# CHAPTER 35

The fire flared in the gusting wind lighting up the faces of the three men sitting in silent contemplation with their backs to the rock face, replete after their fish and vegetable meal.

Radcliff crawled over to the boxes and extracted three tin mugs. Pulling a can of soda from a twelve pack he emptied it into one of the mugs and handed it to Omollo. Radcliff opened a bottle of Scotch and filled a mug for Kurt, then poured one for himself. He gulped down the fiery liquid and refilled it.

Radcliff stood and stretched himself, then took another long gulp from his mug. The wind had freshened considerably. Flashes of lightning lit the eastern sky over the headland.

"Raise your glasses..."

They raised their mugs.

"A toast to Carmen...the most gorgeous creature on God's earth... and to this island."

He returned to the fireside and sat down.

"I can tell you both something which is absolutely certain.... You will be very, very rich before you leave this island. There is more treasure here than you can possibly imagine." He fed the fire with two more logs and turned to look out to sea. A shooting star arced across the western sky.

"Treasure..! How do you propose to get it off the island?" Kurt lifted his arms shoulder height quizzically and then sipped his drink indifferently. "The helicopter radio is burnt out and your radio and generator are both caput...they're full of sea water. We are stranded my friends."

"Someone must know we are here!" Omollo exclaimed.

"It'll take several days before anyone misses us," Radcliff answered. "Maybe Charis Boulevant at Government House will guess where we are. But nobody knows the exact position of the island. We are outside the Seychelles territorial waters and completely on our own."

"I watched you sign that paper in Kurt's office," Omollo said, pointing assuredly at Radcliff. "The authorities will see your name."

"It's here," Kurt pointed to his attaché case beside a food box. "I always take it with me now...I've had four break-ins and as many threats on my life over the past month. About a week ago a couple of French-men wanted me to bring them here. They claimed to be personal friends of yours…as they all do. There was something very suspicious…. no, sinister about one of those guys." Kurt looked into Radcliff's eyes, shakinghis head. "He gave me a look that made my spine prickle."

Radcliff gulped his drink and hung his head. "I'm sorry Kurt. Now you're trapped here with us. You're wife'll be worried sick!"

"I live alone. No one will miss me." He smiled ruefully. "I was stuck on Providence in the Farquar Group for three weeks. The coast guards thought I was on vacation in Europe!"

"Anyway you'll be a rich man. At least I'll get a chance to repay you!"

"Okay!" Kurt laughed. "Let's hear about this fantastic treasure! We've nothing better to do, yah!"

Radcliff told them both about his ancestor's diary, the history of the 'Cross of Goa'; the last voyage of the treasure ship 'Vierge du Cap'; the pirate Olivier le Vasseur; and finally how he had recognised the Cross from Robert's sketch as it stood, slightly askew atop the mountain of treasure.

"Le Vasseur. That name strikes a chord," Kurt mused. "He was called 'The Buzzard' or 'la Buse'. There's a family at Bel Ombre on Mahé still searching for his treasure to this very day. History has it that le Vasseur was captured in 1730. He was sentenced to death…by hang-ing. He was offered a pardon if he told the French authorities on Reun-ion island where the treasure was hidden. Before the trap door opened he threw a scrap of paper to the crowd and cried out: 'My treasure to the one who can understand.' It was a cryptogram that the family on Mahé are still trying to unravel. The treasure is thought to be worth over a bil-lion pounds."

Omollo grinned broadly and shook his head incredulously. "In today's money?" he asked, his bulging eyes rolling skyward. "Does that include the Cross?"

"I doubt it, John," Radcliff broke in. "Not too many people are aware that the Cross exists. It's the treasure that captures people's imagination. The Cross is priceless though." He paused for a second. "I think there's more than just le Vasseur's hoard inside that mountain," nodding towards the rock face and sipped his drink. "I've read about a character called Bernadin Nageon de L'Estang, otherwise known as 'le Butin' or 'the Loot'. He had amassed three hoards of booty. My guess is that the 'Loot' solved le Vasseur's cryptogram and dug up his treasure and buried it here with two other loads he had already had stashed away on Mauritius. Before he died in 1800 he bequeathed the lot to his nephew in France. He sent him all the documentation but neglected to tell him where it was hidden!"

Omollo threw more logs on the fire. Thunder rumbled in the distance. The wind gusted from every direction lifting the tent free of the cliff. It flapped and swung over the fire showering them with embers and sparks. Radcliff tied one rope tighter and fixed the other where it had broken free then hammered wedges of rock into the crevices to hold the tent guy ropes taught.

Kurt poked the logs thoughtfully with a stick, waiting for Radcliff to settle himself beside the fire.

"I know about that white powder gold you mentioned earlier, Alex," Kurt slowly announced. "Your ancestor was right…it is an ancient knowledge. The process was rediscovered accidentally not too long ago by a cotton farmer in Arizona."

"An American…!" Radcliff's horrified expression caused Omollo to chuckle. He tossed Omollo another soda can and refilled his and Kurt's mugs. "Then they know about this already?"

"Yah. They do. The US Government is trying to keep it all very hush hush." Kurt gulped down the contents of his mug. He choked and spluttered, the burning liquid taking his breath. "There was a cotton farmer in Arizona who wanted to improve his crop yield but the soil had a high sodium content which, after the Arizona sun had baked it hard, the soil became impenetrable by rainwater." He paused and looked at them. "The farmer put sulphuric acid on the land to break up the crust."

"Acid!" Radcliff winced, glancing sideways at Omollo. "A bit drastic, isn't it?"

Omollo shook his head sceptically.

"Over a two year period tanker loads of acid were injected into the ground with irrigation lorries following in their wake. The acid and water reacted, bubbling and frothing and breaking down the soil. He added calcium carbonate to preserve the soil's nutrients. What happened after the rainfall was something 'very significant'! When drying in the Arizona sun at about 115 degrees Celsius and almost zero humidity the substance would flare up into a great blaze of white light then disappear completely!"

"That must have looked r-e-a-l-l-y spooky!" Omollo chuckled.

"Yah! The acid couldn't dissolve all the materials in the soil."

"How do you know all this, Kurt?" asked Radcliff.

Kurt grinned. "I was privileged to be associated with some extensive tests in the States during the 1990s researching this phenomena." Their startled looks amused him further. "I haven't always been buzzing around in a helicopter you know."

"You were actually directly involved in these tests?" Radcliff asked in amazement.

"Yah. I'm a professor in nuclear physics. I was doing some research into nuclear halos and anti-matter at the Neils Bohr Institute in Copenhagen. Two other guys and myself were invited to assist the Director of the Institute for Advanced Studies in Austin, Texas."

Omollo sat bolt upright, his lower jaw dropped wide open and the whites of his eyes glowed like twin moons in the firelight.

Radcliff whistled. "Struth, Kurt! Then this white powder gold is the real stuff?"

"It's more common than you realise. The result of our tests concluded that the substance that vanished in Arizona was, as we scientists call it, 'exotic matter'. Hear me out before you look for a straight jacket. This isn't science fiction. It's science fact!"

"What! You can turn gold into powder?" Omollo asked sceptically "Why would anyone want to do that?"

"Good question! The Sumerians and Egyptians believed that it fed the inner spirit or the soul. In the bible it is referred to as 'manna'. It superconducts! Tell me if you've had enough."

"We will," Radcliff smiled.

"PGMs and gold atoms act in the same way…."

"Hang on…PGMs? What are they?"

"Sorry…Platinum Group Metals. These are called noble metals. By subjecting these metals…especially gold…to heat of up to 1100 degrees celsius the nucleuses of these atoms are affected. The electrons, including those in the outer orbit of the atom, are drawn under the control of the nucleus. The strictly controlled heating and cooling process causes its positive screening potential to expand."

"Sorry, Kurt. What *is* 'its positive screening potential'?" Omollo asked with a concentrated stare.

"Most of the electrons rotate around the nucleus within this screen. A few are outside the screen and rotate in the opposite direction to the others. After heating and cooling the nucleus kicks into a high-spin state and the screen expands …influencing the outer electrons to spin in the same direction as the others."

"You said that the heat from the sun was only 115 degrees in Arizona," Omollo queried as thunder rumbled in the distance.

"Yah! That's correct, John. Under natural conditions…everything vanished in a flash of white light! It was the mysterious substance that didn't get dissolved by the acid that the scientists were interested in. By isolating the substance it was then put through these tests to establish what elements it consisted of. We found that the acid reacted with the calcium carbonate to produce this natural phenomenon. It's a state that the Egyptians called the highward fire stone."

"Highward…fire…stone," Omollo repeated slowly, wanting to absorb and understand Kurt's revelations.

"Yah! The atom changes shape. As it increases speed, moving from a low-spin, its norm, to high spin it elongates into a cigar shape. It becomes what is called 'superdeformed'."

"Cigar shaped!" Omollo exclaimed, relieved that he could at last associate with something familiar. "Can you actually see it change shape?"

"Yah. Under a powerful electron microscope. At the point of super-deformity the electrons turn to pure white light and the individual atoms in the high-spin sample metal find it impossible to hold together. They fall apart into a white powder!"

"That's incredible Kurt!" Radcliff raised his voice above a clap of thunder. "How long were you in the US doing these…er…tests?"

"Just over three years. The whole science world was buzzing at the time. Superconductors were '*The Thing*' of the future. It was discovered as long ago as the 1960's that high-spin atoms could transfer energy to each other without losing energy. The white powder is superconductive. The farmer in Arizona had wanted to use this knowledge for the benefit of mankind; he could see its potential in the polluted, poisoned world in which we live. The farmer invested all his own capital into the venture. They were folding back the frontiers of science. He opened the door to what was called ORMEs."

"I remember reading something about ORMEs in a science mag!" Radcliff stated with delight. "It was 1996 or 7. Just before…I…ended up here." Thunder rumbled loudly overhead. "What are they…these ORMEs?"

"It's a bit of a mouth full, Alex. Are you ready for this?" He paused for a second. "Orbitally Rearranged Monatomic Elements."

Omollo chuckled. "I can just picture how the elders of my village would react if they were sitting with us now." His face beamed; his eyes darting back and forth between Radcliff and Kurt. "What a story to hear around the camp fire!"

"What happened to the farmer?" Radcliff asked.

"Fuel-cell technology would render the combustion engine obsolete in one stroke and with it, of course, the giant oil companies. This could never happen unopposed, of course. In his own words, he was 'regulated out of existence'. Tragically he suffered a heart attack."

"The US Government has known about all this but has done nothing!" Omollo's lips twisted strangely, the tone of his deep voice rising to falsetto. "The human race is facing annihilation and the US sits on this knowledge to protect their economy!"

Kurt dropped his head. "Its inertia, John," he said sympathetically. "Change usually takes time! The world economies are like giant wheels. They take time to slow down. It can't happen overnight, John. But there will be change. The bubble has burst already! Meanwhile everyone has to live. It's a hard busy life in most cases just to exist and raise a family." He could see Omollo's expression slowly softening as he spoke. "But the farmer's science prevails, to use a much abused word. Individuals worldwide now have access to this information. Collectively we can influence and persuade governments more effectively than ever before. This is the way forward."

"Time is running out for us," Omollo said sadly. "Africa is the continent that has contributed least to the pollution but suffers the most from its consequences."

"Alex's 'Cross of Goa' could be the answer. Who knows? Man demands something demonstrably powerful placed right in front of his eyes before he sits up and takes notice. We could capture the attention of the world with something of the Cross's magnitude. A superconductor made five hundred years ago producing an undying source of energy. The news would spread like wild fire."

A wide and brilliant bolt of lightning hit the ocean midway between themselves and the horizon. For a few pulsating seconds the whole ocean, the underside of the low storm clouds and the island were lit up menacingly.

"The Cross is a…superconductor?" Radcliff asked rubbing his forehead, feeling the effects of the alcohol.

"Yah. So was the Ark of the Covenant!"

"But *that* was built by the hand of *Allah*!" Omollo protested. "It's blasphemous to presume anything else, isn't it?"

"Yah, in a way, John. The Bible does say that God instructed Bezaleel, the Goldsmith, to build it on Mount Horeb. It describes everything about the Ark: its size; the quantity of gold used, that it was built using highly resinous wood sandwiched between two layers of gold. An excellent insulator between two plates of highly conductive material; it was a capacitor that could generate a charge of thousands of volts!"

"A capacitor!" Radcliff shook his head. "You just said it was a superconductor! Sorry Kurt….I'm a little confused."

"Me too," Omollo confessed.

"A capacitor stores energy. There the similarity ends. A superconductor isn't a conductor of electricity. It doesn't even have a magnetic field. But it is sensitive to the smallest magnetic field. For example: a superconductor's inherent light flows as if in liquid form and creates energy, but a superconductor also creates a field around itself called a Meissner Field. This field excludes all magnetic fields. If you dropped a magnet onto a superconductor it would hover above it…the magnet would levitate! Energy can pass between two superconductors, irrespective of the distance between them, without any loss of energy. The light within it flows continually. It's perpetual motion. It will never stop!"

A thunderclap reverberated in the heavens as if to ratify the statement. Kurt let his two bewildered friends contemplate his revelations.

After a few moments he asked: "I'd like to see that sketch your ancestor made of the Cross, Alex, if I may?"

Radcliff got to his feet. Immediately he began to sway and totter drunkenly, the wind almost blasting him off his feet. Kurt jumped to his aid but Radcliff regained his balance. He stood stiff and erect. He remained statuesque for almost a minute gazing blankly seaward then pivoted on his heels and sagged momentarily. Kurt was ready to grab his waist and pull him back from the abyss when he straightened up and faced the sea once more. He turned and looked at Kurt, his face full of alarm and confusion. Radcliff then proceeded to remove his clothes.

"Leave him, John," Kurt whispered waving Omollo away.

Radcliff stood facing the sea, stark naked, for several minutes. He tottered on his heals then rocked forward, his body as straight as a board. Steadying himself he stooped and picked up a burning log from the fire and threw it over the cliff.

Kurt and Omollo watched the flaming log bounce three times on the cliff face before being extinguished by the sea.

Radcliff lurched as he turned and sat cross-legged before the fire, his head sagging onto his chest, his arms wrapped around his own naked, shuddering body.

Omollo covered him with a sleeping bag and fed the fire more wood, but there was no chill in the intensifying wind. A flash of lightning lit up the small bay and the headland, followed four seconds later by an ear splitting crack of thunder that reverberated within the clouds, its lingering rumble fading into the distance.

"Are you alright, Alex?" Kurt asked, both men cautiously rejoining him beside the fire. Lightning flashes were increasing in frequency and the wind gusted, slamming into the men.

"Sorry…. I'm really very sorry…I shouldn't drink…so much," Radcliff slurred glancing at both men in turn then averting his gaze, having seen the concern in their faces. He stared fixedly into the wind blown flames. "I'm ashamed…" shaking his head as he spoke, "…to lose control like that! I was out of my mind… well you saw that for yourselves… I'm …"

"It's okay, my friend," Kurt gently wrapped an arm around Radcliff's shoulders.

Thunder crashed much closer and the wind gusted raising the embers of the fire, sending sparks flying across their camp.

"In my younger days I used to drink myself into a stupor. It poisoned me. It truly buggered me up, and no mistake! I would've been dead by now if Clive, my agent, hadn't taken control of things. It's an insidious thing… alcohol! *Bloody stuff!* I black out you see," he slurred. "I saw the burning log…" Radcliff thumbed behind him, "…landing in the sea, but remember nothing before that. I always throw a log or a piece of wood,

I'm told. One doctor suggested that I'm throwing the wood for the dog I had as a child. It marks the end of my attack, brings me back to the here and now and, if uninterrupted, I recover almost immediately…except for a blinding headache."

"Yah," Kurt nodded. "My uncle was…like you…he suffered from a type of epilepsy. It's called 'le petit mal'. Have you heard of it, Alex?"

"I believe that's what they called it!" Radcliff waggled his index finger at Kurt with mock reproach. "Jes' Kurt… you amazed me… you're one clever bastard!"

"What happened, Alex?" Omollo asked tentatively, his troubled face screwed up with worry for his friend. "What made you turn to drink?"

"During my twenties. I'd work for days often without food…. keeping myself going on wine and stout…then I'd collapse with exhaustion and sleep for…up to forty eight hours sometimes. I'd awake…then see the mess I'd created…" Radcliff looked away, his face contorted up as if he had chewed on a clove of garlic, "…then I'd feel suicidal."

Omollo shook his head in astonishment.

"You artists…such perfectionists" Kurt watched Omollo wringing his hands anxiously. "You shouldn't denigrate your work…you have a gift. You should rejoice in that."

"I've kept it under control ….I haven't had an attack like that for over twenty years. It's just the drink…"

"Yes, but what happened to you?" Omollo persisted.

"A combination of things, John," he shrugged. Thunder crashed directly above him. Radcliff rocked back and forth holding his head in his hands. He darted an accusative look at his two companions, his eyes suddenly aflame with aggression. "You're worse than those journalists," he slurred. "You're nosey bastards! You know that? My reasons have got buried in time. It all happened a very long, long, long…. time ago."

"All the more reason to get all these things out of your system once and for all," Kurt encouraged.

"What business is it of yours, anyway?" he demanded defensively, slurring badly. Radcliff extended his index finger tauntingly, twisting his wrist back and forth, before Kurt's nose. "I know what you want. You just want the dirt and the scandal."

"Is that the impression you have of me?" Kurt retorted sharply. "You think I'm that low? Is that your opinion of me? If so we'd better stop this conversation here and now."

"Maybe you should leave it, Kurt." Omollo intervened, trying to defuse the situation. "Alex's obviously the worse for wear."

"Yah! I can accept that." He looked Radcliff in the eye. "I just want to know you better, my friend. That's all."

Radcliff shook his head. "John's right. The alcohol's loosened my tongue. I talk a lot of rubbish. You should leave me be, Kurt! I've lived with it for so, so long…. it's far too late for me now."

"Allow us…" a clap of thunder drowned out Kurt's words, "…allow us to be the best judge of that."

"This thing's never really left me. After returning home in December, having been years alone, here on this island, I found the prospect of having to live with other people more terrifying than ever." He rubbed his pounding head, finding it increasingly difficult to talk. He looked directly at Kurt. "Fear is the trigger! I'm sure of it!"

"I think I know you well enough. You're definitely not the type to step away from a problem without a fight," Kurt said softly. "Whatever happened to you must have been… cataclysmic!"

The word 'cataclysmic' reverberated within his fogged and befuddled brain, as if a great gong had been struck.

"Thanks Kurt," he said emotionally, tears welling up in eyes, his mouth twisting up into a half smile. "That's very good of you to say that." He took a deep breath. "Okay, but I warn both of you…I've never spoken about this before… to anyone!"

He wrung his hands, filled with trepidation. Bursts of lightning lit up the whole northern sky, reflecting on the turbulent sea and illuminating the contours and layers of the great billowing cumulous cloud fleetingly with blinding flashes of bluish white light. The nightmarish, but awe inspiring, spectacle brought back to him those terrible days in an instant. A gust of wind blasted into the heart of the fire sending a torrent of sparks across the ledge to the bent trunk of the pine tree.

He told them his story of heartbreak during his youth, which was followed very soon after by the death of his brother. Guilt and fear took a terrifying grip of his mind inducing strange panic attacks and agoraphobia. The guilt he had traced back to a harrowing incident with a paedophile when he was eight years old.

Kurt shook his head slowly and solemnly. "No one recovers from a traumatic experience like that, then superimposed by two tragic losses that happened to you in very quick succession." He looked into Radcliff's watery eyes and said knowingly: "No one knows, unless it's happened to you, what an experience like that can have on the innocent mind of a child. They're things you learn to live with, yah! The guilt remained latent until the crisis of your youth. You are a sensitive person, Alex. For you it obviously had devastating consequences. Life for you must have been an absolute nightmare."

Kurt's words soothed and caressed his mind. He had never heard his own feelings and emotions expressed by another person before and it touched him deeply. With his words he could feel the poison rising up as if drawing puss from a carbuncle: the pain, the horror, the disgust, the fear, the misery, the anger, the isolation, the guilt…. they all surfaced like the bubbles in boiling water… pumping into his upper chest, lifting his shoulders with increasing rapidity. Radcliff clenched his teeth, trying to control the convulsions that shook his whole body until he surrendered to it with a wolf like howl. His chest heaved and tears streamed down his cheeks.

A gust of wind ballooned the shelter up like a sidelong main sail and sent a shower of sparks over Omollo's legs. He leapt to his feet. As he brushed them away he noticed something, lit by the storm, far out to sea.

"There's a ship!" Omollo pointed. "Can you see the green light?"

Kurt and Radcliff joined Omollo and stared into the blackness, the wind whipping at Radcliff's sleeping bag and at Omollo and Kurt's cloths. More flashes of lightning lit up its outline against the churning, steely black ocean.

"It's a yacht!" Radcliff exclaimed casually. "I told you we'd be okay. Maybe they saw our fire. But they should be sheltering on the lee of the island."

"They're heading for the next bay," observed Kurt.

Omollo turned away with a troubled expression and returned to his position beside the fire.

"They're just travellers caught in a storm," Radcliff stated, sensing Omollo's unease. "The headland at the farthest end will offer them some protection."

"We'll have to give our new neighbours a call in the morning," Kurt added. "They can send a signal to Mahé…maybe get another chopper out here for us."

"We'll have to be very careful." Omollo looked up anxiously as the others sat down beside him. "It could be trouble." He fed the fire with more wood.

They all sat in thoughtful silence listening to the wood hiss and crackle.

"Tell me about your family, Kurt," Radcliff asked softly wanting to know more about the extraordinarily talented, unassuming person before him. Thunder rumbled to the southwest beyond the mountain peak.

"My wife divorced me whilst I was in the States. My son and two daughters are living in Amsterdam." Kurt paused, wondering whether he should continue. "I had an affair with a young physicist, you see. She was young enough to by daughter, but we did some great work together. We thought alike and complemented each other perfectly. We had a strength, like all other loving couples do, but it was so…potent. We devised a theory of everything! Would you believe it! It was laughed out of court, as you can imagine. I still believe in it though."

"Can you tell us about this theory, Kurt?" Omollo asked tentatively. Lightning lit up the sea and the bows of the yacht in the next bay.

"Yah. Someday, maybe," Kurt smiled. "It takes quite a bit of explaining,you understand."

"What about you, John?" Radcliff said cheerily hoping to stop him brooding about the yacht. "I'll bet you've broken a few young ladies hearts with that personality of yours!"

"I am a Muslim," Omollo began his countenance uncharacteristically serious and grave. "I have always stayed true to my religion. Ever since I was a boy I've wondered why Christians and Jews and Muslims cannot integrate and live together… in harmony...you know. It's all very good to respect and tolerate all the different cultures in the world but religion is different. Everyone can't have the correct religion, can they? Most of us believe in the one true God. Why can't we all forget the dogma and doctrines and live together in peace."

"That's very commendable, John," Radcliff said. "But what's this leading to?"

"I once knew a young woman." A thunderclap crashed overhead.

"Ah ha! I knew it!" Radcliff chuckled, attempting to lighten the big man's spirit.

"Why haven't you mentioned her before, John?" asked Kurt.

"The same reason you say very little about your family, I suppose."

"Touché!"

"Her name was Sophia. I met her last year during my final week of holidays in Ghana. My father had asked me to go to a village one hundred and fifty miles to the north and buy some special herbs. The roads in Ghana are very bad. They're mud tracks with very deep ruts and potholes. It took me three hours to get there in the Land Rover. I was welcomed by the Chief and the elders; then I was introduced to Sophia, the Chief's daughter."

He was watching flames when an image of her face came vividly to him. He smiled and looked at each in turn.

"When I saw her for the first time my heart actually stopped beating; she was so lovely. She had a beautiful, wide and radiant smile and her voice was as soft and as sweet and as rhythmical as a mountain stream; she was tall and slender and her eyes were nut brown…they glistened with a clarity and a purity…they spoke to me…I couldn't stop looking into them.

"We talked on the way to the herbalist's hut." Omollo's eyebrows rose up reliving the wonder of the moment, oblivious of the noise of the storm, "It was as if we had known each other for years. Our eyes never left each other the whole time she glided beside me. She smelt of jasmine and lilac. I can still feel the softness of her touch when she handed me the bag of herbs. It was electric. I felt weightless."

Omollo turned and faced Radcliff.

"There was a big storm…not as bad as this… and I was invited to stay overnight. We sat together with her parents in the long hut with lightning and thunder flashing and crashing throughout the evening meal. It was dramatic. An evening I will never forget. The rain had cooled the air and it smelt of honeysuckle.

"After the meal I was shown to my hut. Later that night, with the storm still raging, she came to me. It was an experience beyond my wildest dreams. But when I awoke next morning she had gone. The chief, her father, opened the little door to my hut. The sunlight flooded in. All I could see was his silhouette. He told me that I must leave immediately. I asked him if I could see Sophia, but he refused. I hoped that I might glimpse her from the Land Rover, but there was no sign of her."

"Didn't her father know that you were the son of chief?" Kurt asked, feeling Omollo's sorrow and confusion.

"Yes," he bowed his head, choked with emotion and swallowed hard. He then shrugged his great shoulders. "She was a Christian!"

They sat watching the big man wrestle with his emotions.

"What will you do?" Radcliff shouted above the rumble of thunder.

He slowly looked up at Kurt and then at Radcliff. "I'm going back to her village and take her for my wife." Omollo's eyes narrowed and his chin was set forward with resolve. "It will mean that both of us will have to leave Ghana. It will hurt my father badly. I must think of my future. It is with her. I'll take her back to England with me."

"Bravo!" Kurt shouted, toasting him with an empty mug. The first drops of rain hit the shelter roof.

"That's the spirit, John!" Radcliff clasped the big man's shoulders affectionately and shook him vigorously.

"Well, I think that's enough…excitement for one day," Radcliff laughed. "I've enjoyed tonight…very much. I think we should we get some rest and see what tomorrow brings."

"I agree," Kurt crawled across to his sleeping bag and unravelled it. "We'll need some rest before we entertain our new guests in the morning,"

Omollo found a spot to lie down close to the rock face. "I can't see them giving us any trouble before the storm is over," he said.

Radcliff stepped, still naked, into his sleeping bag. "Sleep well!" he called out.

The canopy waved and cracked in the gale. Thick low cloud raced overhead and then the heavens opened. Radcliff turned on his side facing the fire. Carmen's spirit came to him, just as it had countless times before on the island. He slept deeply dreaming of her alone with him on the island beside the Cross of Goa.

The wind fanned the embers into a million twinkling lights. Sparks flew horizontally across the ledge. Ciphered messages sent out into the void to be intercepted by the spirits of the cosmos.

# CHAPTER 36

Radcliff awoke. He shuddered. His sleeping bag was sodden and the fire was out. Kurt and Omollo were snoring alternately and rhythmically as thunder crashed and rumbled around them. Rain hammered onto the surface of the tent like a perpetual roll on a snare drum. Lightning flashes lit up the bending, torn palms on the headland between the two bays and the distant yacht being thrown and tossed in the wild sea. Water poured off the end of the tent and cascaded down the steps leading up to the ledge.

Radcliff descended the steps and the track to the beach and crossed the headland into horseshoe bay. A scimitar of light cut across the horizon heralding the dawn and better weather. Lightning struck the mountain illuminating the area for several seconds. The yacht was clearly visible anchored close to the opposing headland, 250 yards away.

Keeping in the shadows of the coconut palms he sprinted along the beach until adjacent to the yacht, silhouetted against the brightening sky. It was low tide and was able to wade out to a third of the distance then he swam to the craft, tossing and swaying violently on the choppy swell. Treading water 6 feet from its stern he read the name 'Santa Lucia' painted in bold white capitals on the black hull.

Pierre had let go the anchor as near to the beach as possible and then went below. The stench of vomit permeated the air. Jean-Claude was lying prostrate on the settee. The crew were flopped in their bunks amidships. He escaped back to the helm with a bottle of cognac.

With the yacht pitching and rolling Pierre looked shoreward, clutching the bottle close to his chest revelling in the possibility that it could have been Radcliff's campfire burning on the cliff.

He let his body sink to the deck and drifted into a deep, satisfied sleep certain in his mind that he will recover Louis's treasure.

Dawn was breaking when the stern was lifted by a large wave. It passed under the yacht thudding the keel down onto the seabed.

Radcliff was climbing the diving ladder at the stern when the wave came. The jolt that followed as the craft hit the sand knocked him off the ladder. He heard footfalls on the top deck and dived as bullets peppered the sea around him, one skimming his thigh. He swam underwater in a wide arc reaching the beach in the centre of the bay.

Jean-Claude staggered beside Pierre and fired six rounds into the murk.

"Stop shooting!" Pierre screamed.

"Shut up you old fool." A lightning flash lit up the beach. Pierre pulled the barrel of Jean-Claude's rifle as he fired at a figure running for the palm trees.

A bullet whistled passed Radcliff's left ear. He dived behind a palm. Another lightning flash lit up the bay. A small dinghy was being rowed frantically towards the shore.

Close to shore Jean-Claude jumped from the dingy with Pierre on his heels.

"Wait, you idiot!" he screamed, grabbing Jean-Claude's arm and swinging him round to face him. "Think man! Have you considered who this person might be?"

"How the hell should I know?"

"It's Alex Radcliff, you dummy. We need him alive. He can lead us to the treasure."

Pierre watched from shallow water as a figure ascended the cliff face, on the left hand side of the bay, with the agility of a monkey.

"Jean-Claude!" Pierre whispered. "Take Jacques and follow him. No shooting. Catch him alive before he gets back to the others."

"What others?"

"He's not going to be on his own, now is he?"

The wind gusted, but with less severity. He waved his gun barrel towards the far headland. "You two follow me."

They sprinted the entire length of beach. Dawn was breaking rapidly and the rain had ceased.

Radcliff looked down from the cliff top at horseshoe bay. Two men were stumbling and sliding on the wet rocks below him; three others were running towards the camp.

Kurt had heard the gunfire and shook Omollo. "We've got trouble! Big trouble! There's been some shooting…a lot of shooting. Alex's gone!"

"From the yacht?"

Kurt nodded.

"I'll go," the huge man had said peeling off his soaked sleeping bag. "Wait here and guard the camp."

"Take this." Kurt threw him his handgun.

Like a giant panther Omollo climbed the pine tree supporting the shelter, leapt from the top branch, twenty feet above Kurt, onto an overhang and disappeared out of sight.

A single gunshot reverberated through the darkness. Kurt found his bush-knife and had cut down a straight, stout sapling and whittled one end of it into a sharp point. He sat on his sleeping bag and waited.

Twigs cracked in the undergrowth below. Gripping the staff tighter he strained his eyes into the shadows of the steep sloping headland. The light was improving. He saw two men with rifles climbing the cliff fifty meters to his right. Then he spotted another about to climb the steps to the ledge.

Kurt's heart began to pound. He found Radcliff's fishing spear. Propping it against the pine tree he climbed the first few branches taking his own weapon with him.

From above he saw the dark shape climb up onto the ledge. In the growing light of dawn he recognised the old Frenchman immediately as one of men at the heli-port. Kurt watched and waited as the old man checked out their camp, prodding and poking bags and boxes with the barrel of his gun. A second man arrived, also armed with a rifle. But it was not the person had expected to see.

This second man began poking the boxes at the base of the pine with his gun barrel. Kurt seized the moment and jumped onto his back, impaling him with the spear. He crumpled to the floor lanced through the heart. Before Pierre could aim his gun Kurt had grabbed Radcliff's spear and was pressing it against the Frenchman's abdomen.

Omollo had found a pathway taking him towards the sound of a waterfall. Peering round the sharp corner in the cliff Radcliff's face suddenly appeared before him.

"Keep down," Radcliff whispered. "There're two on my tail. Where's Kurt?"

"Back at the camp. Who are they?"

"Don't know. There're five of them…they're French. Three were heading for the camp."

They both descended the cliff to the pine tree. Before climbing down the tree they could see Kurt struggling to his feet. Two men were standing over him with rifles. A third lay inert next to him.

Pierre had pulled out a knife and held it under Kurt's chin. The point broke through his skin and blood began to trickle onto the blade and down his neck. "Where're your friends, eh?" he demanded in English. "There're three sleeping bags here. Tell me who your companions are or you will die." The other Frenchman had him covered with his rifle.

"You take the one with the gun and I'll go for the other," Radcliff whispered.

"Don't move." Jean-Claude commanded from above, his rifle pressed against the back of Radcliff's head.

"Pierre," he called down. "I've two of them up here."

"Get up both of you," he commanded Radcliff and Omollo raising the barrel of his gun. "Come up here Pierre. And bring some clothes with you." He laughed at Radcliff. "We don't want you catching a cold. You are going to lead us to my treasure Mr. Radcliff."

# CHAPTER 37

That Sunday morning an Air Seychelles airliner taxied through the heavy rain towards the Mahé airport building. Four men descended the steps from the Boeing 767, dressed identically in black suits, wearing thick wrap-around sunglasses and carrying bulky black carrier bags. They were all well built with clean-shaven sun tanned heads that glistened in the rain. The tallest of the group and more heavily set led them at quick march across the tarmac.

Once through immigration an airport security vehicle whisked them away to an awaiting DeHavilland Beaver, its engine idling, the pilot ready at the controls. Buffeted by the tail end of a storm, the single engine aircraft landed on Praslin Island, about 35 miles north of Mahé, at just before 10 a.m.

A Land Rover, with headlights blazing, splashed towards them on the tarmac and skidded to a stop. A wiry islander of medium height and build, wearing a red and orange shirt and baggy brown shorts got out of the vehicle. He ushered the four men into a large wooden hut adjacent to the airport control tower that resembled the watch tower to a Japanese P.O.W. camp.

Inside the hut the largest of the four-man group handed the native a folded piece of paper. The native glanced at it quickly then nodded and stood motionless with is hand held out. A wad of Rupee notes was slapped into his palm. The native counted the notes carefully. He smiled quickly acknowledging that the amount was correct and escorted the men through the back door to a covered yard.

The rain beat down on the corrugated roof as the men looked approvingly at the bright red 'Gazelle' helicopter on the concrete beyond. The helicopter's superstructure, glossy in the heavy rain, had a falentron built into the superstructure to enclose the tail blades.

"It's the best in the business!" the native in the colourful shirt proclaimed proudly. "It's a record breaker! As specified, it is fully armed with machine guns and has two Exoset missiles loaded in each port. It has a top speed of over 200 knots and a range of over three hundred miles."

The men said nothing. On the ground lay an array of weapons: hand guns, oozie machine guns, boxes of ammunition; grenades, knives and machetes; blankets, ground-sheets and a four man tent. Each man selected his weapons then skilfully and routinely checked every piece. Satisfied all was in order they began stowing the weapons, equipment and their other luggage onto the helicopter and returned to the cover of the yard.

"It's all 'ere," the leader snarled. "You must 'ave friends in very 'igh places. Maybe they want Mr. Radcliff's arse as badly as we do. Okay! How do we get to this *bloody* island?"

"There's been a terrible storm, sir," the native smiled obsequiously, shrinking away from the big man.

"I can't have *no* delays, you little pip squeak," the leader grinned, his teeth baring viciously, then caressed the native's cheek lightly with his huge open palm. "Is there a problem?"

"There's only one person...." the native's knees had turned to jelly. He squeezed them tight together to avoid embarrassing himself in front of these giant westerners, "... who knows.... where the island is, sir. He has to get here from La Digue. I'll find out how long he'll be.... right now. Oui?"

"You go and find out," he quietly growled. "Me and the boys will be preparing the helicopter. I want someone here to take us to the island by the time we've finished. You've done really well up till now..." he slapped him moderately hard on the cheek; the blow knocked the bony native reeling backwards. "You'd better not disappoint me, son."

The men had changed into jungle combat uniforms and were waiting in the yard when the native crashed through the door soaked to the skin and gasping for breath.

"You're late!" The leader barked. He threw his cigarette to the floor and stamped on it impatiently. "Well?"

"My brother has found the pilot, sir. He will take you to the island." He bowed several times and pulled a grotesque toothy grin.

"Where is he, then?" the man barked.

A tall, slim middle-aged man with a gaunt face marched into the yard in beige overalls carrying a white crash helmet. A bushy white beard and pure white hair pulled tightly into a ponytail accentuated his deeply suntanned face. He advanced to the leader and came smartly to attention, clicking his heals.

"I am to take you to zee island," he announced in a staccato German accent.

"Are you sure you can find it...?" Slaughter snapped derisively.

"Ve attach a radio transmitter to fuselage of Van der Kocke's helicopter...it's south southwest of Frégate."

Slaughter nodded.

"Shall ve go then geentlemen?" He beckoned the men towards the aircraft with an outstretched arm.

The leader waved his men forward. Within minutes the rotor blades were building speed. The corrugated roof of the hut flapped and clattered in the down draft as the helicopter lifted off. The small native watched with relief as they turned towards the southeast and disappeared from sight.

# CHAPTER 38

The four Frenchmen and their captives were gathered on top of the cliff above the pine tree and the camp. The morning sun was trying to break through the thick cloud cover.

"Mr. Radcliff." Jean-Claude produced a long knife and held it to Kurt's throat. "You are a very fit for a man of your age. That's very good, because you will now take us to the treasure. If there are any tricks both your friends will die, starting with this pile of dung."

"We must go back to the waterfall," Radcliff pointed in the direction of the rocky path where he and Omollo had met earlier. He led the procession up the gradient with Kurt close behind.

"They are the Frenchmen..." Kurt whispered drawing alongside Radcliff, "...the ones that came to my hut...."

"Quiet!" Jean-Claude rammed the barrel of his gun into Kurt's back.

Radcliff took the group around a sharp corner of the rock face and onto the wide plateau. About fifty feet to their right the waterfall crashed onto the lake. A cloud of spray rose up from its base. He stopped and looked up towards the domed summit of the mountain.

"Keep going! Why have you stopped?" Jean-Claude demanded.

Radcliff pointed up cliff face. "The treasure is up there...in that crevice."

"You expect us to climb that!" Jean-Claude scowled at Pierre. "If this is a trick, Radcliff, your friends will pay."

"We can reach it..." Radcliff pointed up in the general direction of the ascent route, "...by traversing across that rock face from the waterfall."

Waiting for the two Frenchman to make a decision he looked nostalgically back across the plateau towards the sloping ridge where he had watched so many sunrises.

"Come on then," Pierre waved his gun impatiently at Radcliff, looking anxiously up at the perilous granite ascent. The rising sun had struggled through the cloud and glinted for a second on some overhanging leaves about 250 feet above them. "Let's get going."

"Remember Radcliff, we have your friends here." Jean-Claude shouted up as he watched the two men climb the well-worn footholds next to the falls.

Radcliff stopped beside his cave, pretending to wait for Pierre. The jewels were stacked where he had left them just over a month before. The two climbers crossed the place where the water gushed from the rocks and traversed across the rock face. He turned and signalled to Pierre that he had found the crevice.

The weather was improving from the east, the clouds thinning and more broken. The early morning sun broke through them occasionally cutting diagonally into the crevice, but only lighting up part of the cavern. Radcliff could make out the treasure in the reflected light within the cave. He thought of Carmen, wanting her to be with him. He pushed his head into the slit to get a better view. What he could see looked even greater and more magnificent than he remembered.

"What are you doing? Get away from there you English fool. Let me look." Pierre bellowed from just beneath Radcliff's feet. It was virtually a sheer drop to the beach below them. He climbed up to the crevice and pushed Radcliff hastily to one side.

Radcliff lost his grip. He stopped his slide by pushing his knees into the rock and clawed his way back up to the crevice.

Pierre had his head wedged into the narrow slit in the rock for many seconds. "*Sacre Blur*!" he yelled out as he turned waving down to Jean-Claude. "*Oui*! Oui!"

Having descended back with the others, Radcliff, Kurt and Omollo were lined up against the rock face with one the French crew guarding them with a machine gun. The two jubilant Frenchmen celebrated with ebullient cheering, dancing and raucous laughter.

Pierre sauntered over to them. "Don't look so downcast, Mr. Radcliff. We're going to spare all your lives. Once you have helped us load all the treasure on board our yacht we will leave you to enjoy your island in peace and quiet."

"I like it." Jean-Claude laughed. "It's poetic justice! We give you your lives in return for digging out my family's treasure."

"Jacques," Pierre called out, "take Danny and bring up the box of explosives, detonators, carrier bags and 40 meters of rope from the yacht. Oh yes! And bring the Champagne."

The two men sauntered off.

"*Fast*! Or your share of the treasure will be halved."

The two men scampered across the plateau towards the trees.

Jean-Claude had his captives covered with a machine gun. He and Pierre lounged in the long grass planning, in hushed voices, their strategy for enlarging the crevice. Their monotonous drone would be broken now and then by a burst of excited laughter.

Radcliff, Omollo and Kurt were sat beside the lake, about twelve feet from the Frenchmen. They listened with straining ears to their conversation.

"I heard the words 'ecsplossivo', 'endidoûra' and 'trésor' several times," Kurt whispered. "If they try and blow the crevice they could bury the treasure for good!"

"Maybe not, Kurt. The treasure's tucked beneath the sloping roof of the cavern; if it was to cave in I'm pretty sure the Cross will be safe, at least."

Radcliff gazed up at the mountain summit, which was just visible above the rock face behind them.

"Is there a passage down through the mountain to the cave?" Omollo smiled, reading Radcliff's thoughts.

"There're strange markings and symbols carved on the rocks leading up that ridge…" pointing towards the southern ridge "…and there're more at the summit."

"Those markings are most likely secret signs and symbols in Freemasonry," Kurt explained. "There're on practically every granite island in the Seychelles; probably made by pirates; many of them were well educated ex navy officers…not illiterate by any stretch of the imagination."

The three men sat gazing thoughtfully at the ridge. Light fluffy clouds chased across the clear sky giving moments of respite from the searing sun.

"I've been wanting to ask you…" Omollo's said, his wide grin cheering Radcliff. "…how did you survive for seven years alone on this island? What did you live on?"

"Fish mostly. It took me a while to master the art of fire lighting…my cooking got to be quite good. Hunger makes everything taste sweeter! I made string by soaking pulverised bark and made nets and traps for catching fish and birds. Some of these exotic birds are excellent eating! There're breadfruits, mangos and coconuts, of course. I dug up a twisting vine like plant, which had large tubers growing beneath the surface. I boiled the tubers…they tasted like sweet potatoes. I experimented with just about everything that grows here. I tried a bright red gooseberry looking fruit during my first weeks here…." Radcliff held his stomach and mimicked reaching. "…I was ill for almost a month."

Omollo smothered his laughter, emitting strangulated cackles and breathless wheezing noises.

"You might well laugh, my friend." He smiled, amazed at the spirit of his two companions. "I developed a great respect for every living thing…especially if I could eat it! I'd imagine cavemen…. that's effectively what I'd become….must have had the same regard for the food they ate. There're some pretty nice fruits," Radcliff continued. "One has a spiky skin, a bit like a litchi. It stinks…," clasping his nose between two fingers, "…when you peel it."

Omollo broke into another bout of silent wheezing followed by strangulated squeaks and whimpers. The contagious sounds set off an impulse in the other two men, who struggled desperately to control their laughter.

"Shhhhh…." Radcliff uttered holding his finger to his mouth. He checked that the Frenchman were still in deep conversation. "… but they're very tasty!"

"It looks like paradise, Alex," Omollo said once his laughing fit had subsided. "But I am sure I couldn't survive seven years alone…like you,"

"Paradise," Kurt laughed. "For tourists, yah! Don't you agree, Alex?" He touched Radcliff affectionately on the shoulder. "An English General by the name of Charles Gordon believed that he had discovered the Garden of Eden when he landed in the Seychelles. A huge double coconut inspired his imagination. It's called the Coco-de-mer." Kurt smiled at Radcliff. "Alex knows them well. These nuts, John, get washed up on all the shores surrounding the Indian Ocean. They come from one place only…Praslin Island. Their shape is very similar to the female torso, from the waist to the thigh…a woman's private regions… including pubic hair!"

Omollo smirked, his eyes twinkling as he looked back at Kurt.

"The taller male palm trees…. sometimes over a hundred feet in height and over eight hundred years old…use their long hanging catkin like fruit for fertilization. It pollinates the open flower of the smaller female tree. Legend has it that when the moon is full the male palms creep through the jungle and seek out a female to embrace."

Omollo's grin broadened. "Did you see any of these sexy trees wondering around the island, Alex?" Omollo chuckled. "How did you cope on your own seeing all this sex going on…?"

Omollo's laughter carried across to the Frenchman. Jean-Claude rose to get up but Pierre pulled him back onto the grass. Soon they resumed their discussion.

"Loneliness could drive any man stark raving mad," Radcliff whispered. "I never did see an Eve in my garden. I would've given up more than a rib to do so, I can tell you. I came across an old, gnarled and twisted pine tree stump near the southeastern end of the island. The forest is quite dense up there. In the darkness the stump looked like a person crouching down. It made my hair stand on end. I dodged behind a tree trunk, stricken by fear then peered gingerly around the trunk…"

The two men grinned, imagining the scene.

"Well, I was naked…!" he stated bluntly, "…and it looked so real to me," he added feeling slightly foolish.

"Okay Alex…!" Kurt soothed, smirking at Omollo.

"I never wore clothes…there's little use for them here. I agree, though I must have made a comical sight," Radcliff continued, playing to their merriment. "True, I wasn't quite the Robinson Crusoe type…I crept slowly up to it, spear at the ready," adding actions and expression to portray the apprehension he had felt. "I skirted around the tree stump expecting it to spring to life at any second and attack me. I stalked it to within six feet before I realised what it was."

Kurt and Omollo fought to contain their laughter.

"I sat studying it for the rest of the day and slept there that night. In the morning light I saw the shape of Carmen's torso in the contours and grain of the wood. I felt like Michelangelo after having seen David within the marble slab. I set to work immediately. It took me three months to complete her. Crazy stuff, eh?"

"Crazy enough to keep you sane...!" Kurt remarked spontanously. "I'd like to see it."

"I'll take you to her when we've got rid of these bloody frogs."

"Are you going to let these cutthroats take your treasure?" Omollo whispered incredulously.

"I only want the Cross...although the treasure would be useful. I think we should take any opportunity that might present itself. Agreed?"

"That sounds good to me," said Kurt.

"At the moment it is two against three," Omollo reminded his friends. "One of us could sneak through the grass and get round behind them. Let's take a chance now!"

"What!" Kurt wheezed, holding back a scream.

"They have guns, John. We're expendable. They know where the treasure is."

"I could clutch my stomach as if I was in pain," Omollo persisted. "When they are over here to investigate, you and Kurt could hit them on the head with a rock."

"Alex is right, John. Now is not the right time. Tell us more about your carving."

"As the years passed the tree stump became Carmen. I would talk to her, lay beside her and gaze at the stars through a gap in the tree canopy," the two men glanced at one another significantly, "...yes, of course I would feel her contours...I would run my hands over her shapes. Even though I say it myself, they were very life like. She was a comfort...I found it difficult to leave her.

"I worked out a way of being with her for longer periods at a time by building up a larder of food, enough for two or three days. At first I'd get really excited...exhilarated would be a more appropriate word...I'd wash in the lake and march off over the plateau... singing and whistling through the forest..."

Radcliff noticed their incredulous expressions. He wondered if he had gone too far. "Of course, I would always dream of the day Carmen would be actually here, with me. Anyway, it was that pleasure and the discipline that helped me survive and keep my marbles all those years.

I'm sure of it.

"Towards the end, though, even being there...with the carving... did nothing to help me counteract the growing feelings of despair and hopelessness...they would come suddenly...and overwhelm me. It's strange what solitude inflicts on the mind. I'd lay for days in my cave in deep depression."

"Then you were rescued," Kurt said cheerily.

"Yes, thanks be to God!" Radcliff smiled, released from those memories. "Thanks be to God!" Radcliff said quietly and laughed. "I was rescued in the nick of time! Only a few weeks before I'd tried to do myself in. But then, miraculously, as I was in the process of drowning myself, a vision of Carmen came to me. She guided me to a deep spot in the lake underneath the falls. A pile of jewels shone lustrously in the rays of the morning sun. I traced back the source of the waterfall and found the treasure."

"Incredible! Marvellous!" Kurt slapped Radcliff heartily on the back.

Jacques and Danny staggered back across the plateau laden with bags containing equipment and ropes, soaked with perspiration. The breeze had veered to a drier southerly, the few remaining clouds quickly evaporating under the searing sun. The two returning Frenchmen stripped off their clothes and dived into the cool waters of the lake.

Pierre had unloaded one of bags, prepared the explosives, and then carefully packed the taped, wired bundles of dynamite into a knapsack.

Jacques hoisted himself out of the lake and flopped onto the grass exhausted. Pierre strode to him and the two men talked at length out of earshot of the captives. He then sauntered over to Radcliff.

"We watched you amusing yourselves. We shall find it very amusing when we relieve you of the treasure and wave goodbye to you all. You will now guide Jacques to the crevice and assist him in every way he asks. Remember your friends are down here if you try anything reckless."

Jacques climbed slowly and nervously, acutely aware that the weighty contents of his knapsack could blow the side out of the mountain he was climbing. When they were above the waterfall Radcliff indicated the direction to the crevice pointing out to Jacques the footholds and handholds.

The Frenchman gave Radcliff a roll of cable that he had carried inside his shirt, one end of which was connected to the explosives on his back. He then proceeded traversing the cliff face to the crevice as Radcliff slowly unravelled the cable. With the explosives in place and the fuses connected to the detonators the two men returned to the foot of the rock face.

They all took cover behind boulders littering the base of the rock face on the far side of the lake. Jean-Claude crouched directly behind the captives, his machine gun covering them. Pierre took charge of the detonation.

Sheltered behind a boulder he connected the two bared wires to the small box, wound the handle, braced himself hard against the rock and pressed down the handle.

The ground shook with an ear splitting explosion, sending rocks, smoke and dust bursting from the front side of the mountain. The thunderous blast sent all the bird life in the vicinity shrieking upward in alarm from a thousand hidden perches in the surrounding trees. Fragments of debris rained down for several seconds upon the plateau and splashed into the lake.

Jean-Claude and Pierre ran to the rock face and began to climb, eager to see the result of the blast.

"Oui!" Pierre cried out, confirming their success, once the smoke and dust had settled.

Radcliff looked sadly up at the rock face. The waterfall had vanished. A damp vertical streak a yard wide was rapidly evaporating in the heat of the sun.

He was then pushed from behind and fell headlong onto the ground. Jean-Claude stood over him with his gun barrel pressed into the back of his head.

"Climb up there," he ordered pointing towards a small group of trees sprouting from the rock twenty feet above the smoking hole. He put a coil of rope over Radcliff's head. "Get above Pierre, secure the rope and lower yourself down to him. Come on. Get moving."

Pierre was traversing the rock face and nearing the gaping hole where the crevice had once been.

Radcliff climbed as far as his cave and stopped, stealing another look at the jewels.

"Climb, you English bastard," Jean-Claude yelled up. "What are you doing, bird watching?"

Having secured the rope to a tree trunk Radcliff lowered himself to the gaping, smoking hole and perched himself on the blackened jagged rock. He watched Jean-Claude below yelping unintelligible instructions at him, his arm flailing dramatically.

Pierre translated his commands.

Radcliff threw the remaining length of rope to Pierre, who scrambled over the loose rocks and joined him at the hole. He gathered up the rope and let it drop into the cavern.

"You first, Mr. Radcliff..!" Pierre handed Radcliff a torch. "No tricks! Your friends will be the first to die."

Radcliff took hold of the rope and descended through the smoking fissure into the cool, dusty darkness of the cavern. Looking up from the rocky floor the jagged edges of the eight foot wide hole resembled the open jaws of a shark. The sunlight burst through it illuminating the treasure mountain of countless rubies, diamonds, sapphires, emeralds and coins; the breathtaking sight was reflected in the lake to form a mesmerising, gigantic, sparkling oval shaped ball of colour.

Close up the great pile of jewels was even more massive and the lake seemed deeper. The sun's rays glinted upon the bejewelled Cross, its top section protruding the jewels as if the mountain of treasure was offering it up as a prize to the discoverer.

Radcliff's foot slipped on the loose, broken rocks and he fell sideways, twisting his left ankle. The torch clattered into a crevice and went out.

"What's going on?" Pierre screamed, his voice echoing inside the cave. "I'm coming down."

He rubbed his stiffening ankle, cursing his stupidity then groped in the darkness, searching on his hands and knees, for the torch.

"Hay..! Shine the torch, will you!" Pierre snapped about ten feet from the cavern floor.

Radcliff found the torch between two rocks, clicked it a few times until it relit, then shone it onto the spot where the Frenchman had landed.

"Give me that." Pierre snatched the torch and marched off with Radcliff hobbling behind in the gloom.

Pierre stood statuesque by the lake's edge. Droplets of water rippled the surface giving the whole incredible sight a shimmering lustre. It was the only sound that disturbed the absolute silence.

Radcliff's eyes were transfixed on the Cross of Goa. It was dazzling. The glittering, sparkling rubies, diamonds and sapphires from the largest to the most minute animated the Cross; its exquisite solid gold cross pieces with their flaming suns at each end was identical to the drawing in his ancestor's diary.

Pierre skirted the oval lake. It was approximately twenty yards long and ten yards wide. He could barely contain his excitement, his pace quickening until he was forced to crouch low to get under the slope of the ceiling. He squatted in stunned silence directly opposite out of sight of Radcliff and shone the torch into its shimmering depths. The refraction of light magnified each jewel beneath the surface of the lake. "Louis…Oh, Louis!" he repeated over and over in French. "We've done it old friend. This is a million times more treasure than I ever expected."

Radcliff heard the name Louis and knew from the Frenchman's tone that he had been overwhelmed by the enormity of the treasure. He limped around the edge of the lake until he could see him. Pierre's bulging eyes, lit up by reflected light from the lake, were aflame with excitement, wonder and absolute disbelief that so much treasure could exist in the world.

Pierre looked across the lake at Radcliff. He attempted to stand. His head cracked against the unforgiving rock ceiling. His yelp echoed within the cave. Pierre bounced on his legs, in a squatting position, clasping his head with both hands.

Radcliff wanted to laugh but at that instant he heard shouts of alarm from outside. Pierre crawled back from under the low roof and scurried for the rope, holding the torch in one hand and rubbing his head with the other. He climbed the rope to investigate, leaving Radcliff standing beside the lake.

The faint whirring sound of an approaching helicopter could be heard as Pierre poked his head through the hole. He saw Jacques, who had climbed almost to the hole, with the look of horror and confusion in his eyes pointing at the helicopter advancing straight towards them.

Slaughter had seen the two men at the hole and moved his index finger over a red button. He waited until the last moment before firing two missiles at rock face just above the hole. Before they hit the target the pilot skilfully banked the helicopter clear and towards the plateau.

Jean-Claude looked on in stunned amazement and horror as two white-hot thrusting balls of fire ignited beneath the helicopter. The hurtling missiles were headed straight for the hole in the mountain. He ran for cover along the pathway that Radcliff had bought them earlier that morning and vanished around the corner of the cliff.

The ground shuddered with the force of the explosion.

Slaughter machine gunned Danny, Omollo and Kurt as they dived for cover just beyond the lake but the concussion from the blast jolted the aircraft sending the bullets high above his targets.

Pierre had seen the missiles coming straight for him. He let himself drop back into the cave.

A flash of blinding light lit up the whole cavern for a split second.

Pierre fell to the rocky floor amid the deafening thunderous explosion that knocked Radcliff off his feet. Rocks crashed around him and splashed into the lake as daylight appeared above him for a split second. The whole mountain shook. Then, with a groan, the roof of the cavern collapsed. Falling rock displaced a wave of water from the lake that washed Radcliff nine feet into a gully. Dust engulfed and blinded him before millions of tons of rock fell upon him. The floor shuddered under the impact.

There was an absolute, eerie silence. Radcliff lay still in the pitch darkness, flat on his back wedged into a gully. He moved all his limbs one by one. His ankle throbbed but there was no other pain. Everything was intact. He was unharmed. He tried to roll onto his stomach but the rock ceiling was too low. Touching the roof of his rock tomb with his fingers he estimated its height to be just four inches above his face and stomach.

Radcliff was at first seized by utter panic. He screamed for help. After realising there would be no help he grasped onto the only thing he had left…his senses. He lay quietly in the darkness and tried to think.

Glancing back beyond where his head lay he caught sight of a faint round glow in the rock. Tipping his head back further he could see a miniature moon stabbing the darkness. Pushing and wriggling himself along towards the light source he found that the height of his ceiling was increasing. Soon it was high enough for him to roll onto his stomach. Making more rapid progress he finally reached for the moon.

Kneeling he shone the torch beam all around the small open space. He was surrounded by huge boulders. Pierre's arm lay strangely poking from beneath a rock, severed at the elbow. Next to it lay ten feet of rope coiled like a sleeping snake. Directing the beam back down the gully he realised that he had crawled under what had once been the roof of the cave. There was only one way out, the way he had come.

He crawled and slithered his way back down the narrowing tunnel, with the rope tied to his foot. Reaching a point where his rocky ceiling was too low to continue he shone the torch beam through the rest of the tunnel. It lit up a clear open space just a yard further on.

Radcliff sagged; the torch dropped from his hand. Fear and hopelessness paralyzed his mind. The torch had rolled into a gully in front of him; its beam shone upon deep cracks running along the gully floor. He examined the cracks more closely.

Switching the torch off to preserve the battery he worked in pitch darkness.

He dug out a long slither of rock to use as a chisel. With it he chipped away the cracked rock, pulverized by millions of tons of granite that had collapsed onto it. He wiggled forward inch by inch.

After hours digging and clawing at the broken rock he finally pulled himself out of the tunnel.

He turned on the torch. It lit up a space much larger than he had expected. He could see the back of the original cave. He moved the light beam to the left, following the smooth rock face until it shone on a pile of fallen rock and rubble. This pile filled a space between the collapsed roof of the cave and the original cave wall.

With the torch off and working in darkness once more he excavated a hole through the rubble. He poked his head through it and shone the torch. The beam reflected on the multi-coloured mountain of jewels and gold coins just eight feet away. The great mound of treasure was untouched; even the Cross of Goa remained protruding the summit in the same askew position.

Moving the beam around he could see the treasure was confined inside an inverted 'V' shaped space, the roof of the cavern having sheered and crashed onto the floor where the edge of the lake had been. The water had drained from the lake.

He switched off the torch and the pitch darkness engulfed him. A slow, regular splatter of dripping of water on damp rock broke the absolute silence. Filled with dread and fear he clicked the torch back on.

He shone the dim beam around the space and over the fallen roof. Above that massive slab of rock there was a large gap, half filled with rubble, which sloped steeply upward. From the angle he was standing he was sure it would lead to the freedom. He turned off the torch and contemplated his next move.

The torch and the rope were his only aids. Soon the battery would be flat. The thought of being entombed in total darkness with the greatest hoard of treasure ever seen spurred him into action.

He poked the torch through the hole and shone it onto the Cross for the last time and prayed.

With the torch beam little more than a glimmer he climbed into the chimney and began his ascent into the unknown.

# CHAPTER 39

Omollo, Kurt and Danny had dashed across the plateau making for the trees. The German pilot had banked the red Gazelle into a steep turn. The chopper hurtled down on them within seconds.

They fanned out then dived for cover the moment they heard the ratter-tat-tat from the machine cannons. Bullets ricocheted off the rocks and thudded into the earth, tracing four lines of erupting plumes of dust over the area the men lay.

Omollo glanced back for an instant. Smoke and dust billowed from the side of the cliff, water gushed out from a fissure below a massive hollow in the mountain. He grimaced at the thought of Radcliff buried somewhere inside the mountain under tons of rock.

Kurt tugged at Omollo's arm. "Come on, yah!" He nodded in the direction of the pirouetting chopper making ready for another run at them. The three men sprinted for their lives, the trees just twelve feet away as the nose of the aircraft levelled out. Its four cannons spat out their white-hot projectiles that thudded into the ground erupting neat rows of advancing plumes of death.

Kurt dived to his right with Danny following just behind him; Omollo rolled to his left, sheltering behind a rock. Danny fell just six feet from safety, bullets having riddled his chest; Kurt yelped with pain, his left leg having collapsed beneath him. Omollo crawled over to Danny as the helicopter turned, nose down and prepared for another pass. Kurt, his left thigh soaked in blood, was already at Danny's side. Danny looked up at Omollo, blood seeping from the corner of his contorted mouth.

"Messieurs…(he coughed)…there are guns and…." he choked and blood welled up from his mouth. He winced in agony... "explosives… (cough)… on board the yacht. They are…" gritting his teeth waiting for his agony to subside "…they are in the storage lockers in the bows." His whole body convulsed, then his head sagged to one side. Air bubbled up through the blood oozing from his mouth.

The helicopter was almost upon them, its machine cannons blazing. Omollo lifted Kurt up onto his good leg and together they staggered the final few feet to the trees and fell into the undergrowth. A hail of bullets axed into the tree trunks, ripping the thick broad leaves over their heads into shreds. The helicopter did not turn but continued on towards the bay.

The two men lay sprawled in the undergrowth. Omollo rolled over to Kurt and examined his wound.

"The bullet has gone right through, Kurt. No arteries have been severed...." He ripped the sleeves from his shirt and bandaged the wound.

An explosion ripped through the air, a plume of smoke mushroomed up above the trees in the direction of the beach.

With Omollo supporting Kurt the two men crashed through the trees and undergrowth, picking up the sloping track through the trees to the cliff top and the beach. Emerging from the trees they saw black smoke billowing up from the smouldering wreckage of the sinking yacht. The bows, which faced seaward, were already submerged; flames engulfed the stern half of the yacht. The surf broke over the projecting bridge and smashed superstructure. Trapped air from the hull boiled up as the 'Santa Lucia' slowly and gracefully sank to the shallow seabed of the bay.

The helicopter pilot was hovering above the beach preparing to land.

Omollo grasped the opportunity. He pointed to the top of sloping ridge of the headland up to the right of them. "Take cover up there...wait for me...I'm going down to the yacht and get those guns."

"Don't be a fool!" Kurt protested. "Wait until night fall."

"It's our only chance."

Kurt watched him dart right, climbing and weaving through the trees and thick undergrowth that covered the headland until he was out of sight. Kurt hobbled through the trees, rummaging through the litter until he found a stout stick. He ascended the steep slope to the top of the ridge and slumped onto a spot where he had a good view of the bay.

He saw three armed men, in battle armour, jump from the helicopter and dash for the cliffs and climb to the spot where he and Omollo had been standing just a few minutes before. His eyes scoured the rocks lining the headland. Then he spotted Omollo's head amongst the rocks opposite the wreck of the 'Santa'Lucia'.

Omollo swam the fifty yards to the yacht under water, surfacing above the bows. The surf lifted him around the protruding superstructure towards the stern. Before he sank into the trough of the passing wave Omollo spotted a man standing beside the helicopter with binoculars looking out towards the yacht. He dived immediately.

Slaughter had been scrutinising the wreckage with high-powered military glasses. A black shape, the size of large seal, appeared close to the roof of the yacht. He made a slight adjustment to the lens focus.

"You *bloody* bastard," he muttered. He switched on his radio intercom. "Get back here pronto," he screamed. "I think we have the black bastard down here by the yacht."

When Omollo surfaced the same man with the binoculars was waving his arms furiously at three figures descending the cliffs. In the distance smoke rose up from the mountainside. He said a quick prayer for Radcliff, filled his lungs to capacity and dived to the stern of the yacht.

He wrenched an axe from its fixture and swam the entire length of the lounge. He broke open three of the lockers and smashed open the racks holding the armaments in position. The handguns, rifles, harpoons and knives spilled out, in slow motion, onto the floor. The exertion had taken up most of his air. Fish of all shapes and colours darted before his eyes as he looked around for something to carry the weapons. He pulled the sheets from a bunk and bundled as much as he could into one of them. His lungs were aching for air. With a final effort he broke open the forth locker. Boxes of ammunition cascaded onto the pile of weapons.

He surfaced for air.

Gasping and treading water above the stern he looked ashore. Three men were stepping into an inflatable dinghy whilst the one with the binoculars was scurrying over the rocks that lined the headland, barking incoherent orders.

Omollo filled his lungs once more and returned to the lockers in the bows. He tied the sheet at the corners and carried the heavy, bulky load to the stern and hoisted it over onto the seabed. He walked towards the centre of the bay with the weight of the weapons over his great shoulders. Omollo plodded as many paces as he could before he was forced to drop the bundle and surface for air.

Treading water he was mortified to see that the wrecked yacht was just ten yards away. The men in the dinghy were 25 yards away and paddling frantically.

Omollo dived to the bundle and quickened his pace. Gritting his teeth he accomplished twenty yards before being forced to the surface. With his lungs full and resisting the urge to look back he dived to the bulging sack and tried to do better. Four more times he repeated these feats of endurance until he reached shallower water. The seabed rose steeply up to the beach.

He was nearer the source of air but his burden grew heavier. Staggering out of the water the full weight of the weapons with their sharp protrusions cut agonisingly onto his shoulders and back.

The man with the binoculars spotted Omollo in knee-deep water climbing the beach two thirds the way around the bay. He waved and shouted commands at his men who were diving above the wreck.

Omollo tried to speed up, neither stopping nor looking back. Using up the last vestiges of his energy he reached the cover of the coconut palms and the rocks.

He stole a quick glance over his aching shoulder. He saw the three men in the dingy rowing for shore.

A hail of bullets whistled over Omollo's head and thudded and smacked into the granite cliffs and the thick vegetation behind him. He dived to the left and rolled, with the bundle, into a hollow in the white sand.

Two of the men abandoned the dinghy and waded through the shallow water, firing continuously. Pinned down and exhausted, Omollo loaded two machine guns and two harpoon guns and waited.

The two men charged up the beach, guns blazing whilst the third waded to shore with the dinghy. Omollo curled up as small as he could as bullets whined and screamed all around him, ricocheting off the rocks and palms and splattered plumes in the sand around the rim of his hollow.

Hearing footfalls very close to his position he raised his head, took careful aim with the harpoon gun and shot the nearest man through the neck.

The man fell in gurgling agony, pulling ineffectually at the bolt of metal piercing his throat. The second man fired blind, raking an area to Omollo's right.

Omollo bobbed up with the other harpoon and fired hitting him deep in the chest, the force of the harpoon throwing him backwards with his machine gun blazing.

The third man let go of the dinghy, took a few cautious paces up the beach then crouched. The afternoon sun was searing hot. Advancing slowly, scanning the area carefully he dropped to one knee beside his dying comrade still clasping the shaft of the harpoon with blood soaked hands. Deducing the direction the spear had been fired he checked his weapon and gingerly and silently crawled to his left.

He froze above the rim of a hollow to see a stack of weapons on a white sheet. He rolled into it and bobbed his head over the lip.

Omollo emerged from behind a palm tree holding one of the French machine guns and fired twenty rounds into the back of the third man.

Slaughter had watched the gunfight through his glasses from the headland. Seeing the last man die he screamed curses at them and clambered back over the rocks towards the helicopter.

"Get that chopper up" he yelled at the pilot.

The pilot had been relieving himself in the sea. Not understanding the command he assumed that Slaughter wanted him on the headland.

Omollo saw the pilot leaving the helicopter. He stuffed a clip of ammunition into his trouser top and sprinted for the bright red Gazelle.

Slaughter began waving frantically at the pilot: "Go back you idiot...*Go Back!!*"

Instead the German quickened his pace towards Slaughter.

Omollo had covered fifty yards, but the helicopter was another hundred yards down the beach. The sand was soft and his heavy frame made the going tough. Nearing exhaustion, willing his feet and legs to keep pumping he stumbled over a fallen palm and crashed into the sand like a wounded bull.

"Get back and start that *bloody* engine," Slaughter hollered at the pilot.

The pilot turned in alarm and ran back to the aircraft. Slaughter stopped for moment and scanned the opposite headland with the field glasses, slowly searching the full length of the beach for a telltale sign of his foe.

The helicopter rotor blades slowly began to turn. He looked back along the beach once more with the field glasses and then he saw his man on his knees in the sand.

Omollo's left eye was filled with sand. He groped around the sand for his gun, his right partially blinded by sweat cascading down from his brow and dazzled by the sun reflecting on the glass cockpit.

Slaughter ran for the aircraft and climbed in as the blades gathered speed. The pilot prepared to lift off. He focused the binoculars onto the beach. He saw the black man take aim then flames and smoke spurted from the gun. Bullets smacked and thudded into the fuselage. The pilot slumped forward unto the control panel.

Using the body as cover he took control of the aircraft. Another burst of gunfire thudded harmlessly into the pilot and pinged off the fuselage. With the aircraft airborne, Slaughter turned the tail to face the gunfire, heaved the pilot out of the door and accelerated at full power out over the sea before Omollo could reload.

Jean-Claude Narbonne had seen the whole battle unfold, hidden in dense foliage beside the yacht's dinghy, ten feet from where Omollo stood. He watched Omollo stagger to the water's edge and bathe his eyes then stand motionless looking at the helicopter fade from view. He ducked down when Omollo came back up towards him, still carrying the gun, and then turn towards the cliffs at the end of the beach.

Kurt had descended the slope to the cliff top to greet him.

"I saw it all!" Kurt cried jubilantly. "You were marvellous, John," he said ecstatically. "Yah! Simply brilliant young man..!"

"It was not enough," Omollo said despondently as he hauled himself up to join Kurt.

"You've beaten them!" Kurt shouted, slapping the big man on the back as he hauled himself onto the top.

"Hardly. You don't know this character. He'll be back. I can guarantee it."

"Who?"

"The one that got away...again! Slaughter's his name...and that's exactly what he does for a living! He'll be back I can assure you!"

"At least you saw the bugger off! Yah? He'll not come back in a hurry." Kurt put his weight on the injured leg and the pain shot through his body. He gripped more tightly to Omollo's shoulders. "They were the ones after...Alex, yah?"

"He's alive, Kurt. I know it…"

"The whole mountain side would have come down on him…"

"There's something about Alex. He makes you believe in what he is about…I know it doesn't make sense…but I'm sure his destiny is to bring that Cross of Goa out of the mountain. Not to be buried with it."

"Maybe this Slaughter will believe that he's won…and leave us in peace now?" Kurt said hopefully.

"Always expect the worst. Then you're never disappointed…or caught off guard! My boss taught me that."

With Kurt's arm around Omollo's shoulder the two men made their way back up through the trees to the plateau.

Jean-Claude waited for several minutes before making his move. He burst out of the trees pulling the dinghy and paddled out into the bay. He dived over the spot where the yacht had sunk and salvaged some of the remaining weapons and explosives, emergency supplies, fresh water and a compass from the wreckage.

With his dinghy loaded up he rowed back to shore, hid some of the weapons and provisions in a small cave in the cliff and covered it with rocks and leaves. Taking one loaded handgun, a knife and several bottles of water and tins of food, he returned to his original hiding place, covering his tracks as he went.

Omollo eased Kurt onto the grass next to the lake. "I have to go back to the camp on the ledge. I'll be back soon." Kurt nodded.

Omollo took the machine gun and skirted the rock face, descended the thin path to the top of the cliff and climbed down the pine tree to the ledge. He packed the tent into a carrier bag and loaded another with the first aid kit, tins of food and Kurt's attaché case. On the beach he hurried across the sandy headland separating the two bays. The tide was rising, the sea lapping the burned hulk of the helicopter.

He skirted the three bodies, took one of the automatic rifles from the sheet and stuffed the boxes of ammunition into one of the bags. He folded the sheet over the rest and covered them with sand.

The pilot's body lay face down on the beach. Close by it he saw fresh footprints and the marks of a dingy having been dragged from the sea. He dropped his bags, removed the safety catch on the machine gun and followed the tracks into the palm trees. He found a dinghy with the name 'Santa Lucia' painted on it. The boat had been covered with palm leaves. The light was fading rapidly. Backtracking cautiously to the bags he warily continued to the cliff, checking constantly behind him as he went.

Awaking Kurt from a deep sleep Omollo set to work peeling off the makeshift dressing. The wound was a mess. The blood had congealed grotesquely around the gaping hole in his leg, which was swollen and inflamed. He lit a fire, built a tripod and hung a billycan of water above the flames.

Immersing lint from the first aid kit into the boiling water Omollo gently applied it to the wound.

Kurt hollered with pain.

"It will need cauterising."

"Do what you have to, but do it quickly…. yah!"

Omollo searched the bag and found a bottle of whiskey then heated Kurt's hunting knife.

"I saw tracks in the sand… on my way back," he said slowly, looking up at Kurt, the whites of his great brown eyes lit by the firelight. "Some-one had hauled a boat up the beach."

Kurt thought for a moment, droplets of perspiration on his brow. "He's alive then…the Frenchman…, yah?"

"It has the name of the yacht painted on it. I found it hidden in the trees." Omollo gave Kurt the whiskey bottle. Kurt took a long gulp. Omollo waited a few moments then applied the red-hot knife to the wound.

Kurt's flesh sizzled. He screamed in agony.

Omollo dropped iodine around the hole. "We have to find him before he finds us," Omollo added bandaging up his thigh. "There's those weapons…I must bring them back here." He eased Kurt into a more comfortable position, propping him up against a pile of padded rocks he had arranged next to the fire; he then set about erecting the tent.

"Before I go hunting for this Frenchman I'm going up there," he pointed up to the spot on the rock face where the missiles hit.

Kurt drank some more whiskey. "You think Alex's still alive?" he spluttered, the pain raising the pitch of his voice.

"I'm a believer in fate, Kurt. As I said before, Alex found the Cross of Goa in that mountain and it's his fate to bring it out for the world to experience and see. I'll be back soon."

With only the glow of the stars to aid him Omollo climbed the cliff face, stumbled over the broken and cracked rocks and hauled himself up to the lip of the crater where the mountain had caved in on itself. Perched on the lip he looked down into a deep, gaping crevice. Loose rock and rubble sloped steeply down into the gloom.

"*Alex!*" he called out several times, his powerful voice booming into the night. There was no echo. "Come on, Alex," he yelled into the hole. "I know you're down there and I know you're alive." He choked. "Kurt and me are coming to get you out. Don't give up, Alex. We're coming." His cries were absorbed into the mountain but it gave nothing away.

"I've found a hole above the broken rocks of the cave in," he reported back to Kurt. "I called out, but…"

"Maybe in the daylight you'll see another way down."

"There is. Down from the top of that mountain!"

"What!"

"You heard Alex mention that there could be a way down earlier today. There'll be more rope on the yacht! Maybe I'll salvage other stuff that might be useful as well."

"I'm not going to be much use to you for a few days, John. I'm sorry!"

In the firelight Omollo could see a patch of crimson soaking through the bandage. "At first light I'm going hunting...for that Frenchman. Then I'll see what the yacht has to offer."

# CHAPTER 40

Slaughter had set a course for Mahé but Frégate Island, the most easterly of the main group of Seychelles' granite islands and the most isolated, came into view. Two coastguards challenged Slaughter as he refuelled. They paid with their lives. Taking their charts he plotted a course, island hopping, for Madagascar; the first island on his list was 'Ile Plate'.

An emergency cabinet meeting was convened at Government House, Seychelles. Charis Boulevant put his solution to the crisis to the vote: 'discretion was the better part of valour'. The decision was unanimous.

Every coastguard in the archipelago was ordered not to intercept or impede the rogue aircrafts' progress until they had decided upon an appropriate course of action.

The Seychelles Air Force Commander scrambled two Harrier jets. Their pilots were given an airborne brief: 'to intercept and bring down the Gazelle just before it reached Madagascar airspace; if that objective failed, to proceed under special clearance to observe only from an altitude of no less than 10,000 feet'.

Slaughter landed at Ile du Nord, the southern-most island in the Farquhar Atoll, his last opportunity to refill his tanks before crossing the open ocean to Madagascar. The fuel dump had been destroyed.

With no option but to continue, he had 230 miles of ocean to cross with only a quarter of his fuel remaining. Maintaining an altitude of 100 feet he took full advantage of the strong northeasterly sea breeze.

With the Madagascar coast in sight he put on the headset, switched on the radio and adjusted the frequency to a designated emergency wavelength.

"This is 'Condor' calling base, over...'Condor' calling base...over."

"This is base. What's the problem...over?"

"I'm nearing the north of Madagascar and very low on fuel. I've got company. Two jets above me at twenty thousand feet, over."

"Stand by 'Condor'..."

Slaughter waited.

"Land on Nosey-Be on the northwest..."

"I know it." Slaughter reduced altitude to 50 feet and veered the helicopter to starboard skimming the rocky coastline.

"They'll be expecting you…Over."

The fuel warning light began to flash. "What about the money from the States…over?" A high headland suddenly appeared. He pulling hard on the controls. The aircraft's belly brushed the long course grass.

"Negative. Keep it simple, 'Condor'…the airwaves have ears. Father and family gone for ever…over."

"Tell me your *fucking* joking, Jeb. Get back to Toni Ramaliche. We've lost a dozen men on this caper…over."

"He's gone, too. There's no one left. We're on our own now. Oh, more bad news. Brigitte has left you and taken the kids. Sorry, mate. We'll talk later. Good luck. See you at base…over and out."

"You bitch! You bitch!" Slaughter pummelled the control panel with his free hand until it cracked. "You fucking rotten bitch!" Pain shot up his arm and blood oozed from his torn palm. Holding the control lever between his legs he bound the wound with a piece of rag stuffed in the door pocket.

A mile from Nosey-Be island the engine cut out. The only sound was the air whistling around the cockpit and the dying whirl of the rotor blades. The aircraft was above the steep battered cliffs when it began falling, descended directly towards the relentlessly pounding ocean. He grabbed a life jacket and steered the nose diving craft out to sea. A hundred yards out and six feet above the waves Slaughter jumped for his life and braced himself for the impact.

The helicopter smashed into a solitary rock and exploded on impact. Two jets banked slowly left and returned to base.

# CHAPTER 41

Doctor Bagshot watched Carmen exercising her leg on the parallel bars.

"You're making remarkable progress, Carmen. I think we can take you off the steroids tomorrow."

"Have you any news about my partner?"

"That's why I've come to see you, my dear. Please prepare yourself. It's not very good news I'm afraid. Your man is alright, I'm sure…" he added quickly…fumbling with words. "Last Saturday your partner Alex Radcliff and a young English police officer arrived in the Seychelles. From there they were taken to an island. The pilot and the helicopter have failed to return to base on Mahé. There'd been a terrible storm…."

"¡Madre mia! Do you know if they arrived safely?"

"I think so. They left Mahé in the afternoon and the storm didn't break in that region until late evening. My friend's a physician at Victoria Hospital in Mahé and knows people in high places. He was told that the pilot was highly skilled and very experienced. They think that he probably decided to wait out the bad weather. The good news is that a military helicopter was known to take off from Praslin the following day in search of the island."

"¡Que!" she screamed, apprehension gripping her once more.

"Don't be alarmed, Carmen my dear. They'll find your partner safe and sound on the island."

"Si, Si. Yes, I'm sure doctor. Thank you so much." She smiled and shook Doctor Bagshot's hand warmly. "When can I leave, Doctor? I have some friends arriving on Friday evening and I was sort of hoping…." She flashed her beautiful eyes into his.

He felt once more that glorious skip in his heart rate and the tingle in his loins.

"I think Friday morning. Is that okay for you?"

She smiled appreciatively.

"I'll talk to sister." He turned to leave. "I know you'll continue to working hard at the exercises." He added leaving the gym. He waved his arm affectionately without looking back and was gone.

# CHAPTER 42

Kurt Van der Koche staggered to the summit of the mountain.

Omollo moved to allow space on a long flat rock for Kurt to sit.

Kurt flopped beside Omollo gasping for breath wiping sweat from his brow with the back of his hand. He drank deeply from his water bottle.

"It's like being on top of the world up here." Omollo said casually, sitting bolt upright surveying the view.

Every bay and headland was stretched out beneath them. A vibrant panorama of greens and ochre's rose up all around him from an encompassing, seemingly limitless ocean. The brilliance of the colours was dulled by thickening cloud driven by a strengthening wind. Gusts whipped up the mountainside, bending the dozen or so stunted and gnarled magnolia and other mangled species that somehow thrived on the exposed summit.

"I remember saying to Alex….as we approached…that the island resembled a swimming turtle." Omollo smiled as he spoke, looking at his friend. "It does…don't you think?"

"Yah. It…does, John." Kurt agreed, fighting for breath and feeling Omollo's emotion. "We'll find….him, big man." He gulped down mouthfuls of water. "He's indestructible… that Alex Radcliff! Believe me!"

Omollo noticed the blood soaking through the fresh bandage strapped to Kurt's left thigh.

"The climb has opened up your wound." Omollo looked around him. The southern sky was heavy with rain. "We'd better get back. I'll change the dressing for you. Anyway, it'll be dark soon."

"We've just arrived! Have a heart, John."

"We should head back," he insisted.

"Just a few minutes. You have a good look around on your own. I'll rest up here, yah?"

Omollo heaved himself from the stone. Swaying and staggering in the gusting wind he clasped hold of a pine trunk for support. Ten feet away lay a circular depression ten feet in diameter which offered welcome protection from the wind. Omollo went to investigate.

"There's something over here," he called out to Kurt.

Kurt limped over to where Omollo squatted on the perimeter of the depression.

"Look at that!" He shouted above the gale pointing at a rock carving. Above them the gusting wind whistled through the swaying treetops.

Kurt knelt down and examined it. "It's a compass." He hobbled around the rim of the depression and found another stone carving. "This has an eye..." moving on excitedly with Omollo on his heals, "This one's a set square..." He faced Omollo and stated: "I'll bet you all the tea in China that the next stone will have an open book carved on it!"

They found a stone opposite the stone with the eye.

Omollo checked the carving on the smoothed face of the stone. "How did you know that?" he asked incredulously.

"The stone carvings of the open compass, the setsquare and the open book are positioned to form an equilateral triangle. They represent wisdom, strength and beauty, Yah! These are the 'Three Great Lights' of Freemasonry," Kurt explained casually, recovering his breath.

"The 'all seeing eye' is the eye of God which looks directly at the Bible."

"That's amazing, Kurt!" his eyes bulged in awe and admiration. "Are you a Freemason as well?"

"No. But those tests I told you about in the States opened a door for me. I've read the works of many authors who have spent most of their lives researching arcane and esoteric knowledge and ancient secrets." Kurt shook his head. "What they have uncovered is mind boggling, John!"

The two men rose to stand. The gusting wind knocked Kurt onto Omollo.

"My guess, John, is that they are pointing to the entrance into the mountain." Kurt plotted the centre of the triangle in the depression. "That's where the entrance must be!" They both squatted to examine the ground more closely. It was absolutely flat. "Are you up for a little bit of digging?"

Omollo looked up at the threatening sky. Fine rain had begun to fall. "Tomorrow, Kurt. We'd better get back now."

"You must be joking with me, yah?" Kurt looked about for something to dig with. "You'd better make good use of me. I'm not too sure I could climb up here again; not for a quite a while, anyway."

Both men dug and scraped frenetically, soaked by the fine rain blasted onto them.

"Look!" Kurt excitedly brushed away the wet earth and broken roots. He found a straight division between the rock. "This could be it."

The two men followed the edge in opposite directions until they backed into each other. They stood back.

"It's absolutely square. It can mean only one thing! Come on, John." Kurt said insistently. "Let's open it up."

"We'll need a lever...."

Omollo searched the summit and came back with a four inch thick tree trunk whilst Kurt returned limping badly with a wedge shaped rock. After prizing the three-foot edge of the square slab of stone open Omollo rammed the log into the gap. A strange, but very appealing aroma wafted up from the hole. Omollo raised the slab two feet when the wood cracked. The odour from below intensified. Both men were starting to feel its effects.

Despite feelings of giddiness and high inebriation Kurt scrambled around the summit searching for a suitable prop. Omollo stood holding the slab, before the gaping hole, exposed to the mysterious gas. He watched Kurt being buffeted by the wind and rain his staggering, drunken lurching strides suddenly looked very comical. His urge to laugh almost overwhelmed him. He screwed up his face and pushed his head into the ground. The log cracked once more.

Kurt teetered on the edge of the depression with a stouter log in his hand. Buffeted by a gust of wind he swayed then slipped, rolling next to Omollo. Soaked and covered in mud he lay on his back convulsed with hysteria.

Omollo gritted his teeth, his throat contracting with the effort to suppress his laughter. He snatched the log from Kurt with one hand and thrust it between the slab and the ground. Throwing his log to one side he collapsed into a contorted heap in the mud giving himself up to a fit of laughter.

Kurt playfully grabbed a handful of wet mud and threw it at Omollo. It smacked onto the centre of Omollo's forehead.

Both men sat roaring with laughter with mud trickling down Omollo's nose. Rainwater dripped from their chins. Kurt struggled to his feet. Omollo scooped up sods of earth in his arms and dropped the lot onto Kurt's head. A mud battle ensued, albeit a gentle one since neither man had the strength or ability to lift the lumps of earth. Instead they rolled defensively away in the slime, convulsed and helpless with hysterical laughter.

When the effects of the strange odour had finally wore off they lay exhausted on their backs, the heavy rain lashing across the summit washing the mud from their faces and from the edge of the square slab of stone they had just raised.

"We can get down through there," Kurt suggested.

Omollo was tempted.

Seeing the state of his friend, he shook his head slowly. "Not now. We must get back down to camp, Kurt. We'll need some rope and a torch before we go exploring in there."

"Yah! You're right. We'll have to do this together, John." They both looked down at his bandage, soaked with blood, rain and mud. "It might be a while though, my friend."

Omollo led the way slowly back down the ridge. Neither spoke, both wondering how long it would be before they could climb the summit again and resume their search for Radcliff, haunted by the possibility that when they did it could be too late.

# CHAPTER 43

Radcliff had been entombed within the mountain for seven days.

He lay on his stomach. Daylight touched his spent body. He could feel the sun burning the top of his head. The pleasure of its warmth permeated through every limb of his body; every cell reacting to this sudden influx of energy.

The shrivelled life form began to twitch and move under the loose mounds of rubble and rock. Fingers pulled on stones; legs and feet pushed and kicked themselves free. Hope of life penetrated his body as fast as his lungs could draw in the clean, fresh air.

He wanted to shout for joy but his mouth was swollen and parched; he wanted to move but his arms were trapped; he wanted to see but the glare was too strong. Squinting he lifted, stretched and craned his head tortoise like for as long as his strength lasted then it dropped, painfully onto the stones.

Radcliff had lost track of how many days he had been digging and moving rocks in the pitch darkness. The torch battery had died minutes after starting to tunnel through the loose, fallen rocks above the collapsed roof of the cave. Instinct had driven him onward and upward.

He had become a human mole clawing and tunnelling continuously through the loose stones. He dug and gouged his way in the utter blackness keeping his eyes firmly shut.

The effect of this, besides avoiding grit and dust entering his eyes, was that his body compensated for his loss of sight, stimulating his other senses. They became more acute. He could accurately judge the mass of a large rock barring his way and sense if it would be possible to move it. Then he would chip and work at it until it loosened; levering and wiggling it with unyielding perseverance until finally it rolled free.

There was no end, no victory or celebration when that happened. The joy and satisfaction of winning was no longer relevant. He only had a slight sense of relief before moving inexorably up, digging and clawing and kicking with his torn and bleeding fingers, feet and knees, until the next obstruction halted his progress.

It had seemed an eternity, digging in the blackness. During his slow climb he imagined future treasure hunters finding his dried bones amongst the rubble: maybe they would wonder how he came to be so deep in the mountain; maybe they would somehow understand the full horror of his ordeal. He thanked God for having given him Carmen. He prayed for deliverance so that he could see her once more.

He imagined Carmen at the top of his tunnel waiting for him. There was no day or night, just sleep and work. If he was awake he worked. Time did not exist. Length of sleep had no more relevance than how many hours he had worked digging out the countless rocks he had moved.

With his final vestige of energy he pulled away a large rock, which dislodged an avalanche of smaller ones that cascaded onto his out-stretched arms and onto his head. Another larger rock tumbled down catching him a glancing blow on the forehead and he blacked out.

Several hours later the miracle happened. Regaining consciousness, he felt the warmth of the sun on his bruised head. He saw the clear dawn sky and smelt the sweetness of fresh air filling is lungs.

# CHAPTER 44

Omollo silently dressed Kurt's wound in the light from the camp fire. It was late evening on the Saturday following their first ascent of the mountain.

"How does it look...?" Kurt asked tentatively, fearing the worst.

"It's...not too bad..." Omollo replied fastening the small safety pin securing the bandage.

"I'll be okay to go in the morning, yah?"

"The wound's still open, Kurt..."

"But we can't leave it any longer, my friend. If Alex's still alive... and that's a big *if*, John...we must go...he's been without food and water now...for almost a week..."

"He's *alive*!" Omollo shook his head. "He's *alive*, I keep telling you..."

"Then we must go tomorrow. I'll be okay. You'll drive yourself mad, John if we wait."

"But if... the infection...gets worse...?"

"*Gets* worse! It's nearly a week...you've done a great bit of doctoring, yah...but enough is enough, my friend."

"Okay, Kurt. I'm not too sure I can wait any longer, either. We'll see in the morning, okay?"

When they awoke it was overcast but bright with a light warm breeze from the north.

"It's definitely improving," Omollo announced cautiously binding up Kurt's leg.

"The weather's perfect for climbing too. We must go, John!"

Omollo looked up and nodded.

Both men busily filled their backpacks with torches, a selection of tools that Omollo had salvaged from the yacht, food, water and rope.

Before setting off Omollo presented Kurt with a stout walking stick he had hewn from a pine branch the night before.

Reaching the summit Omollo checked Kurt's wound. Satisfied, they removed the lid covering the square hole and lay it on the ground.

"Look at that!" Omollo pointed to the inscription on the underside of the lid. It read:

*"Vista Interiora Terrae Rectific ando Invenies Occultam Lapidem"*

Kurt studied it for a moment and smiled. "The guy who did this had quite a sense of humour, yah! It is the ancient command to examine oneself...translated it means: 'Visit the centre of the earth and by rectifying you shall find the hidden stone'."

Omollo shone a torch into the blackness. Steps descended beyond the range of the torch beam. He tied a safety rope around Kurt's waist. "You go first."

"Thanks friend!" Kurt grunted, carefully lowing himself onto the first step.

"If I fell you'd have quite a job holding me...!" Omollo chuckled handing Kurt his stick.

"Okay! Come on then...let's go and find Alex!" Kurt slowly descended into the hole. "It's a chimney..." Kurt called back, his torch beam cutting deep into the darkness. "There are steps spiralling around the outside...it cuts at an angle to the left. Be careful, yah! The steps are covered in moss and slime...some are crumbling and breaking away."

Omollo followed keeping the safety rope tight.

Kurt took one step at a time. Both men were chilled by the dank air. Water dripped from crevices and dribbled down the walls of the precipitous chimney. They descended deeper, saying very little, stopping frequently for rests.

At a depth of about a hundred feet they reached the bottom of the chimney. A rock fall blocked their path.

"*Alex!*" Omollo bellowed repeatedly, his deep voice reverberating and echoing up the chimney.

They listened.

Water dripped into a large pool beside the base of the chimney. Kurt moved the beam across the lake. The clear water overflowed into a smooth, mossy gully that ran underneath the boulders and rocks that barred their way.

Kurt watched Omollo stroking the great boulders. His face was creased with a look of utter despair.

"Maybe there's another way into the mountain..." Kurt suggested hopefully.

"Dynamite!" Omollo cried his eyes the size of saucers. "There's a few sticks left by those Frenchmen back at the camp."

"It's worth a try. We could put on a long fuse...give us time to get well above the explosion."

They climbed back up the chimney and hauled themselves out of the hole. They were instantly struck by the sun's searing heat and blinding light. They shuddered as the warmth penetrated their chilled bones.

Back at the camp Omollo checked Kurt's wound and re-dressed it.

"I'll get the explosives," Kurt said, heading for the carrier bag.

A familiar, but very faint, noise was carried on the breeze. He stopped in his tracks, listening with his ear to the northerly breeze. Then he heard it more clearly. He ran to the corner of the cliff. The sound was clear…the unmistakable pulsating beat of rotor blades.

"Look!" he yelled, pointing excitedly out to sea with his stick. "It's a chopper!"

Omollo darted over to him, squinting into the glare. Then he saw it…a black dot approaching fast from the northwest. It overshot the island then doubled back to hover over the bays below them.

Omollo jumped for joy then froze suddenly. He turned and ran for the bag of weapons. He threw a loaded machine gun to Kurt then quickly loaded a gun for himself and stuffed clips of ammunition into his pockets.

"It's okay, John. It's from the Seychelles," Kurt laughed.

"They don't know our position. You said yourself…" Omollo's eyes bulging with alarm. "…it's that devil coming back to finish us off. I know it, Kurt. There're landing in the bay."

"Well let's go down there and see," Kurt smirked.

Omollo hurried across the plateau to the trees, Kurt limping with his stick in one hand and gun in the other.

"Wait for me at the cliff top," Kurt called out to him.

Omollo stopped and faced Kurt. "We'll take up our position on the cliff top…. we can pin them down on the beach."

When Kurt reached the cliff top Omollo was waiting, lying face down peering over the rocks. Kurt lay beside him. The helicopter was descending close to the spot where Slaughter had landed seven days before.

"How many people can you get into one of those?" Omollo asked.

"A Gazelle…eight, maybe nine at a push …including the pilot…"

"We must expect the worst…we'll have to split up…. we'll have a better a chance catching them in crossfire. There's more weapons and ammunition at the other end of the beach."

Omollo started to get up. Kurt clasped Omollo's right arm.

"Kurt…I must go…I'm going back to the camp and down to the ledge…where we camped that night…there's some weapons close by. You climb that slope…" pointing up the hill behind them, "…and pick them off as they climb the cliff. I'll approach from the other side of the bay. Okay?"

The two men watched anxiously as the pilot brought the craft safely down onto a strip of beach between the trees and the shallow waters. Coconut palms nodded and swayed in the down draft.

They counted five passengers, three women and two men, jump from the belly of the craft onto the beach, each carrying a suitcase and ducking low, hurrying to get clear of the rotor blades. Two blonde women were first to reach the cliff directly beneath them. The taller blonde wore a pale pink revealing blouse and brief red hot pants the other had on a more modest beige safari shirt and shorts. The third woman was a dark brunette wearing scarlet shorts and white blouse tied above her midriff.

Behind her followed a tall, heavily set elderly man in safari shorts and white tee shirt. He carried a large canvas bag in addition to a suitcase. They huddled together, the wind from the blades tearing at their clothes and luggage, waiting for the last member of the group, a stocky, smartly dressed man in dark blue shorts and white short sleeved shirt. His right arm was in a sling.

"I know these people," Omollo said, touching Kurt's arm as they lay on the rocks above the beach. "Come on, Kurt. It's okay."

The taller blonde in the hot pants spotted the two armed men climbing down the cliff and let out a piercing scream. The last man dropped his suitcase in the sand and struggled to remove a revolver from his pocket. Awkwardly holding the gun in his left hand he remove the safety catch and fired two shots at the larger man as he jumped from the rocks onto the beach.

"Don't shoot! Don't shoot!" Omollo hollered above the whirring din of the helicopter. Kurt slipped over the last few rocks and struggled to stand up beside Omollo. The two men dropped their weapons and held their hands up high.

The man with the gun ran fast up the beach to join the others.

Omollo stood beaming at the group of new arrivals.

"Detective Omollo! Is that you?" The larger man shouted above the din of the aircraft as the other stockier man cautiously approached, his gun still pointed at Omollo.

"¡Madre mia! It's him," the brunette dashed forward and grabbed Omollo's great forearm. "It's Carmen, Mr. Omollo. Where's Alex?"

"Let's get off the beach," Omollo shouted above the din, pointing back up the cliff. "Do you mind Rod?" Omollo smiled, pushing the barrel of the gun away from his abdomen. "You'd better get your suitcase before the sea does."

"I'm…sorry, John," Rod stammered, still in shock. He turned to see his suitcase floating away towards the helicopter. "Yes, yes," Rod hurried off stuffing the gun back into his trouser pocket as he went.

Kurt had ushered the women up the cliff. The men formed a chain, passing the suitcases and bags up to Kurt at the top.

Omollo led them up through the trees towards the plateau and away from the noise.

Mid way along the beach, hidden behind a fallen palm a pair of eyes watched the five people jump from the aircraft. He ducked when the shots rang out and cocked his revolver.

He waited and watched as the group ascended the cliff then he darted out of the palm trees into the sea. Wading out to the helicopter he climbed into the cockpit door and thrust his gun into the neck the stunned pilot.

"Lift up. Take me to Mahé. *Now!*" he demanded in a thick French accent, pushing himself behind the pilot's seat and deftly closing the cockpit door.

They all heard the pitch of the helicopter's engine change. Rod rushed back to the cliff top.

"Wait! You silly bastard!" Rod shouted, waving his fist furiously at the rising aircraft. "Come back!"

Omollo descended the cliff to the beach with Rod close on his heels.

"It's that Frenchman," Omollo pointed to the footprints in the sand. Kurt hobbled up behind the two men kneeling in the sand.

Rod looked down then angrily watched the helicopter turn and head out to sea.

"What Frenchman?" Rod demanded exasperation bursting from his eyes.

Carmen was the first of the women to join them.

"We've had some trouble…." Kurt began.

"Let me explain Kurt. I know these people."

"*Trouble..!*" Carmen shouted. "What sort of trouble? Where's Alex?"

"Some Frenchman's high jacked our *bloody* helicopter!" Rod stood up throwing his arms up in the air.

"Please…please keep…calm everybody," Omollo raised his hands as Rod turned to meet the other three of his group hurry along the beach. "But first, Kurt, let me introduce you to Carmen Burgos, Alex's fiancé." Omollo put an arm around Kurt's shoulder. "Kurt is the pilot that brought Alex and me to the island…."

"Where is he? Please tell me, Mr. Omollo…. Is he hurt?"

"We've been looking for him, Miss Burgos," Kurt said. "When we get back to our camp we can resume our search."

"Detective Constable Omollo?" the taller man shouted.

Omollo stood to attention automatically. "Yes, sir!"

"What's been going on?"

"I'll tell you…but first I think I should introduce you all." Omollo raised his arm towards Kurt, who was standing close to the blonde in the safari shirt. "This is Kurt…Kurt, this is Arthur Brickman, a friend of the late Chief Inspector Hawkins, and this is his widow, Susan Hawkins…" extending his arm towards the blonde next to Kurt. "These two good people are Patsy and Rod Napier who helped Alex and me, and the Chief Inspector, during…that incident in Australia."

"Okay, mate. That's got the poncy formalities out of the way. Who's that bloody Frenchman? What the hell's been going on John…?"

"Calm down." Brickman interceded. "You Aussies always go in with both feet. Let D.C. Omollo…erm…John explain…."

"We're stranded on this bloody island, Arthur…there's the like-lihood of trouble with a Frenchman and our host is missing! I think we're entitled to an explanation."

"Yes. Yes. I know," Arthur placated patiently. "Don't get so excited! Give the man a chance, Rod, will you?"

"We were attacked," Omollo began to explain, "by some French-men. They were after Alex's treasure. We got rid of all but one. He'd been hiding somewhere on the island. I followed his trail several times… but whenever…"

"What happened to Alex, Mr. Omollo?" Carmen interrupted her eyes wide and frantic.

"Alex was captured and taken inside that mountain," Omollo pointed inland in the direction of the mountain, its summit just visible above the canopy. "Don't worry, Carmen," his deep, resonant voice soothing her. "We're very close to finding him. But first we need to go please…soon the light will be gone ... I'll tell you everything once we're back at the camp."

"But what are you goin' to do about our transport?" Rod asked with growing frustration. "Have you got a radio…at your camp?"

"No. I'm sorry Rod," Omollo shrugged. "We're all going to be stranded here for a little while."

"Oh, *bloody* hell!" Rod kicked a broken branch.

"Come on, Rod," Patsy coaxed. "The chopper's gone darlin'. Noth-ing can be done about that. Let's do what John asks. Alex is lost."

Omollo strode off, leading the group back up the cliff and through the trees to the plateau. Kurt struggled to keep up, hobbling just behind the great man.

"Wow! She's more beautiful than I imagined, John," Kurt said quietly when they were several yards in front of the group. Omollo turned and smiled. "What the devil are you going to tell her, John?"

"I don't know…" he said sadly.

At the camp Omollo slowly gave the group a brief summary of all their experiences since leaving the Seychelles. Kurt watched their reactions and could see disappointment, outrage and horror etched in all their faces. They said nothing, stunned by Omollo's description of events and the news that Radcliff was entombed within the mountain.

"At least we are in no immediate danger," Omollo added.

The statement did little to placate them.

Carmen broke away, alone, and slowly made her way to the lake. The plateau was in shade and the light was fading rapidly. Several minutes elapsed. All their eyes were on Carmen pacing sadly up and down. Patsy and Susan Hawkins went to her.

"We're in a *right…bloody* fix, ain't we, John?" Rod snapped after they had gone. "We came out here to help Alex…help him get his treasure out of the mountain. Now we find out that a French bastard is after it…and to cap it all we've still got that bugger who smashed up my wagon to contend with. What happens when this bloody frog regroups and comes back here for his treasure? He's not going to give that up in a hurry, that's for sure!"

"We've got plenty of weapons." Omollo said encouragingly. "There's more on the beach…and maybe some out in the bay…there's a wreck out there…the Frenchman's yacht…"

"Oh great!" Rod retorted. "We're stranded and we're going to have to fight a *bloody* war!" He shook his head, his hand rubbing the back of his neck. "Why did I let Patsy talk me into this?"

Rod and Arthur Brickman turned away; shaking their heads, muttering to themselves, watching the three women huddled together beside the lake.

Omollo and Kurt strode over to Carmen and the two blonde women. Carmen's lips were quivering and she was clutching her leg.

"Is Alex alive, Mr. Omollo?" Carmen asked solemnly, her large tearful brown eyes pleading for a sign of hope, her hands clasped together under her chin as if in prayer.

Omollo stooped and held her shoulders. He looking straight into her lovely watery eyes, smiled as positively as he could and said, with conviction: "We know that he's alive, Carmen. The sooner we can get back inside that mountain the better."

Omollo darted a glance at Kurt for support.

"We've found a secret entrance at the summit…" Kurt pointed in the direction of the mountain.

"Can we go there now?" She asked.

"Not now." Omollo said hating himself. "We must wait until morn…"

"*Morning*! ¡Que hombré! Show me where Alex went into the mountain …please!"

Omollo led the women around the rock face, with the men following. From the corner of the cliff he pointed out the indentation in the mountain-side.

"Alex's inside there?" Rod muttered, exchanging significant glances with Patsy, Arthur and Susan. Carmen gazed up at the spot, her belief that Radcliff was alive unwavering. Everyone looked on sympathetically but said nothing. A golden glow from the setting sun lit the shoulder of the mountain high above them.

"Have you climbed up there since the…?" Carmen quickly asked.

"I did. After the shooting was over I went up there. I found a deep shaft that had formed above the collapsed roof of a cave. I called out many times…but I don't think he heard me."

"Will you climb up there now with me, Mr. Omollo?"

"Carmen!" Susan touched her elbow. "What about your shoulder… and your leg, dear? You said that you suffered from vertigo. The light is fading. Wait until morning…please," she implored.

"Take me up there now, Mr. Omollo." she demanded.

Omollo looked up. The sky was clear and there was no wind. But the light was almost gone. "First you must call me John."

"Okay…John. Take me to find Alex."

"You'll need a safety rope. We must go right now."

Carmen threw her arms around the big man's waist and hugged him.

Kurt looped the end of the rope around her slender waist and tied a bowline. Her perfume and everything else about her intoxicated him.

Omollo led the ascent up the rock face stopping for Carmen to work her way up to him. At the spot where the waterfall had once gushed they struck out diagonally over the cracked and crumbling rock towards the indentation. Using the fissures and crevices that criss-crossed the whole rock-face he and Carmen slowly worked their way to the lip of the hole.

"You climb very well," he encouraged when she was standing beside him at the shaft. "Are you okay?"

"I want to go down there, John."

"That's not wise, Carmen. We need a safety line secured from above."

She began shouting into the shaft, "*Alex…!Alex…!*" Omollo joined in with his booming voice. They listened for a moment, and then he called again. There was no response, not even an echo; their shouts absorbed into the dense granite.

Omollo put a finger to his lips, his great eyes lighting up in the dusk.

Carmen's heart skipped a beat.

"Did you hear that?" He whispered.

Carmen leaned towards the hole, straining her ears. "What did you hear?" she whispered back, her eyes flickering as fast as her thoughts. Then she heard it for herself. A regular tapping noise was coming from near the top of the crevice.

"It's *him*!" She screamed. "*We're coming, Alex…!*"

"Arthur," Omollo called down. "Bring up some more ropes quickly. I think we've found him."

Omollo and Arthur Brickman lowered Carmen slowly into the hole using her safety rope. She carried a coil of rope over her shoulder and held a torch. She touched the loose floor of the cave and set off an avalanche of stones. She heard a yelp of pain to her right and immediately directed her beam to the spot.

"Is that you, Alex? It's Carmen, cariño mia. I'm here." She heard a weak cough.

"Car..men," Radcliff whimpered no further than a yard away, his hoarse voice barely audible.

She worked her way over to the spot where she had heard his voice.

"Let me down a bit more," she called up.

They lowered her too quickly and her foot hit a mound of rocks.

"Slowly!" she screamed back, hearing a grunt as the loose rocks tumbled in the darkness. "Stop!" she cried. "Where are you?" she yelled franticly, shinning the torch beam repeatedly over the area where she had heard the sounds. "I can't see you, Alex," she cried. Her injured right arm seized up, the ripped and depleted muscles cramping agonisingly. She lost her grip on the torch, which clattered on the rocks, its beam slicing angles of light in the cave as it bounced into the blackness and then went out.

Forgetting the pain in her arm she twisted her body over on the rocks and wildly rummaged the rocks with her left hand until, suddenly, she touched bare flesh.

"Oh Alex!" She cried, tunnelling her arm between his body and the loose stones searching for his face. "I've found you, my darling. I've found you!" She worked her hand upward over his body.

"I can't move," Radcliff's voice, little more than a breath of air, came from above her.

"Pull me up a little," she shouted. She rose slowly over the rubble, feeling with her left hand until she caught his hair between her fingers and dug away the stones around his ears and cheek. "You feel cold, cariño. We'll get you out," she said breathlessly, caressing his face.

Taking the end of the rope from around her neck she threaded it under Radcliff's body. "You're safe now," she said with soft assurance, struggling to perform the task with one hand. She tied a quadruple knot to secure Radcliff then tied the free end about her own waist. "Take me up," she called out to the men above. "They will pull you up in a minute. Hold on cariño. Hold on."

Having extracted Radcliff out of the mountain they lowered his unconscious body carefully down the rock face. Susan and Patsy took his legs and then Rod and Kurt took the weight from the rope and laid him onto a sleeping bag. Kurt felt a week pulse in his neck. Rod shone the torch onto Radcliff's limp, torn and bleeding body. It was almost bereft of clothing. Then he shone it on Radcliff's bloodied, dust encrusted face.

Carmen, Patsy and Susan set about cleaning his face, washing his torn body and bathing his wounds. The men erected both ridge tents sideways to the rock face, near to the dried up lake, with the entrances facing each other. The tent nearest to the lake was given to Radcliff and Carmen; Susan and Patsy took the other tent.

Kurt and Omollo lit a fire and prepared a meal.

The four men slept under the stars surrounded by boxes and bags of provisions, supplies and armaments.

The night was warm. Carmen and Radcliff were together for the first time on the island. They all slept peacefully.

But beyond the northern horizon a tempest was brewing. It would be more devastating than the severest weather system could inflict.

# CHAPTER 45

The following morning on Nosey-Be island, northwest Madagascar, Jeb Chiltern climbed the wooden steps zigzagging up the cliff and entered a thatched hut. The hut had been the home of one of the village elders. It was built on short stilts twenty meters up on a ledge in the cliffs overlooking the sea. Concealed by vegetation and palms, the hut was invisible from the beach.

Slaughter was leaning back on the rear legs of the bamboo chair, one foot resting on the window ledge whittling with his hunting knife. Chiltern tossed a letter into Slaughter's lap and flopped onto a chair at the back of the small hut, sweat dripping from his chin onto his bare chest. Slaughter let the wood he was whittling drop to the ground and cut open the letter.

"The *bitch*!" He threw the knife. It embedded itself, quivering, into the doorframe. "She wants a divorce," he yelled, smacking the paper with the back of his hand. "What a fucking nerve, for fucks sake! I've lost every penny on this job; I've never been so skint and she wants to screw me for me house in Chipstead!" He stood and threw the chair against the wall, paced up and down the hut rubbing his baldhead alternately with both hands then turned on Chiltern, his eyes full of fury. "Who's the bloke?" he screamed.

"He's an actor or somethin'," Chiltern answered indifferently, secretly revelling in the sight of the big man cracking up before his eyes but shrewd enough to keep his feelings well hidden.

"He's dead meat! I'll kill the *fucking* little shit!" he hollered, crimson with rage. The veins in his neck and temple protruded like knotted cord. He stared at his clenched fist shaking before his eyes. "I'll cut you up alive with a chain saw, starting with your feet and work upwards! Do yer 'ear me?" he screamed, his great booming voice reverberating like thunder in the small cove.

"Oh! I almost forgot," Chiltern said; his voice the epitome of calmness and control. "I was at the store when a call came for you."

"You're loving this, aint yer? You little weasel." Slaughter wiggled the knife free from the doorframe, clasped Chiltern's ear and held the knifepoint under his chin.

"Hay! Take it easy!" Chiltern quailed, swallowing hard several times, his larynx rubbing against the blade. "I'm on your side!" He searched his pockets and pulled out a scrap of paper and waved it in

Slaughter's face. "It was from some bloke in the Seychelles. He wants you to ring him back...he said it was urgent."

He snatched the scrap of paper and looked at the number.

"He gave me a code word. You are to say 'Kingfisher'."

"Wait 'ere," Slaughter grunted and went out.

Many of the villagers were gathered outside the hut. They watched the Englishman sprint up the steep coombe and enter the general store perched on the cliff top overlooking the craggy shoreline.

Slaughter stormed into the dimly lit, high lofted thatched hut. Its shelves were bare except for a few tins of foodstuffs, a selection for hardware: hammers, sickles and other tools hanging on the walls. A scrawny native wearing a tattered vest lounged on a high stool behind a dust covered counter on one side of the hut. Boxes of nails, screws, washers, nuts and bolts and rubber tubing were scattered indiscriminately upon it. A barrel stood in the centre of the hut with brooms, shovels and various hoes and digging implements clustered inside it.

"I wanna make a long distance call to the Seychelles." Slaughter slapped a pile of small denomination Malagasy francs on the counter. The native nodded to a new booth at the far end of the hut beside a shuttered window.

Slaughter waited several minutes for a tone, cursing and pacing impatiently. Finally he punched the telephone numbers. He heard a ringing tone. A woman answered and he gave the password. She told him to hold the line. His fingers strummed on the windowsill as the minutes passed. He was about to smash his fist into the wall when someone spoke.

"Listen closely, Mr. Slaughter," the small familiar voice instructed. "I can only spare you one minute. The police have detained a Frenchman who has just come back from the island. He has seen Alex Radcliff's woman there."

"You sure..?"

"I spoke with him myself half an hour ago. He said that Radcliff had been inside the mountain when it blew up. I think we can be sure that Radcliff is now dead as a door nail!"

"Yeh, he's a goner alright. I saw the mountain blow myself. He's buried under a million tons of rock! Nothing short of a miracle could 'ave saved him."

"This man has a way of creating miracles, Mr. Slaughter. You should know that! Very quickly...I have an urgent cabinet meeting to attend. I'll offer you a quarter of a million U.S. dollars if you and the Frenchman join forces and bring me Radcliff's corpse or absolute proof that he is dead."

"Half a million *pounds*!"

"Dollars!"

"You're on mate."

"I'll send a coast guard helicopter to pick you up. Be at Hell-Ville airport in five hours time. I have to go. Good luck, Mr. Slaughter."

The line went dead.

A crowd of jeering, shouting natives were in front of the hut when Slaughter returned. Chiltern was baring their way at the top of the steps. Slaughter shoved his way through the mob to Chiltern's side and faced the crowd.

"All right, calm down." He shouted down holding up his hands. "Listen..!" he snapped "...I know we promised we'd be gone as soon as my dislocated shoulder was better. Well, the good news is... its better... and we are leaving right now...at this very moment. Okay..?"

They argued amongst themselves for several seconds.

"The elder demands that his hut is returned to him immediately," a spokesman shouted. "He said that he will allow you to remove your possessions and then you must go."

Slaughter snarled at the spokesman. "It's okay Jeb," Slaughter spoke from the corner of his mouth. "I'll tell you on the way to the airport. Come on, let's get our things together and get out of here."

The mob followed them into the hut. Slaughter pulled the knife from his belt and turned on them. "You said we could get our things," he said waving the point of his hunting knife under the spokesman's nose. They all stopped in their tracks then backed away. He slammed the bamboo door in their faces.

They left the village on foot each carrying two packed holdalls containing sufficient firearms and ammunition to fight a small war.

On arrival at Mahé they had further access to additional Government weapons and were introduced secretly to the Frenchman by a Government official in a small room at the rear of Government House.

"This is Jean-Claude Narbonne, gentlemen," said the diminutive, impeccably dressed middle-aged man, of Asian descent. "The First Bank of the Seychelles has given Mr. Narbonne unlimited Government guaranteed credit provided, of course, that you men form an alliance immediately. Will you please tell me now if you all intend to join forces and agree to take the island on behalf of our Government, confirm the elimination of Alex Radcliff and pay the Government twenty percent of the proceeds of any treasure you might find."

Instantly both Englishmen weighed up the measure of the Frenchman.

The Frenchman's crooked smile turned into a sneer as he considered his chances of outwitting the two men before him.

"Ten percent!" Jean-Claude fixed the civil servant with an icy stare.

"Fifff..teeeen." the government man tentatively insisted.

"You cannot begin to imagine the magnitude of this treasure," Jean-Claude stated turning his back on the little civil servant. "Ten percent will be hundreds of millions of dollars." He turned and faced him. "You cannot take more than that," he said adamantly.

"Agreed. Ten percent it will be," the native capitulated.

Jeb Chiltern ignored the Frenchman's outstretched hand. "What about our share of the treasure?" he grinned revealing two gold teeth.

"Ten percent."

"Fifteen," Slaughter grunted.

"This treasure belongs to my family," the Frenchman shrugged. "I've documentation to prove it. I would say that several hundred million dollars is more than enough to buy up all the women in the world. I'll pay you a minimum of twelve percent and fifteen percent if Radcliff is found alive and stays that way until we have all the treasure out. I want him to witness something before he leaves this world. "

"Radcliff *alive!*" Slaughter scoffed. "Okay Frenchie. Twelve percent it is. If Radcliff's alive we get fifteen." He stole a glance at Jeb, who was licking his lips. "You'll be sorting the transport to the island?" Slaughter added.

"Oui."

"Good, good," the official said nervously as the three men shook hands. He produced an envelope from his inside jacket pocket and handed it to Jean-Claude.

"This is the exact longitude and latitude of the island. It was in the flight recorder of the helicopter you…" giving Slaughter a sideways glance "…crashed off the Madagascar coast. Bon chance, gentlemen." he retreated quickly down the corridor and was gone from sight.

"Oui. I shall be attending to the transport," Jean-Claude said acidly. "I will be purchasing another luxury yacht, similar to the one you sank… with certain modifications. I shall hire three men to crew the yacht, including a pilot."

"I'll be watching you like a hawk, Frenchie," Slaughter pointed a finger into the Frenchman's face. "A deal is a deal, in my book. You double cross me and I'll cut you into tiny pieces...slowly."

It had taken three days to prepare the yacht for the assault on the island. She sailed under a Greek flag but Jean-Claude had renamed her 'Santa Lucia II'. She was a Duchess type, identical to the previous yacht, but her 2000hp diesel engines had been modified; an additional 3,000-litre fuel tank had been installed. She had psychedelically painted hull and superstructure which had debased the integrity of her design and softened her sharp, elegant lines into a grotesque floating monstrosity.

By Wednesday evening, after several successful test runs to surrounding islands, they were ready to go.

At the last moment Jean-Claude brought several mysterious boxes and cases on board and locked them in the bows.

With her engines throbbing and her lines hauled the pilot gave the order to weigh anchor. The yacht gracefully eased its way through the crowded marina of Victoria harbour, discernible only by its lights moving quietly amongst the myriad of masts and hulls moored into neat rows alongside scores of jetties.

# PART FOUR

# CHAPTER 46

That same evening Radcliff lay luxuriating on his back in one of the tents, his head cushioned on Carmen's left thigh. Her finger tips gently followed the rim of his scalp under the ears, they met at the nape of his neck then caressed and stroked his long thick, greying ginger locks. Every now and then she would let her hands wonder over his shoulders to his bare chest, gently and sensuously stretching her arms to his abdomen.

"Ahhh…hhh!" He sighed. "This is…paradise!...heaven!..ke..ee..ep going, don't stop."

Untiringly she repeated the process, stretching just that bit further each time. He reached up…moaning with pleasure.

"We could…"

"Feeling better, my Tarzan!" she chuckled. "Don't worry I will spend the rest of my life making up for you're…er…." Stretching her fingers deeper, delving a little further under his shorts. "Soooon cariño," She purred, her finger tips caressing him. "It's only been three days…"

He groaned.

She withdrew her hand and hugged his head.

"How long?"

"Don't you remember when I found you?"

"Of course I do. I can't think back…it's like a fog…everything is fragmented and distorted like in a nightmare. I can remember hearing your voice...calling me. It was the sweetest sound…my prayers were answered again."

"For once I was there for you," she leaned over and kissed him softly. "We are here together on your island," she said dreamily caressing his face. "I'll actually be with you…when you get to see that Cross of Goa. I just hope…I don't let you down," she added, very quietly.

"What was that?!" he exclaimed trying to lift his head.

"I hope we can get it down," she leaned over and kissed him again.

"It's there; Carmen…nestled on top of a pile of treasure. Maybe tomorrow we'll go up there………"

"The others are digging out the treasure now. Very soon we shall have the Cross of Goa here…beside you."

"The others? Who…Kurt and John? They're digging out the treasure?"

"They've all been in here…to see you over the last three days. There's the Chief Inspector Hawkins' widow, Susan, Rod and Patsy…"

305

"Rod and Patsy! They're here too?" he said in amazement.

She nodded, her delighted expression warming his heart.

"Who's the guy with the huge head…. he poked it in the tent earlier this morning?"

"That's Arthur…," she giggled. "His head…it's *verrry*…large!"

They both laughed.

"He's Susan's friend." Carmen's smile faded. "She's arranged for a small memorial to be placed on the roadside where her husband died. The police put us in touch with Constable Curtis………."

"I remember Curtis," Radcliff laughed. He winced with a sharp pain in his chest. "I think the gun battle on the Capricorn Highway must have been…." Radcliff choked, coughing and laughing and holding his chest.

"Careful, cariño. You've a few cracked ribs. Your chest…. well the whole of your body…. was with the black and the blue."

"Yes, well I think Curtis thought that gun fight was the biggest thing since Ned Kelly!"

"Who is this…Kelly?"

"An outlaw. He wore steel armour over his head and body…."

"Si…I remember…Mick Jagger played him…."

"Oh, yes. I forgot.You're a die-hard Stones fan aren't you."

"I can remember many events in my life when I hear their songs."

"Well how did you remember how to find the island…did the Stone's give you a clue to that as well…?

"No," she admitted laughing. "You told me…more or less…on the journey out to Australia. From that the pilot was able to reduce the size of the search area."

"We've both been put through the mill, haven't we, sweetheart?" Radcliff sighed then reaching up, ignoring the pain, to cup her face in his hands and kissed her tenderly. He winced as he lowered himself down. "Did Curtis introduce you to Rod and Patsy?"

"Si. Rod told us about the shooting… Susan wanted to know every detail…we drove out to where her husband had been shot. Curtis had all the answers…proudly strutting around, explaining the angles and directions of all the shots that were fired." Radcliff shook his head and smiled. "But he has put a touching inscription on the stone. Rod told us how you turned up at the end of their driveway that morning of the shooting…" She looked into Radcliff's eyes apologetically, "I had to ask them…I couldn't stop myself."

"I'm glad you did."

"They could help us with the treasure, no?" She said excitedly. "I thought the more friends we have here the better."

Radcliff nodded and smiled up at her.

"Patsy really likes you. So does Rod. They couldn't stop asking questions. She is very beautiful, no? If she wasn't married I'd have been very jealous."

"You're incredible," he laughed then clutched his chest. "Where are...they all... now?" he asked with a wheezing cough, struggling for breath.

She stroked his brow. "They're inside that mountain...digging out the treasure. John Omollo and Kurt and Susan..."

"*What!*"

"Si. They have gone down some steps from the summit of that mountain and were digging a tunnel. Arthur, Rod and Patsy are at the shaft where we found you. They're preparing it...they intend to bring the Cross and some of that treasure out through there."

"I must help..." he tried to sit up and collapsed back into her lap with the pain from his chest, his back and stomach muscles cramping with the sudden exertion.

"¡Escuchame, mi cariño!" She said sternly. "You must rest...You must be patient..."

Omollo's beaming face burst in through the tent door, the whites of eyes the size of saucers. "He's awake!"

"This man wants to start digging!"

Her look of exasperation amused Omollo.

"Maybe tomorrow," Radcliff corrected, raising his head slightly from her lap. "How's it going, John?"

"I have seen it, Alex!" Omollo's grin broadened to reveal teeth that gleamed as brightly as his huge eyes.

"You've broken through to where the Cross is!" Carmen squealed with delight, caressing Radcliff's head.

"Yes," he said, crouching low to enter the tent. "It's certainly indescribable," his great voice rising to a high pitched falsetto. "It is way beyond anything I imagined it to be." He shook his head and chuckled for a moment. "It is...it made me feel....it's the most...," the big man inflated with excitement as he struggled for a way to describe his feelings, his bulk stretching the fabric of the tent.

"You were right about the treasure, Alex!" His grin turned to a look of sheer amazement. "It is just unbelievable, Carmen. It is beyond words...I cannot describe it!" He burst into a wheezing chuckle, shaking his head with incredulity his excited eyes darting rapidly from Carmen to Radcliff.

"I'll have to get up tomorrow...just to keep my eyes on you lot!" Radcliff croaked. "You'll be making off with all the treasure and leaving us here stranded!"

"Tie him up, John!" Carmen ordered.

"Some people never seem to know when they're well off," Omollo shook his head with mock indignation. "I think his brain must have received more damage than we first thought," he added, rubbing his chin.

"Anyway, I've something to announce. Kurt and me are preparing a special meal tonight. We were celebrating finding the Cross of Goa, the treasure and last but not least your remarkable recovery, Alex! I'll call you both when it's ready."

At noon that day Omollo's group, using small explosive charges, had cleared a pathway through the boulders from the chimney to where Radcliff had been trapped with the Cross of Goa and the treasure.

Arthur's group had reached the treasure chamber several minutes later and joined Omollo, Kurt and Susan standing in stunned silence before the glittering, glowing, sparkling mountain of treasure. They shot glances at each other, their mouths gaping wide open, astounded by the sheer quantity of precious stones and metals stacked in front of them.

Their torch beams played and danced on the gold and the dazzlingly beautiful gems: rubies, sapphires and emeralds shone out seductively amongst the heaps of diamonds, each reflecting a spectrum of colours, the magical multiplicity of dazzling, sparkling lustre was intermingled with gold and silver coins and bars, bejewelled golden ornaments of every shape and size. The whole spectacle, although breathtakingly vast and expansive, had a subtle equilibrium of colour, a balancing allure that was a feast to the eyes.

"It's a work of art!" Arthur had whispered as if the slightest sound might disturb its arrangement. He raised the beam and shone it onto the top section of the Cross of Goa. They all gasped in unison, its glow having a timeless spiritual language that penetrated to the deepest parts of their souls. Their eyes moved slowly over the bejewelled golden cross pieces glancing at each other occasionally with identical expressions of silent incredulity, wonder and excitement.

Kurt's face peered in through the tent door. "Will the guests of honour, King Alex and his good Queen Carmen care to partake of some food from our humble table?"

"Lead on McKurt!" Radcliff buckled as he tried to lift himself. Kurt crawled up beside him and with Carmen's help they managed to haul Radcliff, grunting and cursing, the multitude of pains stabbing him with every movement of his body. They half carried him to his seat of honour close to a long table of food and near to the roaring fire.

The others stood waiting, their shapes silhouetted against the fire. A solitary clap grew into a crescendo of applause.

# CHAPTER 47

Slaughter had gone onto the bridge and stood menacingly beside the pilot, a diminutive Seychellois native. The wind had lifted the swell and the yacht pitched sickeningly across the run of the waves.

"What's that over there to your right?" Slaughter pointed to a bright glow on the horizon whilst taking a gulp from a can of beer.

"Starboard sir..."

"Whatever." He finished the beer and crushed the can in his hand and tossed it overboard. "What is it then...smart arse?"

The pilot, less than half the size of Slaughter, squinted through the steeply raked window. "It's a light. It could be a fire."

"That's what it looks like to me. Turn the boat towards it."

"I cannot sir, I'm very sorry. It is the owner who gives the orders."

"Jean-Claude," he bellowed. "Get your arse up here."

They heard stumbling and crashing below. Slaughter was about to investigate when Jean-Claude appeared on the deck below the bridge, saliva dribbling from his chin. Slaughter descended the swaying, rolling stairs and hauled him up to the bridge by his trouser belt and shirt, his feet momentarily leaving the deck, and propped him against the window.

"Look out there," stabbing his finger on the glass towards the bright glow on the starboard horizon. "What do you see?"

"A light," he croaked clinging to Slaughter. "What of it?"

"It's a fire. A fire burning on your island...the island that has all your treasure! Now, what d'ya see?"

"Do you want me to change course, sir?" The pilot asked Jean-Claude tentatively.

"Oui, Oui. Change course, Maurice," Jean-Claude submitted, eager to get below and lie horizontal once more. "Just do as he says...head towards that light."

# CHAPTER 48

Your throne, King Alex," Omollo bowed extravagantly, adding a courtly flourish with his arm, beckoning him to a stack of flat stones with a boulder positioned for a backrest and padded with a sleeping bag.

Kurt and Carmen eased him down onto it.

"Thank you." Radcliff shrugged, his arms held out from his sides quizzically, smiling sheepishly. "This is…er….erm…marvellous," he stammered with embarrassment, looking appreciatively at each in turn.

Arthur handed out the mugs. Rod popped two bottles of champagne whilst Patsy filled each of the mugs to the brim.

"To Alex..!" Rod bellowed, raising his mug in the air…"and his nine lives…. and long may they continue to be renewed!"

"To Alex..!" They all cheered in unison. Radcliff, with Carmen at his side, gave them the Royal wave and the group sat down.

A table had been made of upturned boxes and logs laid across collapsible chairs with flattened cardboard on top. Candles had been placed in mugs at intervals between the roasted pork, beef and chicken, potatoes, green vegetables, salads, fresh and dried fruits, nuts and a whole salmon.

They sat in a semi circle facing the fire, Arthur in the centre and furthest from the fire. He had taken charge of the drink: bottles of champagne, wine, spirits and soft drink leaned against a rock close to him. Omollo sat between Carmen and Arthur; Susan sat on Arthur's right, next to her sat Kurt then Patsy and finally Rod.

The flickering light from the raging fire and candles lit the dinner table. It was a magical scene. A breeze from the east fanned the fire, sparks rose up like thousands of glowing insects that danced and played on the rock face.

"We were going to save this champers until we'd got the treasure out," Arthur shouted, "but all of us have witnessed one of the greatest and most amazing feats of human endurance we are ever likely to have the good fortune to see. We all wanted to show…"

"What Arthur's trying to say," Rod bellowed, "in his pommy fashion, is that we couldn't wait to get stuck into the grog!"

"Rod..!" Patsy chided. "Shut up and leave him alone, just for once."

"I know, sweetheart."

"That's alright, me dear," Arthur smiled. "I'm quite used to his banter."

"Thanks! All of you! Thanks very much..." Radcliff beamed shrugging with embarrassment "...it's...marvellous." He sniffed the breeze. "Let's eat. I think there's rain in the air."

During the meal Omollo and Kurt gave a vivid and enthralling account of their victory over their enemy and how they found the secret entrance to the passage into the mountain.

"What about that Frenchie who hijacked our chopper?" Rod asked.

"He did get away, it's true," Omollo confessed. "But I think it's very unlikely he will show up again. The wreck of his other yacht is still in the bay. It will take him quite a while to find the capital to buy another."

"Yah, I agree. It will be many weeks before he can organise another foray." Kurt said convincingly, pacifying the rising alarm in Carmen's eyes.

"Okay," Rod acknowledged. "But what about that bugger...what's his name... you said he'd escaped as well!"

"He won't be back," Omollo lied quickly. "He's finished. If he's alive his credibility will be just about rock bottom by now."

"You were telling me about this character, John," Arthur said. "If he *is* the one responsible for the shooting at the hospital then he's definitely got a cash flow problem."

"What did I tell you?" Omollo said quickly, grateful for Arthur's intervention.

"It was the Mob, John," Arthur continued, "in the States...who were the money behind the hospital attack and they supplied the weaponry. I received a message from the F.B.I. before we left England. The whole Cinisi Family have either been killed or rounded up in a gunfight. The Godfather is behind bars, or will be, and all the missing weapons have been accounted for. With no benefactor left to fund his campaign against Alex he'll have no alternative but to give up and go home."

"You can't be sure..." Rod began.

"Rod!" Patsy snapped. "Give it a rest, darlin' and let everyone enjoy themselves, eh!"

"We've got enough weaponry here to see off a small army, should the worst come to the worst." Arthur added casually.

"Tell us about the Cross of Goa, Alex," Patsy asked. "That's why we're all here after all..."

"And the treasure, honey," Rod reminded.

"And the treasure..." Patsy continued "...Kurt mentioned that it has incredible power...that it's like the Ark of the Covenant!"

"You didn't believe all that baloney Kurt told us in that mountain, did you honey?" Rod scoffed, grinning and shaking his head.

"Kurt was a nuclear physicist," Omollo stated proudly. "His work actually involved the elements that gives the Cross its powers. Isn't that correct, Kurt?"

"Yah!" Kurt smiled. "I can fully understand Rod's scepticism."

"I know what you said, Kurt," Rod bludgeoned on. "You said that the Cross is one third the size of the Ark of the Covenant and that it was made in the 1500's using some ancient secret formulae? As a Jew I was taught to believe that the Ark was built by God."

"With greatest respect, Rod," Kurt began. "The Ark was built by human hand. The goldsmith used two layers of pure gold to make the casement with the most resinous wood available...'shittim wood'...the species is extinct now...they sandwiched it between the gold. It's all in the scriptures...the Torah."

"What you're saying is that any Tom, Dick or Harry could build an Ark if they have the right formulae?" Rod laughed.

"I'll go one better," Kurt declared. "People have! The proof is in its existence! Let me explain..."

Kurt repeated the tale of the Arizona cotton farmer. Omollo left the group and climbed the cliff to retrieve Radcliff's carrier bag, which he had hidden deep within his old cave after the attack. On returning to the group he extracted the diary and handed it to Radcliff.

Radcliff opened the pages to the date: Friday the 13th April 1721. They all gathered around him, some holding candles, to see and admire the work of Radcliff's ancestor.

"That's the lower section," Kurt pointed at the base of the Cross shown in the sketch. "The chemistry begins when the top section is placed upon its base. It becomes a superconductor."

Carmen had slipped away unnoticed.

The breeze had freshened snuffing out the candles and fanning the heart of the fire white-hot, blowing the flames horizontally towards the cliff and scorching the grass. Radcliff looked instinctively out to sea, his nose sniffing the air for moisture, half listening to Kurt's résumé.

Kurt then continued to explain the principals behind his statement and went on to describe the powers of the Cross of Goa and how all of it was at the frontier of nuclear physics.

Radcliff recalled the many great fires he had lit over the years on the plateau; hoping his beacons would attract any passing yacht or aircraft.

"John," Radcliff leaned across Carmen's empty place and pulled hard on Omollo's arm. "Keep the fire low," he whispered. "And take those new logs off."

Omollo nodded, realising suddenly the reason for Radcliff's alarm. Unseen by the others, he levered and pulled the burning logs off the fire.

Carmen had waited until Kurt was finished talking then reappeared wearing a new white blouse tied under her breasts, revealing her fleshy midriff and gorgeous concave naval, and a green and red silk sarong tied low about her hips. She strutted to the centre of the semi circle and began clapping her hands rhythmically above her head. She turned to face Radcliff, who was looking up at her spellbound.

"I said that I would dance for you on your island. Can someone give me a good solid beat:-one-two, one-two-three, one- two, one-two-three-four?"

Omollo picked up two smouldering charred logs and hit them together in the required tempo.

Carmen clapped her hands, complicating the rhythm, but Omollo followed perfectly. As she strutted back and forth her bare feet were stomping soundlessly, but effectively, on the ground and her hips swayed, jerked and thrusted seductively. She rotated first one way with one arm bent and raised above her head. Her head was held high and her back straight, her other arm moved in front of her breasts, her hands gracefully moving and twisting, her fingers clicking cleverly to suggest castanets; then she rotated one way then the other alternating the position of her arms. The strutting, hip swaying, foot tapping movements continued, her actions speeding up.

Omollo quickened the tempo.

Carmen paced in front of the dying fire, turning dramatically and arching her back beautifully. Then she danced in front of Radcliff, her legs and feet tapping and stamping faster and faster. Grabbing the hem of the sarong with both hands she moved it from side to side revealing her bare legs. Then she moved back and forth, her feet stomping at an incredible speed, but still Omollo kept pace. She lifted one arm gracefully and began to turn round and round on the spot, maintaining the tempo of her legs but increasing the rate of her spin. Then facing Radcliff she stamped her feet, raising her knees up high using raunchy, provocative gestures. The stamping stopped and Omollo ceased his beating.

But the dance was not over. Breathless but retaining superb poise she began to sway her hips and stamp slowly, but this time lifting the sarong high revealing all of her thighs and moved tantalisingly around the group until she reached Radcliff where she threw her arms up, arching her back and stood looking up at her arms stretched to the heavens.

"¡Olé!" Arthur shouted and the group burst into spontaneous applause.

Carmen sang two Spanish folk songs and was about to dance again when the rain started. Arthur, Rod and Kurt checked the guy ropes on the two tents and covered the provisions with an old canvas.

Susan and Patsy joined Carmen and Radcliff in their tent.

The rain fell heavily.

Rod was about to join Omollo, Kurt and Arthur inside the other tent when a great stifling hand covered his mouth and dragged him backwards clear of the tents with a pistol held at his head.

Three others, two wearing brown anoraks, ripped up the rear of the tent and pointed their automatic weapons into the men's stunned faces.

The loose canvas cracked and flapped in the gusting wind. It wrapped around one of the attackers covering his face and body. Arthur took his chance and grabbed the barrel of his gun. Omollo was rising, ready to assist.

One of the three, wearing a military combat uniform pounded the butt of his gun several times onto Omollo's head, then repeated the punishment on Arthur until he slumped to the ground motionless.

A fifth man, smaller than the rest and also wearing a brown anorak, entered the other tent and forced the women out at gunpoint. The women crawled out through the door followed by Radcliff.

Slaughter, also wearing combats, released Rod and shoved him onto Kurt, who was sitting between the inert bodies of Omollo and Arthur. Susan and Patsy were dragged over to where the men were held.

"That's our man. Cover 'im." Slaughter pointed at Radcliff, who had collapsed, coughing and gasping onto the soaking grass.

The fifth man held his gun at Radcliff's head. The rain fell in torrents, whipped horizontally by the gusting wind.

The other attacker wearing combats grabbed Carmen before she could reach Radcliff and held a long steel blade to her throat, the point of the blade breaking her skin. Radcliff looked up helplessly as her blood mixed and diluted with rainwater and trickled down her neck and between her breasts. The man in combats sneered back at Radcliff, revealing two gold teeth.

Radcliff struggled but the gun barrel pressed down on his head harder, forcing his face into the wet grass. Two black trainers appeared before his nose. He turned his head slowly sideways and peered up glimpsing, out the corner of a bleary eye, a tall man in black towering above him.

"We meet again," said the Frenchman. "However did you escape? Never mind. It is good to see you alive, Mr. Radcliff. It means that you can get back inside that mountain and recover my treasure!"

Carmen was dragged struggling over to Jean-Claude and held upright in a vice like grip by the other man in combats. Jean-Claude held her chin and lifted her head up. "I will have this treasure now," he kissed her hard on the lips.

Carmen bit hard into his lower lip, her front teeth cutting through his flesh. He yelped, prising her jaws apart and wiped his blood away with the back of his hand. He cursed; fury igniting his eyes, then laughed maniacally sending a chill down Carmen's spine. It was then that she recognised her half brother.

Radcliff was held in a kneeling position. Carmen desperately tried to attract Radcliff's attention.

Before she could utter a sound Jean-Claude waved his bloodied hands in front of her face, chanted quietly in French and snapped his fingers.

"Leave her…," Radcliff coughed.

Jean-Claude kicked Radcliff in the ribs and he fell sideways breathless and shuddering with the pain.

"Eh! You!" Slaughter stepped forward, his saturated uniform clinging to the contours of his enormous, muscular frame. He stood directly before the Frenchman and unsheathed his bayonet. "We 'ad an agreement, you slimy bastard. He's goin' to earn me fifteen percent. You leave 'im be. I'll be the one to finish 'im off!"

Jean-Claude's eyes were aflame with rage. He raised a crooked, maniacal grin through bloody clenched teeth. Taking hold of Carmen's chin he looked into her, blank staring eyes. "Dance for me, beautiful sister," he hissed throatily, his serpent eyes still glaring maniacally. "Come on, dance for me."

"No!" Radcliff cried out. "Take your hands off …"

Slaughter kicked Radcliff twice in the stomach.

"Sit him up. I want him to see his woman come to me."

Slaughter seated Radcliff on the same pile of stones that had been his throne just a few minutes before.

"She is mine now, Mr. Radcliff. You have lost everything. How does that feel?"

Jean-Claude pulled Carmen away from the man in combats and fondled her breasts and licked his blood over her mouth. She did not react. "Dance my gypsy queen." He clapped his hands in a slow flamenco beat.

Radcliff looked on in bleary bewilderment, shuddering with pain and chilled by the rain. Patsy and Susan, Rod and Kurt were opposite him, watching in stunned disbelief and horrified silence as the bizarre, macabre dance began.

Carmen's feet stamped on the soaked ground in time with the rhythm, her arms rising alternately above her head with skilful flourishes, her hands and fingers moving with precision and artistry. The Frenchman's blood dribbled from her chin.

Radcliff's head rolled loosely from side to side, his vision clearing sufficiently to see his woman twisting and spinning left and right, her feet and hands moving intricately as she arched her back and held her head high. She swayed and thrusted her hips and pelvis more provocatively than before and her eyes had become demonic and lustful.

Jean-Claude's depraved bloody grin revealed broken and bad teeth; his black eyes leered at Carmen's soaked body, her blouse clinging to her breasts, the action of her hip movements and her bare torso twisting and arching provocatively aroused him. She looked into Jean-Claude's eyes and was drawn closer to him.

Radcliff struggled to stand but Slaughter held him down.

Carmen grabbed the Frenchman by the hair and drew him down to her lips. Jean-Claude laughed as Radcliff struggled impotently beneath Slaughter's grip.

He watched in horror as his woman turned into a vixen from hell before his eyes. She sucked thirstily on his mouth running her hands up and down his torso whilst her body gyrated and moved with increasing eroticism and sexuality.

Radcliff turned away with loathing and revulsion, crushed by Carmen's betrayal. He sagged sideways against Slaughter's leg, accepting his utter defeat.

"I'm not 'ere to watch you 'ave a good time, Frenchie," Slaughter sneered, releasing Radcliff who, unsupported, slumped to the ground. "There's only one thing to do with a bitch like that, in my book!" Slaughter walked away shaking his head and joined the others binding up the men. He opened the bags heaped up beside the men. "Eh! What about this little lot!" he called out. "Guns, explosives...there's an arsenal 'ere!"

Jean-Claude clapped his hands and the dance stopped. "Take her and their weapons to the yacht," he ordered the other man wearing combats.

"You stay put, Jeb!" Slaughter snapped. "You order your own men about, Frenchie. Not mine."

Jean-Claude looked into the Carmen's eyes. He pointed at the shorter man in an anorak then clicked his fingers in Carmen's face and commanded: "Go with him to my yacht." To the man in the anorak he ordered: "Get her to the yacht and take the bags."

The small man staggered under the weight of the two carrier bags. Carmen followed him through the gusting wind and heavy rain across the plateau.

"Lock her in the forward cabin and stay on board," Jean-Claude shouted after him. "You!" he pointed to one of two remaining men wearing anoraks. "Put those women back inside that tent and guard them.... from inside. One wrong move from either of one...shoot them both."

Slaughter stood beside Chiltern, their guns pointed at the four men tied up behind the collapsed tent.

Radcliff had lifted himself back onto his stone seat. He sat in sickened, tormented silence trying desperately to understand the performance he had just witnessed. Jean-Claude kicked his outstretched leg.

"You will do exactly as I say or you will never see her alive again." He kicked him again and Radcliff looked up. "Do you understand me?"

Radcliff lowered his head in resignation and nodded.

"At first light you and your friends will get inside that mountain and bring out every last jewel and coin there is, including the Cross."

Radcliff was silent.

"I know about the Cross, Radcliff."

"What cross?" Radcliff croaked. "I don't know what you're talking about. There're only jewels and coins...jewels and coins. That's all."

The Frenchman kicked him in the groin.

"You lie! If you lie to me again I will give back your precious Carmen piece by piece. Your friend, Clive Norton-Smythe, told me all about the treasure. He also said that you have found a very special cross."

"You knew Clive?" Radcliff's tortured mind tried to piece together all events that had taken place since Norton-Smythe's death.

"I knew him very well, Mr. Radcliff." He laughed mockingly as he walked away from Radcliff. "Stand him up will you."

"You talkin' to me," Slaughter straightened, his jaw clenched tight and raised the barrel of his gun.

"I've something very interesting to tell Mr. Radcliff. I want to look into his eyes as I tell him. Please could you get him onto his feet."

Slaughter lifted Radcliff and held him up.

"I was Norton-Smythe's chauffeur. I was his confidant. He told me many things about you, Mr. Radcliff."

"I didn't know you cared." Radcliff said venomously, his rasping, whispering voice just strong enough to carry on the wind. His legs buckled under his own weight but Slaughter, who was standing directly behind him, caught him and held him upright.

"I know that Clive loved you. He made you what you are. You owe all your wealth and fame to him. How did you repay him, eh? You betrayed him-you and your Spanish harlot. You should have treated him better. He was a very angry man."

"What do you care?"

"I don't. The point is, Mr. Radcliff, that it took me just one night, it was just before Christmas I think," Jean-Claude gloated. "All it took was one night of submitting to his bestial desires and a bottle of gin. I listened to all of his pathetic troubles. He told me everything."

Radcliff cursed his stupidity. Then he recalled Clive mentioning his new chauffeur. Suddenly a piece of the jigsaw fell into place. "You killed Clive!"

"Since you and your friends will never leave this island, I have nothing to fear." He smiled curiously. "I think of it as an execution. Beautifully planned, don't you think? Right down to the packet of Gauloises cigarettes. I bribed your plumber to leave it there."

Radcliff's head was spinning. He sagged against Slaughter. Lifting his head he glared into the Frenchman's black eyes. "What is Carmen to you?"

"I ask the questions. What is this Cross to you?"

"Nothing...it's part of the treasure."

Jean-Claude pulled out a knife and held it under Radcliff's chin. Radcliff could feel the point pressing on the bone. "You are a dead man, Radcliff. The man supporting you has chased you half way around the world. He will kill you very soon. How and when you die doesn't concern me. The longer your Carmen lives the longer you live. If you lie to me again I shall send one of my men to the yacht. He might cut off a finger...an ear....a toe... or something larger maybe," he snarled dementedly. "I'll ask you once again. What is this Cross, Mr. Radcliff?"

Radcliff remained silent.

Slaughter jerked one of Radcliff's arms up his back into a half nelson and wrapped one of his great arms around the front of Radcliff's neck and levered his head back.

"Yes. Yes!" He cried, yielding to the excruciating pain shooting through his chest. "There is a Cross. It's made from pure gold and has gems that are like no other. It's...it is priceless."

"Tie him up with the others," he sneered.

Slaughter resentfully dragged Radcliff across the soaked grass and dumped him next to Omollo, who was rubbing his neck and head.

"Help me tie his 'ands, Jeb." The two men in combats bound Radcliff's hands and arms.

The wind had veered to the west and the rain seemed warmer taking the chill from the wet ground and their soaked clothing.

"Rest well, all of you," Jean-Claude cackled. "You will need all of your strength tomorrow. I want every piece of that treasure out of that mountain before the sun sets. If you fail your women will suffer." He turned to the last remaining man in a brown anorak. "Stay here and guard them. Shoot if they give you any trouble...except for that one," pointing at Radcliff. "Shoot him in the knee or the foot if you have to, but don't kill him. Understood?"

The man nodded.

Jean-Claude, Chiltern and Slaughter made their way across the plateau and disappeared in the darkness of the trees.

"Who the hell is this French blighter?" Rod snapped.

"A very dangerous individual...it appears," Arthur grunted, clasping his head. "I suggest we keep our voices down."

"Are you alright, honey?" Rod called out to Patsy, ignoring the advice.

"We're both okay," Patsy replied. "Have they gone?"

"No. We've got one guarding us out here."

The guard came over to them, kicked Rod in the leg and shook his head.

"The others have returned to their yacht." Omollo shouted.

Their guard levelled his gun at Omollo. Omollo gestured that he would give no further trouble and the guard moved away. They all sat in silence and waited.

Ten minutes passed when they heard the sound of an outboard motor.

The wind and rain abated. The warm sea breeze helped to dry their sodden clothes.

The guard eventually stood up and stretched his limbs, lit a cigarette and walked slowly and cautiously towards the cliff edge on the rim of the plateau, constantly looking back at his captives.

Radcliff glimpsed the crescent moon before it vanished behind a cloud. He estimated that an hour had passed since they heard the noise from the outboard motor.

"I could creep up on him," Omollo whispered, "if someone else could take care of the one in the tent."

"No. It's useless, John," Arthur whispered. "What about the women? It's too dangerous...if it went wrong they'd take it out on them."

"I'm with you, John." Rod said, his spirited whisper carrying on the breeze. "Give me time. I'm cutting through these ropes, but... they're so... bloody tight."

"Don't be fool..." Arthur hissed in rebuke. "...the first sign of trouble and we'll all be dead! Including Patsy...and Susan! You heard what he said to Alex. We must bide our time. Don't you agree, Kurt?"

"Well, I've nearly got my hands free," Kurt admitted proudly. "I'm almost there."

"Good on yer, mate!" Rod chirped.

The guard stubbed out his cigarette and returned to his four captives. "Stop your talking," he ordered with a heavy French accent. "I'll shoot the next one who utters a word." He passed the barrel of his automatic rifle across the faces of the five men huddled together on the ground then moved slowly away and sat on a flat rock mid way between the women's tent and the men.

Radcliff gazed seaward in the direction of the bay. Barely able to think, his whole body racked with pain, his mind tormented by Carmen's willing surrender to Jean-Claude. Images of her with the Frenchman flashed in his mind and tortured him.

Omollo nudged Radcliff's leg with his foot until he came out of his trance.

"Alex!... Alex! Kurt is free. He's working on Rod's ropes now."

# CHAPTER 49

Jean-Claude, Chiltern and Slaughter emerged from the trees and stopped at the cliff top. The crescent moon broke through the clouds lighting up the silhouette of yacht. It was moored 400 yards out in the centre of the bay.

Slaughter had decided to let the Frenchman control matters until half the treasure had been extracted. Then he would make his move. His contingency back up plan still needed more thought, contemplating the possibility of salvaging the wrecked yacht lying 200 yards nearer the headland.

Jean-Claude flipped open his small radio transmitter. "Maurice!" he yelled into the mouthpiece. "Pick us at the beach. Make sure the woman's locked up." He snapped the radio shut and followed Chiltern down the cliffs with Slaughter following up at the rear.

The dinghy took them swiftly back the yacht, the noise from its outboard motor carried across the bay cutting through the still quietness of the night.

Jean-Claude entered the lounge from the port side door and went to the forward cabin. Slaughter and Chiltern returned to their quarters forward of the engine compartment bulkhead beneath the lounge.

"When do we make our move, boss?" Chiltern asked the moment their cabin door was locked.

"Keep your voice down, you fool. These Frenchies speak our lingo better then what you does. Haven't you got nuffin' between those ears of yours." he snarled. "When I'm good and ready, that's when."

"I could do with a kip." Chiltern flopped moodily onto his bunk.

"I'm hatching a plan, Jeb. Okay. I'll tell you about it tomorrow after I've thought it through. When that lot ashore are digging out the treasure and with the Frenchies occupied watching over 'em, we should get some time alone. I'll tell you then."

"Ooooh! I can't wait!" Chilton delighted in a rare opportunity to wind the big man up.

"Eh! That's enough of that! You do that too well for my liking."

"What's to your liking then, sweaty?" Chiltern blew him a kiss.

"That says more about you, talking like that. Did you know that? You bloody poofter!"

"Takes one to know one," Chiltern muttered under his breath.

"What was that?"

"It's only a bit of fun."

"You watch it...that's all."

"Yes boss," he smiled, turning his back on Slaughter, facing the wall. He was working on his own plan. He had seen five harpoon guns stowed with the other weapons in one of the portside lockers. With a perfect aim he could skewer Slaughter like the shark he had caught in Mozambique. He could then escape back to those sandy shores, shack up with that little native girl who was waiting there for him. It was the simple life for him...fishing for a living and living for sex. A small nest egg of jewels would set him up perfectly. He drifted into a blissful slumber.

# CHAPTER 50

The cabin door burst open. Carmen opened her eyes to see her half brother approaching. Instinctively she wanted to scream, but her mind was completely under his control. She watched with horror as her arms lifted up from her side and beckoned him to her. Jean-Claude sat on the mattress beside her.

"We have all night together, sister. You are all mine now." He began to undress her. Not only was she powerless to stop him but her body was moving to assist the removal of her garments. Her stomach knotted up when he kissed her and when the hideous, loathsome copulation began, her body automatically responding to the stimulus. Her actions were robotic and devoid of emotion, spirit or passion.

He looked with frustration into her empty, lifeless eyes. He had needed more response from her; a sign of his complete domination over her and triumph over her lover, Radcliff. But he was denied that essential gratification. She lay naked beneath him, her exquisite shimmering body totally within his power. But for him it was not enough. Her arms hung loosely around his neck, gazing up at him with utter indifference as he climaxed.

He rolled onto his back bereft of the victory necessary for the fiendish purpose he had planned for his half sister. He slapped her face repeatedly but she neither flinched nor altered her expression. His hypnosis had been too complete. He was about to risk bringing her out of her trance when there was a knock at the cabin door.

"Oui."

"Sorry to interrupt, but we want to go ashore. Now! If that's all right with you Frenchie?" Slaughter bellowed. "We'll wait for you on the beach. We're both getting queasy on this tub."

"Wait a minute," Jean-Claude snapped irritably. He pulled on his trousers and emerged from the cabin. "I've an idea. Follow me."

Slaughter and Chiltern picked up their carrier bags of weapons and followed him to the stern. "Maurice," he hollered as they neared the lounge door.

The pilot was waiting for them as they went out on deck. Jean-Claude gave these instructions in French: "I want you to go ashore with these men and check on the situation at the camp. If there's any sign of trouble I want you to get back here quickly. Otherwise stay with the others. I'll join you at first light. Oh! And take those two coils of rope with you."

"Do we take the dinghy?" Maurice asked in English.

"Leave it here. I'll need it later. You can all swim ashore."

Slaughter tapped Jean-Claude on the shoulder. The Frenchman spun on his heals finding himself face to face with the huge Englishman.

"What's the idea, Frenchie?"

"If Maurice doesn't return in ten minutes we can assume all is well at the camp. Just a little insurance, gentlemen," he shrugged uncomfortably.

"We're taking all our weapons. Any objections..?"

"Just leave the dinghy."

"Don't worry. You can keep yer boat. I can't wait to get back onto dry land."

They each donned life jackets and lowered themselves down the stepladder at the stern. Each weighed down by their luggage the swim was difficult until they reached the shallows.

# CHAPTER 51

Omollo was waiting for Radcliff's response. He could see the torment in his eyes. "Alex! Kurt and Rod are both free now," he prompted. "What do you want us to do?"

"It's a nightmare, John," Radcliff whispered hoarsely. "If we succeed in getting rid of the guards, how can we prevent this bloody Frenchman from slicing Carmen to pieces?"

Adrenaline coursed through his veins; his anguished, searching eyes darted from the group, to the tent, to the guard then up at the mountain and across the plateau desperately searching for inspiration.

"Tell them not to do anything until I give the word." Radcliff's whispering croak was just audible to Omollo.

Omollo passed the message to Arthur. Rod, who was untying the rope binding Arthur's hands, heard the message and passed it on to Kurt, who heard: 'Attack when Alex says the word.' Kurt picked up a rock and found a target.

The guard stubbed out a cigarette and sauntered towards the group. Rod, Arthur and Kurt frantically attempted to reassemble their ropes around their wrists and arms. The guard checked the ropes binding Radcliff's hands and torso and was about to check Kurt's binding when the guard saw someone approaching from the plateau.

The small man in the anorak carried two coils of rope over his shoulder. Radcliff recognised him immediately as the one who had taken Carmen to the yacht. The short man spoke to their guard in French, gesturing towards the yacht. They both laughed. He offered the guard a cigarette and followed him back to the flat rock, talking jovially to each other.

Meanwhile inside the woman's tent Patsy nudged Susan. It had been the second time their guard's head had nodded forward. The sudden jolt had awoken him. He rubbed his fingers into his eyes.

The women were lying on their bags of provisions at the back of the tent. The guard crawled forward and shone his torch onto their faces. Satisfied that they appeared peaceful enough he backed halfway out of the tent. "Hay!" he called out in French. "Cover these women will you. I need a break."

Patsy opened one of the bags she had packed and slithered her arm inside, snakelike. The guard looked back as she was groping amongst the tins and boxes and packages. She froze just as he shone the beam onto her.

"Okay. Go ahead." The other guard answered, leaving the smaller man with the rope and strode to the women's tent. "I'll watch 'em for a bit."

The women saw their guard back out of the tent as heavy footfalls approached. Then a face appeared at the door.

Omollo and the others saw the guard emerge from the tent, light a cigarette and wander towards the edge of the dried up lake, twenty feet away. He drank thirstily from a canteen and splashed water over his face.

Kurt took a firmer grip on the rock in his hand.

The replacement guard had the beam of his torch fixed on the women. Patsy had found what she had been searching for in the bag but could not move a muscle. After a few minutes her outstretched, twisted arm was starting to cramp. Susan turned slightly, cleverly supporting Patsy's arm with her elbow, but the pain was becoming unbearable. Gritting her teeth she managed to keep silent but her arm was visibly shaking from the strain.

Before the guard noticed this, the short man with the rope squatted beside him and whispered something.

Radcliff's breathing came in short shallow gasps, all his senses sharp and on full alert. He desperately wanted to give the order, aware that if they were to attack it had to be at that very moment, but certain also that Carmen would be the one to pay if it went wrong. Then an idea to free her began to germinate in his mind.

"Go!" he whispered. His order reached all four men. Arthur and Kurt rushed at the two men at the tent, each armed with a rock. Kurt was there first and cracked the skull of the one squatting beside the guard. The guard reacted quickly and cried out as he dived inside the tent avoiding Arthur's blow.

Rod and Omollo had almost reached the guard at the lakeside when they heard the cry from the tent. The guard dropped his canteen and took aim at Rod. Omollo hurled a rock at him, catching the guard just above the left temple. He slumped sideways to the ground falling onto his gun; the gun went off, firing ten rounds into his own stomach.

Patsy had drawn the carving knife from the bag as the guard half fell into the tent.

Susan had glimpsed Arthur's face at the entrance. When the guard dived into the tent, she dodged the gun and, using her judo skill, seized the guard's arm. The momentum of his fall combined with his own body weight, brought him deeper inside the tent, prostrate and helpless. Patsy embedded the twelve-inch blade between his ribs.

Omollo and Rod arrived as the two women emerged from the tent.

Arthur folded Susan into his great arms; Patsy found Rod and threw herself at him. Omollo pulled the dead guard from the tent and dragged it to where the other lay beside the lake. Kurt followed Omollo with the smaller corpse.

"Do you think they heard the gun shots?" Radcliff asked anxiously after stacking the guns beside the tent.

"No way Alex..." Rod said, reassuringly, hugging Patsy closer to him. "They'll be tucked up in their bunks and sound asleep, I'll bet. They wouldn't have heard a sound."

"How can you be so sure?" Arthur responded sharply. "The racket from those gun shots would have carried to that yacht easily."

"I'm not so sure," said Kurt returning from the lake. "The shots were muffled by his body."

Rod turned away from the group and put his hand softly under Patsy's chin and lifted her gaze to meet his.

"You okay, honey?" he asked gripping her tightly to him. Her lips began to quiver. "I'm so proud of you, baby." She flung her arms around his shoulders. Rod kissed her head as she squeezed herself against his chest.

"Oh Rod," she cried, her face buried in his chest. "I killed him. *I killed him!*" Her body convulsed into deep sobs. "I felt the knife cut into his ribs." Rod held her as she released the horror of the experience. "Then I heard his life fade away... like a gentle sigh," she sobbed. Rod stroked her blonde hair until she had recovered, then pulled away from her to look into her face. The moonlight glinted on her tearful eyes.

"Look honey. He would have done worse to you. They were animals." He wiped her tears with his thumbs. "It was either him or both of you. You did what you had to do," he consoled her softly. "Because of you we beat the blighters. You helped to save us."

"That's right, Pats," Susan said, rubbing her back comfortingly.

Arthur, Kurt, Omollo and Radcliff gathered around the two women.

"You were both.... fantastic!" Radcliff said as a coughing attack struck him. He stooped holding his chest and took the bottle of water Omollo offered him. "Thanks to God we were all thinking on the same wave length," he said with a choking croak, smiling through watery eyes.

"Yeh!" Arthur laughed. "It doesn't happen often when women are involved!"

"Hay!" Susan snapped in mock indignation bringing a chuckle from Patsy. "We made a damn good team."

"That we did!" Patsy sniffed holding up a hand. "Come on...give me five." The two women clapped their hands triumphantly. "You can always count on a Kiwi!"

"Not their beer, though," Rod goaded.

"Thank God it's only you Aussies who are so sensitive about beer. In Kiwiland we have an identity."

"Jes'! That's a bit below the belt, honey!" Rod sulked.

"You Aussies..!" Arthur laughed. "Never mind the beer…didn't we bring something stronger?"

"Yah! I could do with a stiff drink myself." Kurt began rummaging through their supplies. "Come on you lot," handing out mugs to all in the group then filling them all with whiskey. "Let's drink to our victory."

They all impishly watched Omollo take a large gulp from his mug. They waited for his reaction to the effects of the fiery liquid but there was none. He nonchalantly drank the remainder of his drink then poured himself some water.

# CHAPTER 52

What the hell was that?" Chiltern had sat bolt upright on the sand.

"Nothin'." Slaughter turned away on his side. "Coconuts…or somethin'"

"It was too loud…too much noise…it sounded like a machine gun."

"Maybe they've got trouble up there. There's three of 'em there to handle it. Go to sleep will yer?"

"I'm going up there."

"It'll be light in a couple of hours. Wait 'till then."

"No. I want to make sure." Chiltern took an oozie from the bag. He checked on Slaughter then grabbed a loaded harpoon gun.

Crouching low and keeping within the shadows of the palms he darted to the cliff at the end of the bay.

"Hay!Where you going with that?" Slaughter yelled. "Leave that harpoon 'ere."

Cursing his luck Chiltern increased his speed. Reaching the rocks he climbed to the cliff top.

# CHAPTER 53

Omollo eased Radcliff onto his seat of stones and squatted beside him and waited.

Not able to let another moment pass, Omollo rose up.

"Listen everybody!" Omollo said in a slow, calm but serious tone, his deep resonant voice having developed the assertiveness of command. "Now we must concentrate on finding a way of getting Carmen out of that yacht before daybreak."

"You're right, John," Rod said quickly for the group.

"They'll be coming ashore probably just before daybreak. We could ambush them on the beach," Kurt proposed.

"We need to be certain of how many," Omollo said. "It's vital that we catch this Jean-Claude amongst the landing party."

"What about two or three of us swimming out to the yacht now..?" Arthur suggested. "We could find out their plans…"

"We'd be shot to pieces before we got anywhere near the yacht," Rod said dismissively.

"Not necessarily…," said Kurt. "…it would only need one or two of us to swim out and spy on them."

"What if they've got people on the beach already!" Rod added.

"It's possible," said Radcliff

"What about moving the camp?" Kurt countered. "Say we moved it down to that place on the ledge, Alex…where we camped on that first night. If things did go wrong with the ambush we could fall back to this new camp and regroup. It would give us a second bite at the cherry!"

"That's a pretty darn good idea, Kurt!" said Arthur.

"Shall we put it to the vote?" Kurt suggested.

"Okay," Rod said, looking across at Omollo and Radcliff. "Hands up all those who liked the idea."

"What if the shots were heard," Patsy put in, "and there're already on their way here. They'd catch us when we're divided up…some of us setting up an ambush and some lugging our stuff to this ridge."

"It's a ledge," corrected Omollo.

"It'll be light in under two hours," Radcliff interceded. "I'm not going to be much use in a fight.… the state I'm in. I'm shattered already. I'll stay here with the women. Two of us, John and Kurt, could start moving our supplies to the ledge whilst Arthur and Rod take the guns and ammunition to the cliff top overlooking the beach and wait. As soon as they've moved all our things I'll take Patsy and Susan to the ledge freeing John and Kurt to snoop up on the yacht. They can then fall back to join Arthur and Rod."

"That sounds better!" Susan said.

"Let's vote on it," said Kurt.

The vote was carried unanimously and the group divided up as Radcliff had suggested.

Chiltern had reached the plateau and was about to emerge from the trees when two shadowy shapes bore down on him. He rolled soundlessly into the undergrowth, the two men passing within three feet of him. They continued on, weighed down by heavy bags, stumbling in the darkness, through the trees towards the cliff top.

Chiltern buried the harpoon into the soft earth, blackened his face with the humus then ran, keeping low, in a wide arc around the plateau approaching the dried up lake from the high slopes of the mountainside on its furthest side. From a position perched upon the bank he saw, between intermittent bursts of moonlight, three bodies lined neatly in a row close to the opposing bank. He rolled into the lake and, holding his body just above ground, he worked his way on his elbows and knees across the rocky, uneven surface, his weapon cradled across in his arms.

He bobbed his head above the bank adjacent to where the corpses lay. Muffled women's voices came from the tent twenty feet to his left. Removing the safety catch from his weapon he edged along the bank to get nearer to the tent.

Then a man emerged from the tent and looked out to sea. A broadening knife of turquoise light cut the horizon, its edge bloodied crimson and maroon with flashes of orange and yellow.

Chiltern trained his sights on the silhouette standing at the front of the tent.

"Dawn's just breaking," the dark shape announced, stooping to the door of the tent. "John and Kurt'll be back soon."

Chiltern recognised Radcliff's voice. He decided to seize this golden opportunity to kill Radcliff and extract himself from a situation where the odds were distinctly shortening in favour of the opposition. He took aim and waited for Radcliff to move away from the tent for a clearer shot.

Susan had crawled to the tent entrance and looked up at Radcliff. "She'll be alright, Alex. Carmen's indestructible. Just like you!"

Radcliff glimpsed the radiance of her lovely smile, her sensual lips stretched tight across perfect white teeth. It was a smile that revitalised Radcliff's heart. "She is pretty tough," he agreed. "I think I heard Kurt…." He stood up to leave.

"Don't go," Patsy cried. "Wait here…in the tent."

Radcliff entered the tent. Patsy was lying on her back on one side of the tent with Susan having returned to her position, her head propped up on one elbow.

"Yes, keep us two lonely women company," she chuckled.

Radcliff stretched himself out, easing his aching body onto the space between the two women. "What's that maniac doing to her, Susan?"

"We're sure he has a strong hypnotic power over her."

"I think you must be ……"

Chiltern opened fire, shattering the stillness of the night, raking a burst of twenty rounds into the tent, peppering the canvas with holes. He then scurried back, the way he had advanced, to the farthest side of the lake.

Rod and Arthur heard the gunfire and turned back up the slope through the trees. Omollo and Kurt had seen the flashes from the gun and raced to the tent.

Then there were spine-chilling screams that pierced the darkness.

Omollo and Kurt reached the tent as Radcliff crawled out of the tent with Patsy scrambling around him screaming hysterically. Radcliff turned on his knees and clutched her in his arms. She fought him, trying get free.

"Easy, Patsy! Easy!" Radcliff held her tight, although her wriggling, squirming body was difficult to control. "Rod will be here in a moment. Easy! Easy!"

"What happened?" asked Kurt.

Omollo did not wait for an answer. He dived into the tent.

Rod and Arthur were near the perimeter of the plateau when they heard the blood curdling screams.

Rod froze in his tracks. "Patsy!" He was about to run to her but Arthur grabbed his left arm.

"Wait!" Arthur held him fast. "You'll do her no good getting your-self shot. Whoever was shooting is still out there. He'll have to come back this way. Let's get a bit higher, crouch low and keep our eyes peeled."

Rod nodded.

The two men crawled through the undergrowth that skirted the fringe of the plateau.

Chiltern crawled back to the far bank of the lake then sprinted across the open ground the way he had come, towards the mountain slope and the cover of the trees.

Rod held up his hand, gesturing for Arthur to stop. The two men crouched motionless.

"What is it?" Arthur whispered.

"I saw someone…" Rod pointed to a spot high on the plateau ahead of them and to their right. "You're right. He's going for the trees. He'll be coming our way soon."

They set up an ambush: Arthur going deeper into the trees, Rod using the tall grass on the plateau for cover.

Soon they heard light but fast moving footfalls approaching them in the undergrowth. Both men trained their sights of their rifles towards the sounds.

The barrel of a gun pushed against Arthur's head.

"Don't move!" A deep growl commanded from behind. "Drop your weapon. That includes you hiding in the grass," the voice shouted out, "...I've got your man covered. Get your hands up high. *Now!*"

A man approached from the trees.

"Jeb?" he called out.

"Yeh." came the reply.

"Get the bugger in the grass. He's just to your left."

Arthur saw Rod slowly rise from the grass, twenty feet away, with his hands in the air.

Slaughter frisked Arthur then pushed him using the muzzle of his gun towards the open plateau.

"What's been goin' on?" Slaughter growled.

"They've got all the guards! They're all dead!"

"That'll be interestin' when Frenchie finds out."

"We don't need 'im now. We know where the treasure's hid. Just polish off the rest of 'em and clear out!"

"Where's Radcliff?"

"I've just killed 'im!" Chiltern proclaimed proudly. "He was in the tent with the two women…"

"Oooooh… 'I've killed Radcliff'…" Slaughter mocked with extravagant camp gestures with one arm akimbo. "Women, maybe…but Radcliff…. I think not, you little poofter. Strategy's never bin' your strong point. Has it, Jeb? That's why I gives the orders and you don't."

"He's dead, I tell yer!" Chiltern yelled squaring up to Slaughter, erupting with tormented rage.

"Go and get Frenchie up here, pronto," he ordered dismissively.

Chiltern remembered the harpoon. He let his gaze drop to the ground, his fury assuaged by thoughts of sweet revenge. He could wait. He ran off down the slope towards the beach.

"Make yourselves comfortable, gentlemen," Slaughter motioned them to sit with a wave of his gun. "We'll have quite a wait. I should make the most it, if I were you. The Frenchman is going to be pretty pissed off with you lot."

The four were silent around the small shape lying on the dried up lake bed near the rock face. Susan was inside a sleeping bag, at her feet Patsy sat huddled in Radcliff's arms, Kurt and Omollo, weapons by their sides, were sitting on the bank close to her head.

Omollo and Kurt had elected not to pursue the gunman across the plateau knowing Rod and Arthur were out there somewhere hidden in the trees.

The minutes passed. They strained their ears for sounds of the two men returning to camp but the only sound that broke the silence was that of an outboard motor approaching the shore.

Chiltern arrived at the plateau where Slaughter sat covering his captives with Jean-Claude labouring ten yards behind, carrying a large carrier bag.

"What's been happening?" Jean-Claude shouted up to Slaughter.

"Nothing I can't handle. Hasn't Jeb told you anything?"

"Non!" Jean-Claude gasped when he reached the Englishmen. He dropped the huge bag and bent over clutching his knees, recovering his breath. "I heard some shots. That's all I know."

"They've killed all your crew, including the pilot."

"What!" Jean-Claude screamed, drawing a pistol from his trousers and held it at Rod's head. "Breath your last!"

"Jeb here thinks he 'as killed Radcliff and the women," patting him, mockingly, on the shoulder. He saw the Frenchman's look of horror and added quickly. "Don't worry. He's up there somewhere."

Slaughter rose to his feet and nodded towards the plateau. He picked up the Frenchman's carrier bag. "Hey! It's as light as a feather," he laughed. "What've you got in it, Frenchie? Fresh knickers?"

Jeb burst into a fit of manic laughter, which cut through the early morning stillness.

"Six hundred bags…" he snapped, still gasping for breath, "…to carry…. the treasure in. Come on," he demanded, "let's get up there and see what damage they have done." Jean-Claude sneered. "Make those two walk in front."

They all heard the eerie, menacing laughter carried on the breeze from the edge of the plateau. Omollo jerked his head up; Radcliff and Kurt looked anxiously at Omollo.

"Who's that laughing?" Patsy asked frantically, her grip tightening onto Radcliff's shirt. "They've got my Rod." She cried. "We're done for…aren't we Alex?"

"Don't worry, Pats," Radcliff comforted. "He's with Arthur. They'll be watching them and waiting. We've still got the upper hand."

Radcliff seized his chance to put his plan into operation. He scurried to the bullet torn tent and found the remaining bags of supplies. He pulled out a sheathed hunting knife which he stuffed inside his shorts, loaded a rifle and grabbed as much ammunition he could pack into his pockets.

Radcliff felt an iron grip on his shoulder. "Allah will be with you,

Alex." Omollo said with a broad toothy grin. He saw the warm glint in Omollo's eyes and felt the bond between them strengthen.

Heartened by Omollo's gesture Radcliff's weak heavy limbs seamed lighter as he staggered and stumbled to the path beside the rock face.

"Yah! Go with God, Alex!" Kurt said quietly under his breath as Radcliff vanished around the corner of the cliff.

Out of sight of the others, Radcliff's strength failed him and he fell, slipping and rolling to the cliff edge. Digging his feet and hands into the wet, rocky ground he managed to halt his slide to certain death. He lay absolutely still, not daring to move, until his strength returned.

# CHAPTER 54

Kurt and Omollo had taken a weapon each from the pile near the tent. Omollo offered a handgun to Patsy. She reached out to take it but withdrew her hand quickly as if it had been red hot. The gun dropped to the ground. She kicked it away.

Silently dismantling the tent and packing the last of the supplies into bags the three were ready to move on to the camp on the ledge.

"Put down your guns," a heavily accented voice shouted across the plateau. "We have two of your people here. They will die in thirty seconds if you don't throw down your weapons and come towards me with your hands in the air."

Omollo dropped his gun and Kurt reluctantly did the same. The three forlorn figures, the two men flanking Patsy, slowly moved through the tall grass with their hands held high towards the dark shapes approaching them.

Dawn had broadened its brush stroke across the horizon. They could easily see the unmistakable outlines of Arthur and Rod leading the procession.

Patsy ran to him. Both Omollo and Kurt were too slow to react. There was a gunshot and Patsy fell to the ground.

Rod started to run to her but Chiltern was ready and cracked the butt of his rifle on his head.

"Pick him up," Jean-Claude commanded Arthur.

Omollo reached Patsy before the encroaching Frenchman. He knelt beside her prostrate body. Stroking her head he felt blood above her right ear.

"Get up," Jean-Claude gestured to Omollo with movement of his pistol. Chiltern and Slaughter searched both men for weapons.

"Where's Radcliff?" Slaughter demanded.

"Dead," Kurt answered quickly, injecting bitterness into his tone and looking as mournful as possible. "He was shot."

"Where's the other woman?" Jean-Claude's eyes searched the darkness behind Omollo.

"She's dead too," Omollo muttered.

"Alright then…we'll go back and we shall see."

"What about her?" Kurt looked down on Patsy.

Jean-Claude pointed his revolver at Omollo, "You! Bring her."

At the lakeside Jean-Claude checked the corpses.

Omollo had laid Patsy on the ground close to the lake and felt for a pulse.

"She's alive!" he whispered to Kurt.

Kurt backed away to where Arthur was standing with Rod in his arms.

"Where's Radcliff?" Jean-Claude snarled at Omollo.

"He was over there, by the tent," Omollo pointed.

Chiltern ran to the tent, with Slaughter on his heels, leaving the Frenchman alone with the captives.

Kurt and Omollo were both concentrated upon the Frenchman. Arthur had read their minds and was ready to act.

"There's plenty of blood but no Radcliff." Slaughter shouted back. He turned on Chiltern. "You shot him, eh? Where the hell is he then, smart arse?"

Jean-Claude laughed. "You'll find him searching the yacht for the woman. Neither of them are of any use to me. He's too weak to work and she's completely within my power."

"Well I want him," Slaughter roared, stomping back to the group. "I want that son of bitch dead!"

"You're welcome to him. These four will have to work twice as hard for twice as long to get the treasure out."

Slaughter ran off back over the plateau.

"Don't be too long," he yelled after him. Then he turned onto the hapless group. "There's all my treasure to be brought out of that mountain, so I think you'd better get moving. I want every last jewel down here by sunset. And that includes Radcliff's Cross."

"Impossible!" Arthur protested.

Patsy groaned. Omollo was supporting her upper body in his lap.

"This woman will be praying you do the impossible! If you don't… her fate will be more terrible than you can imagine." He tossed the black bag at Kurt's feet. "I want all the loose gem stones and other jewels in the light blue bags and the gold and silver coins and bullion go in the yellow. *Get moving…!*"

"Tie her hands and feet and take her over to the edge of the cliff," he ordered Chiltern, "and watch her. One hint of trouble from anyone and she goes over."


Radcliff had dragged his beaten and battered body along the cliff edge, his chest on fire with every rasping breath he took, until he saw, in the half-light, the pine tree that towered over the old camp on the ledge. He slipped and rolled most of the descent to the pine then, clinging to the trunk he slowly lowered himself, branch by branch, to the ledge. He hid the gun and ammunition under loose stones surrounding the roots of the pine. Armed solely with the knife, he followed his well-trodden path to the beach.

It was high tide. The twisted skeleton of Kurt's wrecked helicopter protruded above the surf.

Once in horseshoe bay he could clearly see the yacht against the brightening sky. His strength and spirits lifted now she was in sight. His weakened limbs were revitalised and responded when he ran, stiffly at first, along the beach. Adjacent to the yacht he waded then swam to it.

Slaughter had stood on the cliff top scanning the beach and the yacht in the dim predawn light for a sign of Radcliff. He descended to the beach, found the dinghy and ran it into the surf.

Radcliff was two thirds of the distance to the yacht when he heard the phut—phut—phut of an outboard motor failing to ignite. He increased his stroke rate, hauled himself up the stern diving ladder and looked back at the beach. In the growing light he saw someone rowing a dinghy about mid-way to the yacht.

With no time to search for Carmen he lowered himself back into the water and swam towards the headland. The pains in chest were intense. By using the kicking action of the breaststroke he propelled himself by improvising the doggy paddle. Mid way to the headland he glimpsed through the breaking surf the roof of the submerged wreck.

Fifteen feet from the roof he trod water and looked back. The light had improved. He could clearly see Slaughter at the stern of the yacht scanning the beach with binoculars. Then he turned the glasses in his direction.

Radcliff dived. Swimming underwater, with his chest on fire, he reached the yacht. He dragged his exhausted body up to the roof. Clinging to the edge, the surge of the waves tugging at his body, he caught sight of Slaughter rowing back to the beach. He rested on the roof watching the man in the dinghy.

Arthur and Rod worked together extracting the treasure beneath the collapsed roof of the original cavern. They scooped up the jewels in both hands, slowly pouring them into a blue bag, extracting the gold and silver bullion and coins, which they packed into a yellow bag.

The bags that were full were carried to the base of the shaft, where Kurt was positioned. He put a single bag into a purpose made sling that was tied to the end of a rope. Two tugs on the rope signalled Omollo stationed outside at the mouth of the fissure to haul it up over the smoothed out floor of the shaft.

Omollo then unfastened the bag from the sling, weighted the sling with a rock and dropped it back down the shaft for the next bag of treasure.

He then fastened the treasure bag into another sling and lowered it to the ground, 100 feet below.

The cave had three distinct chambers: the treasure chamber, Kurt's loading chamber at the foot of the shaft and the chamber that included the pool and the chimney leading to the summit of the mountain.

A profusion of oil lanterns and torches were positioned on ledges and in hollows. The jewels and the gold sparkled and glowed, almost animated by the soft flickering lights of the lamps. These magical reflections were projected onto the walls of the chimney, a myriad of colours dappling the rocky surface, which were in turn mirrored in the pool next to the chimney.

Jean-Claude had opened the first half dozen blue bags that Omollo had lowered, his fingers penetrating and feeling the glittering contents, lifting up handfuls of the gems closer to his bulging, mad eyes.

"Slaughter's comin'," Chiltern called out. "He's running and he don't look too 'appy."

"Bon," he said indifferently retying a yellow bag of coins and then opening another.

"I almost caught... the little shit," Slaughter proclaimed bitterly, gasping for breath. "He'd been on board... I saw 'is wet footprints...he must've seen me..." He gazed at the bags at Jean-Claude's feet. "Is that all they've got out? Eight *bloody* sacks!"

"Oui," Jean-Claude shrugged. "We need you to work out a way of getting the bags to the beach."

"We've got plenty of rope. We'll make a hoist and stretcher. Jeb and me can lower 'em down the cliff face." He pointed at Patsy perched groggily on the edge of the cliff, her hair matted with dried blood. "It's a sheer drop to the beach where she's sitting."

"But that's the wrong beach!" Jean-Claude sneered.

"Move your *bloody* yacht then."

"I can't do that," he cried effeminately. "That bay's too narrow. I've never driven a boat before."

"Well, we do have a dilemma, don't we, Frenchie!" Slaughter laughed sarcastically. "Okay. I'll tell you what we'll do." Slaughter winked at Chiltern. "Give me the keys and I'll move the yacht for you."

The Frenchman thought for a moment. "Make the hoist first."

"Look here Frenchie!" Slaughter stabbed his index finger into Jean-Claude's chest. "Let's get one thing absolutely clear! Me and Jeb are not filling in for your dead bleedin' crew! We want a bigger slice of the treasure if we're to do all this extra runnin' around!"

"As much as you want!" Jean-Claude grinned raising his arms agreeably, his eyes narrowing into slits. "We are fewer in numbers.... no?"

Slaughter took an axe and his machete and marched towards the mountain ridge where the trees were closer. Half an hour later he had hauled back three pine tree trunks and eight shorter thinner logs to the cliff. His bare torso glistened with perspiration…droplets collected on his chin and dripped down his chest. He dropped the axe, tossed the machete at Chiltern's feet then grabbed a one and half litre bottle of water and drained it dry.

"You finish it!" He gasped, wiping his mouth with the back of his hand.

"What! Build an 'A' frame? On me own?" Chiltern complained.

"You call yourself an ex-Marine? Get Frenchie to help you," thumbing towards Jean-Claude unloading a blue bag from the sling. "How many bags 'ave we got?" He shouted over.

"Another eight...sixteen in all. How many can we get onto your hoist?"

Slaughter lifted the nearest blue bag: "…. Weighs about 30 pounds." He lifted a yellow bag. "Mmm…. that's heavy. I'd say that weighs more like 70 pounds. It should take five blue bags, tops…four to be safe. Jeb's buildin' it! Well…do you want me to move this yacht or not…?"

Jean-Claude threw him the keys. "Take two bags with you to the yacht."

"Yeh, okay. Why not?" He stuffed the keys in his combats and zipped up the pocket. With the bags cradled in his arms he set off over the plateau. "What about the woman?" he called back.

"Leave her alone." He watched Slaughter swagger towards the trees, pleased with the way things were progressing. "Move the woman over to the rock face," he ordered Chiltern.

"What do want done first, Frenchie?" Chiltern responded fiercely.

"Okay! I'll do it. You carry on building the hoist. Just keep an eye on the bags," pointing up to the yellow bag that Omollo was lowering on the rope.

Rod sagged onto the bottom step in the chimney and rubbed his aching right shoulder. He gazed into the pool beside him. Falling droplets of water from above gently rippled its mirror like surface, blurring his reflection. For one glorious instant he imagined Patsy there beside him.

His vivid imagination was tormenting him. His clenched fists began to shake with frustrated rage.

A bubble, the size of a basketball, rose up from the centre of the pool and burst, emitting a sweet aroma. Then a series of smaller bubbles came to the surface and burst, leaving the air heavy with a pungent sickly smell. He felt dizzy and light headed. He chuckled involuntarily, whilst at the same time fighting back an overwhelming urge to scream with laughter.

Kurt's nostrils flared as the sweet air reached him. He was securing a yellow bag into the sling. A few seconds elapsed before he recalled where he had smelt the aroma before. He noticed Rod rocking back and forth on the step beside the pool holding his stomach. Arthur was clutching his lumber region with both hands. He straightened up to ease his pain and smacked his head against the sloping rock ceiling. He doubled up, staggered backwards, grasping his head and then his back. He toppled and fell onto his knees, yelping in agony.

Rod let out a bellowing burst of stifled laughter, which echoed strangely within the confines of the three chambers.

Arthur glared at Kurt with fury and indignation at the Aussies outrageously unsympathetic reaction to his situation.

Kurt could do nothing but collapse into convulsions of hilarity, emitting throaty, choked up squeaky sounds and long silent wheezes that added to the reverberating noise of laughter coming from the cave.

Rod watched Kurt's shuffling dance and intricate footsteps that were just managing to keep him upright. He disintegrated into further helpless swaying and bowing movements as his body struggled to expel the laughter building up inside him.

Then the smell reached Arthur. Stricken by the gas he still tried to sooth his aching torso whilst sinking to the ground, doubled up, in hysterical laughter. Each man watched the others with incredulous fascination: the multitudinous comic attitudes and positions and contortions they were involuntarily adopting; the emission of strange unearthly whimpering and squealing noises that startled and tickled the others. They rolled and fell about with contorted helplessness; tears streamed down their faces totally incapacitated by the rib tickling effects of the gas.

All their efforts to stop their laughter failed. The volume of their combined raucous hilarity echoed up through the shaft to Omollo.

"What's happening?" Omollo called down, worried what reprisal will be inflicted on Patsy for the lost minutes getting the treasure bags down to the Frenchman. "Have you all gone completely mad? Keep it down or there'll be trouble. Think of Patsy!"

"Why have you stopped lowering the bags?" Jean-Claude screamed up to Omollo.

"Where have you taken Patsy?" Omollo demanded.

"Never mind her..! Why have the bags stopped coming down?"

"Kurt!" Omollo shouted down the shaft, his hands cupped around his mouth. "What is going on? He wants to know why the bags have stopped coming up."

Kurt staggered back to the shaft, holding his stomach, his guffaws and whimpering cries reaching Omollo.

"Have you been drinking?" Omollo yelled down, then inhaled a waft of the sweet smelling gas rising up from the shaft. It was the same strange sweet aroma he and Kurt had encountered after prising open the slab on the summit. "Kurt! That smell…!"

Kurt sniffed between bouts of drunken giggling.

"What are you doing..?" Rod managed to ask before sliding helplessly down the rock wall once more clutching his abdomen.

A full minute elapsed before Kurt could answer him, his face frozen into a contorted grimace around his nose as if ready to sneeze. Concentrating on the word he brought his jaw up to pronounce the letter 'f' whilst holding back his hilarity, acutely aware how ridiculous he looked to the others. Then suddenly, his nose wrinkled up and his mouth elongated, the word was emitted:

"Sniffing…"

Seeing Rod crease up on hearing the word Kurt's legs buckled and he slid to the ground helplessly.

Arthur had regained some measure of control until Kurt's 'sniffing' reply. Seeing Kurt sag to the floor was too much. Arthur folded up against the rock wall holding his stomach.

Their laughter echoed up the chimney; the sound being amplified by the chambers of the cave and then released up the shaft. The contagious noises affected Omollo profoundly. He bit his lip and drew away from the shaft.

"What's going on?" Jean-Claude screamed. "Answer me or the women dies."

Omollo turned away from the shaft and took several deep breaths. "They've been gassed," he shouted down to the Frenchman. "Kurt," he bellowed into the shaft. "It's gas! Get out of there!"

Omollo watched Jean-Claude cursing and pacing back and forth beneath the rock face. Then there was total silence from the shaft.

"We're okay now, John," Kurt shouted up at last, tugging twice on the rope. "Sorry. It was this gas…it must have been nitrous oxide…. laughing gas! It bubbles up from the pool."

"Hurry, Kurt. He's getting very agitated. I'll throw down another rope and sling."

"We want to start removing the Cross, John. Can you help us?"

"Impossible, Kurt," he yelled, throwing down the new rope and hauling on the other. "Just send more bags up here fast."

Omollo removed the weighty yellow bag from the sling and held it up for the Frenchman to see.

"Get it down here, fast!" Jean-Claude screamed up at Omollo. "It's almost ten thirty and all you have to show for it are eighteen bags!"

Chiltern leered at the woman propped against the rock face, trussed up from head to toe. The ropes were tight across her breasts and hips, her garments snared in the twists revealing titillating areas of bronzed flesh. Salivating, his blood racing, he licked his lips and moved towards her, his fingers reaching for her blouse.

Patsy pushed herself back against the rock, squinting as he came at her, the glaring sun directly behind him.

"Get away from her," Jean-Claude yelled, waving his handgun at Chiltern.

"If you're goin' to point that at me," Chiltern snarled, "you'd better be prepared to use it."

Jean-Claude took aim, his finger squeezing on the trigger.

"Okay, okay," Chiltern backed away and resumed his work on the 'A' frame.

Patsy relaxed as the man in combats moved away. "Water…I need water," she pleaded but Jean-Claude ignored her, totally preoccupied with the yellow bag being lowered to the ground. He stretched up ready to clasp it even though the bag was still twelve feet above him.

The morning sun pounded remorselessly onto Patsy's aching head. From where she sat she could see the flattened grass where the tent had been. Beyond that was the rocky bank of the dried up lake where Susan's body lay.

She recalled the conversation they had during the air flight to Victoria. They were both stretching their legs at the rear of the aircraft when Susan had said awkwardly:

"Patsy…soon we'll all begin living together, confined on that island. I need to ask you a couple of things."

"Ask away," Patsy had said breezily, a little shocked by the seriousness of Susan's tone.

"Arthur is very taken with you. You know that, don't you?"

"I know he likes to look at me. All men do. I like men looking at me. Don't you?"

"Yes, but…." she had paused thinking how best to put her next remark. "Do you have to flaunt yourself like you do? Arthur lost his wife six years ago and well…

I think your husband is getting very…. how should I say…. upset by Arthur's attentions."

"Rod! You haven't got to worry about him. We know each other, Susan. We're soul mates him and me. No one can get between us. I love sex, Susan, and I love feeling sexy. Everyone should. It's life isn't it?"

"Yes, but you could moderate what you wear. That's all I'm asking."

Patsy had seen the hard manipulative mind working behind Susan's eyes. It was the same look that her mother's eyes had had. Her father was a good man but nowhere near ambitious enough for her mother. She had wanted him to get the Manager's job at the Bank and improve their social standing within the small town of Palmerston North, on the north island of New Zealand. Her mother had nagged him constantly until life at home had become unbearable for him and for Patsy. She had left home and travelled to England at the age of nineteen.

"What do you suggest I should wear?" Patsy had said indignantly.

"Undergarments would be a start," Susan had answered quickly.

Patsy's eyes had narrowed at her audacity but she held her composure in view of her recent loss and out of respect for Carmen and Radcliff. To defuse the situation and her growing animosity she resorted to self-deprecation.

"I'm terrible," she had agreed. "I love nudity or to feel as close to it as possible. I should remember that not everyone wants to live the way I do. I promise to think about what you said."

"Thank you, Patsy," Susan had flashed one of her beaming smile that had touched Patsy deeply. "There's another thing I wanted to ask you. What did you make of him?"

"Who..?"

"Alex, of course," Susan had laughed. "You met him in Australia, didn't you?"

"Oooh y..e..s!" Patsy's face had lit up with the memory of that morning alone with him under the veranda at home. "Very good looking…"

"I know," Susan had said, smiling in a typically dismissive way. "I've seen photos. What was he like? What did you make of him?"

"He doesn't look the hero type," Patsy had said, realising that Radcliff had been the main purpose behind the talk. "He looked to me like a regular guy. Rod and me were amazed when we found out what had happened to him and who he really was. He's well mannered and…" she had recalled how she had caught him looking at her breasts and giggled. "…well I gave him some tea and… well I wasn't wearing much, just a frock…the look he gave me turned my knees to jelly!"

"You're a married woman!" Susan had said with disdain. "How long have you two been married?"

"One year this coming May," Patsy had retorted, raising her head with pride. "Rod and me…we are free spirits. We trust each other implicitly. We got married because we loved one another. I don't want him to change, ever. He's the kindest man I've ever met. He has a heart of pure gold. If he were here now he would tell you that he would never ask me to change either! How can you tell each other you love one another then get married and spend the rest of your life trying to change them?"

Patsy had noticed Susan's lips tighten before turning away quickly, feigning interest in the view through the window of the emergency door.

# CHAPTER 55

Radcliff had swum to the headland from the roof of the sunken yacht, clambered over the rocky shore to the beach and found the dinghy. He then rowed out to the yacht, tied it to the Yacht's stern handrail, climbed the diving steps and entered the lounge. It was devoid of furnishings except for a built in bar at its far end. Forward of the lounge were four cabins. Using a fire axe he broke open the lock to the first one on the right.

Carmen was inside, lying naked on her back. Her clothes piled on the floor where they had fallen the night before. A bowl of fruit, two water bottles and a packet of biscuits, all untouched, were on the bedside table.

She lifted her head dreamily then let it flop back onto the pillow. The sheet was blood stained under her legs. It was then that he saw the extent of her injury to her right thigh for the first time. Half of her muscle had been destroyed by the gunshot wound.

"Carmen, it's me, Alex." She lay absolutely still, staring blankly at the ceiling. "Come on my sweet." He shook her gently. "We have to go. I'm not sure I can lift you....you'll have to help me." He shook her more vigorously, but still no response.

He crouched beside the bed, his back facing her and slowly pulled her onto him. Her weight pinned him down for a moment. Raising himself onto is knees he crawled, with Carmen lying prostrate on his back, to the door and turned left into the lounge.

Outside, at the stern, he let Carmen roll gently from his back onto the deck, and then returned to the cabin for her clothes, the fruit and the water.

The outgoing tide had turned the yacht around, its bows facing the shore. Leaning over the handrail he spotted someone running from the beach into the sea. He tossed the food, water and clothes into the dinghy then lowered Carmen gently down. She crumpled onto the floor of the dinghy like a rag doll. Radcliff cast off and rowed frantically towards the headland beyond the wrecked yacht.

He reached the headland just as the man completed his swim to the yacht. Still having precious seconds before the man climbed aboard the yacht he pulled hard on the right ore and turned the dinghy towards the beach.

He followed the figure on the bows of the yacht whilst rowing with the last vestiges of his strength. The man on the yacht levelled a gun at them; Radcliff cut into the rocks and threw the water and food ashore. Holding Carmen and grabbing her clothes he capsized the dinghy at the instant a burst of bullets peppered the upturned hull.

Cupping his free hand under Carmen's chin he kicked his feet for the shore. A wave lifted them and carried them hard against the clam-covered rocks. Wedging her body behind a rock with her head held above water he turned expecting to see the gunman preparing to rake the rocks with gunfire.

Instead he heard the great engines of the yacht growl into action and the vessel slowly turned towards the opposite headland.

# CHAPTER 56

With several bags of treasure stock piled with Omollo the three men worked furiously to move the dazzling top section of the Cross.

"Come on you blighters pull," Rod shouted through gritted teeth.

"It's no good," Arthur pleaded. "It won't budge."

"Yes it will, you weak kneed pommy bastard!"

Slowly the Cross began to slip, bulldozing a trench through the glittering mountain.

"Stop!" Kurt shouted. "Shhhh," lifting a hand to his mouth. "Listen!"

Then they all heard distant calls from the chimney. Kurt grabbed one of the torches and shone it up the spiral steps into the pitch darkness.

"I'm going up," Kurt said. "Give me a coil of rope."

Rod and Arthur watched the light gradually fade as Kurt circled up the chimney and waited.

"More bags." Omollo's distant voice reached Rod and Arthur via the shaft. "I've got three left."

"Is Patsy okay?" Rod shouted up the shaft tying a yellow bag to the sling. He pulled twice on the rope.

"I can't see her. They've moved her...they've built a hoist...on the spot where she was sitting...keep the bags coming, Rod."

"We've moved the Cross..." Rod yelled back up the shaft.

"It's Alex!" Kurt called down from the chimney. "Help me, Arthur. Get up here quick!"

Arthur disappeared up the chimney whilst Rod tied a blue bag to the sling, and tugged on the rope. It silently moved up the shaft.

# CHAPTER 57

Slaughter approached the camp from the plateau watching the Frenchman and Chiltern struggle with the hoist. The blonde was leaning semi-conscious against the rock face.

"That *bleedin' fucker's gone!* He's taken the woman."

"So, what! Radcliff has the woman...we have the treasure!" Jean-Claude smirked.

"He'd nicked the *bloody* dinghy," Slaughter bellowed. "I 'ad to swim out to the yacht for a shooter. When I found the dinghy it was shot up pretty good. He's got 'er in the trees somewhere. I'll get that bleeder… if it's the last *fucking* thing I do!"

"When we've got all the treasure on board," Jean-Claude said impassively. He was studying Patsy then checked the dried blood around her head wound. He lifted her chin up. Her face was badly burned and her lips were swollen with dehydration. He ripped open her blouse and caressed her breast. "She will be perfect for what I have in mind." He kicked the 'A' frame. "Can't you improve this hoist? We tested it with four bags and it practically collapsed!"

"Water," Patsy begged, looking up at them. "Please give me water."

"I can't get it to take more weight," Chiltern had shrugged.

"That's because you are an idiot!" Slaughter untied the rope securing the 'A' frame. "Take hold of the frame."

Chiltern did so.

"It has to be more upright." Slaughter climbed the rock face searching for a suitable anchor for the rope.

Omollo was lowering a blue bag to the ground.

Twenty feet up the rock face and several yards to the right of the rope with the blue bag daggling from it, Slaughter put his hand into a deep fissure. It cut across an overhang in the rock face. Below it a knob of rock protruded upward at an acute angle. He secured the 'A' frame guy rope to it.

Chiltern waited for Slaughter to return. "The yellow ones weigh a ton," he advised.

"Okay. Try it with three blue and one yellow."

The three men gingerly lowered the cradle down the cliff face. The 'A' frame, now more upright, had brought the cradle closer to the cliff. It bumped and bounced on the protrusions and snagged on the scrubby bushes clinging to the cliffs. Six feet above the beach the cradle turned over and the bags plummeted to the beach. They heard the sound of coins pouring onto the rocks.

Slaughter threw an empty yellow bag at Chiltern. "Go and sort it, Jeb,"

# CHAPTER 58

Kurt and Arthur helped Radcliff over to the treasure.

"Amazing isn't it!" Radcliff exclaimed, feasting his eyes on the sparkling mountain. "It looks even more dazzling in this flickering light...you've moved the Cross!"

"Did you see Patsy?" Rod asked hopefully. "...is she alright?"

"They had her propped against the rock face. I couldn't see much, Rod. I was on the ridge. I'm sorry. They've built a hoist to lower the bags to the beach. Slaughter...the big bloke...he's moved the yacht into the next bay...nearer to the hoist."

"Where's Carmen?" Rod asked.

"She's well hidden." Radcliff looked at the three in turn. "She...she doesn't seem to...know me."

"He's got some powerful hypnosis over her, Alex," Kurt said softly. "Or its drugs..."

"You're probably right," Radcliff said mournfully. "You always are." He waded into the heap of glistening gems. "She'll be okay now I've got her back." He stretched across and touched the Cross. "Come on. Let me give you a hand to get the Cross out!"

They all pulled together. It slid down the slope, ploughing a trench as it went embedding itself deep into the side of the glistening mountain of precious stones and coins. The four men lifted it, staggering under its weight, shuffling inch by inch, knee deep in jewels, until they could swing it onto the rock floor.

"Jes, mate! That's sold gold, and no mistake," Rod groaned rubbing his shoulder and back. "Kurt, do us a favour mate. Send up another bag."

The three men stood before the Cross, mesmerised by its beauty and fascinated by its ingeniously conceived and intricate design. They each in turn ran their fingers over the Cross, feeling its countless jewels and then caressed the four golden swan neck supports and touched the hands outstretched over the flat golden slab that would be the lid for the base section of the Cross.

"It certainly is an incredible piece of work," Rod said admiringly. "Look at the intricate carving ...and the placement of the gems. It's magnificent!"

"I can see how it works now, Alex," Kurt said rejoining the group. He pointed excitedly to the piece of polished stone set in the centre of the intersecting crosspieces. "That crystal is crucial when harnessing its power. It's amazing to think that in medieval times they knew the properties of these materials.... and they acquired that knowledge from civilizations that existed thousands of years ago!"

"Send some more bags up," Omollo shouted. "Slaughter's threatening to come up."

Kurt tied the last filled blue bag to the rope and it disappeared up shaft.

"I think Arthur and me had better get back to work," Rod said, taking a yellow bag from the pile.

"I'm going to have a look for the base section of the Cross," Radcliff said wading into the glittering mound. He was thigh deep in jewels when he began digging, ferret like, into the gems pushing rubies, diamonds, sapphires and every other precious stone imaginable down to where Arthur and Rod were working.

"I've got it!" he cried from deep within the hole, completely hidden from view of the other three.

"We can't stop, Alex. We must keep the bags moving." Arthur said handing Kurt two more blue bags.

"Okay...I can handle this on my own." Radcliff scooped the gems out of the base. Then his fingers scraped on a small box. Remembering the diary he clasped the edges of the base and lifted. It held fast.

"What will.... you do...about Carmen?" Arthur gasped, filling the blue bags with incredible speed.

"There's a place overlooking the marshes on the south eastern end of the island. I'm going to stay with her there."

"Kurt knows where there's some weapons," Rod said.

"Yah...." Kurt shouted from the shaft. "...in horseshoe bay not far from the headland separating the two bays. John killed three of Slaughter's men there...the weapons are wrapped in a sheet and buried in the sand.... do you know where I mean?"

"John told me about it. I'll find them." Radcliff waded back to Rod and Arthur then dragged a blue bag over to Kurt. "The base of the Cross is showing, Kurt. You remember me telling you about the small box..."

"Containing that white powder gold," Kurt chuckled. "I know... we'll get the base out. Good luck, Alex."

Radcliff took one of the torches and climbed up the steps disappearing into the gloom of the chimney.

"Show those buggers a thing or two, Alex m' boy..!" Rod shouted after him, the sound of his bare feet slapping on stone receding up the chimney.

It was late afternoon; the sun had sunk behind the mountain, when Radcliff was back beside Carmen. She was lying where he had left her, propped against the carving he had made of her.

# CHAPTER 59

Jean-Claude's exhilaration and excitement had grown with each successive bag lowered safely to the beach, all the problems of the past eradicated from his mind. He leaned against a leg of the 'A' frame rubbing his hands together gleefully.

"How many bags do have we on the beach?" he asked.

"Five more than a few minutes ago," Slaughter barked.

"Oui. But how many are there now?"

"Didn't they teach you how to count in frog land either, Frenchie?" Slaughter snapped repulsed by Jean-Claude's childish elation. "There's one hundred and forty blue and twenty one...no...twenty two yellow. *Fucking* remember that...I'm not about to tell you again. Anyway you should be thinkin' of a way of getting' the bags to the yacht before the tide gets up again...." Slaughter chided "...you're going to lose some of your precious jewels...piling 'em up like that!"

"You've got the keys," Jean-Claude retorted. "Go down there and work it out."

"You've got a *fucking* nerve! I told yer that the *bloody* dinghy's buggered. We'll need to make a raft or some..."

"So...! You're the ex-marine...get down there and make one." Jean-Claude commanded effeminately, his eyes narrowing maniacally.

"*What!*" Slaughter bridled and moved menacingly on the Frenchman.

Chiltern grabbed his arm. "I'll give you a hand, boss," he volunteered slyly. "The sooner we can get this treasure to the yacht the sooner we can finish up here. You can ferry the treasure to the boat whilst Frenchie and me continue lowering the bags..."

"I'm amazed, Jeb!" Slaughter laughed. "That's the first bright suggestion you've made in your life! Let's go."

Half way across the plateau Chilton stopped.

"I've forgotten me machete," he said.

"That's no problem." Slaughter swaggered on. "I've got mine. You can do the lashing."

"I'll get it, all the same," Chiltern insisted, starting back across the plateau. "I'll catch you on the beach."

Chiltern watched Slaughter swagger on and disappear into the trees. He waited for him to get well clear then sprinted to the spot in the trees and dug. There was nothing. He dug in another spot. He recounted the steps from the bush as panic took hold of his mind. He got down on his hands and knees and dug frantically, the excavated dirt and stones rising up between his legs.

"Looking for this?" Slaughter towered over him, the harpoon pointing into Chiltern's face. "Get up, you little prick. So you actually believed you could out smart me, eh! You had better hope I still need you, Jeb." Slaughter lowered the weapon. "Go on…. fuck off fast back to that idiot Frenchman."

Chiltern scrambled to his feet and scurried through the grass, knowing the limited range of the harpoon.

Slaughter pulled the trigger watching the harpoon shaft glinting in the sunlight for a millisecond before burying itself into the centre of Chiltern's back. He fell on his face writhing in agony; feeling for the shaft with one hand then sagged and died.

He threw the hilt and firing mechanism in the direction of Chiltern's body and continued on to the beach.

The shadow of the rock face had engulfed the plateau when Jean-Claude finally took a break from stacking the bags up beside the 'A' frame. A pile of fifty bags, mostly blue ones, had accumulated on the cliff edge.

He knelt before Patsy curled up by the rock face. The rope had bitten into her flesh and her exposed skin had been badly burned by the sun. He ran his fingers over Patsy's bare hips and abdomen.

She was too weak to react.

Controlling his lust he moved to the cliff edge and watched Slaughter, waist deep in water, finish loading his raft with bags of treasure. The weight of the twenty bags had submerged the logs, the water level lapping the first layer of stacked bags.

"Where's your compatriot?" Jean-Claude shouted down.

Slaughter continued checking that the bags were secure then inspected the knot holding the raft to the line running to the yacht's winch.

"Answer me!" The Frenchman screamed with rage.

Slaughter waded out, for the sixth time, alongside the rope extending to the yacht.

Jean-Claude decided to make his move.

"Stop!" he shouted up at Omollo. "No more bags! I'm going back to the yacht. We'll begin again at first light. The woman is coming with me…no more tricks or she dies a long and painful death."

Jean-Claude untied Patsy's feet and legs. He dowsed her face with water until she revived sufficiently to stand.

He heard the great engines of the yacht growl into action once more. He gripped her arm and dragged her to the cliff edge to check the bags of treasure. Below he saw the partially submerged raft being hauled slowly towards the yacht.

The light was fading rapidly as Jean-Claude pulled Patsy along with him over the plateau towards the trees and the beach. She whimpered when Chiltern's body came into view. The eyes of the bloody corpse were frozen into a startled, horrified expression and its mouth was contorted with agony.

Jean-Claude pulled her away from it and held her close to him as a shield. With his gun pressed hard against her temple they edged nearer to the trees.

Radcliff was lying in the undergrowth clutching one of the two automatic rifles he had found buried near the headland. Patsy cried out with pain, her eyes full of terror, the gun barrel rubbing her head wound.

Jean-Claude gripped her close from behind, turning in slow circles as they moved down the pathway towards the cliff top and the beach.

Radcliff could only watch this macabre dance from the cover of the trees with the two guns slung over his shoulder. He waited for an opportunity to strike until they reached the cliff top but the Frenchman's gun was pressed hard against Patsy's head. He prayed silently for her then made his way back through the trees. Crossing the plateau he tripped, falling headlong in the grass. Rolling to one side he came face to face with Chiltern.

Patsy stumbled at the foot of the cliff pulling Jean-Claude onto her. He quickly rolled on his back and forced her to stand. Keeping his back to the sea he pulled her across the beach to the neighbouring bay.

Slaughter saw them coming as he secured a mooring rope from the raft to a palm tree. He sat on one of the fifteen remaining bags of treasure stacked against the cliff and waited.

"Take us out to the yacht?" Jean-Claude shouted as they approached.

"What kind of mug do you take me for?"

"You take her then. I'll swim behind."

"Oh! You'll swim, eh? I've worked my butt off down here, Frenchie! Take her yourself. By the way! I now want half of all that treasure."

"We agreed a third...."

"I've got the keys." He dangled them before his nose. "I could leave you here to rot. There's enough treasure on board the boat for all my needs."

"You won't do that. You need Radcliff and that money. You won't see a cent of it if you kill me and leave without Radcliff's body." He let Patsy drop onto the sand and aimed his gun at Slaughter's face.

"Now that's very impolite. And we were getting on so well, too. Here're your fucking keys." He tossed them at Jean-Claude's feet. "Go and have a good time with your blonde. I wouldn't mind a piece of that myself," he salivated, leering at her for a long time. "A piece of that would be just fine right now."

Jean-Claude stooped and picked up the keys. He directed the gun towards Patsy. "Get on the raft."

She weekly hauled herself up and rolled onto it.

He swung the barrel towards Slaughter. "Stand back!" Jean-Claude backed off into the sea.

"You make sure you have a good time, Frenchie," Slaughter jibed. "When I've finished my business with Radcliff I'll be after you!" He looked across towards horseshoe bay. "Right, Radcliff! Your time has come." Slaughter picked up his weapons and made his way to the marshes in the southeast to begin his sweep of the island.

# CHAPTER 60

That night the group of six sat in a circle between the rock face and a roaring, crackling campfire. A warm northerly sea breeze whipped up the flames A thousand sparks spiralled upward within the vortex, climbing above the rock face to mingle with the star filled firmament. The remnants of a meal was scattered on the grass. They all stared in silent reverence at the magnificent prize that lay before them.

In the middle of the small group, set side by side upon a flattened cardboard box, were the two sections of the Cross of Goa. The flames played upon the golden base casting a mesmerising warm glow over each of them; the gold and jewels of the Cross' upper section gleamed and sparkled in the firelight, their reflections dappling their faces mystically with an effusion of colour.

Carmen lay on the grass, her head and torso resting against Radcliff's chest. She had on her blouse and green and red silk sarong, oblivious of Radcliff and of everyone and everything surrounding her. They had their backs to the fire.

Omollo was seated on Radcliff's right with Kurt and Arthur next to him, with their backs towards the rock face. Rod completed the circle. He lay haggard and exhausted, propped on one elbow pensively pulling at the grass, with the dried up lake just behind him. The light from the fire intensified the deep lines of torment and worry etched into his face.

Earlier Radcliff had crossed the plateau climbed the rock face up to where the giant Omollo was stood at the mouth of the shaft. Kurt, Rod and Arthur were hauling themselves out from the shaft on the ropes they had used for extracting the treasure.

They had all been gathered at the mouth of the shaft when Radcliff told how he found Chiltern's harpooned body then went on to explain how the Frenchman had Patsy covered with a gun as he dragged her to the beach.

Rod had pulled on his arm.

"You let him take her!" Rod had screamed with rage.

"There was nothing I could do, Rod,"

Arthur restrained Rod from an actual physical attack.

"He had a gun at her head the whole time…it was too risky, Rod."

"Why didn't you follow them? There would have been a moment when…" He had looked around for support from the others, but Arthur had shaken his great head sorrowfully.

"Alex was right, Rod," Arthur said carefully. "Only a trained gunman could have hoped to take out a man in that situation."

"That Frenchman would've killed her," Kurt said slowly. "Discretion is often the better part of valour, Rod." He put an arm around Rod's stiffening shoulders. "We've released Carmen, now we must save Patsy. We can do it. We just need to keep our heads clear. It's now two against seven. Good odds, yah!"

"I'm so sorry Rod…" Radcliff began, but realised that there was nothing more he could add.

"I think we should try and get the Cross out now, while we have the chance," Kurt suggested.

"To blazes with the *bloody* Cross," Rod screamed. "What about *Patsy*?" he shrieked. "We should attack the yacht and get that evil son of bitch before he………" a mental image of Carmen's strange, raunchy dance flashed into his mind, "….if there's only two of 'em left…we could do it!"

"We need to keep calm," Arthur soothed. "I know what you're going through…"

"No you *bloody* don't," Rod snapped, glaring up into Arthur's deep set, shrewd eyes.

"We need to have a plan, Rod." Omollo said slowly. "We need to find out what this Slaughter is doing…."

"Yah! Exactly! Don't you see?" Kurt looked imploringly at Rod. "It's all coming to a head. This Slaughter will want to take everything, but first he'll be looking for you Alex. He needs to finish you off!"

"Now that's really comforting to hear!" Radcliff retorted with mock indignation.

The group had stood in silence at the mouth of the shaft waiting for Rod to deliberate.

"Okay! I can go along with some of that!" Rod had said at last. "What the devil do you need the *bloody* Cross for? We should be able to track down this blighter Slaughter and then we attack the yacht."

"The Cross is vital, Rod," Kurt had insisted.

"Why?" Arthur scratched his head, equally perplexed. "I don't understand it either. I agree with Rod…"

"Thanks mate!"

"Let's sort out these two buggers, get Patsy and then we'll have all the time in the world to get the Cross and the rest of the treasure," Arthur had suggested.

"I'll answer that…" Radcliff had quickly stepped in "…there's something very sinister about this Frenchman. He has control over Carmen and by now…sorry, Rod…he'll have Patsy under his spell as well. I need him to break this spell he has over them. We need to tread very carefully…for the sake of both women. I think we should find out what the Frenchman is up to before anything else."

"Yes, but why do we need the Cross to do that?" Arthur had persisted.

"If we get the Cross out we could use its powers to help us. Kurt knows more about that than me…"

"Alex is right, Arthur," Kurt had turned and faced Rod. "You've seen what that box of powder can do. Well, by using it we could get the Cross out very easily. With the Cross assembled, Rod, we will be invincible …and we'll save Patsy for certain. I'm sure of it!"

Rod turned to Arthur.

The Englishman's thick, bushy eyebrows pushed up deep furrows on his brow. He lifted his shoulders in resignation.

"I guess another hour or two won't matter too much," Rod had agreed. "But once the Cross is out I'm going to be on that yacht faster than…"

"No! Sorry Rod," Kurt had stated firmly. "You'll do her no good in your condition. You and Arthur have had it for one day."

"Now look here…." Rod begun.

"He's right, Rod," Arthur had acknowledged. "We've worked over fourteen hours in that bloody mountain filling those *sodding* bags. Even I just had the strength to climb out…"

"All right! All right! But when we nail the blighter, I'm going to hang him up by the balls…" Rod had slapped his right fist into his left palm, "and then crush 'em between two rocks!" They had all watched him battling to contain his emotions. "I just want to see…" his lips tightened across his teeth into a determined grimace, his chin quivering, "…to see… my Patsy again."

It had taken the five men just over two hours of delicate manoeuvring to extract both sections of the Cross and lower them to the ground. Kurt, Omollo and Radcliff had used the cover of darkness to cross the plateau to the beach leaving Rod and Arthur to prepare a fire.

With seven fish skewered on his spear Radcliff had waited in the shadows of the cliffs, close to the headland. An hour later he recognised the unmistakable silhouettes of Omollo and Kurt returning from the yacht.

"Over here," Radcliff had called out.

"That Frenchman's…up to…something. It's all…very weird," Kurt had said breathlessly, shaking his head gravely.

Omollo nodded, the whites of his eyes bulging larger than ever.

"The lounge has…no furnishings. In its centre he has a blackened area…about twelve feet square…surrounded by…red silk sheets…laid down on the floor." Kurt raised his eyebrows. "He had painted…two white circles, one within the other on the black area." Kurt bent over and leant on his knees fighting for breath. He saw Radcliff's spear with the neat row of fish impaled upon it.

"You've…been busy, Alex!" Inhaling deeply he had stood erect. "Between the white lines of the circles," he had continued, the alarm in his voice intensifying, "he had painted…the signs of the zodiac. Within the inner circle there was a pentagram… each blade had a metallic bowls with flames…burning from them. Black candles were everywhere, Alex! The walls and ceiling were covered with all kinds of mystical symbols and weird writing."

"I've seen this sort of thing a few times before," Omollo had said, his eyes shining white in the starlight. "There had been a murder in a north London cemetery…the victim was a human sacrifice. I've seen some strange things in Benin too. There they practice Voodoo and black magic…but that was very messy…"

"Where was Patsy?" Radcliff interrupted. "Did you see her?"

"No," Omollo shook his head. "The lights were too dim…"

"Yah! The lounge was lit by very low red and green lights…. there was no sign of the Frenchman either. Tell Alex about the treasure bags, John…"

"They were one side of the lounge door. I went into the lounge… not for very long… and I saw them in the shadows stacked against the back wall. There must've been more then hundred bags! There was no sign of Slaughter either."

"He must be out there somewhere!" Radcliff had stood and scanned the island. "Carmen's on her own! Here take the fish. I'll bring her to the camp." Radcliff had scurried up the cliff face and was gone.

# CHAPTER 61

Slaughter had worked his way around the mountain slopes to a position above the camp. In the glow from the campfire he had searched for Radcliff. He recognised the two men preparing the meal and had overheard one mention that Radcliff would be bringing some fish back.

From his vantage point he could see an overhang from the rock face and a plan begun to hatch. Then shadowy shapes had approached the camp from the trees. Slaughter backtracked to the plateau, returned to the beach then swam out to the yacht. Eerie red and green lights emanated from the lounge which lit up the stern of the vessel and shone on the steps down to his cabin below the lounge.

He took a knapsack from under his bunk, filled it with explosives, a handgun and the remainder of his ammunition from his locker and climbed the steps to the lounge deck. A hand grabbed his arm.

"Where are going with that?" Jean-Claude had emerged from the lounge in a black robe with scarlet bands around the hem and the hood. A golden chord was tied around his waist.

"What *do* you look like..?" Slaughter had smirked mockingly. "...some kind of high priest!" He eyed the Frenchman up and down. "High priestess, more like! I'm getting off this yacht, away from you...and all your black magic!"

"Leave the raft. I'll need that in the morning!"

"Well I need it too, you great French berk. I'll bring the bloody thing back," Slaughter untied the rope securing the raft. "I'm takin' some jelly with me."

"Why do you need that?"

"I've got an idea," Slaughter had grinned throwing the bag onto the raft then jumped down himself. "It's my own Big Bang theory!"

"*What*!"

"Don't worry. I know what I'm doing." Slaughter then heaved on the rope tied to the palm tree and raft slowly moved away from the yacht.

"There's still more treasure inside the mountain!" Jean-Claude had cried after him. "Be careful...you've already blasted it with two missiles! I want those jewels! They're mine and I intend to get them."

"Ours!" he had shouted back. "Just don't sacrifice my share to the devil... along with that blonde."

Jean-Claude had gone back inside and went straight for the bar and drank half a bottle of vodka. He ogled Patsy's hypnotised and naked body lying on her back invitingly on the bags of treasure. He salivated, restraining his lust. He consoled himself with the thought of taking her later when Carmen, his Queen, would be at his side. Then the blonde woman's blood would bind them forever. Together they would rule the universe.

He had then grabbed Patsy's arm and dragged her across the lounge floor to a position above the white circles enclosing the signs of the zodiac where a scarlet sheet was placed. Two crimson cushions lay the other side of her. Jean-Claude lay her on the sheet. The flickering lights from the candles and flaming bowls played on her naked body. Kneeling on one of the cushions he snapped his fingers. Her eyes had flicked open instantly. He lifted her head.

"Drink my beauty," bringing the half empty bottle of vodka up to her lips, "Drink."

She had gulped all the remaining liquid thirstily.

# CHAPTER 62

The green wood crackled and hissed on the campfire.

"We could assemble the Cross now," Radcliff suggested.

"Yah. But the moment the lid is in place," Kurt said cautiously, "the Cross will become a very powerful superconductor. The energy it'll generate will be unimaginable... it will continue doing so indefinitely. We must not be too hasty."

"That goes beyond any laws of physics that I know of," Arthur scoffed. "Its design is unusual, I grant you but it's only made of gold and a few precious gems."

"It's the way it has been put together," Kurt explained. "Observe the hands on the lid; the index figures almost touching. They are its electrodes. The base works as a capacitor...provided, of course, the wood sandwiched between the gold hasn't rotted!"

"Then you're not completely sure the Cross will work!" Arthur gazed at Rod, who continued pulling at the grass, staring blankly at the Cross. "Patsy's life is in the balance here! We're not conducting one of your scientific experiments!"

"The Cross will work, Arthur," Radcliff stated assuredly. "I've a diary...I have it here in one of these bags...written by my ancestor, Robert William Radclyffe." He spelt out the old English spelling of his surname. "He wrote it two hundred years after the Cross was built... he described in detail its incredible potency. The wood that was used is the most resinous they could find. It is sealed, sandwiched between two layers of pure gold."

Radcliff went on to briefly explain to Arthur and Rod why the Cross had been constructed, by whom, and what secrets it concealed.

"Honestly Alex! How the devil could this Portuguese goldsmith possibly know how to build a scale model of the Ark of the Covenant?" Arthur asked irritably. "And replicate its powers...?" He added incredulously.

"Bloody right..!" Rod sat bolt upright. "I think you're taking a mighty chance with this thing."

"You've already seen what the white powder gold can do! Do you both remember those fragments of clay we found inside the base?"

Arthur nodded.

"If they were not Sumerian then they were from an earlier time. They gave precise instructions for making the white powder gold and how to construct the Ark."

"Yeh! But how did this Portuguese goldsmith come by 'em?" Rod persisted.

"The Templars brought them out of Jerusalem in 1125, possibly with the Ark itself," Radcliff proclaimed. "The tablets were given to the Knights of Christ for safe keeping. As I said, that's why the Cross was built.... to keep the secrets from those blood thirsty devils of the Inquisition."

"Okay. But how could your ancestor know all this, Alex?" Arthur asked.

Radcliff answered slowly: "From the Archbishop of Goa in 1721..." He told them how pirates seized the 'Vierge du Cap', the treasure ship that carried the Cross. "Robert and his new wife and the Archbishop were passengers on that ship. The Archbishop befriended Robert and told him everything he knew about the Cross and its secrets."

"1721!" Arthur ran his left hand threw his thick, black curly hair. "Did this ancestor of yours have a brother?"

"Yes," Radcliff answered, surprised by the question. "There's an inscription by his brother in the front of the diary."

"His name wasn't Charles by any chance?"

"Yes. It was."

"He was a very important feller in the history of Freemasonry. I was once a Mason." Arthur admitted with a trace of an apology in his voice.

"You bloody pomms get up my nose with your brotherhoods and secret societies," Rod snarled. "I know they give generously to charities but in my book it's just a way for the rich and affluent to keep their wealth intact under the pretext of being bloody do-gooders whilst two thirds of the world's population are on the bread line. If you want to do good deeds why don't you just get on with it?"

Slaughter had carefully worked his way back to his position on the rock face above the campfire. He could clearly see Radcliff in the firelight. Five others including the woman were seated in a circle around two golden objects, one of them clearly a cross.

He overheard some of the conversation below him, which amused him, whilst he prepared to bury Radcliff and all his 'toffee nosed' friends under tons of rock.

"Freemasonry started in Scotland, Rod!" Arthur retorted. "The Scottish Rite was probably Templar inspired and closely associated with the Jacobite cause. Charles Radclyffe was the Earl of Derwentwater and the illegitimate son of Charles II. He was of course a Jacobite through and through."

"I'm sorry, mate. Snobbery niggles me that's all." Rod thought a moment. "Jes,' that makes Alex royalty!"

"I have often wondered," Radcliff smiled, "if Robert was ever involved with the crowning of Bonnie Prince Charlie as King Charles III."

"Rubbish!" Arthur admonished.

"But Charlie was on his way to London to take the throne of England," Radcliff persisted.

"He turned tail...he never took the British throne," Arthur added quickly. "He left England with his tail between his legs!"

"Well, not quite...," Radcliff began.

"Who gives a monkey's...," Rod broke in impatiently. "Look, can't we get on with assembling this Cross and stop wasting time."

Omollo fed the hungry fire several more branches. It licked its meal ravenously, flaring on the dry bark and emitted appreciative sparks which swirled and climbed to the stars.

"Before we begin assembling the Cross," Radcliff said seriously, "we must observe the safety rules for handling and transporting it. These rules have been passed down from Vasco da Gama to Robert Radclyffe via the Archbishop of Goa."

"The Levites wore special breast plates of gold with studs of polished stones when they carried the Ark," Arthur mentioned casually. "And they had to walk bare foot."

"Once the top section of the Cross is in place," Kurt stated, "its power will begin to generate. Removing it later will result in the sudden release of its energy. It could be catastrophic!"

They all stared at the Cross.

"It seems very dangerous to me," Arthur rubbed his chin apprehensively. "We are playing with fire here."

"You're a mason *and* a policeman!" Rod mocked. "Come on Arthur, where's your spirit?"

"It *will* be very dangerous." Kurt looked earnestly into eyes of his friends. "We know that the Cross is one third the size of the Ark but it functions on the same principals. During our tests in the States we found that a superconductor releases Gamma rays when discharging energy. They have the smallest wavelengths and the most energy in the electromagnetic spectrum. Gamma rays can release more energy in 10 seconds than the Sun will emit in its entire 10 billion-year lifetime!"

"In other words-they're a bit dangerous!" Rod quipped.

Loose rocks tumbled from the overhanging rock above them.

Slaughter pressed himself against the rock keeping absolutely still, clinging onto the edge of the fissure. The leg that had broken the rocks free hung suspended in space.

Arthur shone a torch up the rock face. The group followed the beam as Arthur scanned it across and around the overhang then widened his search up the shattered rock face to the shaft.

Carmen had remained leaning passively against Radcliff's body.

"It's nothing," Radcliff shrugged. "Its just loose rocks...it happens all the time."

"I think we should move," Kurt pointed up at the overhang above them. "That looks rather threatening."

"Help me with Carmen," Radcliff gently lifted her torso under her arms as Kurt took her legs. "The rest of you start bringing the stuff?"

They carried her beyond the fire.

Kurt spotted a deep hollow with boulders either side of it.

"Lay her here!"

"There's a bigger one further up," Radcliff said. "It's about level with the end of the lake."

With Carmen safe they returned for the Cross.

Slaughter set the fuse to detonate the explosives in four minutes. He ascended the rock face to the shaft and climbed the rope, retracing his steps to the ridge.

As Arthur, Omollo and Rod trudged back and forth with boxes and bags Radcliff and Kurt peered into the base section of the Cross.

"I've an idea." Kurt took two glass pâté jars from a bag. "Hand me the gold box." He broke the seal and emptied some of its contents into the two jars and screwed the lids firmly down. Replacing the box, he put one jar in his pocket and wedged the other under one of the gold hands reaching across the lid of the top section. He stuffed mud and grass around to hold it secure. He called Omollo over to them.

"Alex and me will take the top section. You follow us with the base."

They placed both sections of the Cross inside the hollow where Carmen lay. Arthur and Rod staggered towards them loaded up with carrier bags and boxes of supplies. Rod stacked his boxes close to the end of the dried up lake and returned for more. Arthur fell headlong into a bush, spilling the contents of the boxes onto the grass. He began picking up the tins of food.

"Leave it all there," Kurt called out. "Alex and me will collect it. Get the rest of the stuff."

Arthur lifted the last three boxes, staggering under their weight and was about to skirt the fire. Rod was carrying a couple of bags just a few paces in front of him.

A cataclysmic explosion shook the ground. The rock face heaved up and outwards amid a flash of white heat. Within a split of a second the two men were engulfed in smoke and dust as tons of rock was blasted out of the mountain.

Radcliff dived onto Carmen as Kurt and Omollo took cover behind a boulder. They were enveloped by a cloud of dust and smoke. Radcliff covered Carmen's face, as rocks and stones pummelled their bodies followed by a deluge of smaller needle like fragments raining down upon them.

There was a deathly quiet for several seconds. All that broke the silence was the sound of a few loose rocks and stones tumbling down the rock face. They looked up but they could see nothing through the pall of smoke and dust hanging over the area.

"Slaughter...!" Omollo growled. "This is his work..."

Kurt lifted himself up. "Rod and Arthur! They're out there..."

Omollo clasped his shoulder gently. "They're gone, Kurt. They were right in the middle of it. We've got to get this Slaughter...before he kills us all."

Radcliff eased himself off of Carmen, his dust covered face streaked with blood from a graze on his head. "You two okay?"

Kurt nodded.

"Slaughter will be back to finish us off," Radcliff said kneeling beside Carmen. "We must get away from here...now."

"Yes, but where to, Alex?" Kurt asked.

"Get everything to the trees. We'll decide there. You bring all the stuff, John, and anything you can salvage. Kurt and me will take Carmen and come back for both parts of the Cross."

"Shouldn't we check on Rod and Arthur, first?" Kurt asked.

"We haven't time," Radcliff stood and began lifting Carmen up by the shoulders.

# CHAPTER 63

Slaughter had reached the ridge when the explosives detonated. He pulled out a small set of binoculars from his combats and scanned the area. It was in total darkness. Eager to see the results of his work he hurried down the ridge. His foot caught in a root and he fell headlong over the narrow path and rolled down the steep slope, smashing his head on a rock. He struggled to his feet then collapsed unconscious, rolling under a young eucalyptus tree.

Kurt and Radcliff laid Carmen beneath the trees. She groaned. It was the first sound she had uttered since Radcliff had rescued her.

"What is it my sweet?" Radcliff lowered his ear to her quivering lips.

"Water...give her water," Kurt suggested.

Radcliff supported her head as Kurt tipped a few drops onto her lips from his water bottle. Suddenly her eyes glared demonically at Radcliff. She clasped Kurt's wrist with an iron grip and pulled the bottle to herself and drank thirstily, her wild eyes remaining riveted on Radcliff. Having had her fill she snatched the bottle from Kurt and threw it to one side then returned to her former state as if nothing had happened.

Radcliff searched Kurt's face for an answer, but he had none.

"Leave her, Alex. Let's go back for the Cross."

Omollo searched the debris littering the plateau piling up salvaged boxes and bags as Kurt and Radcliff brought the two sections of the Cross to where Carmen lay.

Kurt returned with Omollo to where they had last seen Rod.

The dust had settled. Great boulders had buried the camp and obliterated the fire. Many more littered the area beyond. Wisps of smoke rose up out from the rocks and boulders covering the spot where the fire had been.

Omollo's eyes filled with tears. He looked to the heavens as Kurt said a prayer.

"Look!" He pointed up at the shaft.

Kurt looked up. He gasped at what he saw in the starlight.

Above them a yawning black hole looked down on them.

"The explosion...it's blown away the mountain side...!" Omollo exclaimed in utter amazement.

"Those missiles must have fractured the rocks covering the cavern…" Kurt deduced incredulously "…and weakened the rock supporting the mountain side."

"Come on, John. We need to get back to Alex."

They hastily collected up some of their supplies lying strewn amongst the boulders and returned to the cover of the trees.

Breathless, the three men stood over the two sections of the Cross.

"We can't assemble it here," Kurt stated. "The canopy's too thick. We need a clearing. Is there a clearing nearby…any ideas, Alex?"

"Hay, what about all the weapons and things we've left on the ledge?" Omollo asked suddenly.

"We can get them later," Kurt replied dismissively.

"I know the exact spot! We need to head up towards that ridge…" Radcliff pointed south deeper into the trees "…we'll carry her as before, okay John?"

Omollo collected up the boxes once more and followed Kurt and Radcliff in the pitch darkness through the trees. Radcliff led holding Carmen's legs battering a path through the dense undergrowth whilst Kurt held her shoulders lifting her high over the semi trodden vegetation.

Radcliff stopped. They lowered Carmen gently down pillowing her head with leaves. She lay next to Radcliff's carving of her.

The canopy was thinner at that altitude. The general shape of Radcliff's carving was clearly visible in the starlight.

"So this is the famous sculpture, yah?" Kurt said, recovering his breath and running his hands over the smooth sanded surface of her breasts. "It feels very good, Alex!"

"I think so." Radcliff raised a chuckle.

"I'll look forward to seeing this in the daytime," Omollo remarked after scrutinising it for a long time. "The wood looks beautifully smooth…it's wonderful, Alex."

Having trudged back and forth bringing the Cross and all their supplies to their new location Kurt said breathlessly as he scrutinized the canopy: "We'll need…a better clearing…than this if…we are to assemble the Cross…Alex!"

"Follow me." Radcliff led them higher up the slope, striding through the thinning vegetation, for about fifty yards to a small clearing on the edge of an escarpment. It had an uninterrupted view overlooking the marshes and the whole southeastern end of the island.

"Shouldn't we hunt down this Slaughter first?" Omollo said.

"It'll be too risky in the dark," Radcliff said searching the eastern horizon for a glimmer of dawn. "We'll be safe here 'till then."

"Slaughter won't give up until he's seen you dead, Alex." Omollo persisted.

"You're right John. What about the Cross, Kurt?"

"Okay, let's get the Cross up here," Kurt agreed.

The three men brought the two sections up to the clearing and lay them side-by-side on a flat rock. Kurt checked the area inspecting the trees and measuring distances between the trees to find the optimum location for the Cross to be assembled.

Kurt found a lone fury barked spindly tree growing well inside the boundary of the clearing.

"We'll need to position the Cross well away from that tree. It could be a danger and interfere with the Cross. Also it's very precious. I'm a bit surprised to see one here."

"That's my pharmacy!" Radcliff chuckled. "I used to come here a lot. I've cured many ailments using that tree! I used to soak the bark in water as a painkiller. It tastes quite good too…quite intoxicating!"

"I know. It's a 'Neam' tree," Kurt stated. "There's a specimen on La Degue island, but it comes from South East Asia. They call it the wonder tree…but enough of the natural history lesson…let's take the Cross further over to the left…closer to the edge of the slope."

With the Cross in position, about six feet from the escarpment, Kurt knelt beside the base and peered inside.

"Those inscriptions…" he marvelled "…that Frederico de Silva the goldsmith was a master of his craft, yah…" his tone was as soft and warm as the sea breeze "…to have the forethought to copy the formulae from the clay tablets into the gold for posterity should the tablets be destroyed. I've made my own copy…just in case…I wanted to take my time and make a better copy…

"Okay gentlemen, are we ready?" Kurt looked up at the two men.

# PART FIVE

# CHAPTER 64

Kurt gingerly loosened the mud around the glass jar of white powder, easing it from beneath the golden hand and stood it on the lid. Taking the other glass jar from his pocket he placed it beside the first.

Radcliff and Omollo glanced at each other, feeling Kurt's excitement.

"You and John lift the top section and hold it just above the base."

The white powder gold within the jar made the task easy.

"Hold it there," Kurt commanded with a lilt. "That's it…now clasp the top using those curved supports…keep your fingers away from the edge of the lid……get a firm grip."

He waited.

"Let it down slowly. Yah…yah…slowly...*stop*!" Kurt adjusted the position of the top so that it lined up perfectly with the base. "Okay… gently now…"

The lid slipped into place with a hiss of expelled air then seated itself with a heavy clunk. Kurt immediately pushed the glass jars off the lid with a piece of wood, skirted the assembled Cross and retrieved the jars.

Radcliff and Omollo backed away several paces. Kurt hurried to join them.

The three men stood in silence before the magnificent Cross. They could feel its power building, the gold radiating a strengthening invisible force that suffused the three men. They experienced both exuberant elation and extreme terror that rooted them to the ground.

"We are the first to see the Cross…" Alex whispered reverently "…complete that is…for almost three hundred years,"

"It's…it's…incredible…Alex." Omollo said as though in a trance, grappling with the reality of the moment whilst simultaneously feeling delectable uplifting, tingling sensations with surges of deep apprehension and regret that they had chanced putting the cross together at all. His great bulged eyes were riveted upon the Cross of Goa.

"Look how it sparkles in the starlight...the colours are amazing, yah? Its gold surface has an alien sheen to it!"

Each man watched the other in mystified wonder as these sensations continued to elevate their limbs and minds whilst unnerving reactions caused strange fluttering sensations in their abdomens. Despite their anxiety they could not suppress what seemed to be juvenile elation drawing their spirits inexorably together, rekindling a knowledge and certainty that had long been hidden and forgotten in some deep recess of their psyche. Overwhelmed by the intensity of this power each man wanted nothing more than to embrace the other. They did so; enraptured and bound in this blissful joy that each felt had been denied them for too long.

Whilst in that brotherly embrace Radcliff recalled suddenly the words in Robert's diary...the words that the Archbishop of Goa had written: 'Will anyone ever have the joy of standing before the Cross of Goa again? Will anyone ever feel again that extraordinary uplift of the spirit and enrichment of faith? Will it ever be recovered in one piece?'

A blinding pillar of light emanating from the edge of the cosmos descended upon the Cross, lighting up the whole island and the ocean surrounding it with the brilliance hundreds of times brighter than a mid-day sun.

The three men reeled away turning their backs on the Cross. They crumpled to their knees shielding their eyes with their arms. The light had the withering heat of a foundry furnace which seared into their backs and sucked away the air around them. After 60 seconds exposure they were about to ignite, their clothes scorching and smouldering, then the dazzling light faded and darkness returned.

With their backs to the cross they gradually rose to their feet. Omollo slowly peered over his shoulder. Then the others turned slowly.

The whole clearing was enveloped in a dense fog. An eerie effulgence grew rapidly outlining the Cross in silhouette within the cloud. Then two figures began to materialise. They stood just before the escarpment... their dull, fuzzy shapes quickly becoming distinct. They wore white robes, neatly trimmed beards and shoulder length hair.

The three men were transfixed.

The glowing mist was being rapidly sucked into the Cross through the infinitesimally small space separating the base and the upper section.

The two robed figures slowly approached the three men, stopping just before the Cross. They emitted a visible aura of warm luminosity that surrounded their whole bodies, the one to their right had fine golden hair and a long flowing blonde beard; the other had rich auburn hair and beard of equal length and colour. They reached out their arms, beckoning the men to come closer.

"Do not be afraid," the figure on the right said, smiling softly. "No harm will come to you."

They remained silent, transfixed and awestruck.

"I have been waiting for this moment for a very long time," the same figure added, his extended smile brimming with benevolence and warmth.

Radcliff wanted to speak but his jaw had locked shut.

"Yes, Alex," he said. "I've been waiting for you." His arms reached out to Radcliff. "I am Judas Thomas."

His sweet mellow voice touched their hearts, but did nothing to decrease the terror in their eyes.

He turned his golden head slightly to his right. "This is James... better known as James the Just. It was our destiny to be here with you at this critical time."

James bowed his head gracefully. As he did so his smile extended slightly betraying amusement at their fearful expressions.

Each man glanced hopefully at the other waiting for one to volunteer to be the spokesman.

Kurt's mouth twitched, curling nervously up at the corners. "You say you've been waiting. Do you mean that you've been waiting for Alex to assemble the Cross?"

"Kurt," the auburn haired figure to their left laughed, opening his arms out wide. "You are truly blessed with great perception." He spoke more crisply, in a slightly higher pitch than his companion.

His confidence returning, Kurt asked boldly: "Where are you from?"

James stepped closer.

The three men backed away.

He stopped and held out his arms beseechingly. "Come. Take courage." He smiled. "I will not harm you..." stepping back. "...we are from another dimension, Kurt...from a place beyond any human conception and imagination. You can thank your forefathers... the ones who built the Cross... that we could be here in this hour of your need."

"The Cross has brought you from another dimension?" Kurt's face screwed into a grin of delight. "This is incredible science. You have actually tele-transported yourselves to Earth...?"

"In a manner of speaking," Judas Thomas smiled, dropping his arms gradually to his sides. "You have a genius that has yet to be recognised, Kurt. Your 'Theory of Everything' is very close to the truth..." he said joyously, but then added seriously, "...for your dimension." Kurt was about to speak but the blonde robed figure continued in the same mesmerising soft clear tone. "As you know, Kurt, these 'Superconductors' ...as you call them...can transfer infinite energy and matter from one to another over infinite distances.

"The Cross has absorbed a massive surge of energy to bring us here. That energy is intensifying as we speak and will continue to do so until we use it to return to our...dimension. As you will also know, Kurt, these devices are very dangerous," his countenance suddenly changing to one of severity. "The precautions you have taken were woefully inadequate. The Gamma rays alone could have vaporised you all in an instant. You should have known better, Kurt!"

"You are Judas Thomas?" Radcliff croaked, his dry throat clearing slowly. "One of…the apostles…*of Jesus?*"

"I was called Didymus, the Greek term for 'the twin'." The robed figure moved forward.

"The twin..!" Kurt exclaimed with a lilt, still smarting from the severity of his chastisement.

"You will hear many astounding things during our time with you, I can assure you, my son. But now you must act quickly. We will talk much more later on about the truth that you seek…but we have come to warn you that you are in very grave danger. When I say 'you' I mean everyone…in your whole universe."

"*What!*" Radcliff exclaimed.

"Yes, Alex! You are in imminent danger!"

"What kind of danger?" Radcliff asked in alarm.

"There is a force of incredible destructive power manifesting itself in the yacht as we speak," James answered sharply. "The whole of creation…every living being, star and galaxy in your universe is threatened!"

"What is this force?" Omollo asked, his mind flashing back to the harrowing crime of black magic in a London churchyard. He shuddered recalling the sight of human remains butchered on tombstones, their severed heads impaled on inverted crosses.

"Provided you act…" Judas Thomas began.

"Carmen has gone!" James broke in. "She has returned to the Frenchman."

Machine gun fire cut through the stillness of the night startling roosting birds, their wings pounding the canopy leaves.

Radcliff scrambled through the trees and undergrowth back to the stump.

"She's gone!" Radcliff cried out. He picked up her white blouse and green and red silk sarong and stared into the blackness of the forest.

Kurt and Omollo turned and were about to follow Radcliff.

"*Wait!*" James held up his hand. "Alex," he called. "Come back. You'll not catch her. Carmen is unharmed."

Judas Thomas waited for Radcliff to return.

"The gun shots came from the man you know as 'Slaughter'. He heard her running through the trees and opened fire blindly into the darkness. He missed! He is in pursuit, but he will not catch her."

"Time is running out," James said with compelling urgency.

Judas Thomas pointed his finger at the Cross. A shaft of white light shot from his fingertip and struck the point where the cross pieces intersect. A diamond shaped crystal, an inch and a half wide, was dislodged and fell at Radcliff's feet. They looked down at it in amazement.

"Cut some bamboo, Alex," James demanded urgently. "It must be seven feet in length and wide enough to grip and hold the crystal. Someone unravel a length of rope."

Radcliff ran off down the escarpment towards the marches with a machete.

Kurt stooped to pick up the stone.

"*Don't touch it!*" James cried out in alarm. "It will be very hot!" he said softly with a grin.

"It cannot be...! Is it a replica of King Solomon's 'Stone of Foundation'?" Kurt asked hesitantly, unsure that an incorrect presumption might cause offence and further rebuke.

"No!" James laughed. "It is the actual crystal! The Templars uncovered it and took it to France with the rest of the Temple treasures. Their Portuguese brothers, the Knights of Christ, found the perfect hiding place for it... wouldn't you say?"

A few minutes later Radcliff returned with six canes. Choosing the one most suitable they wedged the stone into the end of the bamboo and applied pine resin to hold it secure then lashed it with the cord unravelled from a piece of rope.

"Each of you must listen very carefully," said Judas Thomas, his tone sombre and grave. "We are dealing with a force from another universe and we haven't much time to explain in detail. Kurt will understand all what I am telling you and can explain everything to both of you later. The cane is your wand. But it will only function if the person wielding it has in his possession some white powder gold. The 'superconducting' powder will extract unlimited energy from the Cross and transfer it through your body to the crystal. Your body, the Cross and the crystal will become one instrument. Your thoughts alone will direct the energy, determining automatically the magnitude required and when it should shut off. Kurt will know how to find the most vulnerable point of his target once the force materialises.

"Kurt, you will, of course, be in control of the cane, but give one of the jars of white powder to Alex."

"Do you have any questions?" James asked crisply.

"I presume... that this force we're up against originates from.... a universe where.... anti-matter predominates?" Kurt asked tentatively.

"It is more prevalent," Judas Thomas corrected. "But do not presume, Kurt, that it is quite as simple as a battle of matter against anti-matter. This power originates from a much more complex universe than yours. What is your strategy, Kurt?"

"It's difficult to say. I need to see exactly what we're up against."

"As I said before, Kurt, your 'Theory of Everything' is very close to the truth," James said encouragingly. "When you face your adversary you will know what to do. The cane and the crystal will be with you. They will prove your theory."

"Remember your calculations, Kurt," Judas Thomas smiled "It is the seventh Quark, the centre Quark that exists only in your universe.

Humankind could not have evolved without it. You are God's children who are experiencing His creation. You were right, Kurt, the seventh Quark is the driving force within the atom. As it spins it vibrates stimulating and conducting the other six quarks into a sub-atomic concerto. The sequence of notes creates a field through which symmetrical particles pass and are given certain mass depending upon the music the quark's produce. The symphony of your cosmos is as beautiful to hear as your shinning, blue jewel of a world is to look at. "

"Kurt," James interjected, "you must aim for the nervous system where the atoms are most vulnerable. Find the nerve, think of nothing but your Quarks and your aim will be true. You will obliterate its anti Quarks setting off a chain reaction that will cause its own universe to collapse in on itself."

"It will be reborn," Judas Thomas smiled reassuringly.

"Yes. Like all universes," added James casually, "it will begin again as a primordial blast of light. You call it the 'Big Bang'. The newly born universe could have the seventh Quark intact this time." He laughed loudly having noticed the three men gawping at him with bemused incredulity. "It is the cycle! It is continuous transformation and creation...contraction and expansion! We know that you understand all of this, Kurt."

"Yah! Thank you," Kurt fumbled for words. "That is....erm... exactly what I'll do...I'll bombard its most vulnerable areas...in its nervous system.... with matter until an anti proton is penetrated by the one particle that will smash its subatomic structure to smithereens."

"Excellent Kurt..!" James nodded in appreciation. "I know that this wonderful universe of yours is safe in your hands!"

Radcliff and Omollo exchanged looks of awe and admiration for their friend.

"First you must hit your mark with your first attempt," Judas Thomas stated emphatically. "Failure and the element of surprise will be lost. It will instinctively protect that area you are targeting, making your task next time close to impossible. Second you must complete the destruction of this force before sunrise. Failure and the force could grow too large and too strong for even the Cross to overcome. Third you must remember that the unlimited power of the Cross is transferred automatically to you through the white powder and the crystal. You will be victorious if you believe *that* with all your heart. Then your aim will be true. Kurt, you are the present day David fighting your 'Goliath'. Your staff will be the sling, but the 'Goliath' that is awaiting you has the strength of unimaginable magnitude."

"But as I said there are complications," James added gravely. "I'll be brief. Your great scientific minds are already discussing the possibility of multiple universes, which you have called membranes, or 'branes' for short. You must abandon any conceptual idea of how another universe might be structured. There are twelve universes: each having one planet that supports intelligent life; for each life form there is a God; for each universe and each God there is a supreme God that created everything there is, that was and ever will be. That supreme God sent us to you."

"Then science isn't too far from the real truth?" Kurt said.

"You are close to understanding your own universe, but you have no concept of how the other universes are structured and how they interact with your own. Love and fear are the two extremes, not good and evil... which are inadequate representations of the Alpha and Omega of the extremes. Similarly right and wrong and hell and heaven are human inventions. The force you will encounter has emanated from a universe where fear predominates. The God of that universe is a tyrannical, malevolent and sadistic one."

Radcliff coughed. "Sorry to interrupt this fascinating flow of scientific and theological knowledge, which are revelations to John and me...but if we partially destroy this thing, can it materialise again? Can it reform itself?"

"It will do so very quickly," Judas Thomas answered emphatically. "It has absorbed energy from three other universes during its existence and is, as a consequence, very strong and adaptive. Its universe is very advanced but the life forms, when they materialise are very primitive.

"I will be here to assess the situation and help you if you should be unsuccessful in your first attempt to destroy it. Remember that '*love*' is the key weapon. *Use it!* In the battle to come it will have as much potency as the cane you carry. Think of everything and everyone on your Earth that you love and hold dear. You must fight with your hearts and souls as much as your minds. Love and God are supreme. God will be your guide."

# CHAPTER 65

Slaughter sat nursing his head in his hands. Lightning struck the ridge a quarter of a mile below him, its bolt unusually straight and wide and its blinding light cast daylight over the island for more than a minute until it slowly faded and darkness returned.

He looked skyward. It was bereft of clouds. He immediately thought of the Frenchman. "That stupid son of a bitch!" he muttered to himself as he hurried down the side of the ridge to the plateau.

Carmen hurtled naked through the trees, flying faster than a leaping gazelle towards the beach.

Slaughter reacted firing blindly into the blackness of the forest.

Guided by an unknown external force, Carmen's feet barely touched the ground. She descended the cliff and sprinted across the bay over the headland and swam with Olympian speed towards the yacht.

Red and green lights flooded from the open lounge door. The sharp silhouette of Jean-Claude stooped over the handrail of the yacht watching Carmen approach.

She climbed the ladder, her body glistening in the strange light, her chest heaving for breath.

"Come with me, sister," Jean-Claude said with a demonic gleam in his eyes, ushering her towards the lounge door.

Dripping wet, her voluptuous body shimmering as she walked gracefully into the lounge with Jean-Claude following her water trail.

"You will be my Queen," he proclaimed, closing the door behind him.

They slowly strode ceremoniously through the lounge, hand in hand, skirting the flaming bowls in the pentagram. The red and green lights were turned towards the windows leaving the interior lit by thick black candles that burned around the pentacle, in its centre flames danced from a large golden bowl.

"*Carmen!*" Patsy screamed out. "*Help me! I can't move! Help me, please...!*"

Patsy was absolutely still, paralysed from head to toe by the venom of the taipan snake, lying nude upon a scarlet sheet placed across the top of the pentacle.

Carmen desperately tried to overcome the force controlling her actions and turn her head to signal Patsy, as she had tried to do with

Radcliff, but Jean-Claude's power was too great. Instead she could feel her facial muscles tighten involuntarily across her mouth into a sadistic grin.

Jean-Claude stooped over Patsy's head and waved his hands before her eyes and she fell silent.

Carmen moved indifferently and impassively around Patsy's head and sat cross-legged on one of two cushions overlooking the pentacle and Patsy's body. She held her head majestically high, her wet hair clinging to her shining body. It fell in thick strands over her firm breasts and down her back, her spine curving at the base thrusting her abdomen sensuously forward. Her open hands rested on her thighs, palms upward.

Jean-Claude strode swiftly to the base of the pentagram where seven bowls had been placed in a row parallel to Patsy. Each bowl contained potions and mixtures of herbs, dead insects and animal parts. He took a long dagger from his robe, held it against his forearm and ran the blade across his flesh. Blood ran freely from the wound onto the blade. He picked up the central bowl and let his blood to drip into it, chanting in an unintelligible tongue.

He took the bowl to Carmen, his chanting more vociferous, and lacerated her arm letting her blood mingle with his. He held the bowl up above his head. "Mon maître…mon maître…mon maître" he cried out devotionally placing the bowl of blood at Patsy's head.

Jean-Claude returned to the base of the pentacle and took the seventh bowl, chanting once more. He produced a small cloth bag from his robe and emptied its powdery contents into it. Separating Patsy's legs wider apart he brought the bowl up between her legs and cut her inner right thigh letting her blood drip onto the powder. He mixed the contents of the bowl to a thick paste and slid the bowl up to her crotch.

Carmen remained still throughout, facing the lounge door her eyes fixed on a spot above the door where a green mist was forming.

Using a long taper Jean-Claude then ignited the contents of the five remaining bowls. Thick blue smoke billowed up giving off an obnoxious, putrid smell. Excited by the odour he watched the green mist slowly absorbing the smoke. He cast off his robe and cavorted around the pentagram, chanting and calling whilst throwing a grainy substance into the bowls as he pranced by. When the lounge was clear of blue smoke he sat, breathlessly, next to Carmen, sweat dripping from his nose and chin. He clasped Carmen's right hand and raised it up wailing eerily in a strange tongue.

A vortex of clean air descended over the central golden bowl, fanning and sucking the flames upward. The vortex grew in strength. Yellow smoke filled the room. A hurricane force wind blasted into the bay and entered the lounge to feed the whirling wind inside the lounge. Mysteriously the candles and the fires around and in the pentacle continued to burn unaffected by the terrific wind.

Slaughter had reached the headland between the two bays when the wind struck. Fronds were being torn from bending Palms and blown against the cliffs. He clung to the trunk of a palm tree as a hail of coconuts pounded the sand around him. Three struck him in quick succession on the crown of his head. He slithered to the sand unconscious. The wind ceased immediately.

The swirling yellow smoke inside the lounge was sucked suddenly into the green mist. The mist condensed into a sphere the size of a basketball which hovered above the lounge door, rotating slowly on a vertical axis.

Jean-Claude picked up the bowl above Patsy's head, stood astride Patsy's waist and drank some of the blood. He held the half empty vessel high above his head and chanted in tongues then offered the bowl to Carmen. She stood up, took the bowl and drank whilst he continued to chant. His arousal was becoming increasingly apparent as he knelt between Patsy's legs and drank thirstily from it.

Carmen was seated once more on the cushion, her eyes set on the revolving green orb over the door, unaffected by the rape that was taking place before her.

The first mark of dawn had sharpened the ocean's black horizon with a cutting edge. A narrow tapering fiery band of scarlet, orange and yellow melded upward into a watery, delicately infinite turquoise.

Radcliff had carried a rifle and a coil of rope over his shoulder and Kurt had clutched the cane with the crystal fastened into the end of it. They leaped through the trees, the jars of powder making them semi-weightless, mindful of Omollo struggling to keep pace. He guarded their rear, occasionally running backwards, sweeping the barrel of his automatic rifle in great arcs expecting Slaughter to pounce at any moment.

Cutting through the trees on the headland, Radcliff stumbled over Slaughter's body and fell sprawling headlong into the sand. Kurt jumped to avoid both bodies.

When Omollo arrived the two men were kneeling over Slaughter. Omollo held two fingers against his bloody neck.

"He's alive!" he grunted.

"Tie him to the palm tree." Kurt said.

Omollo dragged him to the palm and propped him against the trunk. Radcliff hastily lashed him to it whilst Kurt filled Slaughter's mouth with pieces of palm frond.

"Come on!" Radcliff pulled Kurt's arm. "We haven't much time."

The three men waded into the sea. Kurt fell sideways, buffeted by something in the sea. It hit Radcliff's legs and hurled him into the air. Omollo saw the giant black shape coming and dodged out of its way.

"Sharks!" Omollo yelled in alarm.

"Keep absolutely still!" Kurt shouted back. He inserted the end of the cane into the water in the direction of the shark. The shark vanished.

They swam towards the yacht. But then a fierce wind blasted seawater into their faces, forcing them back into the shallows. The wind turned into a tornado, its twisting funnel skirted the yacht and came straight at them churning and lifting the water ahead of it. The three men fled, cutting across to the headland dodging the twister as it continued into the bay. It turned at the cliff, dislodging the cockpit section of the helicopter embedded in the cliff and hurled it at the three men. They dived behind a palm. The wreckage smashed into the palm that Slaughter was bound to, a piece of cockpit sheared off from the impact hitting Omollo across the head, shoulders and back.

Kurt scrambled to his knees, hugging the palm as the tornado dragged the others into its fearsome, rumbling vortex. It scythed through the palms, sucking up sand, water and vegetation as it approached them. Kurt pointed the cane into the wind and it ceased immediately.

Radcliff gently lifted the wreckage from the unconscious Omollo and carefully rolled him onto his back.

"Come on, Alex! Dawn will be breaking soon. He'll be okay. We'll have to leave him here."

The two men charged into the sea and swam for the yacht. Slowed by their weapons and ropes they rested, treading water. Approaching the yacht the sinister reflections of red and green lights stretched out across the black surf to meet them like a strange shimmering, multi-coloured carpet.

Kurt climbed the diving ladder with Radcliff close behind him. On deck Kurt held out a hand to Radcliff. At that instant the yacht began to shudder, the sea around them ruffled into tall plumes and the cliffs opposite shook hideously, rocks and trees tumbling into the bay.

Radcliff clasped Kurt's outstretched hand and hoisted him aboard. Kurt directed the cane at the crumbling cliffs, then at the sea but the earthquake continued. A strong blast of air made Kurt spin on his heels. Radcliff was pointing at the approaching rumbling horror with his mouth wide open.

A tidal wave 60 feet high loomed down on them. As is neared the shallows it was gaining height, its crest ready to crash upon them.

Kurt pointed the cane towards the great wave. The yacht rose up with breathtaking speed, teetered on the brink of the crest then slowly descended as the wave rolled under them and continued on into the bay dragging the yacht with it. The wave smashed against the cliffs the surge of water sucking the yacht back out to sea. The ropes securing the yacht to the palm tree creaked, twisted and groaned under the strain, squeezed seawater squirting from its fibres.

On the eastern horizon the dawn was intensifying. With the ship steadying, Kurt and Radcliff peered through one of the rectangular deck windows into the lounge. The macabre scene was made more horrific by the sight of a strange green ball levitating in the room.

Back on the Island, a finger picked at the ground underneath a boulder. Its movement was slight but effective. The hole grew large enough to allow more fingers to gouge at the soil. Eventually a hand forced its way through and fresh air gushed into to hollow. The air helped the hand become more effective and soon an arm reached out and clasped a stone. The stone loosened the earth and speeded up the digging process until exhaustion took its toll and the hand and arm withdrew back beneath the huge rock.

Kurt and Radcliff tentatively entered the lounge. The levitating green glow they had seen through the window was a sphere of gas. It hovered above a mound of human flesh stacked midway along the starboard wall. The gaseous globe was two feet in diameter and growing perceptibly with a pulsating red core the size of a golf ball developing at its centre.

Jean-Claude, Carmen and Patsy had been hurled across the lounge when the wave had struck. Jean-Claude lay on his back across Patsy's inert body and Carmen was sprawled across him. The pile of human flesh was stirring.

The two men charged at the green sphere, Kurt clutching the cane like a warrior with a pikestaff. Skidding to a halt they stood transfixed before the green gaseous orb.

Kurt aimed the cane at the rotating translucent ball, searching desperately for a target. Blue gossamer threads weaved amongst the outer layers of gas like blood vessels of an eyeball. The threads stemmed from its red centre.

He had found its nerve system but the strands were too tightly packed together to be distinguishable, forming clumps of nerves stems at its centre.

Jean-Claude screamed unintelligibly at the ball, kicking Carmen away, pointing in Radcliff's direction. Carmen moaned as her head hit the floor.

The ball remained stationary, revolving upon its vertical axis, its red core pulsating more frequently.

Then, with alarming suddenness the flaming bowls, the candlesticks, the cushions and the sheets came flying at the two men. The sheets clung to their bodies and faces like elasticised cling-film.

Tearing the sheets from their eyes, standing back to back, they gazed around the lounge. At the stern some sheets were on fire illuminating the stacks of treasure bags. The green ball, Carmen, Patsy and the

Frenchman were gone.

Radcliff beat out the fire with a sheet whilst Kurt searched the forward cabins.

Kurt ran to Radcliff's side. "The Frenchman has the women locked in the cabin with him."

"No sign of that green…thing?" Radcliff asked, tossing the scorched sheet onto the treasure bags.

"It will have found itself some dark corner to hide in." He nodded to the window. "The sun's almost up. Let's go. There's nothing we can do now until sunset, yah! Maybe our robed friend will have the answer."

The green ball hovered above the dried up lake over the exact spot where the three corpses lay under tons of rock. It span into a long wisp of smoke, permeating the spaces and devoured them one by one. Above the rocks it reformed into a green ball, twice its previous size. It needed for more food. It searched under the other boulders that were strewn across the plateau, stopping at the base of one boulder. A cry of pain was lost to the morning air. The ball whirled into a vortex above the huge rock lifting it a foot in the air.

Dawn had penetrated the shadowy remains of night lingering on the plateau.

The ball vanished. The boulder fell back to the ground, but not into its original position. A smaller rock had held the boulder up leaving a small space between its base and the ground.

# CHAPTER 66

Kurt and Radcliff swam towards the headland. In the growing light of dawn they could clearly see the raft held fast by the ropes. A man lay spread-eagled on the deck.

Kurt held his cane out before him as they tentatively waded the final few feet to the raft.

"It's John!" Radcliff shouted climbing up beside the great man.

Kurt reached for Omollo's arm and felt for a pulse. "He's okay... he's unconscious."

"He's hurt...!" Radcliff pointed at Omollo's leg. Blood was squirting from a deep laceration across his thigh. He cut a length of rope and applied a tourniquet.

Kurt inserted a jar of powder into Omollo's pocket, rolled him onto his shoulders and carried him ashore.

Only three bedraggled palm trees remained standing on the headland and around the bay. The great wave had scoured everything else from the beach. Broken branches, fronds and palm trunks littered the sea and the shore.

They made a stretcher from the debris. As they lowered Omollo onto it he raised his head.

Radcliff beamed, gripping Omollo's shoulder firmly.

"This man's like you, Alex..." Kurt chuckled. "...bloody indestructible, yah!"

"It'll take more than a little wave to kill me!" Omollo grinned. "At least I fared better than him!" He nodded towards the palm further up the headland.

Slaughter had been ripped in two. Only his torso and left arm remained tied to the stump of the palm tree. The first rays of the sun glinted upon the contents of a split yellow bag half buried in the sand.

The two men gave Omollo an account of the extraordinary events on board the yacht as they carried their bulky load back to where they had camped.

"Did you...manage to get...it, Kurt?" Omollo asked his great eyes as wide as saucers. "Whatever it was?"

"We will tonight! Yah, Alex!"

Radcliff propped himself against his carving of Carmen.

The three men slept through the morning.

The two robed figures of Judas Thomas and James the Just waited motionless for them to awake, standing in the shadows midway between the men and the clearing. The sun was high, its rays bursting through the thin canopy.

Radcliff was the first to awake.

"Alex," Judas Thomas rushed forward. "You must hurry. We have much to prepare." James strode up to his side.

Radcliff shook Kurt awake. His grunts stirred Omollo.

They looked up at the robed figures. Their smiles were warm but their eyes were full of dread.

"It has grown," James said in a characteristically sharp tone, but had greater incisiveness and urgency. "It will be much harder to destroy. You cannot fail tonight."

"At least now I know what I'm up against, yah!" Kurt said winking at Radcliff countering the alarm the robed figure had engendered.

"It's big...and green...and round!" Radcliff smiled. "Oh! It's red centre grows and throbs!"

Omollo giggled.

"If it has grown larger..." Kurt nodded, "...then I'll be able to get a good look at its core. I'll see the nerve ends more clearly." He turned and faced Radcliff and Omollo. "I'll need just one clear shot...that's all I need.... and I'll finish it off for sure."

"It has consumed three bodies lying in the lake," Judas Thomas stated. "It has grown appreciably, Kurt. At present it is hiding below deck, behind the engine compartment. The centre...the red core as you put it, Kurt.... is bigger. It is much more developed...in every way."

"If that's the case, then I'm positive we can finish it tonight."

"It will be more powerful!" James reminded. "It will know your strategy! It will protect itself this time!"

"We'll be on board the yacht before night fall. We'll ambush it in the lounge."

"But it could go anywhere!" James snapped. "There are...." his tone mellowing "...the bodies of your friends to think of. They are also there near the lake. It will find them...very soon it will have accumulated a force that will surpass the powers of the Cross of Goa...when that happens, dear friends, we shall be forced to leave you to your fate."

"Abandon us..! Kurt objected.

"We are sorry," James shook his head slowly. "But you will have to fight this force on your own."

"If we have to leave you before you confront your...your Golieth," Judas Thomas explained kindly, "it is because we must limit the energy within the Cross. By keeping the Cross' power to a minimum will have the effect of restricting the size of your enemy...for a while at least."

"The ball will be fooled into a false sense of security!" Kurt exclaimed.

"Exactly..!" Judas Thomas grinned.

"If we fail…what will happen to us?" Omollo asked impassively. "How does this thing intend to take us?"

"The core has a high concentration of platinum. It is what you call a 'superconductor'," James explained with usual clipped and precise diction. "It will absorb every particle of your universe and 'transport it back through…what your scientists term…'a worm hole'. Really what happens is that everything will vanish and reform instantly in the universe from which this force emanates from. The galaxies, suns and planets…you, everyone and everything…the trees, the mountains, the seas…. nothing will exist here. Your universe will reform in that universe. You will be subjected to the whims of that God. Your lives will become a living hell."

"I think I'd better keep my eye on the ball! Yah..!"

"I think you will!" Judas Thomas added confidently.

"Will you return?"

"I will come back on my own to help if necessary. We had hoped, before the manifestation of this force, to use the Cross to 'pave the way', as it were, for an event that will eclipse any that have gone before on your planet. Your priests have known about this for many years but sadly, for reasons best known to themselves, they are refusing to tell the people of this joyous but also very important news."

Radcliff had been tenderly caressing his carving of Carmen the whole time Kurt had been talking with the robed figures. He looked up suddenly. "Are you referring to the Garabandal apparitions of the 1960's?" he asked tentatively.

"When you have won your battle, my friends, all of you must spread the word."

"Carmen said that it will be the greatest miracle that Jesus ever performed."

"When will it happen?" Omollo asked, his great eyes bulging to the size of golf balls.

"No one knows precisely, John," Radcliff said quietly, recalling that incredible Easter he and Carmen had shared together eight years before. They had sat on the bench before the pine trees, their backs to the village one hundred feet below on the mountain slope. Carmen had told him the full story of the apparitions. He could hear her gentle voice coming to him on the breeze.

"Only one of the girls," Radcliff cleared his throat, desperately wanting to repeat her words correctly, "…who experienced the apparitions …she's a woman now of course…she knows the exact year it will occur. She has given us clues. The miracle will occur at 8.30 p.m. on a Thursday evening between the 8th and 16th days of March, April or May."

Radcliff paused and looked up at the robed figures. There was no sign of reproach.

"She will let the world know eight days in advance of the exact day this will happen," Radcliff continued. "It will coincide with a great ecclesiastical event. It will be seen by everyone…no one will escape it. During the miracle everyone will see…the error of their ways; they will feel bitterly remorseful. Many will prefer to die than experience the pain of all the wrongs they have done. The miracle will be life changing. A permanent mark will be left at the sight of the miracle for ever more."

"Well done!" Judas Thomas beamed. "When you all return home with the Cross you will be able to spread the Garabandal prophecies throughout the world. The media will give you the publicity you need to reach the masses. You must make the people aware of this great event. Encourage them to make the pilgrimage and experience it for themselves."

"That is *the* most important condition of our being here," James stated. "Whatever the outcome, the Cross of Goa must be brought back to England. It is to be housed within the walls of your castle, Alex. Your *whole* story must be told to the world. Many aspects of the coming battle will be difficult to prove, but we will assist you in that respect. You will always have the power of the Cross of Goa to support you.

"My master and brother, Jesus, said: 'Let one who seeks not stop seeking until he finds. When he finds, he will be troubled. When he is troubled, he will be astonished and will rule over all'; 'Recognise what is before your eyes and the mysteries will be revealed to you. For there is nothing hidden that will not be revealed'."

"Was Jesus the Son of God?" Radcliff asked tentatively.

"I must congratulate you on that excellent question!" James crisply replied with an unexpected grin. "The answer to that very question will go a long way to bringing unity between the great religions of your world. It was imperative that Jesus was seen to fulfil the ancient prophecies. His purpose on earth was to strengthen and reinforce God's laws. He never claimed to be the Son of God. He was the anointed one…the 'Messiah'! He was descended from the house of David through Joseph. But he was also the 'Messiah' in a priestly sense being the son of Mary, a direct descendent of Aaron. He was a double Messiah…the 'Messiah of Aaron and of Israel'.

"When He was about to be stoned by the Jews, Jesus said to them, 'I have done many good works for you to see…for which of these are you stoning me?' The Jews answered him, 'We are not stoning you for doing a good work but for blasphemy: you are only a man and you claim to be God.' Jesus answered, 'Is it not written in your Law: I said, you are gods? So the Law uses the word gods of those to whom the word of God addresses.' When you understand this, when you clearly see this truth, when your hearts accept this very possibility then this revelation will bring about change to your lives here and now. It is a forgotten concept that will move you all to a higher spiritual existence.

"What I tell you is this: that God is in each of you; that you are all gods; that everything that exists in the universe is all part of what you call God; that it is all one giant soul. You are all fragments of that soul. Jesus was a Jew and it was never his intention for a new religion to be founded in his name. The Old Testament is sacred to Muslims as much as it is to the Jews. Put down your petty differences and live simply in order that others can simply live!"

"That is exactly what I believe!" Kurt stood up with a joyous, animated expression. He reached out with his arms as if to embrace everyone. "When my calculations revealed the possibility of the seventh Quark I remembered Paul Dirac when he said: 'A physical theory must have mathematical beauty'. Suddenly everything fitted together. Even the string theories and the 'brane' theories were acceptable to me. My addition to Murray Gell-Man's group theory opened the door to the possibility of explaining gravity itself."

"Well the 'CERN' experiments might one day endorse your theory," Judas Thomas said. "Congratulations, Kurt!"

"How *do* you explain gravity?" asked Omollo.

"That's the sixty four thousand dollar question, and no mistake, John!" Radcliff sighed and looked away. "It will inevitably be beyond our lowly minds. If Kurt says he can explain gravity, then I believe him."

"Gravity...the last unexplained force in physics," Kurt began dramatically. "It differs from other physical forces. Einstein's theory of general relativity says that massive objects bend spacetime..."

"We are wading into very deep water here Kurt," Radcliff sighed.

"Carry on Kurt," Omollo insisted. "I've always wanted to understand this."

"Well the curvature of spacetime tells objects how to move. It is this influence we call gravity. In his famous analogy Einstein stretched a rubber sheet and rolled a tennis ball across it. It travelled in a straight line. Then he rolled a bowling ball across the sheet resulting in the sheet being stretched. If the tennis ball is then rolled across the sheet once more it will follow a curved path. They are at present endeavouring to detect gravitational waves given off by merging galaxies or black holes.

"But more importantly I want to explain how we can defeat the force we are facing hear and now. Most massive objects in our universe form themselves into spheres. On a much smaller scale we witnessed this phenomena last night...that alien green ball!

"Well hydrogen was the first and simplest element: One atom and one electron. The nucleus is positively charged, the electron is negatively charged. The nucleus has one proton and one neutron; within those are particles called Quarks. There were thought to be just six of these: up, down, strange, charm, top and bottom. My theory is that there are seven Quarks.

"You see vibration is the key. The quarks spin, vibrating like guitar strings. The seventh Quark is like a twelve-string guitar which produces chords and single notes on two or more levels. It not only leads the music, it decides what music to play. The 'maestro'! God! Symmetrical particles are given an identity, their unique mass, as they pass through the quarks musical field. Everything in the universe was initially formed and given direction by this magnificent symphony of the cosmos!"

"That sounds magical, Kurt!" said Radcliff.

"What was it Shakespeare wrote…?" Omollo looked at Radcliff and then at Kurt for an answer.

"'If music be the food of love, play on!'" Judas Thomas laughed, breaking the silence. "From act one of 'Twelfth Night'."

"Yah! Very good! The quarks are linked together by a mighty force, which behaves rather like elastic or a strong spring. Murray Gell-Mann found that the harder he tried to dislodge a quark the tighter that elastic force became. But every atom wants to fuse with other atoms to produce better music, to augment and harmonise. The more they accumulate the greater the pressure and the hotter the music! Our sun and the earth are examples. The earth's core is molten iron…the most stable of the elements.

"The vibrations are more sustained and structured, the heat generated increases with volume. The elastic force keeping the vibrating Quarks together pulling on other particles; they want to join in the music and pass through its harmonic field. The process is perpetual and perfect!

"Wow!" Radcliff wiped his brow with an exaggerated sweep of his hand.

"I can't believe that you said all that!" Omollo exclaimed shaking his head, grinning from ear to ear. "It was music to my ears…food for my mind. It completes the circle for me. The universe is a vast auditorium for music! Incredible, Kurt! Simply incredible..!"

"You have not explained properly why gravity is so weak," James said critically. "It is such a gentle force compared to the dynamic forces of nuclear fission…when the atom is split."

"Yah! But there are limits…yah…to what any one person can absorb in one time, yah! Galileo is the man! Way before his time! But millions of people watched that experiment on television…when David Scott, the Apollo astronaut, was on the moon..."

"I remember that!" Radcliff said eagerly. "When he dropped the hammer and the falcon feather at the same time…they fell at the same speed and hit the surface together!"

"I did not see that," Omollo stated, wriggling his body for a more comfortable position.

"A bit before your time!" Radcliff mused with mock indifference.

"It is the collective vibration, the harmony, of the atoms, caused by its subatomic structure—the Quarks, which draw matter to it or push it away to hit the correct note."

"Fantastic! Marvellous! But you must be absolutely sure how you are going to deal with this green ball tonight, Kurt?" Omollo stated. "We trust you implicitly. But what makes you so sure you are one hundred percent right? If we fail again it will not be just the end of us."

"Well said, John!" James applauded. "Tonight will be your last chance, Kurt. Are you absolutely positive this will work?"

"This green ball has no seventh Quark. The beam from the cane will be guided by my thoughts. It will enter the anti proton in its most vulnerable spot...its central nervous system. The seventh Quark from our beam will smash its very structure to pieces. It will be like releasing a stretched elastic band. The chain reaction will spread back to the dimension from which it originated and collapse into itself."

Radcliff looked up at the sun. "We have about six hours until sunset."

The boulder rested on the smaller stone. There was sufficient space to allow both arms to dig at the ground. One arm had been severely burned; dirt had clogged the open wound. Wearily the arms hacked down hard into the ground with a stone tool. Minutes later the same hands expelled the loosened soil from the ever widening hole. Those hands laboured all day.

At dusk the arms emerged and thrust down on the edge of the hole. A man heaved himself out and dragged himself, imperceptibly at first, towards the trees.

# CHAPTER 67

It had been several minutes since the sun had sunk behind the mountain, its silhouette sharp against a brilliant evening sky of hazy bluish yellow.

Judas Thomas raised his hand slowly. "Very soon we shall have to go." His tone was soft and gentle. "You must remember this... Charles Darwin would have said that your species is too intelligent and resourceful to allow the threat of extinction to continue unchecked; the sciences have revolutionised your knowledge of the universe and all it contains; the Apollo Moon missions have changed the psyche of everyone whether consciously perceived or not. The story of your survival will unite the world in its epic struggle to minimise the effects of climate change." He paused, smiling warmly.

Radcliff tentatively raised his arm "I have a question." He stared at the ground awkwardly for several moments. "I have been racked with guilt most of my life. Why is mankind generally affected by guilt and has the burden of a conscience. Living alone on this island I had none of those emotions. After my rescue these feelings returned. Guilt and conscience constrain natural development. They are perverse tools of the civilised world. From infancy through to childhood and on to adult life our religious leaders begin by telling us that we are all sinners...that we must pray for forgiveness. How can we be born guilty?"

"An excellent question...!" Judas Thomas smiled. "Jesus was trained in the ways of the Therapeutae, believers in the 'One Devine Reality'. They were healers. He learned also the Asian powers of the mind and used all his powers in the glorification of God. He was a Master of his craft attaining a level that no other mortal soul has ever reached...or ever will again.

"The celibate, divine role model of Jesus Christ was invented in the fourth century when Christianity became an accepted religion. The invention of the Holy Trinity had the same effect. It separated Jesus from humankind.

"It was, therefore, declared that everyone is a potential victim of the devil and are all therefore sinners from birth. This idea stems back to Adam and Eve and the forbidden fruit. It is interpretation of the scriptures that has been at fault not the scriptures themselves. Guilt is repressive. Life is meant to be experienced at the highest spiritual level ...the highest that any one person can possibly attain.

"My brother, Jesus said this: 'If you bring forth what is within you, what you have will save you. If you do not have that within you, what you do not have within you will destroy you.' You men are our messengers. God will be with you always."

Judas Thomas moved closer to James.

They stood with their arms reaching out, beckoning to the three men. "Goodbye dear friends," they said in unison.

In an instant they were gone.


The man had dragged himself inch by inch across the plateau. Night had fallen. Movement and feeling had returned his legs. He lifted his weary body onto his knees and crawled.

He blundered into Chiltern's decomposing corpse, recoiling in horror away from the putrid body. Lifting his head above the level of the grass he could see the trees just a few yards ahead of him. Hauling himself up onto his knees he looked back across the plateau. The silhouette of the mountain had changed. The extent of the change shocked him.

Then, from nowhere, a green ball four feet in diameter appeared. It hovered for several seconds above the boulder he had escaped from. Suddenly it darted straight for him. He charged on his hands and knees for the trees, smashing and entangling himself in the undergrowth finally crashing into a tree trunk.

Peering back through the leaves he saw the pulsating green sphere hovering over Chiltern's body, its glowing red centre throbbing intensely and growing in size.


Kurt and Radcliff were on the yacht, inside the lounge, hidden behind a barricade of treasure bags next to the entrance. Omollo had remained at the camp guarding the supplies.

The yacht began to pitch and roll violently.

The two men heard movements in one of the forward cabins and cautiously peered over the bags. Kurt gripped the cane tighter, waiting for the Frenchman to emerge from the shadowy corridor leading to the forward cabins. Radcliff's eyes darted rapidly back and forth from the dark, cavernous gloom ahead to the lounge door three feet to Kurt's right.

The rocking ceased as suddenly as it started.

Radcliff nudged Kurt with his elbow. The green ball was hovering above the lounge door. Its pulsating red centre had increased to the size of a soccer ball. Kurt waited.

A cabin door unlocked. The Frenchman appeared from the corridor.

The two men watched Carmen follow him into the lounge. She was clasping a length of rope. She was leading Patsy whose hands were tied in front of her. Patsy's mouth was gagged. All were naked.

Kurt and Radcliff ducked low behind the bags as Jean-Claude

busily retrieved all the candles, bowls and the remaining unburned sheet and replaced them in and around the pentacle. He laid the scarlet sheet across the top. He relit the candles and bowls and returned to the cabin. The two women stood absolutely still.

Kurt gripped the cane keeping the crystal pointed at the red centre of the green globe. The hideous green glow from the ball mingled with the light from the flames. The pungent odour from the multi coloured smoke of the burning bowls drifted towards Kurt and Radcliff.

They could see Carmen and Patsy clearly in the flickering lights.

The Frenchman returned now clothed in a black robe. He waved his hands in front of Patsy's eyes, untied her hands and led her to the scarlet sheet. She lay down before Carmen, who was seated on one of the cushions. Jean-Claude strode to the centre of the pentacle and threw a substance into it. The bowl exploded into white light. The light glinted on the surface of a long knife that was held in his right hand.

Radcliff gritted his teeth, glancing at Kurt.

Kurt's eyes were concentrated upon the red nerve centre of the green ball.

The Frenchman chanted as he threw more material into the centre bowl causing fresh explosions. He moved to the base of the pentacle, chanting loudly, and lifted his arm up and reopened the wound from the previous day. He picked up the centre bowl from the row of seven and let his blood drip into it. Then, screaming in tongues at the green ball, he took the bowl to Carmen.

Radcliff grabbed Kurt's arm. "Do it now. Kill this...thing," he hissed in a desperate whisper.

"I can't...its core...is getting hotter." Kurt mouthed with virtually no sound at all. "I can see the nerve ends...they are clear...like little black dots. I'm tracing them back to where they converge." He looked Radcliff in the eyes. "Then we pray...!"

The Frenchman began chanting again with increased volume. He opened the wound on Carmen's arm letting her blood mingle with his once more. He held the bowl up above his head. "Mon maître...mon maître...mon maître" he repeated again and placed the bowl of blood at Patsy's head.

Jean-Claude returned to the base of the pentacle and took the seventh bowl, chanting once more.

Kurt nodded to Radcliff that he was about to attack and took careful aim.

The green sphere suddenly darted towards Kurt and descended upon his head.

"Alex! Take my powder and... think of the seventh Quark..."

Kurt's head and shoulders disappeared into the ball.

Jean-Claude screamed in rage and frustration having seen the ball move.

Radcliff grabbed the cane whilst gripping Kurt's shorts. His torso was being sucked rapidly into the green pulsating mass above him. Kurt's shorts broke loose. Radcliff wriggled the jar out through the pocket watching helplessly as his friend's feet disappeared into the slime.

Radcliff raised the cane, aiming at the ball's red centre.

The core was turning white hot and had grown rapidly. His brain was crying out: 'Kurt, where are these black dots? How do I think my aim? What do I *think* of?'

Kurt's voice came to him as clear as if he was still beside him: 'I'm all right Alex. Wait for the black dots to appear. Follow the nerve threads to where they converge. Then you must think about nothing but the image you've built up in your mind about my seventh Quark. Point the cane at the spot where these threads converge.'

'But Kurt, what does a Quark look like…' Radcliff's mind yelled back.

The green ball was growing. It was moving, encroaching upon Radcliff. He backed away aiming the cane at its evil looking heart.

The Frenchman dashed back to his cabin and returned with a gun. He ran to the spot where Radcliff crouched behind the treasure bags.

Judas Thomas' calm mellow voice came to Radcliff: 'You must aim for its central nervous system where the atoms are most plentiful but more vulnerable. Find it then think of nothing but Kurt's Quarks. Your aim will be true. We are here to guide you, Alex.'

He found the black dots in its bloated white-hot centre and followed them to where they all converged, a translucent, kidney shaped nerve centre. 'Kurt was right,' he thought to himself.

The ball was descending upon his face. He sunk to the floor, making himself as flat as he could and took aim.

At that instant a bullet struck the treasure bag and slammed into the metal wall behind him.

Radcliff held tight to the cane thinking of his image of a Quark. All he could imagine were snooker balls. Then he remembered what Kurt had said, that Quarks are linked together by a mighty elastic force.

He closed his eyes, thought of Quarks as snooker balls, six red balls grouped in a circle with one blue ball in the middle. The blue ball was vibrating the elastic that connected the red balls. As he released the energy from the crystal he visualised Kurt's seventh Quark shooting at its target like a cruise missile.

The green orb exploded in front of Jean-Claude, the detonation sending him flying across the lounge onto the bar with Carmen and Patsy blasted on top of him.

Radcliff lay in a pool of green and red slime with Kurt, soaked in the glutinous muck, lying on top of him.

# CHAPTER 68

The man had staggered through the trees, following the pathway to the cliff top. Seeing the eerie lights emanating from the yacht he half slid half climbed down the rocks to the beach and plodded heavily and wearily across the bay.

Reaching the headland a flash of green light rocked the vessel violently. A second later he heard an explosion.

Filled with a sudden burst of Herculean strength the man staggered, crawled and clawed across the headland, his aching limbs too weak to bear his weight for too long. Spurred on by an inner voice crying out to him nothing could have stopped him reaching that yacht.

He began wading out to the vessel, half blinded with sand and sweat caked around his eyes. He saw the blurred images of three people diving from the yacht. They were swimming towards him. He continued wading out to meet them but their pace was superhumanly fast.

He had no time to think.

The first stopped swimming and ran through the water towards the beach, the blade of his knife glinting in the starlight. The swimmer did not look once in his direction. Two women stood waist deep in the water twenty feet to his left.

"Patsy!" He cried. Then he recognised Carmen.

The three friends remained gazing at each other until a gunshot rang out from the yacht.

Carmen and Patsy crashed through the water at the same incredible speed following the first swimmer towards the shore.

The man stood transfixed, gawping at the two figures fading into the darkness.

Then a green sphere, the size of a tennis ball, shot past him. It hovered above a palm stump for a second then rose up, slightly larger, and disappeared over the cliffs.

Radcliff and Kurt had watched in horrified fascination as the green residue and slime covering the floor and their bodies began to coalesce, like magnetised mercury. Gathering up their weapons they escaped outside.

From the stern they had watched the Frenchman passing someone as he flew through the water. Radcliff fired a warning shot from the Frenchman's gun before jumping from the stern. Kurt followed. They were halfway to the man standing statuesque in the sea when the green ball whizzed over their heads.

"Rod!" Radcliff bellowed pushing his body through the final six feet of water to greet him. "I can't...believe...it!" He hollered breathlessly, clasping and shaking his shoulders.

"Alex!" Rod gasped.

He sagged onto Radcliff, who buckled under his weight.

Kurt reached out and held Rod. "I've got him, Alex."

Radcliff tucked his head beneath Rod's left armpit, Rod's arm clenched across his chest. He looked into his friend's exhausted eyes. "You look all tuckered out, mate!" He exclaimed.

Rod's mouth stretched into a grin "Yeh! I suppose I am. And that's for sure."

Kurt wrapped Rod's other arm around his shoulder and the two men helped their friend to the shore.

On the beach the two collected up more broken branches for a stretcher.

"What happened to your arm?" Kurt asked, kneeling at his side twisting his right arm slightly to see the wound more clearly in the starlight.

"It's nothing! What about Patsy? I saw her...she looked straight at me, fellers! She just followed that bloke ashore." His eyes bulged with horror. "She didn't know me!" He added slowly his words fading into long sigh.

"It's the Frenchman," Kurt said. "She's...well she's under his spell..."

"Yeh. I guess so..." Rod's eye lids sagged.

"Better get him back to camp, yah?"

Kurt tucked a jar of white powder in Rod's trousers and the two men trudged with Rod on the stretcher across the headland.

Slaughter's remains had gone. Only a coil of rope remained tied around the palm tree.

Omollo heard them approaching. He was standing beside the carved tree stump, propped against a makeshift crutch with a fire blazing a few feet behind him. His great beaming smile greeted the two men, with Rod on the stretcher, as they emerged from trees.

"Allah be praised!" Omollo said spontaneously. He manoeuvred awkwardly with his crutch around the carved stump to get closer to Rod. "You've come back to us." Omollo took Rod's limp hand and squeezed it tight.

Radcliff and Kurt lowered the stretcher close to the fire with Omollo still clutching Rod's hand.

"This looks very cosy and welcoming," Kurt said cheerily. "I think

Rod could use something to eat."

"I saw Patsy…" Rod struggled to lift his head.

Omollo's great hand grabbed at a rolled up bag and stuffed it under Rod's head for a pillow.

"She didn't know me, John!"

"It's still not finished, John!" Kurt whispered. "Alex hit the mark…" Kurt's arms flew open. "It blew up…."

"It came back to life!" Radcliff added heavily. "We saw it…. it was much smaller…it shot across the bay."

"What about Slaughter?" Omollo asked.

"He's dead," Radcliff said with indifference.

"Dead and gone…literally!" Kurt added.

"Where's my Patsy?" Rod cried. "Where's that bastard taken her?"

"Inside the mountain," Kurt answered. "He'll want to be near his treasure?"

"That's a possibility!" Radcliff was strangely comforted by the thought that Carmen was also in the cave amongst the treasure.

High in one of the trees overlooking the clearing and the escarpment a green glow hovered on the branch of a tree. The Neam tree. The ball had feasted and was growing rapidly in size.

Below the tree the Cross of Goa was absorbing a massive surge of energy.

"I think we should finish that green thing before we tackle anything else," Omollo said.

Radcliff turned to Kurt. "What was it like…inside that thing?"

A look of horror crossed Omollo's face.

"I was contained inside a membrane…it was rather like a transparent chrysalis. I had just enough air. It can't consume living tissue. But what I saw was astonishing. From the outside it looks like a green eyeball. But inside you enter another dimension. It was huge…it appeared to be over twenty yards across. There were several decks. I was on the centre deck in one of the blocks of shelves…they looked like bookcases…. divided into a honeycomb of compartments. Four were occupied with chrysalises like mine. Strange disjointed music played. It was similar to Chinese music but the notes and chords sounded very unpleasant. Between the top of the shelves and the ceiling there was an array of screens. I could see you clearly Alex. Your thoughts were being transmitted over loudspeakers. What was really spooky was hearing my own thoughts telling you what to do. I even heard Judas Thomas's encouraging words."

"Then it must have known what I was aiming at!"

"You were thinking of snooker balls. It had no way of knowing what they were and how you associated that to its nerve centre…"

A white glow lit up the trees. They turned to see Judas Thomas standing next to the fire.

"I have very little time," he said, his hands held tightly together in a praying attitude. "You must take everything you wish to take with you to the yacht now. Kurt, you *must* ensure that you take your bag containing your copies of the inscriptions you found in the base of the Cross."

"What's happening?" Radcliff asked.

"Do what I bid you to do. I will answer all your questions later. I can tell you now that I am setting a trap for this green monster. The Cross of Goa will release the repugnant odour of rotting flesh and concentrated negative energy that will be irresistible to it, and also to any other creature subservient it. This plan involves an enormous sacrifice on your part."

"We'll do anything...of course..." Radcliff turned to the others. "Agreed?" Omollo nodded.

"It will mean that the Cross...will have to be destroyed. There is no other way."

There was a long dumbfounded silence, each man wrestling with the implications of what Judas Thomas had said.

"It's irreplaceable...it's too valuable..." Radcliff began, turning away shaking his head in dismay.

"Are you certain...?" asked Kurt.

"I know what the Cross means to you. And I know what it means to the world. Better than you do. There is no other way to destroy this force entirely. Its ability to replicate itself was not expected. We underestimated its strength. We are so very sorry.

"But you can make another, Kurt. You have all the gold that you need. You have the skill and the knowledge."

Kurt considered the possibilities. They all watched and waited.

"I could do it," he said at last. "I'll need somewhere to build it."

"My home," Radcliff said quickly. "It'll be our headquarters. We'll use the chapel. It's secure enough."

"A Chapel..? In your home..?"

"I own an old castle. It's in Sussex."

Kurt turned to Omollo in amazement.

Omollo nodded.

Kurt chuckled. "You never cease to amaze me! Sounds the perfect place Alex..!"

"What about my Patsy?" Rod croaked weakly from behind them.

"The Frenchman will be lured to the Cross," said Judas Thomas. "The women will follow him." He looked at each man in turn. "It is the Frenchman's soul that has been taken. The women are slaves to him only. Once he is...dealt with...they will be safe." He paused for a moment. "Are you are willing to make this sacrifice?"

They all nodded.

"Then I think we will be victorious. God bless you all."

He vanished.

The men sorted out the essentials from their supplies and belongings and stuffed them into bags and boxes. Omollo loaded himself up with a haversack, a rifle slung over his shoulder, a carrier bag in one hand, the crutch held in the other he hobbled down the slope through the trees.

Kurt and Radcliff helped Rod back onto the stretcher. They gave him both jars of white powder to hold then stacked the stretcher with as many essential bags as possible and followed Omollo to the beach.

The Frenchman arrived at the clearing, with the women following just behind him. When he saw the green orb hovering in the tree he raised his arms high into the air and bowed in homage whilst chanting once more.

But the Cross of Goa distracted his concentration. His nerves and mind were affected by its strange power. He paced around it first one way then the other, trying to understand it, wanting to push it over the edge of the escarpment but unable to. He felt nauseous and giddy, his mind in turmoil and his stomach churning sickeningly.

He backed away and leaned against a tree to steady himself. He clicked his fingers and Patsy obediently came forward and lay between Jean-Claude and the Cross. He clasped the knife with his teeth and clapped his hands high above his head. Carmen came forward and sat facing the Cross with Patsy lying in front of her.

Jean-Claude began chanting once more, this time louder and more purposeful. The green ball descended slowly and hovered above the Cross. He knelt beside Carmen and took her hand.

The green orb leapt into the air, repelled by an invisible force. The irresistible lure compelled it to persist but each time it reached the Cross it was repelled away.

Jean-Claude, in desperation to continue with the ceremony reopened his arm wound with the knife and then cut Carmen's arm, holding their wounds together, commingling their blood. The green ball excitedly moved down to Patsy, hovering above her abdomen then rose up above Jean-Claude and Carmen.

The couple bowed low.

The green ball touched both heads then returned to the treetop.

Jean-Claude laid his Queen beside Patsy and proceeded to consummate their marriage.

Omollo, Kurt and Radcliff had returned to the camp, having left Rod on board the yacht. They searched the bags and boxes for more essential supplies and managed to fill one last bag.

"I'd like to see the Cross of Goa just once more before it gets destroyed," Kurt said.

Three men went to the clearing.

*"Oh my G.....!"* Radcliff tore away from Omollo, who toppled onto Kurt, and charged at Jean-Claude, knocking him off Carmen's body. The two adversaries were locked in combat, but this time on equal terms. The Frenchman fought like a woman, scratching and pulling at Radcliff's hair as they rolled across the clearing. Radcliff punched him hard repeatedly in the ribs. Jean-Claude grabbed one of Radcliff's arms and embedded his teeth into his forearm. Radcliff kneed him in the groin three or four times then landed him a hefty blow in the abdomen. Jean-Claude's jaws released their grip. Radcliff nursed his bleeding arm.

Meanwhile Kurt had taken Patsy back to the camp.

Omollo held his crutch above his head like a club ready to strike the Frenchman. The green ball landed upon his face and was sucking him into it.

Radcliff had got to his feet and held onto Omollo. But his head had gone completely, his arms flailing helplessly.

*"Kurt!"* Radcliff screamed out. *"Come back! Bring the cane!"*

Kurt picked up the cane and hurtled through the trees and under-growth. At the clearing he saw only Omollo's crutch lying on the ground. Carmen lay still beside the Cross of Goa.

He heard distant groans coming from deep below the escarpment. Peering over the steep slope he could see two shapes moving amongst the pine trees. Then he saw the familiar green glow hovering high in the trees close to the shadowy figures.

Sliding, falling and rolling down the slope keeping a tight grip on the cane he smashed into a tree. Sprawled in the dirt, the wind knocked out of him, he saw Radcliff about to strike the Frenchman with a log.

The Frenchman ducked and charged at Radcliff's lower body, knocking him off his feet. The Frenchman picked up a rock and hurled it down at Radcliff's head. Radcliff rolled sideways dodging the blow. He got his feet and slammed the log against the Frenchman's back. He fell with a grown. Radcliff then cracked the log down on the Frenchman's head.

Jean-Claude lay still.

A brilliant white light lit up the clearing high above them. Kurt looked back.

"Go and save Carmen, Alex," Judas Thomas said, standing beside Kurt. "Hurry man! Before the Frenchman recovers…and he will!

Judas Thomas pointed up into the branches of a nearby tree. "Take aim with your cane, Kurt."

Kurt did so.

"You have to do this with your imagination. See its nerve centre in your mind and aim the crystal using your feelings."

Kurt closed his eyes. The crystal was aimed straight at the centre of the green ball.

"You can stun it for a few minutes…that's all…Kurt. It will give you time to get away."

Radcliff was hauling himself groggily up the slope.

"Hurry, Alex!" Judas Thomas called out. Then to Kurt he said: "When you've hit your mark your friend will be released. I will remain here to help you both get to the yacht. Then I must return immediately to the Cross. I have to be back in time to set the trap."

The ball deflated as if pricked by a pin and Omollo fell out of it. Judas Thomas held out his hands and the big man floated to the ground.

Kurt picked up Omollo's semi-conscious body as if it were a feather and bounded back up the escarpment completely weightless with Judas Thomas following close behind with his arms outstretched wide.

They overtook Radcliff who was staggering with Carmen in his arms.

"Take Patsy to the yacht, Kurt." Judas Thomas commanded after reaching the camp. "Give John your other jar of white powder and go. Now! All of you."

Omollo followed Kurt and Patsy bounding almost weightlessly through the trees towards the beach.

"I will have to go very soon," Judas Thomas explained as Radcliff arrived. "I'll help you carry Carmen for as long as I can." He opened his arms to Radcliff and Carmen. They began to levitate before their robed friend then they sped through the trees. Close to the edge of the plateau their robed friend vanished.

Radcliff and Carmen dropped heavily to the ground, rolling over one another with inertia. Radcliff lay breathless and stunned in the grass.

Carmen had cracked her head against a tree trunk and lay unconscious in the undergrowth. Radcliff, close to exhaustion, struggled to lift her. He staggered a few steps with her in his arms but his knees buckled to the ground.

Judas Thomas was at the clearing. The green ball was up in the tree overlooking the Frenchman lying prostrate before the Cross.

The green ball stirred, seeing an opportunity to feed.

Judas Thomas remained hidden waiting for the right moment to strike.

Radcliff picked Carmen up and staggered a few more steps. He rested again. They were close to the edge of the plateau, where the pathway from the beach emerged from the trees. He could see the rock face and remembered hearing the glorious, life saving sound of the waterfall.

The waterfall was dry and the rock face disfigured. But he had Carmen. Then an idea came to him. It filled him with a new strength. He lifted her limp body high up to his chest.

"We're together on my island, my love," he said as carried her over the plateau towards the treasure mountain. "It's just you and me now. And here we'll stay...forever more."

With superhuman strength he carried her over the fallen boulders covering the campsite and climbed the rock face, made easier by the devastation caused by the explosion. He reached the grotesque, gaping black hole in the mountain. Stumbling and wobbling with Carmen in his arms he trod across the mass of broken rocks and gravel which descended gradually into the depths of the cave.

Recognising the wedge shaped mass of granite to his left, he lay Carmen on the rocks for a moment and went deeper into the cave to investigate.

The mountain had collapsed onto the old shattered roof of the cave. It had protected the remainder of the treasure from being smothered. Seeing a way down the rock fall to the chambers where they had extracted the treasure, Radcliff returned for Carmen.

Kurt had climbed to the bridge and had started the mighty engines, their roar breaking the still air of the early morning. He throttled back. The great engines idled with a rhythmic throaty throb. Weighing anchor he reversed the yacht slowly back into the bay as far as he dared and waited for Radcliff and Carmen to arrive.

"Maybe he's decided to stay," Rod had suggested.

"Not without saying something," Omollo called up as he climbed the stairs to the bridge. "Where do you intend to take us all, Captain?"

"Coetivy Island. We'll go 'round the northern end of the island and head west. Once we get into deeper water I'll plot the course."

"I suppose you read the stars as well," Rod jibed.

"This time of the year I use Hydra and the Southern Cross as my guides," Kurt laughed. "Look!" He swung from the handrail and pointed directly above them. "See that cluster of stars?"

Rod stood on the steps squinting up into the heavens. "Yeh. It's a pity Patsy's crook. She would've loved all this."

Omollo had joined Rod on the steps and followed his gaze. "I can see it!"

"That's the water snake's head. Just below them is a bright star... that's Alphard...follow that line and you will see the snake's body."

"Oooh yes!" They each said in turn.

"You see that wide line of stars...?" he pointed south over the port side of the yacht, "that's the Milky way. Now look there." they followed Kurt's finger, "at those four brilliant stars...?"

"It's a cross!" Omollo said in amazement.

"That's the Southern Cross," Kurt proclaimed proudly. "It's an hour after midnight and with the stars in that alignment I can estimate our position with some degree of accuracy."

The Frenchman had crawled to the edge of the clearing, naked and alone, nursing his wounds. He was compelled against all his will to remain in the clearing. The Cross before him was making him physically sick. But also it exuded a strange warming energy. Suddenly and inexplicably many childhood memories came flooding back to him.

The green ball watched and waited from high in the treetop for its prey to fall asleep. It could feel the power of the glistening object below and knew that a titanic struggle was inevitable. It needed sustenance to overcome it.

Judas Thomas would trigger his snare the moment the ball had consumed the Frenchman. He watched intently.

At first the Frenchman had been in considerable pain and discomfort from his fight with Radcliff, but his condition had deteriorated rapidly. He developed a fever and had fits of violent shaking.

Jean-Claude was being drawn inexorably closer to the Cross.

Judas Thomas knew that the Cross was gradually soothing the troubled mind and soul of the naked wretch before it. He prayed continually for his soul.


"When Alex and Carmen are on board, John," Kurt said, adjusting the yacht's position to keep them clear of the beach. "We'll do exactly what Judas Thomas said we should do."

Rod had brought Patsy up to the bridge. She stood passively by his side with Omollo next to her. They were all standing in a line behind Kurt.

"What! Build another Cross," Rod said sceptically.

"We can do it, Rod!"

"If Kurt says we can do it, Rod, I am not going to be the one to argue with our great scientist here," Omollo's grin broadened with every word he uttered.

"There are some magnificent quotes from our great leaders and scientists of the past. We can be guided by them!" Kurt was feeling inspired. "Gandhi had said: 'Be the change that you wish to see in the world.' An excellent one, yah! We are all responsible, yah!

"Then there's John F Kennedy…

"Okay mate! You win."

"Anyway Kennedy said: 'Divided, there is little we can do. Together, there is little we cannot do'."

"Yeh. I've heard that one as well, sport."

"We've been set one of mankind's greatest challenges, my friends," Kurt continued in full flow. "We've been tested and found worthy of this great task, we have the tools and I know how to build another Cross of

Goa. Let's get to work!"

"Bravo maestro!" Rod exclaimed derisively. He turned to Patsy, expecting her to scold him. She remained silent. He bowed his head desperately wanting to hear her voice.

"I'm disappointed in you Kurt," Omollo said with mock disapproval. "With your style and wit I would have expected three quotes to set us on our way!"

"I didn't want to bludgeon you all with anymore," Kurt laughed. "The last one then: R. Buckminster Fuller, who lends his name to complex carbon structures called Buckminsterfullerene…under the microscope they look like soccer balls, John! Buckminster Fuller said: 'You never change things by fighting the existing reality. To change something, build a new model that makes the existing model obsolete.' Is that good enough my friend?"

"*Now* I know that we can do it, Kurt!" Omollo grinned. "After what we have been through it will seem like child's play."

"Well you can certainly make people want to get up and try!" Rod chuckled.

"Yah! Well with you with us, Rod we cannot fail!"

The stern was bathed in white light. Rod opened the lounge door to see the robed figure before him once more.

# CHAPTER 69

Kurt and Omollo came down from the bridge.

"You must leave right now. Alex and Carmen are not coming with you. They are staying inside the mountain. If you leave now you will survive. Hesitate for an instant and you will all surely die. You must return to Alex's home and build another Cross, Kurt. Your story must be validated before you publicise it. This is vital. Do you understand?"

"Yah! What will happen to them?"

"The island will be vaporised. I'm sorry. Alex and Carmen's spirits will live on. They will be with us, at God's side, dwelling in his house forevermore. They will never be forgotten. There will be a permanent marker. A rainbow will be seen arcing over this spot at the 8th hour, on the 8th day of the 8th month of every year until the end of the time.

"A *marker*! A *bloody*...! Sorry!" Rod looked away apologetically, wanting to bite his tongue. "I'm sorry...but a *marker*...! Can't you do *anything* for them?"

"I'll have only a fraction of a second to make my escape before the Cross is destroyed. It is their choice to stay. We must respect that." Judas Thomas gazed into Omollo's beseeching great eyes. "I'll do what I can, I will promise you that. Now, please dear friends, I must go. It will happen very soon. There are no words to express how much is owed to all of you. God knows how much was at stake. Please! You must go now. God is with you all."

Kurt climbed silently up the stairs to the bridge, his heart heavier than at any other time in his life. With tears flooding from his eyes he did not linger. If they must go, he thought, then we should get it over with. Quickly he accelerated the yacht out of the bay.

Omollo stood silently beside him, watching Radcliff's Island gradually recede and fade from sight.

Rod, weeping freely, held Patsy close to him as they gazed at the dark outlines of the island. She instinctively comforted Rod although appearing indifferent to any of the events that were taking place.

Judas Thomas returned to the clearing.

The Frenchman was sitting a few feet from the Cross, rocking back and forth, his arms folded tightly, deep in thought.

Jean-Claude was reliving a period in his life when he had been truly happy. He was a child playing in the streets of Marseilles. They were

405

warm, trouble free memories of his early school years and his friends, Jacque and Pierre and little Nichole. He had loved Nichole. She had been six, two years younger than him. He had never loved anyone more in his whole life than Nichole.

She had been tragically killed in a road accident outside his apartment block.

These memories brought him in touch with his real self. The real Jean-Claude Narbonne. 'Where did it all go wrong', he pondered miserably. He imagined for one blissful moment that it was possible to be that person again. But when he realized where he was and what he had done he felt deep remorse and regret for the first time in his life.

Then that terrible day when he was eight years old came vividly into his mind. It had been two weeks after Nichole's funeral. He had answered a knock on the door. His estranged mother was standing before him. He knew instinctively that it was she from old photographs he had secreted away in his room. She had looked so beautiful. Her auburn hair was long and wavy framing a heart shaped face. She smiled when she had seen him, her generous lips parting to reveal perfect white teeth. Jean-Claude leapt into her open arms. She squeezed him so hard he remembered wishing that she would continue squeezing him until he was inside her body once more.

The tears flowed freely down Jean-Claude's face as he felt again her sweet kiss on his cheek.

Then his father, out of mind with drink, burst into the room. He had slapped her several times. She stumbled backwards from the force of the blows and fell into an armchair, close to the French window. He then picked her up by the shoulders, screaming at her and shaking her like a rag doll. She was crying and pleading with him. She noticed the little Jean-Claude watching them. Her expression of sorrow and a desperate longing to protect him had remained with him all his life. It was the last time he saw her.

The father swung open the doors, picked her up from the armchair and swung her over the balcony.

Jean-Claude had run to the window to see her lying in the road close to the spot where Nichole had been killed.

His father staggered back into the lounge, his eyes wild and furious. He glared at the small boy.

Lifting Jean-Claude up he screamed: "You saw nothing boy…do you understand? Nothing..! Is that clear?"

Jean- Claude had nodded. A great steel door in his mind slammed shut. He had not shed a tear since.

Jean-Claude rolled onto his side and sobbed.

"Très désolé ma soeur…Forgive me my sister…" he repeated many times stroking the smooth rock lying just in front of him. He sobbed himself asleep.

The green ball swooped from its high perch to a position a few inches above the Frenchman's head. It hovered there for a moment then began jumping and vibrating erratically. Judas Thomas watched for several minutes as the ball countered the affects of the Cross. Finally it steadied itself, its small red centre glowing brightly and began to consume its prey.


Patsy had been lying on a bunk in one of the forward cabins. The monotonous crash and thud of the yacht's hull breaking the surf had kept her from sleeping.

Her mind was suddenly freed, unshackled from the Frenchman's spell. The notes of Etude 'Tristesse', her favourite Chopin piece came into her mind. The notes were clear and soothing.

Eager to find Rod she dashed through the lounge. She bumped into Omollo. Clinging to his shirt she shouted joyously: "I'm okay…I'm okay, John! Isn't it wonderful!"

Without waiting for his response she burst through the lounge door.

Rod had been watching the horizon, holding on to the stern flag-pole, when the door crashed open behind him.

Omollo watched from the doorway as Rod took one step towards her and caught her leaping body and engulfed her into his arms.

"Oh, honey…"

They kissed and hugged. Omollo approached them, grinning broadly, and wrapped his great arms around both of them.

"Where's Alex and Carmen?" She asked.

They returned to the lounge and Rod gently broke the news to her.

Carmen lay close to the pool at the foot of the chimney with only Radcliff's tattered cloths and empty treasure bags covering her.

Radcliff had all the torches and lanterns burning. The chambers of the cave were exactly as he had remembered, untouched by the explosion, but silent and empty.

Radcliff brought handfuls of precious stones and gold coins to Carmen and covered her with them. He stepped back to admire his glittering recumbent Queen. She took his breath away. Her beauty was more stunning than Cleopatra, more mysterious than Nefertiti and more serine and spiritual than Isis. He knelt before her, as a knight paying homage, and pressed her hand to his lips.

She turned her head and drew him to her, her watery eyes pools of love and warmth.

A succession of bubbles burst from the pool releasing large quantities of the nitrous oxide gas into their grotto.

The gas affected them immediately.

Radcliff engulfed her into his arms. As he squeezed her to him he could

407

feel her shuddering with the same restrained emotions and controlled hysteria.

"I have you now…" he managed to utter before he was doubled up over her by a long breathless wheezing laugh. She kissed his neck and chin between her own fits of hysterical giggles. Tears of joy cascaded down their cheeks. She found his lips with hers and they drank thirstily from each other whilst giving one another their undying love, stopping only to release a build up of rapturous laughter.

Radcliff brushed away the jewels and coins and removed her covers whilst kissing with increasing passion and intensity, pausing to giggle like amorous children on their first sexual adventure. With their bodies entwined, they rolled across the rocky surface, Carmen gripping his cheeks, drawing him deeper into her.

They rolled into the pile of treasure, their gyrations and writhing boring them deeper and deeper into the jewels, making love with a wild, unfettered passion and blissful euphoria. They held their erupting climax at bay, both slowing and relaxing their movements…. she looked up into his ecstatic eyes. Ravel's 'Bolero' came into her mind. She resisted an urge to hum the music unaware that Radcliff had the same music caressing his soul. "Cor..az..ó..n!" She breathed out in a long sigh. "I love you so much."

Feeling weightless imbedded in the jewels, their hearts and souls freed from the shackles of earthly restrictions they gave themselves up to a paradise that was beyond their wildest imagination.


The green sphere had remained close to the Cross of Goa, attracted by the scent of decay and the irresistible vibration emanating from it.

Judas Thomas emerged from the trees, directing the crystal at the Cross. For one fleeting instant it levitated, perfectly still, in all its glory, looking magnificent in the star light. Then it moved suddenly and swiftly to the escarpment and tipped over the edge. The ball bounded after the Cross, following it as it tumbled and slid down the slope. The concentrated superconductive energy within the base was at its zenith. But the Cross remained intact. Judas Thomas had only a moment to act.

Then the cross bounced diagonally towards a great rock.

Judas Thomas vanished.

The 'Fiery' Cross of Goa struck the rock ripping the top section from the base.

In that instant a cataclysmic blast of indescribable force was released from the base. The heat from the explosion was a million times hotter than the sun. A blinding flash of white light, flecked with a hue of scarlet, orange and violet, shot across the surface of the sea then expanded to transform the whole night sky into daylight.

Radcliff and Carmen had been entwined, their thrusts harder and slower as they laughed and groaned through an endless climax. A white light engulfed them as the mountain shook for the last time their personal Bolero enriching the heavenly concert that played endlessly throughout the cosmos

# CHAPTER 70

The detonation flashed across the eastern horizon, its blinding light bursting across the sky one thousand times brighter than any sunrise.

Kurt had taken the yacht safely beyond the effects of the devastating explosion, which had vaporised everything within a ten mile radius of the island. He secured the helm and joined Omollo, Rod and Patsy at the stern.

They watched in stunned silence, horror struck by the intensity of the blast and mesmerised by the flaming pillar of smoke and dust rising up from the vicinity of the island many miles below the horizon. The pillar continued to rise into the stratosphere, held erect by a narrow force field.

All of them had an image of Radcliff and Carmen in their minds eye:

Omollo remembered them laughing together in the tent after Radcliff had been rescued from the mountain.

Patsy saw Carmen dancing the Flamenco in front of a mesmerised Radcliff but her first image of Radcliff, at her home in Boguntungun, was the one she treasured the most.

Rod could see their laughing faces as Rod told Carmen of the time he had first laid eyes on Radcliff.

Kurt had his own strong image of Radcliff. It had been the day of his rescue from the island three months before. During the long helicopter flight back to Mahé and to civilisation they had both talked throughout the whole journey. His tanned, bearded face had lit up when Kurt told him that the island he had been stranded on for seven years was uncharted. They had both become firm friends. He would always picture Carmen on the beach just after the group had landed. She was the most beautiful woman he had ever seen.

The pillar of smoke emitted a pure white phosphorescent glow.

Patsy clung to Rod's side.

The sea around the island had been instantly vaporised momentarily revealing the seabed. The granite had turned white hot before disappearing into a fog of smoke and dust. Then the sea gushed in to fill the void billowing up clouds of steam. Air rushed into the vacuum above the island.

"You can feel their music, Yah?"

Patsy buried her face into Rod's chest sobbing uncontrollably.

Rod bit his upper lip, his chin quivering with pent up emotion. "Do you think…he managed it? Judas Thomas…I mean."

"Come back to us, Alex," Omollo murmured, tears streaming over his great cheeks and dripping from his chin. "Please come back."

A hurricane force wind hit the yacht head on. The great wind whipped the sea into vicious waves that slammed into the lurching yacht. All the lights went out. The yacht was in darkness except for the port and starboard lights linked to an auxiliary power supply.

Kurt grasped the handrail and bounded up the steps to the bridge and steadied the helm and closed the throttle.

When the great engines eased to an idle the small group took cover inside the lounge.

Patsy was first to enter. She froze in the doorway.

Rod and Omollo clung to the doorframe, steadying themselves against the swaying rocking movement of the boat.

Patsy's arm was waving frantically in the air pointing at something inside the lounge. Her mouth moving but was unable to make a sound.

Rod and Omollo squeezed themselves inside and squinted into the gloom.

Two green shapes were writhing on the floor.

"Who…who…is…it, Rod?" Patsy clung to him in terror.

The waves were almost broadside to the yacht and the small boat pitched and tossed in every direction.

Omollo tentatively moved forward clinging to the starboard side of the lounge. He could see the green shapes more clearly. They were entwined as he approached; then they became still. Warily he backed away.

Rod and Patsy were crouching silently amongst the treasure bags stacked along the back of the lounge.

The green shapes slowly and breathlessly began to sit up.

Omollo could depict the outline of the pentacle half illuminated in the green light. The shapes were in the centre of it. He could think only of the Frenchman. Fear began to churn deep within his stomach.

The pitch of the boat sent him staggering back towards the stern.

"Who are they?" Rod hissed.

"Go and get Kurt," Omollo hissed as he lay on his back. "Quickly! He's the only one who can deal with this."

"Is it him? Has…he…come…back?" Patsy whimpered.

"Shhh! Take it easy, honey. Stay here with John."

The green shapes began to move into a couching position.

Kurt burst into the lounge with Rod close behind. A torch beam cut through the darkness searching the floor and walls. "Where are these green men?"

The beam lit up one figure then shone on the other. Their startled faces were unrecognisable.

"It's a man and a woman," Kurt uttered in amazement. "They're both... naked."

"What do yer want?" Rod shouted.

One of the figures spoke: "They can't be angels, sweetheart."

"I know that voice," Omollo chuckled. "You've...you've come back!" Omollo lumbered towards them, his arms outstretched, but the yacht lurched and he was tossed against the side of the boat, crashing and clattering into some pots and pans.

Rod, Patsy and Kurt inched towards them, gripping firmly onto each other, Kurt's beam still full on Radcliff's face.

Omollo pulled out a scarlet sheet tangled up with the pots and pans. As he lifted himself up he noticed that his arm was tinged green. Outside the starboard light glowed through the window.

Radcliff was kneeling on his right knee, his nude genuflect brilliantly illuminated, shielding his face from the powerful beam.

Kurt turned off the torch.

Omollo came forward with the scarlet sheet.

Radcliff suddenly burst into a fit of hysterical laughter, still intoxicated by the gas. Carmen was soon to follow, giggling uncontrollably.

"I..." Radcliff began as though breaking into song, the warbling sound rising to a haunting wail that became a constricted throaty gurgle fading into a long breathless side splitting wheeze. Carmen was contorted with hysteria, sagging over Radcliff's left leg emitting a muted cackle that could have come from a broody hen.

"I...." He began again, wheezing breathlessly again, "I...th... thought." Carmen took a rasping intake of air and he was lost again. Regaining his concentration he continued, "after m...m...mooove..." he creased up again with laughter, tears streaming down his face.

"It's the gas, yah?" Kurt laughed.

Carmen stood, averting her eyes from Radcliff her back stiffening with resolve and determination to compose herself.

"Af...af...after moving th...th...th...the mountain." He sagged to his knees helpless with laughter.

Carmen doubled up screeching with laughter, leaning on Radcliff for support. The yacht pitched violently. His feet were too slow to compensate for the movement and they both collapsed into a heap on the floor.

Radcliff pulled himself up then lifted Carmen to his side. Radcliff adjusted his stance to take her weight and maintain balance.

"We thought we would be in p...p..," Radcliff breathed deeply, holding his concentration thinking of nothing but the next word. "Paradise," he managed to blurt out. He turned to Carmen. Their eyes met for a second then they both faced the group, their expressions suddenly very stern. "Instead...we are here...with you!"

Radcliff and Carmen watched the others as their expression changed from joy to sadness. There was enough nitrous oxide in their bodies for one more fit of the giggles.

Patsy took the scarlet sheet from Omollo and offered it to Carmen.

Carmen recoiled away from her. "No…no. I'd rather be naked than have *that thing* next to my skin."

Rod pulled Patsy closer to him. "You don't seem all that pleased to see us, Alex. I am right?"

The yacht lurched on the swell. Carmen clung to Radcliff. His expression was grave.

"Neither would you, my friend. We know what is to come. We'd sooner be out of it, thank you very much."

"But we are alive, Alex," Omollo encouraged, his deep voice as warm as his smile.

"Yah. We won Alex!"

"Yes, but what's the point if…when we get home…we all end up locked away in a loony bin…or worse. No one is ever going to believe what's happened here…."

"This doesn't sound like you, Alex. You're exhausted, yah!"

"They're in shock," Patsy added, glancing up at Rod.

"Try and understand will you…I found this woman…" he pulled her close, loving the feel her skin against his, "…eight years ago…torn apart for seven…I almost lost her twice…now all I want…we want…is some peace. When we saw that bright light shining on us we thought… well never mind what we thought."

"It's not your destiny, Alex. You weren't meant to end your lives. Neither were you meant to live the cosy, peaceful life by the fireside with your woman beside you knitting. You and Carmen were born to bring change to the world, yah. You have no choice in the matter."

"Judas Thomas spoke to us…it was like in a dream…it seemed that he talked for a long time …he told us what to expect when we get back…"

"But Alex, it can't be worse than what we've been through already …yah!"

"Hear me out for Pete's sake….It will be very difficult, Kurt. The human race is on the very brink, okay. People with money and influence are going to do everything possible to hang on to what they have; their status, their possessions, everything... *I mean everything!*"

"I know that, man. There's always going to be those rich bastards… but there are many, many more who aren't like that. Have faith...we've got Obama, yah! There are the millions and millions who are living on the bread line. They will listen, yah?"

Radcliff glanced at each in turn, then he asked: "Are you sure you can build another one…another Cross, Kurt?"

413

Kurt looked Radcliff squarely in the eye. "I can...I'm absolutely positive, Alex. I have all I need… copies of the inscriptions that Federico de Silva…the goldsmith…carved in the base...my own notes…there're all inside your diary."

"But we'll need protection…a small army even…"

"You already have a castle," Omollo grinned.

"That's right, mate. You three fought off a bloody invasion…missiles …the lot. You cannot quit now!"

"We're going to need more people behind us. People we can trust. We *must* reach all those people who want to listen to us."

Rod said: "Doesn't it say in the Bible…'those who have ears to hear. Let them hear.'"

"That's right darlin'. My Rod knows his Bible."

"Come on, Alex. Lighten up, mate! Me and Patsy want to invite you two love birds to a Barbee at our place. Let's have a bit of a celebration! What'yer recon, eh?"

Radcliff turned to Carmen. She was looking up at him. He melted into her eyes.

"Count me out, Rod." Omollo said bashfully with a wide grin.

"A previous engagement, eh!" Patsy teased. "Who in the world could that be?

"We don't need three guesses…that's fer sure. Sophia's her name. Good on ya mate! It gives the rest of us something more to celebrate!"

"Ah, yes," Kurt said thoughtfully. "Sophia. Quite a name that!" Kurt slapped Rod on the back. "Little green men, eh! On board *my* ship!"

"Crikey Kurt.... It was dark. You were…."

In their laughter their thoughts simultaneously turned to those who were missing.

The waves smacked rhythmically against the hull.

"I'm going back up to the bridge," Kurt announced. "Now the weathers improved we want to get to Coetivy Island pronto, yah!"

Radcliff turned to Carmen. "Let's find some clothes. Can anyone fix the light?"

"Yeh. Leave it me mate." Rod opened the rear door. "Hay, Kurt. Throw down that torch."

Omollo retrieved Radcliff's bag from amongst the treasure sacks, "Here, Alex...take this..." Radcliff reached out and took it. The whites of Omollo's eyes widened, matching his great toothy grin. "I'm glad to be rid of it…too much responsibility for me!"

The edge of the diary poked through the semi fastened zipper.

Radcliff moved the zipper and extracted the diary. Sheets of paper poked out from between the pages. He opened it. Kurt's notes were at the page of Robert Radclyffe's sketch of the Cross of Goa.

# THE END


*Jesus said: "If two make peace with each other in a single house, they will say to the mountain, 'Move from here,' and it will move."*

The Gospel of Thomas
Text adapted by Elaine Pagels and Marvin Meyer

TO PLACE AN ORDER:

You can order further copies of the book directly from either
Winchester Boson Publications or by visiting the book's website.

FREE DELIVERY!

To order further copies of the THE CROSS OF GOA please visit website at:

www.thecrossofgoa.co.uk

Alternatively please email us at:

wbp-crossofgoa@hotmail.co.uk

On receipt of your email we will send you an order form and payment instrcutions.